THE IRISH SPY

A Novel of the Irish War of Independence

Front cover image of British Union Jack painted on wall with bullet holes by Piotr Krzeslak, used under license from Shutterstock.com

Back cover image of RMS Titanic ready for launch in 1911 from Robert John Welch (1859-1936), official photographer for Harland & Wolff, used as work in the public domain.

"The Irish Spy - A Novel of the Irish War of Independence," by Douglas Clark. ISBN ISBN 978-1-947532-54-0 (softcover); 978-1-947532-55-7 (hardcover); 978-1-947532-56-4 eBook.

BY DOUGLAS CLARK

BELFAST

TAKE FIVE

SHELL GAME

EVERMORE

CRITICAL MASS

FAULT LINES

PROVOKE THE DEVIL

THE IRISH SPY

To Josie

THE IRISH SPY

A Novel of the Irish War of Independence

DOUGLAS CLARK

"Let no man write my epitaph; for as no man who knows my motives dare now vindicate them, let not prejudice or ignorance, asperse them."

—**Robert Emmet,** Irish nationalist from his speech after being sentenced to death for treason by a British court in 1803.

CHAPTER 1

FIRST WORLD WAR - NORTHEAST FRANCE – MARCH, 1918

In the pitch dark early morning hours of March 21, 1918 the steam locomotive crawled along slowly without headlamp to hide its advance from any German aerial observation. The train was approaching the front lines of the Western Front. A distant rumble began at 4:40. A massive artillery barrage.

The sound increased as the train traveled east toward the River Somme. As daylight broke the terrain only added to the sense of impending dread. A surreal landscape as far as the eye could see. Gray ground meeting a gray sky. No trees, no vegetation, only upturned soil pockmarked with shell craters. Partly buried destroyed military debris poked out from the ground. An apocalyptic scene created by years of some of the war's worse fighting. Any suggestion of human habitation long since obliterated.

Positioning of opposing forces along the River Somme varied little over the course of the war. Each side pushed the other back to occupy the enemy trenches in great offensives resulting in thousands of casualties. In a later battle, the opposing side retook the same ground leaving countless more thousands of fallen young men. Unimaginative generals repeatedly threw their armies in massed assaults employing the same unsuccessful tactics.

1

The train operated by American Army engineers arrived midmorning at a British Army supply depot three miles to the rear of the front trenches. The artillery volume so heavy the noise sounded almost continuous with little interval between explosions. German artillery rounds were landing only a half mile distant.

"Seems a bigger than normal barrage. What do ya think is going on, Sir?" The sergeant handling the locomotive's throttle shouted to the officer standing next to him.

"I'd guess a new German offensive," the American Army captain said. "This time the Germans, next time the Brits. Been this way for four years. Does sound like something big going on though."

This time would prove different. The Germans were intent on breaking through the Allied lines to end years of stalemated trench warfare. Heavy long-range German guns lobbed shells well behind the British lines west of the town of St. Quentin, France intending to disrupt British artillery batteries and supply lines. The weight of this unprecedented artillery bombardment lasted five hours then abruptly ended signaling the German infantry assault. Unprepared, nearly one million German troops overwhelmed Allied forward defensive positions.

The captain added, "Poor buggers in the trenches are now catching hell from German mortars. The infantry assault comes next."

"Can't imagine being in one of those stinking trenches, Sir," the sergeant said.

"Neither can I, Sergeant. Keep the boiler steam up. We're exposed this close to the front. Want to reverse out of here soon as we're unloaded. Got a bad feeling."

———

The British Third and Fifth Armies fell into strategic retreat as seventy-two German divisions launched what was to become known as the Spring Offensive along a 45-mile front. This was the latest in a series of great battles fought along the meandering River Somme in northeast France. The first clash between German and French forces occurred early in the war in 1914. That failure of the Germans to penetrate the French lines resulted in both sides constructing defensive trench positions. The Western Front extending through Belgium and France from the English Channel to the Swiss border would define the Great War.

Later years saw enormous clashes of million-man armies between the Germans and the allied forces of France and the United Kingdom. The front lines eventually solidified into ever more permanent trench fortifications. During the Battle of the Somme from July to November, 1916, the Allies advanced their front lines by only seven miles. The cost was 623,000 British and French casualties, 465,000 German. An average of 8,000 men falling each day.

The United States entered the war on the side of Britain and France in 1917. A future threat to the Germans since the United States at the time had only a small standing army. It would require time to recruit, train, and equipment an army sufficient to impact the European conflict. By early 1918, the United States had yet to field a sizable fighting force. Eventually the Germans knew the great industrial power would pour men and materiel into the conflict. Four years had exhausted all the European combatants. America would decisively tip the advantage to the Allies.

General Erich von Ludendorff, chief strategist of the German high command, recognized by 1918 that Germany could not win this continued war of attrition once the United States weighed in on the Allied side. But the overthrow of the Russian Tsar months earlier resulted in the new Bolshevik government signing an armistice with Germany ending the fighting in the East. This allowed shifting substantial manpower and supplies to the Western Front. This convergence of circumstances led Ludendorff to attempt a massive offensive at the River Somme.

Penetrate deep into France. Capture the strategic city of Amiens. Split the British and French forces denying the ability of a combined counterattack. Break out of the accursed trenches.

3

Achieve improved territorial leverage from which to negotiate better terms under the unavoidable armistice.

On March 21, 1918, Ludendorff began the attack of *Operation Michael*. Much of the terrain was already a vast wasteland of destruction resulting from two years of war. Tactically Ludendorff counted on not only superior manpower strength but deployment of new tactics. On the Eastern Front the Germans developed mobile open-warfare tactics using elite infantry units. Shock troops, *Stoßtruppen*, consisted of select soldiers used in rapidly advancing small units to infiltrate and disrupt enemy essential support operations behind their front lines.

At the beginning of 1918, only four American combat divisions were on the front lines. Deployed under British and French command, they remained in quiet sectors to gain combat experience. However, American engineering units arrived in France months earlier to reinforce Allied supply capabilities. Among these were railway engineering regiments. The staggering volume of food, ordnance, and timber necessary to support millions of troops required construction of new rail lines.

———

On that first day of the German assault the British Fifth Army fell back under the weight of the German onslaught overwhelming the twenty-six British divisions.

The five-hour preceding artillery barrage surpassed anything previously experienced. The Germans fired over 3.5 million shells. German trench mortars concentrated poison gas rounds of mustard and chlorine gas on the forward British trenches. Adding to this new vision of hell, heavy fog blanketed the battlefield disguising the clouds of deadly gas.

Captain Trevor Sullivan of the 12th Engineers Light Railway Battalion of the United States Army commanded a train resupplying the British with ammunition and provisions. His train arrived at a supply depot close to the front near the town of Saint-Quentin. As offloading started, wounded spread in growing numbers over an acre near the tracks waiting evacuation. A continuous stream of arriving wounded stretched from the direction of the front as far as he could see. He estimated their numbers would soon exceed the capacity to evacuate by this train alone. A massive battle was raging.

By ten o'clock in the morning, the artillery barrage stopped. The thunder became replaced by sounds of gunfire, grenade explosions, and the rattle of machine guns. By early afternoon great numbers of retreating British soldiers poured into the immediate vicinity of the supply depot. The noise progressively sounding closer. The front was collapsing.

To a wounded British junior officer Sullivan said, "What's happening at the front, Lieutenant?"

The young man was walking with his arm in a sling and a blood-soaked bandage covering an ear.

"Germans have attacked in strength. Overran our lines. Never seen anything like it. My colonel said the *Krauts* didn't have the means to mount a serious offensive. Bloody fucking idiot."

"Has the front stabilized?" Sullivan said.

"Stabilized? Fuck no! If reserves aren't thrown in soon no telling where this'll end."

Sullivan motioned to one of his own officers.

"Lieutenant, start loading the wounded immediately. And get the Limeys to hurry up offloading those supplies. Once the cars are loaded with wounded we're out of here regardless where the unloading stands. Where the hell is that goddamn captain of theirs?"

Sullivan was no fan of the British, especially being Irish. American-Irish from Brooklyn. But his family also had a strong *Fenian* background, Irish republicans dedicated to an independent Irish republic. Freedom from British rule. Two uncles participated in the failed Eastern Rising of 1916 in Dublin. Both executed by the British.

Yet Sullivan found himself attached to the British Army. Combat troops of the American Expeditionary Force had yet to come up to strength in France. In the first vanguard, U.S. engineering battalions arrived in late 1917. His battalion was assigned to support the British Expeditionary Forces fighting in

5

northeast France. Build new rail lines. Run trains transporting supplies to the front and remove the wounded to the rear.

Sullivan eventually found the British captain commanding the supply depot. The stereotypical British officer with traits that irked Sullivan after working alongside them for months.

West Point trained, Sullivan considered the British general staff criminally incompetent in prosecuting the war. Unimaginative, dull-witted, seemingly unconcerned by the extent of their own casualties. Bred of the best schools. From the *right* families meaning wealth or influence. An elitist officer class promoted by other than merit.

"Captain, I suggest your troops get a move on with unloading. Many of the wounded are in a bad way. Their numbers rapidly growing. We must get underway."

"I believe we shall finish soon, Captain."

Sullivan persisted. "According to some of the wounded, the front has become fluid. Some say the Germans have deeply penetrated the British lines in places with small units of elite troops. Not stopping to consolidate their gains, they just keep on advancing. One fellow said they were ambushed from behind as they fell back. You need to prepare your men."

"Captain Sullivan. Have you ever been in combat?"

"What the hell does that mean?"

"I mean that I have. Three years' worth of war. Soldiers invent all sorts of fanciful stories. Rumors abound."

"My point is we have no idea where the front is. If there even is a front anymore. And if the Germans are making deep penetrations our position here may soon come directly under attack. Your position, Captain. This supply depot."

"I think that's unlikely. The front is still some distance. This is a rear supply depot. If a threat were imminent headquarters would be making arrangements to reinforce our position. There has been no communication or warning."

Inept fool. Before Sullivan could lose his temper the sound of battle erupted close by. Small arms fire at first, soon followed by the unmistakable rattle of machine gun fire. Then a few errant rounds struck the train cars. That meant fighting just hundreds of yards away.

Sullivan left the bewildered British officer on the run moving toward the train's engine. Along the way he yelled orders to any officer or NCO within earshot. "Get the stretcher wounded onboard immediately! Anyone not capable of firing a rifle. We'll leave once we have steam."

Swinging up into the cab of the engine he told the three-man crew, "Get the steam up, Sergeant. Once you're ready we're reversing the hell out of here."

Two soldiers began furiously shoveling coal into the boiler.

To the credit of the British wounded there was no panic. Several wounded officers rallied those capable of holding a rifle to move toward the sound of the approaching assault. Taking up defensive positions some distance from the train, most realized they were now a rear guard. Even if they survived they would not be among those evacuated on the train.

Sullivan quickly assessed British troop strength guarding the supply depot as light. Unlikely to be reinforced with the front collapsing. Walking wounded could not defend this position if the Germans penetrated this far with any strength.

He ordered two of his men to run forward up the tracks towards the fighting.

"Once you see any Germans get your asses back here on the double."

To his two lieutenants, "Gentlemen, I sent two men forward to act as lookouts. If they return it'll be on the run. I'll signal the engineer to sound three blasts on the whistle. Then he'll immediately put the train in reverse. Warn the men. When the whistle sounds, stop loading wounded and jump on board. It means we're being overrun."

With that Sullivan took up a position a short distance in front of the engine.

Within minutes the two American soldiers came sprinting toward him. One soldier screamed as he approached Sullivan,

"Lots of Germans, Sir. Right behind us. The Brits have been overrun!"

Sullivan could now see many British soldiers in full retreat. Many bandaged from previous wounds expecting evacuation to the rear. Poor bastards.

He signaled the engineer hanging out the cab window with a winding motion of his upraised hand. Three blasts of the steam whistle followed.

Sullivan took off at a run behind his two soldiers. The train was slowly moving in reverse as he reached the engine. Looking down the length of the train he could see his American soldiers climbing onboard. Hundreds of wounded remained unloaded. Nothing he could do. Must save as many as possible.

Small arms rounds began hitting the engine right next to him. Two lone German soldiers clumsily ran toward him in their hobnail boots weighed down by heavy field kits. Bayonets fixed to their rifles.

Dropping to one knee he took up a classic firing position. A long distance shot for his Colt M1911 .45 caliber pistol. He rested his left elbow on his knee supporting the butt of the pistol in his left palm. A single shot dropped one of the Germans at over thirty yards.

The other soldier stopped running to take aim at Sullivan with his Mauser rifle. With his target stationary for just a second, Sullivan placed a shot into his chest followed by a second to the head.

Behind the two soldiers came an officer at a full run. Firing his sidearm while closing on Sullivan, one round found its mark hitting Sullivan's steel helmet.

The round did not penetrate the helmet but jerked the chin strap distracting Sullivan for a second. With the German now within only a few yards Sullivan fired three rounds slamming him backward.

The first soldier that Sullivan shot rose to his knees trying to recover his rifle. Sullivan sighted his last round delivering a kill-shot to the throat.

This sequence of events happened in the span of only a few seconds. The sergeant engineer frantically waved Sullivan to climb aboard. As he grabbed the handhold swinging up into the cab the sergeant let out the throttle. The steam engine's drive wheels slipped a few turns on the rails before eventually catching hold. The train steadily accelerated.

The Americans narrowly escaped the near disaster. Managing to rescue only some British wounded, it was difficult to look at the wounded left behind as the train sped past.

"That sure as hell was close, Sir," the sergeant at the throttle said. "Saw you drop all three of those *Krauts*. Damn impressive shooting. Were you lucky or are you that good a shot, Sir?"

Sullivan loaded a fresh clip into his pistol. "Some of both I'd guess, Sergeant. I was sidearm champion at West Point my last two years. Just a knack I guess. But only against targets over ten years ago. When someone's shooting at you it's a whole different matter. So yeah I got lucky."

The sergeant turned to the two soldiers feeding coal into the boiler, "Ain't that somethin', lads. We got Wild Bill Hickok for our captain."

CHAPTER 2

After two weeks the German offensive stalled in early April. While penetrating forty miles into Allied lines they failed to take Amiens and split the British and French forces. The captured shell-cratered desolate terrain from earlier battles was of little strategic importance.

A poor return for the prohibitive cost to the Germans. While inflicting 250,000 British and 80,000 French casualties, the Germans suffered 250,000 casualties. Numbers they could ill afford, including irreplaceable elite troops.

The British poured in reinforcements. Replacement artillery, tanks, and machine guns reequipped Allied losses. Not only was the Allied defeat indecisive, the Germans lacked the capability to resupply troops, food, or ordinance. Soon fresh well-equipped U.S. Divisions would enter the fight. Ludendorff's failed *Operation Michael* proved the beginning of the end for Germany.

———

The magnitude of the carnage was not made public at the time. Both sides feared a populist backlist in reaction to such incomprehensible carnage. At the front, the continual attrition of their comrades demoralized soldiers of every rank. Dehumanizing filth and boredom in the trenches punctuated by interludes of seemingly sacrificial violence. A stalemate along a semi-fixed front. The war into its fourth year, the end not yet in sight.

For Trevor Sullivan it was no different. The idea of continuing his career in the army less certain. He was an engineer, a builder at heart. The army had been good to him. A first class education at government expense. A professional skill. Opportunity. Prestige. But this? Tens of thousands dying in these stinking trenches. The generals are too old, applying tactics of the last century while deploying twentieth century killing technologies. The machine gun and the airplane alone changed the face of warfare. Young men sacrificed unnecessarily.

Would General Pershing deploy American troops differently? Were senior American officers any better leaders than their European counterparts? No soldier envisioned such a war. The blunting of the German offensive at the Somme resolved nothing. The war would continue. The American Expeditionary Force would soon have their own day of blood.

All this weighed on Sullivan's mind when granted his first leave in May, 1918. Leave of course meant Paris. A brief semblance of normalcy after months witnessing unrelenting horror.

Even with rumored food shortages in Paris anything was better than British field rations. The staples of corned beef, called bully beef or a disgusting concoction of fatty meat and vegetable stew called Maconochie. Rock-hard biscuits that needed to be soaked in water to be made chewable. The only pleasure tea masking the tainted flavor of the drinking water.

Paris offered great sights seen only in photographs. Architecture. Art. Wine. And of course beautiful French women.

Sullivan disembarked the train at Paris' Est Train Station in the 10th arrondissement. Finding a taxi outside the station, he asked the driver "*parlez-vous anglais?*"

"*Oui, Monsieur*. You are American soldier? An officer?" The ebullient driver said with a broad smile.

"Yes. A captain. Been in France for six months. First time in Paris. I only have a few days leave. What's the best hotel? Somewhere near the River Seine and all the sights."

"Ah, there are many fine hotels in Paris. The Ritz, the Crillon, *certainement*. Might be difficult to get a room. If I might suggest another hotel, *monsieur*? Some say it's the grandest smaller hotel in all of Paris. The desk clerk is my cousin. The Hotel Lotti. Very near the Jardin des Tuileries and the Louvre. All on the Seine. Perhaps I can persuade him to offer an American *capitaine* a special rate."

Although wary Sullivan agreed, subject to seeing the place. It proved an immediate delight on entering the lobby escorted by the taxi driver. Indeed the driver at least knew the desk clerk as he embraced him then introduced *Capitaine* Sullivan. Whether a special rate or not, or just a way of getting a large tip, the room was within his means.

That first afternoon he wandered down to the Seine. Taking in the iconic architecture of the Louvre, Notre Dame Cathedral, the Conciergerie, and the graceful bridges. As a civil engineer he marveled at photographs of Paris' sublime artistic melding of form and function.

In the distance the Eiffel Tower dominated the skyline. Erected as a temporary structure for the 1889 World's Fair, artists of the time derided it as ugly. Now, a cultural icon celebrated as the endearing symbol of Paris.

That first night consisted of a long hot bath followed by dinner at the hotel. After a couple of whiskeys the fatigue brought on by the stress of the last weeks made it difficult to keep his eyes open. The first decent meal in months and a real bed put him out soundly for the next ten hours.

The next morning he felt reborn. A clean uniform. Real coffee with pastry. A sunny spring day in Paris. The Eiffel Tower was his must first stop. The foundations for the massive sloping legs held his professional interest. Taking the elevator to the highest observation platform at 900 feet provided a breathtaking sight.

After lunching at one of the ubiquitous outdoor cafes he walked to the Louvre Museum. He held fond memories of childhood visits to the Metropolitan Museum of Art in New York City. While no expert, he appreciated art in all its forms. High on his list were the works of Leonardo da Vinci.

He became drawn to da Vinci while studying engineering. Captivated by looking at translated reproductions of da Vinci's notebooks. Drawings of his visionary inventions. Were prototypes ever attempted? Da Vinci's grasp of mathematics, physics, and anatomy advanced beyond his time. Yet more renowned as one of the greatest visual artists of all times. The archetypical Renaissance man fascinated Sullivan. The Louvre housed many of Leonardo's most famous works.

Sullivan eventually came to the celebrated *Mona Lisa*. Like most first time viewers he was surprised by its small size. At only 30 x 21 inches it was smaller than most other works displayed nearby. Yet only the *Mona Lisa* held a small crowd trying to get close enough to appreciate da Vinci's nuanced creation.

Working his way closer, Sullivan asked a nearby uniformed museum docent if the museum might have any of Leonardo da Vinci's codex on display.

"*Je ne parle pas l'anglais, monsieur. Je suis désolé.*"

Sullivan nodded and smiled his rough understanding that the docent did not speak English.

"Excuse me, sir. May I be of help in translating your question?"

Sullivan turned at the woman's voice. Was her accent Irish? A remarkably pretty woman his own age. Something about her face. Particularly her large expressive eyes. Magnetic. A fortuitous opportunity to talk to this attractive woman.

"Why yes, *mademoiselle,* that would be most kind."

"You asked about a *codex*? What is that?"

"Da Vinci's notebooks. His sketches and observations. I've seen reproductions but it would be something to see the originals."

She conversed in French with the docent for several moments then returned to Sullivan.

"He believes not. Says the best known of these codex are in various other museums throughout the world but not the Louvre. So sorry. But I hope you enjoy da Vinci's paintings. Personally I think the *Mona Lisa* is overrated. I like some of his other works better."

"You have a favorite?"

"Yes. *Bacchus*. A much larger format than the special lady."

Sullivan couldn't help smiling looking at this woman. "Excuse me but are you Irish? Your accent. My family is Irish."

"Yes, I'm Irish. I believe you're an American soldier?"

"Yes, mam. Captain Trevor Sullivan of the 12th Engineering Battalion, U.S. Army. From New York."

"And I'm Maureen O'Farrell. Originally from Derry, Ireland. Would you be knowing where that is, Captain?"

"As a matter of fact I do. In the north. Ulster. My father came from Belfast, my mother from Limerick."

"So as all Ulster Irish ask, what are you?"

Sullivan looked puzzled.

"Catholic or Protestant? Not sure religion has much to do with it."

"I see what you mean. Especially in my case. My father's family is Protestant, my mother's Catholic. At least back in Ireland. We never went to church so it never meant much to me."

O'Farrell smiled coyly. "Then it wouldn't be clear how to anticipate your feelings about the nastiness going on in this latest push for Irish independence."

Sullivan was attracted to this woman. Certainly didn't want to prejudice that by being on the opposite side of her political views. And no wedding band so possibly unattached?

"Oh it's a big deal for Irish-Americans too. Personally I'd like to see Ireland independent. I'm not fond of the British. Would hate to see it come to open rebellion though. Ireland will suffer."

"But if Ireland is to be free of Britain how else than by the gun? Political means haven't worked for hundreds of years."

"You favor an armed revolt?"

O'Farrell took on a serious expression. "I truly hope it doesn't come to that but I expect it will. Things have become worse since the Rising in 1916."

14

"Miss O'Farrell, might I be so bold as to request you have lunch with me? I would love to hear more about Ireland. Never thought I'd meet a pretty woman from Ireland my first day in Paris."

O'Farrell's expression appeared serious. Clearly she was debating whether to carry this encounter further. But why not? A free lunch. Wine. A handsome officer. Polished calf-high brown boots, matching leather Sam Browne belt, with the uniquely American Stetson flat-rimmed campaign hat set at a rakish angle. And an Irishman.

"Lunch would be nice, Captain Sullivan."

"Wonderful. Perhaps you could choose a place. Somewhere that you particularly like."

The Louvre no longer on his mind.

"Well then, game for little walk, Captain?" O'Farrell said. "Left Bank cafés are quainter. The place I have in mind is called Les Deux Magots. Famous as the haunt of artists and writers. Located on the other side of the river at Place Saint-Germain-des-Prés. Perhaps a twenty-minute walk."

"Is this one of your favorite places, Miss O'Farrell?"

"Not exactly. I'm a struggling student. Finishing my art studies at the Sorbonne. Need to be frugal. Dining at cafés is a rare treat."

It was a beautiful sunny day. Perfect for outside dining. Les Deux Magots was Paris as Sullivan imagined. Especially in the company of an attractive woman.

"So once you complete your studies what will you do?"

"Hope to get a job at a museum. Maybe then go on for an advanced degree. A better job, perhaps even teaching art at a university."

"Do you have a job that helps pay for college?" Sullivan was certainly fishing to understand how a young single Irish woman made her way in Paris.

O'Farrell knew the game. What she did not want was to leave an unfavorable impression. More than a little taken with this American, that seemed important.

"I'm a dancer. The pay is adequate. Most of all I can work nights. Leaves the daytime available for classes."

"I'd like to see you perform. Would that be possible?"

She dare not guess at his reaction. Regardless that was who she was.

"I perform at the Folies Bergère."

Sullivan knew of this venue. From soldier talk. Beautiful women in scanty costumes. Surprise must have shown on his face.

"Are you familiar with the Folies, Captain?"

"Yes. At least I mean I've heard of it."

"Are you shocked?"

"Certainly not. Why should I be?"

"Come now, you must know that the dancers perform in very revealing costumes. Some would even call it nudity. Do you find that scandalous?"

"No. Scandal is what politicians do. Victorian so-called propriety is just another stupid legacy of the English. The Louvre is full of paintings and sculptures of naked women and men."

"Oh it's more than just Victorian propriety. It's just another way to subjugate women. Men aren't bound by the same rules. Nonetheless, I intend to live my life by my rules."

O'Farrell searched Sullivan's face for a clue to his reaction. Had she gone too far? Telling this complete stranger she danced semi-naked? Then declaring herself a women's rights advocate. Might get her a bed partner but not good form to foster something more serious.

Sullivan understood he needed to convince her he found nothing objectionable in her revelations. To the contrary her assertiveness captivated him.

"I think that's fine that you pursue life as you like. Your dancing is artistic expression. It hurts no one. As to women, of course they are subjugated. Men run things. They have the economic power. They're not going to welcome giving anything up. Women will have to force change to make things different.

"As for me, I don't feel threatened. But many men are. So don't apologize, Miss O'Farrell."

Over lunch their conversation switched to O'Farrell describing Paris to Sullivan's endless string of questions.

"Now tell me about yourself, Captain Sullivan. How did you wind up in France?"

"I'm that rare breed, a career soldier. I go where I'm ordered. I'm an engineer. Assigned to building railroads supplying the front. Been in France for months."

"An engineer? Did you study at a university?"

"Oh yes. One of the best. The United States Military Academy. That's how I became an officer."

"You're from an important family then?"

Sullivan laughed. "Heavens no. Working class family. Father was a railroad man. Died in an accident when I was young. But he had the foresight to buy a small tavern in Brooklyn. My mother and sister run the tavern. A good living but certainly not wealthy."

"Then how was it you got into the military academy? In France and England only the sons of the privileged class attend these schools."

"Probably why they turn out poor military leaders. In America merit determines attendance at the army or naval academies. You must have excellent academic qualifications and then be recommended by a member of congress.

"I was an exceptional student. Especially mathematics. But so were many others. My chance came because of an Irishman that was sweet on mother. The Brooklyn borough president no less, Keith Flanagan. He'd come around to the bar often. Took a liking to me after I consistently beat him at chess. I liked him too. He was good to my mum.

"Anyway, he had political connections. Used his influence to have our local congressman nominate me for West Point."

"Did she marry him?"

Sullivan shook his head. "No. She was tempted. Flanagan made her laugh. But then he was arrested. Convicted of embezzling public funds. Sent off to prison. Soon after, the newspapers reported his suicide."

Changing the subject Sullivan said, "You never told me back at the Louvre which side of the Irish political argument you favor, Republic or Union? So I'll risk my own revelation. Like I said, events in Ireland are of major concern to Irish Americans. So many of us are first or second generation. Parents or grandparents from the old country. Starving Ireland giving up its youth to American opportunity.

"My family is more actively connected to Irish politics than most Irish-Americans. You see my uncle, my mother's sister's husband, was the rebel Thomas Clarke. Know the name?"

O'Farrell registered surprise. "One of the leaders of the Easter Rising in 1916?"

"Yup. A real old-time Fenian to the core. Spent a good part of his life in British prisons for terrorist acts. After being released from prison he came to America. He lived in Brooklyn during my teenage years. My sister and I called him crazy Uncle Tom. An intense humorless man. My mother said it was the rough treatment in prison that made him a little odd.

"Eventually of course he returned to Ireland to join in the thick of things. Signed the independence proclamation. Executed a few days after the collapse of the 1916 Rising. My mother's younger brother, Ned Daly was also executed by the British Army. So that's my family background."

O'Farrell shook her head. "Well that is something. Of all the people to run into in Paris. An Irish-American Fenian. Of course I know of Tom Clarke. My father reveres the name. You see my father and two brothers are active in the Irish Republican Brotherhood."

"Really? And you?"

"Me? I favor a free Ireland but I'm not part of the fight. But it's more than about just freedom from the Brits. In the northern counties it's about discrimination against Catholics. Jobs, equal justice, a decent life. The Unionists are Protestants. They see their power connected with remaining part of Britain. But for me and for a good many women, Ireland is a bloody backward brawling place. That's why I left."

"My good fortune that you did."

"But your father is Protestant from Belfast you said. How was that?"

"He was only a Protestant because of his parents. To say he was not religious was an understatement. We never went to church, Protestant or Catholic. Never knew why. He died when I was only ten. Mother never spoke of his political leanings. She only said he never talked much about his family. I suspected it probably had to do with his marrying a Catholic.

"More wine? This bottle's about gone."

"I think not. It's getting late. Unfortunately I must work to-night. Can't be tipsy."

An awkward moment for both. Does it just end with lunch?

"Miss O'Farrell, this has been a delightful day. Don't want it to end. Might I come to see you perform?"

With some trepidation she said, "Of course."

———

Sullivan offered a taxi to take O'Farrell first to her apartment then on to the theater. She declined. Not about to have Sullivan see her cramped apartment near the university shared with two gossipy roommates.

"Must be getting to work. I'll take the metro as usual to the theater. Need to arrive well ahead of the first show for makeup and costume preparations. You can come backstage after the last show ends at midnight."

Sullivan wandered the Left Bank after escorting O'Farrell to the nearest metro station. He couldn't get her out of his mind. What a stroke of fortune. Unfortunately only three days then back to the front.

The Folies Bergère nightclub turned out to be quite an experience. The audience by no means all men. Women in evening gowns sipped champagne with gentlemen in evening attire.

Feeling somewhat underdressed in his uniform, Sullivan remained at the bar after seeing the show. An upscale place by the exorbitant price of whiskey. But the show certainly delivered. Beautiful young women displaying bare breasts, midriffs, and legs in elaborate customs. The well-choreographed review with a large orchestra transcended any feeling of a lewd spectacle. This was not a New York strip club.

Maureen O'Farrell baring her physical charms was riveting. Her figure better than many of the others. Some he thought slightly heavy in the hips. Not O'Farrell, especially with her long legs.

After the show he made his way backstage. Somewhat disconcerting once inside the dancers dressing area with so many women in various stages of undress.

"Captain Sullivan, over here," O'Farrell said raising her hand from a dressing table halfway down the long room.

She was wrapped in a robe preparing to remove the heavy stage makeup.

"Did you enjoy the show?"

"Captivating. You looked particularly lovely."

"Not shocked?" She said coyly.

"Not at all," smiling and shaking his head. "Perhaps we might have a late drink somewhere?"

"I wish I could but I have a class tomorrow morning. And I must also work again tomorrow night. Somewhere in between I need some sleep."

Sullivan appeared deflated.

"Certainly. I understand. It's just that ..."

O'Farrell interrupted seeing his disappointment, "But the day after is Sunday. No classes, no work. I have the whole day free."

She looked up with an expression he took as hoping he would agree. He beamed.

"That would be wonderful. Shall I pick you up?"

"Let's meet for coffee at the same café, Deux Magots. Say nine o'clock in the morning?"

"I'll be there."

He wasn't sure why she did not want to reveal where she lived. Hoped it wasn't a complication of some sort. But he'd take what he could. "I'll say goodnight then, Miss O'Farrell."

"Call me Maureen, Trevor. See you Sunday."

CHAPTER 3

FIRST WORLD WAR - NORTHEAST FRANCE – SEPTEMBER, 1918

It was wrenchingly difficult for Sullivan to return to the front after those few days in Paris with Maureen O'Farrell. They spent that entire Sunday together. Each shared personal details of their lives. His ten years in the army as an engineer, his duties since arriving in France. She commented on his good fortune avoiding service in those appalling trenches portrayed in the newspapers.

As for her, why she left Ireland, the politics only a part of it. More about having a life not confined to a stereotypical woman's role. Marriage, children, with no intellectual dimension. She needed something more. Difficult for women everywhere but Ireland was especially backward. France seemed above Victorian convention so it made sense to seek a life here. Attracted to art from an early age caused her to think how she might make that a career.

While sitting at a café she sketched Sullivan. A striking likeness. Yet it was the background setting rendering that gave it real quality. Showing other sketches within her sketch pad revealed her to be a talented artist.

"These are remarkable, Maureen. I'd love to see your paintings. These sketches are more interesting than all those enormous paintings at the Louvre."

"Thank you. But my work is nothing like the art found in the Louvre. Most people don't know that the Louvre does not contain *objects d'art* of later vintage than the mid-19th century. Most of those paintings you refer to are 15th and 16th century religiously inspired subjects. An era of much different style. As an art student I appreciate the talents of the older works but they don't invoke an emotional response.

"Personally I'm more attracted to artists of the movement called Impressionism. A Paris-based school of painting of only the last forty years. Too young for those artists' work to populate museums. But they will someday. You should see them. My favorites are Sisley and Pissarro. I like Monet too."

Sullivan smiled. Maureen was clearly animated. "So how is this Impressionism different?"

"Oh my. In so many ways different ways. Impressionist painting is first about light. The depiction of light acting on ordinary scenes. Short thick brush strokes rather than defining detail like those paintings in the Louvre. Good art invokes emotion."

"Therefore the name Impressionism?"

"Exactly."

"So where do you view this art?"

"Salons, galleries, exhibitions."

"Perhaps you can show me when I next return to Paris on leave?"

"I would like that very much, Trevor. I mean about your returning to Paris."

A difficult farewell late that night. He must return to his unit the following day, she to classes and her night job. This time she allowed him to escort to her apartment building near the Sorbonne.

"I would ask you up but I have two roommates, Jeanette and Natasha. Not very private."

"I understand," Sullivan said relieved that she was not harboring some secret life. "This has been wonderful meeting you, Maureen. May I write to you?"

"Of course, Trevor."

That night ended with O'Farrell initiating a passionate kiss.

"My sketch will let me picture your face."

They kissed again with Sullivan vowing to return. Captivated by Maureen O'Farrell, he felt her reciprocal romantic feelings.

Sullivan experienced the same depression of any soldier ending leave and returning to the war. A cruel transposition from Paris back to the stink and horror of the trenches? At least his duty placed him somewhat in the rear. The German Somme offensive that landed him in the thick of any infantry attack was a fluke.

———

After supporting the British for eleven months, the U.S. 12th Engineers transferred to American control in July. A different kind of army and a different location on the Western Front further south. After working alongside the experienced British Army, Sullivan's engineers complained about the lack of the American's military experience.

General John Pershing commanding American Expeditionary Forces finally felt ready to commit a predominately American fighting force in a major offensive against the Germans. Three corps of the U.S. First Army massed southeast of Verdun alongside French colonial troops. In support, the 12th Engineers constructed miles of main track and a network of spur lines to shuttle ammunition, artillery, water, and rations.

The American attack commenced near Saint-Mihiel with the objective of breaking through German defenses and taking the fortified city of Metz. Manpower superiority of the fresh U.S. Forces pushed the Germans back. After the Battle of Saint-Mihiel in September the 12th Engineers followed the victorious First Army north to a position facing the German's Hindenburg Line. Here the American First Army joined the Second Army with two French armies on their left flank. 1.2 million Allied troops poised for a major offensive against less than half that number of exhausted German troops.

By September, Sullivan's unit found itself north of Verdun on the edge of the Argonne Forest. Although exhausted, the Germans were not yet beaten. Having captured the Argonne Forest in the early stages of the war, during the intervening years they constructed a daunting defensive network within the heavily wooded terrain.

Their forward line consisted of trenches and listening posts. Once past this forward warning position, advancing Allied forces needed to push through dense forest clogged with undergrowth. Beyond that the Germans' first main battle line consisted of well defended trenches with extensive barbed wire entanglements. Behind that a final defensive line used natural and man-made barriers supported by interlocking machine gun positions.

The Germans massed artillery further yet to the rear, presighted to their last defensible line. Any attacking force successful penetrating that far must move quickly or risk annihilation by a last-ditch German artillery bombardment.

After a massive Allied artillery bombardment lasting twenty-four hours, the attack began. The green American troops believed the bombardment would neutralize enemy resistance. Having witnessed these exchanges of artillery while supporting the British, Sullivan knew better.

The Allied offensive made advances of several miles that first day. Sullivan's construction unit followed by laying light-gauge rail track to move supplies closer to the advancing Allied forward positions.

The fighting proved bitter. The artillery did not destroy German entrenched fortifications. The Germans retreated to successive lines of defenses. As everywhere else in this war, defensive artillery and machine guns harvested terrible numbers of casualties from attacking forces moving in the open. After five days the Allied offensive stalled.

———

Sullivan received an unusual order to report to the forward command tent for the 77th Infantry Division. The 77th anchored the western end of the American line where it linked with the French sector. What could this be about?

"Captain Sullivan, I have a special mission for you," Colonel Stacy commanding the 308th Infantry Regiment said. "You will be temporarily attached to my command."

Sullivan saluted Stacy.

"May I ask why I've been attached to your infantry regiment, Colonel?" Sullivan said.

"Of course, Captain. You're an engineering officer. Specifically a railroad man. Regular Army. West Point. Highly recommended. Let me explain our mission."

Stacy leaned over a map spread over a folding table. Tracing with his finger along the map, he said, "Two of my battalions have advanced to here. They're now within striking distance of an important strategic objective here.

"Their mission is to capture and hold the Binarville-La Viergette Road part way up a line of hills at a junction here at Charlevaux Mill. They'll advance up the Ravin de Charlevaux then cross a shallow stream to assault the objective. The French will be advancing on our left flank. On our right is the American 307th Regiment.

"Now parallel to the Binarville-La Viergette Road is a rail line. It is vital to German resupply. We need someone familiar with railroads and demolition. That's you. Depending on our success, we either destroy it decisively or turn it to our own use if we can hold the terrain."

"Yes, Sir," Sullivan said gloomily. What shitty luck. Part of an infantry attack into the teeth of German defenses. Hilly densely wooded ground undoubtedly within German artillery range. Killing ground that favored the Germans.

Stacy said, "You're to set off and join Major Whittlesey commanding the 1st and 2nd Battalions. You will give him these orders."

Sullivan stuck the orders inside his tunic wondering what he was in for. He recalled with unease the general order of the 77th Division commander General Alexander before this offensive

26

commenced. *No retreat. Defend any ground taken. Attack forward, ignore your flanks.* Sounded like a stupid order more typical of the British general staff. But at the time he didn't think that affected his railroad engineering unit.

The offensive was into its fourth day when Sullivan set off at dawn to join with Whittlesey's command. He was accompanying a relief company joining Whittlesey's main body.

The Argonne Forest seemed more a jungle than forest. A continuous tangle of nearly impenetrable undergrowth between the larger trees made slow going except by defined trails. It posed a natural defensive line when joined to the man-made German Hindenburg line of trenches that stretched north all the way to the English Channel.

Sullivan hoped the sergeant leading the column knew the way. Easy to get lost in this twisting maze. Impossible to see a concealed enemy.

"What happened to Lt. Colonel Smith? I was ordered to report to him. Thought he was in command of the 308th not this Colonel Stacy?" Sullivan asked the lieutenant commanding relief column, K Company as they set out.

"You don't know? Smith was killed yesterday. They're not sure what happened. But Smith was leading a small detachment the same way we're headed."

Holy shit.

The trek lasted less than one hour. Signs of recent fighting became evident. Shell craters. Splintered trees. With each step the sounds of battle appeared closer. Although sound direction can be deceiving, Sullivan felt it came from not only in front but also either side. Unfortunately that later proved to be the case.

Nothing could prepare anyone for combat. Once K Company joined Whittlesey's command it was clear that these soldiers had been through a terrible fight the last several days. Everyone moved about by crawling. Periodic cracks of rifle fire punctuated the threat of German snipers.

Sullivan eventually made his way to Major Whittlesey in a vacated German dugout.

Whittlesey was tall and slender. Wire rim glasses, professorial in appearance, soft spoken, a slight resemblance to President Wilson. A former lawyer, he joined the army a month after the United States entered the war. Now he looked gaunt and dirty.

"Captain Sullivan 12th Engineers reporting as ordered, Sir. Orders from Colonel Stacy."

Whittlesey took the orders without saying anything. After reading the paper and shaking his head with an expression of disbelief, he handed the orders to another officer. "Read this George."

After a moment, the other officer, a captain said, "This is ridiculous. Headquarters has no idea what shape we're in. Or what we're up against. You need to push back."

"I agree. Sergeant, get me a runner. Someone from K Company who knows their way back."

While Whittlesey penned his argument against the order to assault the ridgeline to the north, the other officer introduced himself to Sullivan.

"Captain George McMurtry. Glad to have you with us. How long in the army?"

"Over ten years. West Point '07. And you?"

"Harvard Law. Same as the Major. Citizen soldiers. A couple of New York lawyers. But I fought in Cuba with Teddy Roosevelt's regiment so I've seen a bit of action in my time. How'd you end up here?"

"Apparently because I know railroads."

"Well you certainly got the shit end of the stick being assigned to the 308th, Captain. Did you piss somebody off?"

In contrast to Whittlesey's slender stature, George McMurtry was a barrel-chested burly man. Outgoing, even smiling although having undergone days of vicious combat. How could he joke while obviously stuck in this desperate situation? And with orders that apparently sounded suicidal.

The sound of an intense firefight erupted to the rear of their position. An hour later a corporal arrived to report to Whittlesey. The runner from K Company.

"Sergeant Butler told me to report we've been cut off in the rear. He's in command of K Company now. Lieutenant's dead. I couldn't get through to headquarters. Butler says our left flank is exposed. No sign of the French. He thinks their advance stalled. We're now stuck well out in front he thinks. Exposed on our left."

"Very well, Corporal. Get back to Butler and tell him to dig in," Whittlesey said.

With the runner lines cut, Whittlesey resorted to sending his reply to his new orders by carrier pigeon. He received a reply from headquarters the following morning.

The original orders carried by Sullivan remained unchanged. Whittlesey's new orders specifically read: *Proceed through a gap in the German defensive line along the ravine of the Charlevaux Creek and take up a position below the Viergette-Moulin de Charlevaux road and the parallel railroad track. Objective must be taken today regardless of casualties, regardless of lack of support on your left flank.*

Whittlesey shared the latest orders with McMurtry and Sullivan. Reconciled to obeying his orders, Whittlesey replied to headquarters: *Understood but I don't know if you'll hear from us again.*

With most of his officers killed, Whittlesey said, "Captain Sullivan. Will you take command of D Company?"

"Yes, Sir," Sullivan said. His thoughts turned to Maureen O'Farrell. No time to write a real letter. Maybe just draft a few lines to be found on his body. A shock after his other letters over the last three months recounting the war's horrors as witnessed from relative safety.

Within the hour Whittlesey gave the order to move forward. What would later be known as the *Lost Battalion* was a composite command consisting of seven infantry companies plus two machine gun companies. At that it was still below strength of a normal infantry battalion with fewer than 700 men when they advanced on October 2.

German resistance was relatively light. Except for unfortunate A Company. Of the original 205 men when the assault initiated five days earlier, previous fighting had reduced it by half.

That afternoon they lost 90 more. Only 18 men remained when the day's objective was achieved by evening.

Whittlesey positioned his troops along a deep depression at the bottom of a steep slope below the road. Surrounded by heavy forest with dense brush, it provided the best cover from which to spend the night. His battalion now consisted of only 554 men.

A patrol from Sullivan's first combat command, D Company, returned after surprising and neutralizing a German forward position. The dense undergrowth afforded advantage even to the attacking Americans.

The sergeant heading the patrol came up to Sullivan, "Look what we got here, Captain. A sniper rifle. Wonder how many of our boys been killed by this one?"

Taking the rifle by the barrel the sergeant was about to smash it against a rock.

"Hold on, Sergeant. Let me see that."

Sullivan took the rifle. Not the ordinary field issue. He examined it closely sighting on a target through the mounted scope.

"This is a Gewehr 98 Mauser, Sergeant. Mighty fine weapon wouldn't you say?" Sullivan said, "And this Zeiss scope. Good German optics."

"You seem to know your weapons, Captain."

Sullivan decided to keep the weapon. This fight would only get worse. His sidearm wouldn't be enough.

"Find me the ammunition for this rifle, Sergeant."

As Whittlesey's men dug in eating the last of their limited rations none realized their precarious position. The arrival of K Company with Sullivan in tow was the last direct contact from regimental headquarters. It was only Whittlesey's command that successfully penetrated the German's first defensive line. Allied forces on both flanks had stalled their advance under German resistance. Although the fighting was bitter, Whittlesey's battalion had exploited a weak section in the German line. The Germans recovered then closed that gap behind Whittlesey's advance. Cut off, the battalion was now also surrounded.

The situation worsened the following morning. German artillery began shelling at 8:30AM. Reconnaissance patrols returned to advise Whittlesey that enemy patrols were sighted on both flanks. No friendly forces in evidence. E Company returned after engaging a large German force taking 20 casualties. Only 18 men returned. They confirmed that the command was completely encircled.

Mortar rounds then began falling uncomfortably close. While the German artillery was not directly threatening because of their position on the reverse side of the east-west slope, a mortar with its high vertical trajectory could be devastating.

"Captain Sullivan, the Germans have set up a mortar somewhere about here," Whittlesey said pointing on the map. "I need you to send a platoon and neutralize it."

Sullivan's D Company numbered no more than two platoons. He was the only officer along with just one sergeant. As with the whole 77th Infantry Division, better known as *New York's Own*, his soldiers consisted mostly of new recruits and conscripts. Taxi drivers, clerks, tailors, and factory workers. And this battalion led by two Wall Street lawyers. No regular army veterans other than himself. Sullivan must therefore take personal command of the patrol to neutralize the mortar.

He selected twelve men. Even though soldiers for only a year these young men were disciplined. In a short time they had seen their share of death. They didn't need any instructions from an *engineer*, regular army or not.

Sullivan took the German sniper rifle.

His senior man, a corporal, deployed his men in groups of four each. One group would advance while the others provided cover.

After advancing a couple of hundred yards they could hear the thump of the mortar as it launched its explosive round.

Sullivan said to the corporal, "Get me to where I can see the mortar crew. Doesn't have to be too close. Just in range by maybe two hundred yards."

"Yes, Sir." The young soldier's expression suggested *what the hell did this stupid officer expect he was going to accomplish just because he had this rifle with a telescopic scope?*

Pistol shooting was Sullivan's specialty at West Point. But he was no slouch with a rifle. He understood the principles of marksmanship even though never having any training in long range sniper shooting. There was no such training in the U.S. Army. Only a few good marksmen had even been issued scoped rifles.

He gave the corporal his field glasses to spot their target. Slithering on their elbows in the concealing brush, Sullivan followed ten yards behind.

Eventually the corporal stopped. In a whisper he said, "German infantry. Spread on a line from that group of trees on the left to that big rock on the right."

"How many do 'ya think?"

"Can't tell, Sir."

"The mortar?"

"Can't see it. Must be behind those guys out front."

Sullivan sighted through his scope to assess the target. After several moments, "Here's the plan, Corporal. I'm going to crawl to the left to that little hillock. Want to see if I can spot the mortar crew. You bring up the rest of the platoon. Put them to our right.

"Tell them to open up on the Germans once I fire first. When they're in position get back to me. You'll be my spotter."

The corporal gave Sullivan another questioning expression then set off.

Sullivan's new position proved perfect. A dense clump of brush allowed good concealment. The slight rise provided a much better view. Once situated he spotted the three-man mortar crew. About two hundred yards.

Returning to Sullivan's position ten minutes later, the corporal said, "They're in position, Sir."

"Good. I can see the mortar. My first shots will target the crew. I want you to spot the infantry positions with the field glasses. Call out some reference so I can pick out the target quickly."

His first target filled the scope eyepiece sufficient to place the crosshairs on the German's head. Well within range. Problem was he didn't know this weapon. Was it still sighted in accurately by the dead German sniper or had it been damaged? Had the sniper adjusted the scope for different windage or elevation? Was he a good enough shot?

No wind. He guessed at the elevation adjustment for the distance. Just have to take the shot and see what happens. Target the torso for the largest possible target.

"Get ready, Corporal."

The target was standing carrying a mortar round. Sullivan let out his breath slowly and squeezed the trigger.

The rifle recoiled up.

"Shit, you got him!" the corporal said in whisper.

Firing to their right erupted. Immediately he sighted on another of the mortar crew and squeezed off a shot. The second German went down. The third crewman scampering out of sight realizing his position was compromised.

"Corporal! Target?"

"Two yards to the right of that double trunk tree at one o'clock."

"Got it."

Another hit. A beautifully lethal weapon this Mauser.

Ten minutes later Sullivan downed another. As the Germans pulled back attempting to remove the mortar, he shot another.

"Corporal, advance the men and drop a grenade down the mortar tube. Then let's get the hell out of here."

Once back with the rest of the command reporting to Whittlesey, the corporal couldn't contain himself excitedly saying, "You should have seen it, Major. Captain Sullivan took out five Germans with that sniper rifle."

CHAPTER 4

By the afternoon the American makeshift redoubt came under sniper attack. They were out of food. Ammunition low. Water must wait for the cover of darkness to scavenge from the stream. Risky business since the Germans pre-sighted the area.

Whittlesey's effective fighting force had dwindled further to now less than 400. A 25 percent casualty rate in the last 24 hours. Night brought some relief with only enemy harassing action. More distressing though was the agonized moaning of the American wounded. Nothing could be done to ease their agony. Along with gnawing hunger and the damp cold, sleep was impossible.

Since their initial penetration of the German line, Whittlesey's *Lost Battalion* was lost only in the sense they appeared doomed. They knew their location and so did regimental headquarters. As crude as it was, carrier pigeon communications effectively relayed their circumstances. Other American units tried unsuccessfully to break through the reestablished German entrenched positions to mount a rescue.

Sullivan fought alongside his depleted D Company. He ordered his men to wait until they could place a target in their sights to conserve dwindling ammunition. Crisp *yes sirs* followed with newfound respect for this marksman officer.

34

His corporal turned out to be a sharp-eyed spotter. Sullivan tasked him with locating German snipers. He believed he took out two.

"Sir, two o'clock a hundred and fifty yards. Large rock," The corporal said.

"Don't see him," Sullivan said after identifying the position. "Corporal?"

Sullivan turned his head. Next to him the corporal lay dead. A bullet through his left eye.

In the afternoon friendly incoming artillery commenced. As the rounds landed progressively nearer it became evident the target coordinates were wrong. Total disaster was only avoided when a wounded carrier pigeon named *Cher Ami* managed to reach division headquarters to correct the error. But not until friendly fire claimed 30 more Americans.

———

The next night was colder. No rations for over thirty hours. Leggings were unwrapped for the three beleaguered medical aides to use as makeshift bandages.

The following day they knew their exact position was known to headquarters. Low flying American aircraft attempted to drop much needed supplies. Most missed the *Lost Battalion* but the brave attempt by the aviators fostered a glimmer of hope. Enough of a spark for the beleaguered doughboys to turn back a determined German grenade attack late in the afternoon.

From the cliff above, grenades began raining down on the American position. The emboldened Germans came out from cover to throw grenades. Exposed, they made good targets for Sullivan.

———

Another terrible night. Even retrieving water from the stream was abandoned because of concentrated German machine gun fire. Without food for days, Whittlesey ordered no more burials of the dead to conserve his men's strength.

With ammunition all but gone, the end seemed near for the *Lost Battalion*.

If you were still standing you were lucky. Luckier yet if you were also not wounded. Along with many others, Sullivan's luck eventually ran out that afternoon.

After Whittlesey refused the enemy commander's surrender request, the Germans mounted their most aggressive attack yet.

Sullivan's D Company now numbering only 22 anchored the west end of the Americans' pocket below the hill. With their limited ammunition they must wait for clear targets. That meant allowing attacking Germans to get very close. In this dense underbrush it also meant the probability of engaging the enemy with bayonets.

Machine gunfire savaged D Company's position prior to the German assault. Next came hand grenades. The German *Model 24 Stielhandgranate* was a concussion grenade. An offensive weapon effective in the open since it relied on concussive blast effect instead of fragmentation.

A nearby grenade knocked Sullivan unconscious. Recovering after a short time he realized his position had been overrun. Some of his men engaged the Germans with their bayonets. Extracting his .45 pistol he picked out targets close by. Dropping several Germans disrupted consolidation of their assault.

His own men rebounded at the sight of Germans dropping under Sullivan's amazing rate of fire hitting target after target as he expended two magazines of ammunition.

Until Sullivan also went down.

A bullet struck the left side of his abdomen. The impact spun him around. Like being hit by a hammer. Terrible pain. Quickly his shirt and service tunic soaked with blood.

Realizing that he couldn't count on help, Sullivan unwrapped one of his leggings to bind up his chest. A dirty handkerchief forced to serve as a bandage.

Still conscious, Sullivan watched in amazement as his exhausted men repelled the Germans. He had no idea the extent of his injuries. When he moved, pain nearly caused him to pass out while coughing up blood. Must have been hit in the lung. Little chance of medical help. Everyone still functioning was too depleted by thirst and hunger to do anything beyond their own needs. Many still able to hold a rifle showed evidence of wounds. Dead and dying lay everywhere.

Nothing to do but just sit here and wait for the end. If bleeding internally he would probably not last much longer. Another German attack would finish them anyway. This night would be their last.

But as darkness fell enemy fire abruptly dwindled. Quiet fell across the woods broken only by the distressing cries of the wounded. After such a heavy attack what did this silence signify?

To Whittlesey and McMurtry's surprise an unknown officer accompanied by several fresh American doughboys arrived at their command bunker.

"Lieutenant Tillman, Sir. There are three companies of the 307th just a hundred yards from here. We're here to reinforce your command, Sir."

———

Those 307th reinforcements were just the advance of a successful broader American counterattack in the Argonne. The Germans fell back. American ambulances even began arriving along the Charlevaux Road at the top of the crest above the position of the *Lost Battalion*.

Major Whittlesey assembled the remaining soldiers able to walk. 194 men of the more than original 700 marched slowly back to regimental headquarters. Those soldiers moving up to replace them at the front stopped and in silence saluted as the survivors of the *Lost Battalion* passed.

A field surgeon informed Sullivan he should survive barring infection. The bullet passed through his abdomen breaking a rib and ripping out tissue. Seemed to have missed any organs. Except for a shattered rib puncturing his lung. A nasty scar but no debilitating impairment after surgery to correct the damage.

In the aftermath those of the *Lost Battalion* learned their ordeal made news throughout the world during those terrible days in the forest. Eventually seven Medal of Honor citations were awarded, and thirty recipients received the next highest decoration, the Distinguished Service Cross.

———

Evacuated to an American hospital in the small town of Revigny thirty miles south of the battlefield, Sullivan immediately posted letters to his mother in Brooklyn and Maureen O'Farrell in Paris.

Convalescing in an adjacent bed was George McMurtry. Like Sullivan his wounds were not life-threatening. Within days, Charles Whittlesey visited the wounded of his ill-fated command.

After speaking to his friend McMurtry, Whittlesey turned to Sullivan.

"The surgeon says you're going to recover, Captain."

"Well I hope the war ends before I recover enough to be put on the line again. Can't say I'd want to go through that meat grinder again, Sir."

Whittlesey offered a weak smile. "I heard several accounts of what you accomplished, Captain. I've recommended you for the Medal of Honor."

"Damn glad you joined our merry band, Sullivan," the ever ebullient McMurtry said while propped up in his bed. "Why you're as deadly as that Tennessee sergeant named York that captured a whole company of Germans up the line north of us. Happened the same day that we got pulled out. And you're not even infantry. How'd you learn to shoot like that?"

Sullivan just smiled and shook his head. Changing the subject he said, "And what are you and the Major going to do after the war?"

"Back to practicing law. And you? You're regular army aren't you?"

"Not when this war ends. Years of boredom now the horrors of this war. I've experienced enough of both as a soldier. I like the idea of being just an engineer a lot better."

A few days later tears ran freely down his cheeks at the sight of Maureen O'Farrell striding down the aisle between the rows of beds. Heads of the wounded doughboys turned at the rare sight of a pretty woman not wearing a nurse's uniform. A few whistles caused her to bless them with a big smile which brought cheers.

More cheers followed when she bent down and took Sullivan's face in both hands and kissed him.

"You've some explaining to do, Trevor Sullivan. I thought you were safe running about on your trains. All of Paris knows of the American *Lost Battalion*. Then I suddenly receive your last letter saying you had been in the thick of that fighting. In a hospital wounded. A terrible shock."

He was grinning at the sheer joy of being close to Maureen. Surviving the odds. The prospect of a life.

"Got shanghaied, Maureen. Just bad luck. But that's all over now."

"Your wounds? How bad are they?"

"Got shot in the side. No lasting damage. A broken rib punctured my lung but I'll recover fully."

She sighed with relief. "What happened? The newspapers said so many American soldiers were killed?"

With a somber expression he said, "Not easy to explain. Words can't easily express what it was like. Later on I'll try to tell you more details. Even I need to sort it out."

"How long must you stay here?"

"A few weeks."

He took her hand. "Once I'm out of here I'll meet you in Paris."

"I'd love that, Trevor."

"Maureen. What I mean is I'm staying for good. Here in France. Paris. I'll find a job. God knows France will need engineers to rebuild from the war."

"You'll leave the American Army?"

"Yes. That I've decided. As soon as the war is over. That'll be soon."

"That would be grand, Trevor. I mean that you're staying in France."

Rising on an elbow he said, "I'm not saying this very well, Maureen. What I mean is I'm in love with you. I want to be with you."

"Oh my," she replied but quickly broke into a smile. "I don't know what to say. We barely know each other, Trevor."

"I know enough. Never met a woman like you."

"Well, Trevor Sullivan, I admit to being quite taken with you myself. When you get to Paris let's see what develops. I'll be waiting. Anxiously waiting."

They kissed prompting another round of cheers from the wounded doughboys.

———

By the end of October the Allies pushed the Germans back to the pre-war border. Supplies of every kind exhausted. Food particularly scarce. German manpower reserves used up while 10,000 new American troops arrived in France each day. The German civilian population rose up in revolt against the monarchy. Widespread military mutiny threatened. With no way for Germany to mount a successful defense, it only remained how the war would formally end.

On November 9th the German parliament declared Germany to be a republic. Kaiser Wilhelm abdicated going into exile in the Netherlands. On November 11, 1919 an armistice was signed ending the Great War. A war that claimed an estimated 10,000,000 military deaths. The dislocations and the aftermath would shape the world for the remainder of the twentieth century.

For Trevor Sullivan, like thousands of others, their personal world was irrevocably changed. Nothing would ever be the same. Remaining in the U.S. Army no longer remained a career alternative. A life with Maureen O'Farrell hopefully now his future.

When Sullivan reported to his regimental headquarters two weeks before the Armistice he was greeted with effusive fanfare. A genuine hero. The following day his battalion assembled on parade to witness his decoration ceremony. A rare occurrence for an army engineer to be highly decorated for valor.

After a brief address, the commanding officer of the 12th Engineers announced Sullivan's promotion to major, presenting him a set of gold oak leaf major's insignia. The decorations for valor followed. The United States Medal of Honor was followed by a French colonel looping a ribbon around his neck carrying the French Croix de Guerre.

But the accolades meant little. He ached for the war to end so he could be with O'Farrell. Once she knew Sullivan was going to recover she returned to Paris for degree finals at the Sorbonne. They each wrote several times a week. After professing his love, Sullivan was delighted by the increasing intimacy of O'Farrell letters.

One letter received immediately after the Armistice formally ended hostilities confirmed her degree of affection.

My Dearest Trevor,

Now that this ugly war is over when can we be together? I greatly miss you. I recall those first days when we met. Everything now seems to be looking brighter. I passed the finals for my degree. I was then accepted for post-graduate studies. Best of all, I have a new job. In the arts! Isn't that wonderful? I'm the new administrative assistant to the curator of the Musée du Luembourg. Close enough to walk from my apartment or the Sorbonne.

By the way, with my new job I quit the Folies. No more dancing naked. But for you, Trevor I'll make an exception. How about that for shameless boldness! See what liberating Paris does to Irish prudishness.

Will you be able to spend Christmas in Paris? I do hope so my dear. My roommates have left so the apartment is ours.

I love you, Trevor,

Maureen

Not only did he spend Christmas with Maureen in Paris, he formally resigned his commission from the U.S. Army. Although the regiment was preparing for return to the United States within a couple of months, Sullivan was not essential. His recuperation limited him only to light administrative duties. His Colonel attempted to dissuade his resignation pointing out that he had a promising military career beyond the demobilization. He was regular army, West Point, and a decorated hero. Should make colonel in a few years. Sullivan graciously declined.

No regrets over the decision. He could still make a career as a civilian engineer. And why not in Paris? But the brightest prospect was Maureen O'Farrell.

CHAPTER 5

PARIS, FRANCE – 1919

Sullivan returned to Paris on Christmas Eve afternoon, 1918. From that first meeting the previous spring Maureen O'Farrell dominated all his thoughts. With the separation caused by the war, their romance blossomed through letters. Then the shock of Sullivan's letter telling of his ordeal in the Argonne Forest crystalized O'Farrell's affections after seeing him in the hospital.

O'Farrell was waiting for his train. Sighting him stepping off the train she rushed to him. Falling into his arms she wept with joy.

"You're in uniform. But you're done with the army aren't you?"

"Absolutely. But I haven't gotten around to purchasing any civilian clothes. Last chance to wear my major's oak leaves."

"Let's go home. I've fixed up the apartment a little. I hope you like it. Didn't have much money. It's quite small."

"I'm sure I'll love it. We can shop for some things together. I've a little money from my mustering out back pay. Some savings back in New York. It'll see us through until I find a job."

O'Farrell stared into his eyes for several moments.

"What it is, Maureen?"

"Just looking at you, Trevor Sullivan. Wondering what it'll be like being together."

He kissed her while embracing her tightly. Felling her breasts press against his chest aroused him. He could feel his erection pressing against her thigh."

She did also. "Let's take a taxi and go home, Trevor."

Once inside the apartment they embraced again. This time they made no attempt to disguise their mutual desire. His hands ran down her backside. She grabbed his erection.

She walked him to the bedroom. Both started to undress.

While hurriedly undoing buttons, she said nervously, "You'd think that women's clothing would do more to show off a woman's charms. But instead it covers everything. Made for ugly old ladies. Men can't tell the difference in all these layers of fabric. I like my Folies costume better."

He smiled becoming ever more aroused as she got down to her garter belt, hose and brassiere.

Standing there only in his under pants with his erection obvious, she said, "See how more practical a man's clothing is?" Pointing to his underwear, "Aren't you going to remove those if we're to make love?"

As he slipped down his underwear. She looked at his fully erect member making a pleasingly surprised expression with her eyes as she removed her bra.

He knew she had magnificent breasts having seen her show at the Folies. But looking at her fully naked this close was more erotic then anything ever fantasized. He had been with other women but never with this effect.

Lovemaking lasted all afternoon.

Wearing only her unbuttoned blouse and still naked underneath, O'Farrell brought a bottle of wine and glasses back to the bed.

"Well that was truly spectacular," she said while pouring wine for each. "To our life together, Trevor Sullivan."

He kissed her. "More than spectacular, Maureen. You're an extraordinary lover."

Looking at him coyly she said, "You're not the first but that shouldn't matter does it? I'm sure I'm not your first either."

His experience with oral sex was limited. Apparently not for Maureen as evidenced by her exploitive techniques giving a broader dimension to their intimacy.

"Of course it doesn't matter," she said breathlessly. "See, I'm just as progressive as you."

Not sure how she acquired her lovemaking skills. Clearly not from a traditional Irish upbringing. Perhaps just a natural ability once Victorian and Judeo-Christian orthodoxy was shed. Of course he didn't care. He agreed with her feminist philosophy. Stupid sexual taboos were imposed on women by men. And men didn't know what they were missing.

———

The next several months were the best of Sullivan's life. Deeply in love they developed a domestic routine suiting the interests of both. For O'Farrell her days and often nights were consumed with her museum job and her studies. He diligently studied French while she was at work knowing he must be able to read fluently if he intended finding employment.

Although not much of a cook, he made sure there was always food available to assemble a simple meal. Venturing out each day forced him to develop his verbal skills. Lovemaking became the day's reward.

And all this in Paris. Like O'Farrell, Sullivan fell in love with the city. So different from Brooklyn and the many boring army postings.

They eased effortlessly into a domestic routine. A forerunner to marriage but neither raised that issue directly. Still weighty matters to be sorted out. O'Farrell certainly wasn't the domestic type. She intended to have her own career. He had no idea where she stood on the issue of children. For that matter he wasn't sure how he felt. Children could change so many other things both found important.

With O'Farrell's tutoring, Sullivan's verbal French advanced to a level sufficient to seek employment.

In March he secured a managerial post with the Ministry of Finance which had responsibility for industry and much of the task of rebuilding after the war. His wartime credentials and engineering experience related to railroad operations made him a valued asset. The rail infrastructure in the northeast required extensive repair from war damage. Shipments of materials for rebuilding towns, roads, bridges would place unprecedented demands on the national rail service. Although his responsibilities entailed frequent travel, his base office would be within the ministry in Paris, housed in the Richelieu Wing of the Louvre Palace.

After a decade of bachelor officer quarters and a year of war mostly in tents, their small apartment felt like a real home. A typical Left Bank Parisian street view with two windows looking down onto quiet Rue Laplace just west of the Sorbonne.

While Sullivan and O'Farrell enjoyed a period of settled bliss in their adopted city, things were much different for their families back home. For Sullivan's family the 36th state ratified the U.S. constitutional amendment to prohibit the sale of alcoholic beverages in January, 1920. Prohibition would officially be the law one year later. His mother's tavern in Brooklyn supported not only her but Sullivan's only sister, her husband, and three children. Not sure what Prohibition meant to their economic future.

For Maureen O'Farrell's family the political situation in Ireland continued to worsen. Ever since the ill-conceived British executions of the leaders of the Easter Rising in 1916, Westminster's arrogant bungling continued to fan the fire of Irish rebellion. The British move to impose military conscription on the Irish in the last year of the Great War provided the final impetus. The militant Irish nationalist political party Sinn Féin swept the 1918 parliamentary elections, ousting the established Irish Parliamentary Party. The newly elected Sinn Féin members of parliament then refused to take their seats in the House of Commons of the United Kingdom in London. In further defiance they established an Irish parliament, Dáil Éireann, in Dublin.

A provincial Irish parliament was previously abolished in the Act of Union of 1800 which bound Ireland to the United

Kingdom. Therefore this was a direct rebuke of British rule. British Prime Minister Lloyd George outlawed the upstart Irish Dáil Éireann. But unlike the 1916 Rising which held little popular support, the election of 1918 expressed an overwhelming rejection of Britain by a large majority of Ireland's population. The exception being the Unionist-Protestant concentration in six counties of the northern province of Ulster.

By 1919, the tensions progressed to outright rebellion. This time in history the Irish people seemed sufficiently united in seeking some form of autonomy from Britain. Violence instigated by an armed guerrilla insurgency quickly escalated overshadowing political negotiation.

With the possibility of Irish autonomy came heighten tensions in the northern counties of Ulster. Sectarian conflict between Catholics and Protestants there was not new. Now those lines became drawn not only culturally but as pro-republican for a sovereign Ireland versus pro-union to remain part of the United Kingdom. Protestant pro-Britain unionists overwhelmingly held economic and political control of industrialized Ulster. Those entrenched interests became potentially threatened if the six northern counties with protestant majorities were joined with the twenty-six Catholic majority counties.

The unique situation in the North placed O'Farrell's family in the midst of the swirling antagonisms. Derry to the Irish, or Londonderry as it was officially known, was the second largest city in Ulster. Catholics here represented a majority in the city while Protestants held a majority across all the six northern counties, including its largest city Belfast. Ulster's factional antagonisms created a more complex political environment than the rest of Ireland. As if in a civil war, no Ulster citizen could remain neutral.

—

The Irish War of Independence began on January 21, 1919. On that day the Sinn Féin elected representatives assembled in Dublin forming the parliamentary First Dáil. They drafted a Declaration of Independence reaffirming the 1916 proclamation of an Irish Republic. Punctuating that political statement with action, Irish Republican Volunteers acting on their own initiative killed two Royal Irish Constabulary officers in County Tipperary.

The militaristic volunteers considered the RIC to be the means by which Britain exercised control over Ireland. The RIC was composed of ethnically both Protestant and Catholic Irish. Politically the Constabulary consisted of officers favoring both positions of Irish autonomy and continued union with Britain. This was an Irish police force but the British administration in Dublin directed their control. Therefore most Irish viewed the RIC as an instrument of British oppression. Regardless of their political views, RIC officers soon found themselves collectively reviled as a British institution.

The violence would center on this conflict between the Irish Volunteers soon to be known as the Irish Republican Army, or IRA, and the RIC. Éamon de Valera the President of the outlawed Dáil Éireann made that a matter of official policy in April by passing a motion calling on the Irish people to ostracize the Royal Irish Constabulary.

The British government faced a dilemma. Putting down this insurrection solely with British troops was politically unacceptable. Furthermore it played into the republican position that Ireland was nothing more than a British colony. The British recourse was to bolster the RIC with *auxiliary* resources, ostensibly a police force but in practice poorly controlled non-Irish paramilitary mercenaries. The worst of both alternatives that would define much of the violence in the Anglo-Irish War.

While the rebellion enjoyed wide public support, lack of guns and money severely hampered military operations. Éamon De Valera went to the United States to raise money to fund the fledgling rebellion. Highly successful given the large ethnic Irish American population, he would remain in the United States until the end of 1920.

In De Valera's absence Michael Collins assumed control of the Volunteers and directing the operational aspects of the war against the British. Although officially the Minister of Finance of the shadow Irish government, Collins's extraordinary organizational abilities extended his portfolio more broadly. Brilliant, driven, and ruthless he became the symbol of the revolution both to the IRA and the British enemy. As Director of Intelligence for the Irish Republican Army he essentially ran military operations circumventing the Chief of Staff with whom he had differences.

By 1920 British efforts to quell the uprising remained unsuccessful. The Anglo-Irish War progressively worsened as the IRA continued to exploit the fundamental British dilemma. To successfully defeat this guerrilla enemy required disrupting its vital base of material support provided by the population. British tactics of intimidation by terror served only to harden Irish resolve. The IRA grew stronger gaining new recruits, evolving into an effective fighting force by developing tactics proving successful against the better equipped Crown security forces.

———

Trevor Sullivan and Maureen O'Farrell spent their first year enjoying a new life. They planned to marry in the spring of 1920. Depending on job advancement opportunities for Sullivan, they planned on continuing to live in Paris. They discussed the possibility of New York but Sullivan lobbied for Paris. Maureen suggested the idea of visiting his family in New York. Perhaps have the wedding there. A short honeymoon. But Sullivan said a two-way passage would be too costly. Nor could they leave their jobs for that many weeks.

"What about having the wedding in Derry? You'll want to have your family attend won't you?"

"You're joking? About Derry I mean. You've been following what's going on in Ireland. Derry's one of the meanest places in this rebellion. Not about to have my most special occasion in a place like that. And not by some damn priest. That's what mother would want. Then of course they'd want to know if you're a practicing Catholic. Were you ever even baptized? Since you have no religious feelings that would only make matters worse. I may be Catholic but I won't let the Church run my life."

"Okay, I see what you mean. But you're close to your mom and dad so how about this. We get married here in Paris by a magistrate. Have a grand party with all our friends. Then we'll go visit your family. The deed will be done. It'll be just a visit.

"We'd be gone only two weeks from our jobs. I've never been to Ireland and you haven't been home for a couple of years. A honeymoon of sorts. Along the way we can stop and see my aunt in Dublin then train up to Derry."

She thought for a moment warming to the idea. "Yes. That would be grand. Let's set a date. How about April? What better time to marry than springtime in Paris?

CHAPTER 6

By 1920 the Irish rebellion moved into a new phase. Although engaged in guerrilla hit-and-run tactics, the IRA became a disciplined military organization. Brigades were comprised of battalions of various sizes. Company designated units operated within their home geography. Each unit had a military structure with a commander, adjutant, intelligence officer, and quartermaster, all elected. Some fielded active service columns known as flying columns. These were the IRA's mobile strike force of disciplined gunmen. But chronic shortages of weapons consistently placed them at a decided disadvantage to Crown forces.

IRA strength came from broad backing by an angered majority of the population. Essential for any successful insurgency, popular support provided IRA fighters with food, shelter, and most of all, intelligence. Because of overwhelming resentment toward the British, lack of even the most basic cooperation with the British controlled Royal Irish Constabulary hampered police intelligence. Even civilians that did not support the IRA feared reprisal if suspected of collaboration with the government. Ostracized and blind, the RIC flailed about or hunkered down within their barracks.

Sinn Féin represented the political foundation of the rebellion. Many IRA such as Michael Collins were also active Sinn Féin members. Women formed their own militant support or-

51

ganization, Cumann na mBan, providing material support to the IRA.

As never before in their long troubled history with Ireland, the British now faced the entire Irish population turned against continued rule by the United Kingdom. A population that developed well organized institutions now standing in open rebellion. To the rest of the world it looked like a colonial struggle for independence.

The British government's own actions further inflamed Irish antagonism. A total reversal from the situation following the failed 1916 Rising where there was little popular support. Over the course of this new insurrection, the British security forces unintentionally reinforced support for the IRA. The application of repressive measures growing out of their colonial history. Inflicting collective punitive measures, destruction of property as reprisals, police harassment, internment without trial, martial law supplanting the rule of law, and throughout the conflict, extrajudicial executions.

From the beginning British security forces were on the defensive. By 1920 the RIC numbered over 9000. With the intensifying violence, public ostracism, living under virtual siege, and with divided loyalties within its ranks, retirements and resignations increased. New recruitment was choked off to a level insufficient to compensate for the attrition.

The British government's answer to the policing manpower crisis was to begin recruiting in January for the Royal Irish Constabulary Special Reserve, the RICSR. Coming largely from the unemployed ranks of former British soldiers serving in the Great War, these temporary police became known as *Black & Tans* for their mixed police and former military uniforms. Eventually their numbers would grow to 9,500 by the end of 1921. Ex-British Army soldiers with no police training. Foreign invaders to the Irish.

The British created yet another entirely separate counter-insurgency force. This force comprised of ex-British Army officers. This elite force was officially known as the Auxiliary Division of the Royal Irish Constabulary, or ADRIC, or more simply just the *Auxiliaries*. While the RIC and Black & Tans staffed barracks throughout Ireland, the Auxiliaries would operate with mobility where needed. These shock troops, moving about in armored cars with mounted machine guns, eventually numbered 1,400.

Relatively unrestrained, the Black & Tans and Auxiliaries began a reign of terror. Their principle tactic was to inflict collective damage on the population in acts of reprisal to IRA attacks. Torture and simple murder became commonplace.

To add sheer weight of military numbers, by January, 1920 there were also 20,000 British regular troops stationed throughout Ireland.

Short of a full military occupation of Ireland with regular troops, British Crown forces could still only react to IRA attacks. Those reactions progressively became more oppressive serving to escalate the war by further solidifying civilian support for the rebellion.

While twenty-six counties overwhelmingly sided with independence and supported armed rebellion, the situation was more complicated in the six counties of the northern Provence of Ulster. Over half the population there was Protestant actively supporting to remain part of the United Kingdom. Protestants controlled the industrial economy as well as the political power of Ulster. In a region with historic sectarian divisions, they feared becoming a minority into a predominately Catholic Ireland ruled from Dublin. Ulster unionists denied the rebels the widespread civilian support fueling the insurgency in the South. Protestant-unionist paramilitary groups joined with British Crown forces to suppress what they saw as a Catholic fueled rebellion.

The British government continued to mishandle the Irish problem. Continuing along the path set by the Act of Union in 1800 uniting Ireland with Great Britain became increasing untenable. To provide a measure of Irish autonomy Parliament passed the Third Home Rule Bill in 1914. However that same year the Great War in Europe erupted forcing suspension for the war's duration. At war's end, the British House of Parliament resumed debate of yet another Irish home rule bill seeking an approach to appease competing Irish aspirations while preserving British hegemony.

Unlike the bill passed in 1914, the Fourth Home Rule Bill also proposed partition of Ireland with two home rule parliaments; one for the six counties of northeast Ulster and the other for the remaining twenty-six counties. The solution satisfied nothing. Sinn Féin members of parliament declared open rebellion by refusing to take their seat seats in the British Parliament.

———

This was Ireland when Sullivan and O'Farrell arrived in Dublin in late summer of 1920. They had closely followed events since the start of hostilities in early 1919. Heartbreaking for both. Both felt their Irishness. Both were Irish nationalists at heart. Even some guilt tinged their conscience for not taking some part in the *struggle* as they corresponded with family.

Announcing their marriage provided a much-needed diversion from the politically soaked letters from both mothers. Both women were staunch Irish republicans.

After reading the most recent letter from O'Farrell's mother, Sullivan said, "She's afraid for her sons and husband. Circumstances sound different when they're personal accounts of what it's like."

O'Farrell just nodded. She closed the book she had been studying. "That's why I left. Couldn't live like that. Feel guilty I guess though for not being there. As if I saved just myself."

"Don't feel that way. Your brothers and father chose to go to war. Your mother stands with them of course. I suspect she's afraid every time they leave the house. Every soldier makes a great thing about honor and duty. Until they have to kill somebody, or somebody tries to kill them. Hard enough on a battlefield. Can't imagine what it's like where you live."

"It's young Dillon I'm most afraid for. He's only twenty. Can be a hothead. Not cautious like Terrance, or Daddy. I know all of them have taken up the gun. Mom doesn't disguise it that well in her letters. She must worry herself sick when they're out doing whatever. Still want to visit bloody Ireland?"

"Of course. Even I should see my Aunt Kathleen. Been a long time. She spent a year in a British prison not long ago."

"Oh my God. For what?"

"Accused of being involved in a conspiracy with Germany against Britain toward the end of the European War. Released just last year. She's close to my mother so it'll be good to pay her a visit. May be a bad time for Ireland but it shouldn't be dangerous for us."

"Not so sure that's the case in Derry," she said. "But we need to honor our responsibilities. Wouldn't be right not to see family. Besides I want to show off my new husband."

Booking passage on a freighter out of La Havre, they were among a dozen other passengers bound for the two-day passage to Dublin. Blessed with good weather they passed the time reading outside on the sundeck before and after lunch. Lovemaking in the afternoon followed by a nap made it seem like a honeymoon.

They arrived in Dublin on a Sunday. As the freighter moored dockside, Sullivan recognized Aunt Kathleen waving. He had not seen her in many years since she left New York to return to Ireland in 1907 with her husband Tom. In her early forties, she appeared older with all she endured the last few years. Wearing wire-rim glasses now, her hair in a matronly style. Not only was her husband executed following the failed 1916 Rising, her younger brother Ned faced the firing squad the next day. Pregnant at the time with her fourth child, she miscarried. All this while being active in the rebellion as a founding member of the women's Cumann na mBan.

From his mother, Sullivan knew Aunt Kathleen remained a hardened militant republican.

Sullivan descended the gangway ahead of Maureen. His aunt rushed to embrace him. Tears ran down her cheeks. "My dear, Trevor. It's been so long. So much we must …," breaking off her words to acknowledge Maureen.

"Aunt Kathleen, my wife Maureen. Good republican stock from Derry," Sullivan said as the women embraced.

Kathleen said, "I'm so delighted to see you both. Wish the circumstances were different though. John, come over here. Trevor, you remember your cousin my eldest son don't you?"

A good looking young man of eighteen walked over. After greetings all around, John Clarke said, "We heard about what you did in the war. Medals and all. You're a major in the American Army?"

"I was, John. Just an engineer now. Left the army when the war ended."

Kathleen Clarke said, "I'm afraid things are a little difficult here with our own war, Trevor. We'll have to take some unusual precautions in order to enjoy your visit."

"Is there some danger, Aunt Kathleen?"

"No, it's not that. Don't want you to get involved that's all. Don't stare, but do you see that man over there in the gray suit holding the newspaper?"

"Yes," Sullivan said taking a brief glimpse.

"Dublin Municipal Police. They follow me. Not all that clever about it. I think they may want me to know. I'll explain in the car. John will drive us. Now let's collect your luggage."

Once underway in the sedan, Sullivan said, "How are you feeling, Aunt Kathleen? Your heart I mean."

Arrested in May, 1918, she spent nine months in Holloway prison in London. British intelligence in Dublin Castle alleged Sinn Féin was conspiring with Germany to start an insurrection to divert resources from the Western Front on the Continent to Ireland. As a Sinn Féin leader, she was among 150 jailed without trial. Release came only after she suffered a heart attack.

"Much better. Doctors say I should avoid stress. And how is that possible with all that's going on? One must live life by the dictates of their conscience not the limitations of the body.

"And how's your mother doing. Never dwells on troubles in her letters. Just like her. And with the difficulties of making a living with a pub in a country that now prohibits liquor. How stupid is that?"

"I think America regrets it already. Anyway, mom and my sister and her husband have adapted. Make a bigger deal out of serving food now. But they converted a back room into a bar. They're called speakeasies. Keep it for their regular clientele. They buy smuggled liquor from Canada from black market guys called bootleggers. Mother couldn't image an Irish neighborhood without a pub."

"Good for her. Keara always had a sense for business."

Typical to how he remembered his fiercely strong-willed aunt to divert the conversation away from herself. He knew from his mother's letters that his aunt was fully engaged in the rebellion but his mother didn't know any details. Given the chance, Kathleen Clarke would have fought alongside her husband with a gun in 1916. Her three sons were living with relatives in Limerick. He was surprised to see John her eldest now with her in Dublin. Probably meant he too was active with the IRA.

"How is it you can afford a car like this, Aunt Kathleen."

Kathleen laughed. "Gracious no. It's not mine. Belongs to Cumann na mBan. Donated by Countess Markievicz. Know her?"

"Know the name of course. Fought with Uncle Tom and Uncle Ned in '16. She wore a uniform and fired a gun. Went to prison didn't she?"

"Sentenced to death like the other leaders by a stupid British court martial. Came to their senses and commuted it to life imprisonment because she was a woman. Released a year later in the general amnesty. Then she was arrested along with me two years ago in that stupid nonsense about us conspiring with the Germans. You'll meet her later."

Sullivan turned to look at the car following close behind. The Dublin Police plainclothes officer from the dock visible in the passenger seat.

"So I take it you're actively involved in this new rebellion?"

Kathleen turned to look at him in the backseat, "In the thick of the fight, Trevor."

After the short ride, John Clarke pulled up in front of a Catholic church on Haddington Road.

"Don't worry, Trevor we're not going to mass. Need to abandon our police shadow so we can have a proper visit. John will take your luggage along to the house."

After entering the church, Kathleen led the way briskly down an isle alongside the pews. A sparse crowd of mostly women sat waiting for the one o'clock mass to begin. Approaching the altar Kathleen hurriedly genuflected while making the sign of the cross then moved to the left entering the sacristy. Repeating the ritual, Sullivan and Maureen followed.

In the sacristy a priest and two altar boys looked momentarily surprised. Recognizing Kathleen Clarke, the priest nodded and made the sign of the cross but said nothing. All three exited a door into the rear courtyard. An idling car with a driver was waiting a short distance away.

The drive took them several scenic blocks as they motored next to the Grand Canal, a minor waterway running south from the port and the Liffey River. The car pulled up in front of a long row of houses reminding Sullivan of Brooklyn brownstones. Getting off at an intersection, Sullivan and Maureen dutifully followed Kathleen wondering where they were headed.

Kathleen headed to the alley in the rear of a block of houses.

"Our driver will make sure we weren't followed," Kathleen said.

"My god, Aunt Kathleen, are you that important?" Sullivan said.

"I don't think so. But the people I associate with are. Some have a price on their head. The British follow me hoping to catch bigger fish. Not particularly imaginative. But the British rarely are."

"So where are we going?"

"The home of a close friend. Three houses down this alley. Back door of course. Thought I'd show you what I'm up to in this war.

"The same war we started in 1916, Trevor. That was just the opening battle. This time we'll win. Tom and Ned and all the others didn't die in vain. We may have lost that battle but the people are now with us. Lots of things have changed.

"Anyway, thought this might be a more interesting after-noon for you and Maureen than chatting over tea with your old aunt. Having never been to your homeland I wanted to show you what this is all about. We'll have time for a proper family visit tomorrow."

Turning to Maureen, Kathleen said, "Trevor told me of your family background, Maureen. So you won't be surprised by my friends. With my husband gone, they're my family now. Hope you don't mind sneaking around Dublin."

Maureen smiled, "Not at all, Mrs. Clarke. I like adventure."

Sullivan looked at her with an expression conveying *I have no idea what my aunt is up to.*

At a back door several houses down the row they were greeted by a woman with the appearance of a younger version of Kathleen Clarke. Same stern countenance. Wire rimmed glasses, utilitarian hairstyle, dressed in a high-neck white blouse and long skirt.

"This is my friend, Sorcha Rogers," Kathleen announced as she embraced Rogers.

Rogers escorted them through the kitchen into the parlor. Two women and two men were seated in the large sun-filled room. A tea service sat on a sideboard. A serving platter offered an assortment of scones with jams.

Everyone present knew Kathleen Clarke by their cheerful greetings. All stood and kissed her on the cheek.

"Let me introduce my nephew Trevor Sullivan and his wife Maureen. Trevor's from Brooklyn, Maureen's from Derry," Kathleen said. "Both make their home now in Paris of all places. After distinguished himself in the Great War Trevor met Maureen there and love took its course."

To Trevor she said, "Everyone here trusts you and Maureen with your families' republican backgrounds. But of course it's best not to mention to anyone in Ireland that you've met any of us during your visit to Dublin. All of us are doing our part to win independence for Ireland."

With that Kathleen introduced everyone.

"This is Constance Markievicz, or I should say Countess Markievicz as she is known to the world. You know her story of course. No one more fearless, man or woman."

Markievicz was tall and regal in appearance. Older than Kathleen Clarke but still a handsome woman. She smiled and shook Sullivan's and Maureen's hands.

"And this is Mary Gibney and her fiancé Dick McKee," Kathleen said. "Don't let Mary's age and beauty deceive you. She's also a veteran of 1916. Ran messages under fire."

"And this handsome man is Dick McKee. Brigadier of the IRA Dublin Brigade. Right hand of Michael Collins. A real escape artist and swashbuckler."

Sullivan thought how young McKee was to hold such a position. But then again, Collins was not much older. All wars are fought by the very young, but in the case of the IRA, even the leadership was youthful.

"And this is Sorcha's husband Tom. Both work directly with Michael. Tom is a solicitor. Assists Michael in financial matters. Michael is of course Minster for Finance of our new parliament, Dáil Éireann. Obviously Michael wears other hats making him so wanted by the British.

"All of us have to take these precautions just like our short trip here to lose my police tail. Even this is a *safe house*. Sorcha and Tom live in the adjoining house and maintain this for … well gatherings like today. There's a secret doorway if the need should arise. Provides some chance of escape if we were to be raided."

Sullivan looked at Maureen with an expression of concern.

"Please don't worry, Trevor. We should be safe here. You and Maureen are in no danger yourselves. But you see how things are in Ireland."

The conversation turned to these revolutionaries wanting to hear about Sullivan and Maureen. How did two Irish meet in Paris? What was living in Paris like?

Constance Markievicz said to Maureen, "Kathleen said you're from Derry. Certainly been a bad time there these last couple of months. How is it for your family?"

"As good as could be expected for any Catholic. My father and two brothers are IRA. Mother too in her own way. More involved than other folks I suspect. But I only know what's going on by mother's letters. Never specific of course. I've been living in Paris for three years so I'm out of touch. This is my first time back. A sad time."

"I'd say difficult not necessarily sad," Markievicz said. "This time we'll win. The people are behind us this time. We have an effective fighting force. International support. Funding. We'll simply outlast the British."

"Hope you're successful," Maureen said. "I'm all for Irish independence but things are different in the north. Half the population is Protestant Unionist. Armed to the teeth. Can't see Ulster Protestants ever joining the South in a republic made up of mostly Catholics. You might drive out the British this time but Ulster is a different matter.

"I left because Catholics and Protestants can't seem to live together. That won't change by whatever happens in this war for independence. And I wanted a career not a family. Victorian views oppress Irish women. Paris is freer for a woman than Ireland."

"I know the attraction of Paris. Met my future husband there while studying art at the Académie Julian," Markievicz said. "You're also studying art I understand?"

"Constance is an accomplished painter in her own right, Maureen," Kathleen Clarke said. "That landscape on the wall over there is by her,"

Maureen rose from her chair to examine the oil painting.

"This is excellent work, Countess," Maureen said. "Impressionist style. Reminds me of Alfred Sisley. I work at the Musée du Luxembourg where we have many of his landscapes."

Kathleen knew everyone wanted to hear about Sullivan's war experience so she said, "Trevor you know served with the American Army in France. Decorated for valor."

"Yes, your aunt said that you fought in the Argonne Forest," McKee said. "But how did an engineering officer operating railroads end up on the front line?"

"Just bad luck. I was assigned to a unit whose objective was to capture a rail line. Got caught in a salient. Military term for an overextended position. Cut off from our rear lines for days. Two thirds of the command fell as casualties. Trapped in difficult terrain with exhausted supplies, and ammunition. The fighting was something fierce."

McKee said, "I understand you also received decorations for killing a lot of Germans. You know something of weapons?"

Sullivan nodded. "Yes. Apparently born with the skill. Had expert training at the United States Military Academy. In France a German sniper rifle fell into my hands. Out of necessity I seized the opportunity to turn it against the enemy. That's how I received the metals."

"Wounded also Kathleen said?" McKee said.

"Yes. Painful experience. Fully recovered though. No permanent damage."

Maureen smiled and touched his hand. "Scared the hell out of me. Thought he was just playing with his trains. Then I get this letter saying he's in a hospital."

"Played on her sympathies to convince her to marry me," Sullivan said.

"You're right you careless lout. Here you go and get yourself shot while telling me you weren't in danger. Clearly you needed watching over," Maureen said.

A knock on the back door turned everyone silent. McKee opened his suitcoat revealing a holstered revolver. Through the door came a muffled voice, "It's Harry."

"Maybe he has the Big Fellow in tow. I was hoping you'd get to meet him, Trevor," his aunt said.

Sullivan had no idea who she was talking about.

Tom Rogers opened the door. A well-dressed man entered and removed his hat as he shook hands with Rogers.

Behind him a taller man pushed through also removing his hat.

"Move your arse, Harry. Don't want to be hanging about at the back door attracting attention."

Kathleen said, "And here's my surprise, Trevor. The Big Fellow, Michael Collins."

CHAPTER 7

Michael Collins and his good friend Harry Boland greeted everyone before approaching Sullivan and Maureen. Collins' presence dominated the room. Charismatic in every way. A tall well-built handsome man, but the nickname 'Big Fellow' was as much a reference to his political stature.

"And this pretty woman must be the new Mrs. Sullivan," Collins said as he kissed Maureen on the cheek.

"Major Sullivan. Congratulations. You're a lucky man apparently in both war and love."

Collins said Boland, "Maybe we can recruit the Major, Harry. Good Irish republican stock. And Mrs. Sullivan's father and brothers I've been told are with the Derry City battalion."

Sullivan shook hands with Collins and Boland. From newspaper reports both had prices on their heads. Aunt Kathleen indeed ran in dangerous circles. Yet here they were socializing on a Sunday afternoon in the midst of conducting an insurrection.

"Just in Ireland for a family visit, Mr. Collins. Celebrating our recent marriage. Had enough of war. Besides I'm an American and no longer in the army."

"Well there's almost as many Irish in America as in Ireland. Thanks to the Great Famine eighty years ago. Abetted by British landholder greed and aggravated by British colonial subjugation since then. Not surprising that a fair amount of our funding

64

comes from America. If you're born Irish your heart will always be here."

Like all Irish, Sullivan new the story of the famine in the late 1840s. Each generation handed down their own anecdotal memories of the horrors that killed a million people and drove perhaps another million to emigrate. It laid the foundation for the modern hatreds directed at the British. During the famine colonial British landholders continued to sell grain under protected pricing while the Irish working class starved. The British government never fully mounted relief of the suffering.

The Great Famine lay at the heart of Sullivan's feelings about the British. To avoid encouraging Collins, he did not respond.

Turning to Sorcha Rogers, Collins said, "Sorcha my dear, would you be having any whiskey about? The tea and scones look inviting but I'll wager a couple of fingers of good Irish nectar would be especially welcomed."

Sorcha Rogers smiled at Collins and produced a bottle of Jameson from under the sideboard. Collins himself ducked into the kitchen to get glasses.

Collins poured generous shares all around to the men seated around a dining table.

Dick McKee said to Collins, "Mr. Sullivan is an engineer but obviously knows weapons, Mick. Obviously a crack shot too. Saw enough action to win medals."

"Graduate of West Point according to your aunt," Collins said. "Impressive background, Mr. Sullivan. I wasn't joking when I said we could use men like you for the cause."

"I've had enough of war, Mr. Collins. The Constabulary is Irish not British. They outgun your IRA. A war fought among the Irish people not some open field of battle. It'll continue to get uglier. All of Ireland will suffer, perhaps for years. Your only hope is British lack of resolve. Of course that assumes they don't send in the army in great numbers to put down your rebellion."

"They won't do that," Collins said. "They fear world condemnation. The British public wouldn't stand for it. So they instead masquerade former British soldiers as police calling them

Royal Irish Constabulary Special Reserve, these bloody Black & Tans. Unemployed dregs turned mercenaries with a license to murder and loot.

"They've also recruited ex-British Army officers into something called the Auxiliary Division of the RIC. They're to conduct counterinsurgency operations against us."

"To my point. Not only outgunned but up against a numerically superior force. You could be in for a long war. Tough on all Irish citizens. Eventually you'll make enemies among your own supporters. A disaster to the Irish economy."

"Casualties are a cost of freedom. Ireland has been under the thumb of Britain for over three hundred years. This is the first time that independence is within our grasp. The Irish people are tougher than you think, Mr. Sullivan."

"And since I'm Irish from a Fenian family I sincerely hope you succeed. But I'm also American. I don't live here. Don't share the deep personal conviction that all of you do. At least not enough to take up the gun again in your cause, Mr. Collins."

"I understand. Can't blame me for trying," Collins said. "But forgive my poor manners. You're here visiting family on the occasion of your recent wedding. A toast to Mr. And Mrs. Sullivan."

Everyone raised a glass or teacup.

Collins was always charming and engaging but he never rested. He was a one-man force directing the Irish Republican Army that grew out of the secret fraternal Irish Republican Brotherhood founded in the mid-19th century. In addition to his formal function as Minister of Finance of the rebel parliament Dáil Éireann, Collins assumed broader responsibilities. With his unique organizational skills and audacity, Collins intruded into all corners of the rebellion.

The proclaimed Irish President, Éamon de Valera, was in the United States raising money for the rebellion. The nominal chief of staff of the IRA, Cathal Brugha had long-running differences with Collins therefore Collins regularly circumvented Brugha's authority. As Director of Intelligence for the IRA, Collins wielded wider command of military operations. Since Collins remained President of the Irish Republican Brotherhood, which included a good many IRA fighters, his power base transcended his officially designated role.

"I understand you're off to Derry to visit your family, Mrs. Sullivan," Collins said. "The North has seen a lot of fighting these last couple of months. The Ulster Volunteers are a nasty bunch of cutthroats. They've organized to bolster the forces of the Constabulary. But they're out of control."

"We know that all too well, Mr. Collins," Maureen said. "The last letter from my mother spoke of the violence these last few months. The UVF is allowed a free hand to attack Catholics in Derry. It's more a civil war in the north."

"Under the circumstances I hope you still have a pleasant visit. Even though your family is IRA, I'll give your husband a personal note to the Derry City Independent Battalion Commander. It might become useful should you encounter any difficulties. I'm sure your family will know how to contact him. Name's Peadar O'Donnell."

Collins scribbled with a pencil in a notebook from his breast pocket, tearing out a page and handing it to Sullivan.

The rest of the afternoon passed with Maureen regaling the women about Paris. She and Countess Markievicz especially hit it off with their mutual involvement in art, at times even commenting in French to each other.

The men probed Sullivan about his war exploits. They all shared a good laugh at Sullivan's recounting of British incompetence during his near-disaster at the supply depot. After much probing Sullivan eventually explained his narrow escape.

"Good grief, with a handgun? Perhaps we could get you to at least train some of our lads? Some of them couldn't hit a cow in the arse with a shotgun at five paces," Collins said jovially.

Later in the afternoon the same driver returned to drive them to Aunt Kathleen's residence located above her tobacco shop at 77 Amiens Street.

The next day was devoted to Sullivan's cousin John driving them about Dublin with Aunt Kathleen pointing out the sights. She gave them the grand tour of the historic events and places as they happened on Easter Monday, 1916. Her personal tragedy. The ill-fated beginning of what now held the possibility of finally driving the British from Ireland.

The following day they made their farewell as they boarded the train to Belfast where they would change trains to go on to Derry. Even though both Sullivan and Maureen followed the Anglo-Irish War by newspaper accounts, being here brought an uneasy pall to what should be a joyous trip. In both Derry and Belfast, violence became a daily threat for much of the citizenry. A different kind of war not visible in Dublin.

—

Kathleen Clarke's tobacco shop and residence was only a couple of blocks walk to the Amiens Street rail station. Clarke saw them off. In their short stay in Dublin there was little evidence of a guerrilla war taking place. The RIC visible everywhere but Sullivan had no comparison to less troubled times. However it was shocking to witness his aunt being followed by the Dublin police. A bizarre experience to then sit down with wanted rebel leaders for a Sunday social gathering.

Aunt Kathleen's last words as they boarded the train to Belfast, "You two have a good visit in Derry but be careful. Everyone there is in peril. Worse for Catholics. Shootings, burnings, looting. Even those not in the fight suffer. Don't be out and about."

A disturbing warning emphasized once they disembarked in Belfast to change trains to continue to Derry. Not only were RIC officers more visible at Belfast's Great Victoria Street station but armed British Army soldiers also patrolled the platforms in fours.

They took lunch at the Belfast station during their one hour layover.

Sullivan said, "Do you suppose Derry will be like this?"

"Might be worse from what mother says in her letters," Maureen said. "Derry is more Catholic. Makes the Prods more nervous. Remember mother writing about the riots in April. Been bad since then. Danger comes from these Ulster Volunteers. Protestant thugs. It's back and forth attacks between the IRA and the UVF. A reprisal of some sort follows every attack. I'm already nervous, Trevor."

Sullivan touched her hand. "Just a family visit. Only a couple of days then we're back to Paris."

The three-hour train trip to Derry turned out to be five.

The last leg of the journey from Coleraine to Derry provided spectacular water views of the northern coastline of Ireland and Lough Foyle. A sunny day with broken high clouds. Difficult to imagine violent conflict tearing apart such place of beauty.

After exiting a great tunnel almost a half mile long through a cliff on the northern coastline west of the village of Castlerock, the train came to an abrupt stop. An emergency stop with the screech of metal on metal as the locked wheels skidded along the rails. Sullivan opened the window and leaned out. Nothing visible toward the front of the train. They were stopped in a rural section of the line. A scattering of trees and brush ran along one side of the tracks, the North Atlantic on the other.

Moments later a British Army officer with drawn revolver came rushing down the aisle of their car followed by six soldiers with rifles at the ready. Sullivan watched as the soldiers exited running alongside the train toward the engine. Seconds later came the sound of gunfire.

"Shit! Maybe an IRA ambush?" Sullivan said.

He stood up and stepped past Maureen in the aisle seat. "Sit down on the floor."

"The floor?" I'll do no such thing."

"Maureen, there might be bullets flying about. Now do as I say. Please?"

"What are you doing?" she said while settling to the floor. Other passengers doing the same.

Sullivan stood opening his duffle bag on the overhead rack.

"Don't intend to be caught in a firefight unarmed."

From his bag he pulled out his .45 Browning service automatic and slipped it into his waist in the back.

The sound of small arms fire continued for over thirty minutes. After it ceased all remained quiet for some time before the train started to move again.

Eventually the conductor came into their car and announced, "We'll be late arriving in Derry folks. An obstacle placed on the tracks. Been cleared away now. An IRA attack it seems. All safe now. Soldiers drove off the attackers."

Sometime later the British lieutenant returned to Sullivan's rail car. To his soldiers, "You lads station yourself two each between these last two cars. One to each side. Keep on your toes for any sign of more of these IRA blighters."

As the lieutenant approached, Sullivan said, "What was that about lieutenant?"

"Just a stupid attack by the IRA. Seems they didn't expect we'd be onboard in force," he said with a grin. "Three platoons. Dorset Regiment returning to Ebrington Barracks in Derry."

"But you're sure it was the IRA not this other crowd the UVF?"

The officer's expression stiffened. "And you are, Sir?"

"Name's Sullivan, Major Sullivan. Formerly of the United States Army serving in France."

The officer's expression relaxed as he came to attention saluting smartly, "Sir. Definitely IRA. They've started to turn their attention on the trains. Usually just tamper with the signals to make them display red. Usually at night. Train stops, they mount their attack. Looking to kill police or soldiers. Steal arms and goods. This time the nasty bastards meant to derail the train. Removed a section of rail. Engineer saw it in time."

"All the Sinn Féin sympathizers driving the trains have gone on strike. Refuse to operate trains carrying war goods or military personnel. They've had to bring over engineers from England. Glad this British chap was at the throttle."

"Casualties?"

"Two soldiers wounded. But we killed one attacker and captured two of their wounded."

Sullivan looked over at Maureen, "Welcome home."

CHAPTER 8

As the train pulled into Derry's Waterside station Sullivan felt the weight of his growing unease. Since setting foot in Ireland the ominous climate of the Anglo-Irish War as the newspapers called it, became increasing pervasive. Hardly a honeymoon, not even a holiday. Neither he nor Maureen would be here except out of family obligation. He hoped that would not prove a mistake.

"You okay?" He said to Maureen.

"I guess so. I already miss Paris. Life there was difficult during the war. The uncertainty. News of the terrible carnage at the front. Those terrifying German long range shells falling without warning. The prospect of the collapse of the French Army threatening mutiny. Food shortages the last year of the war. But this feels worse."

Sullivan put his arm around her shoulder.

"Just a few days then we'll be returning to Paris. It's about seeing your family. Too bad it's under these circumstances. But we'll get through it."

The train tracks followed the east bank of the River Foyle for a grand view of the waterway on the right with the station on their left as the train pulled into Derry.

"Oh my god, there's Mom and Dillon!" She said seeing them on the platform as the train eased to a stop.

Sullivan took down their two pieces of luggage from the overhead rack. Maureen exited the train jumping down briskly running to embrace her mother.

Mrs. O'Farrell looked the part of the teacher which she was. Releasing her daughter, she came up to Sullivan. "Oh my aren't you the handsome one? Welcome to the family, Trevor."

She hugged him tightly, kissing him on the cheek.

"My youngest, Dillon," She said as Maureen released her embrace of her younger brother.

"Hello, Sir. Heard a lot about you," He said extending his hand.

Sullivan smiled and said, "Good to meet you, Dillon. Please call me Trevor."

Dillon O'Farrell was a good looking young man of twenty of average height. Took after Maureen in appearance.

"Your train was two hours late," Mrs. O'Farrell said.

"Sorry you had to wait, Mother. The train was stopped outside of Castlerock. An IRA ambush we were told."

Dillon O'Farrell said, "What happened?"

Maureen turned to Sullivan who answered, "A British officer said some sort of attempt was made to derail the train. Engineer saw it in time. The train was full of British regulars. Dorset Regiment from Derry. Anyway there was a firefight."

"Was anyone hurt?" Mrs. O'Farrell said.

Sullivan said, "No passengers. According to the officer, one of the attackers was killed and two others captured. Some soldiers were wounded."

Mrs. O'Farrell covered her mouth with her hand. "I'm so sorry. And here you're coming home to celebrate your wedding. I fear ... well never mind. We shall just make the best of it."

"We will, Mrs. O'Farrell. We'll have a wonderful visit," Sullivan said. "Both Maureen and I know what's going on in Ireland. Breaks our hearts though to see our families' suffering."

Mrs. O'Farrell nodded. Changing the subject she said to Maureen, "Your father, Terrance, and Nora are at work at the mill. But we'll all have a grand supper together tonight to celebrate."

To Sullivan she said, "Hope you don't mind taking the bus home. We don't have a car. We live across the river in the Bogside. Not too many Catholics livin' here on the east side of the river."

"The bus will be just fine, Mrs. O'Farrell."

She locked arms with her daughter and led off through the rail station.

Dillon O'Farrell picked up his sister's suitcase and fell in beside Sullivan.

"Maureen's letters say you're a war hero. An officer in the American Army," Dillon O'Farrell said.

Mrs. O'Farrell said, "Dillon, don't be pestering your brother-in-law with questions. Give him a chance to catch his breath. Been a difficult day I should say."

—

Along the route of the short bus ride disturbing scars of the recent rioting were evident. Boarded windows. Piles of wrecked furniture at the side of one street. A burned section of several row houses. Maureen looked at Sullivan with moist eyes just shaking her head. For Sullivan this wasn't the total destruction of villages seen in France but nonetheless, it still had the unmistakable look of war.

Life here was insecure for everyone. For all of Ireland for that matter. Reading accounts in newspapers could never impart what it was like to live under constant threat of violence. Without saying anything to Maureen, Sullivan regretted their coming to Ireland. They should be celebrating a future. Instead he felt they were becoming emotionally sucked into a vortex.

The O'Farrell house was at the end of a long stretch of brick row houses. A working class neighborhood just a few blocks west of the great 17th century walls of old Derry. Few cars or lorries about. In the street, several young boys in dirty clothes kicked a soccer ball.

The inside of the O'Farrell home proved pleasant. Worn furniture but everything tidy. Some of Maureen's earlier oil paintings proudly displayed on the walls of the small sitting room.

Eoin O'Farrell arrived home early that evening. A joyous occasion having not seen his daughter since she went off to Paris. He greeted Sullivan with almost the same display of affection.

Mary O'Farrell said, "They had a spot of trouble on the train over from Belfast, Eoin. An IRA ambush west of Castlerock. Driven off by Dorset soldiers riding the train."

Eoin O'Farrell's face dropped.

"Was it your unit, father?" Maureen asked.

Her father said nothing for several moments.

"Come now, father. Trevor knows that you and the boys are IRA. It's alright. I told you his family's background. Besides, you'd never guess who we met in Dublin. Introduced by Trevor's Aunt Kathleen."

Eoin O'Farrell remained uncomfortable openly talking of his IRA affiliation to his new son-in-law.

"Kathleen Clarke. Tom Clarke's widow. She's still in the fight. It was her that invited us to take Sunday tea with Michael Collins himself."

"What! You met Michaels Collins?"

"Yes we did. Trusts Trevor enough to give him a note to Peadar O'Donnell. I suspect you know him?"

Trevor showed him the slip of paper from Collins.

"Good lord! A note from Collins himself. Yes, O'Donnell commands our battalion. But no it wasn't our unit that attacked the train. Might have been those boys out of Belfast. McCorley's flying column maybe. He's headstrong. Bent on attacking the British wherever. Usually operates closer to Belfast though.

"Any civilians hurt?"

"No, sir," Sullivan said. "Never even saw what happened. Just heard the gunfire. But a good thing the train wasn't derailed."

"Mary, we'll have a glass or two of whiskey before dinner. Especially after that adventure. And we've a lot to celebrate.

Never thought I'd see the day when you'd be married, Maureen."

"Now, Eoin you shush that kind of talk," his wife said.

Mary O'Farrell brought out a platter with a new bottle of Bushmills and glasses into the parlor.

"Well it's the truth," Eoin continued. "None of the local lads suited her. Had to go off and see the bright lights of Paris."

"Father. I left because women are second class in Ireland. In Derry, Catholics are second class. I don't mean to diminish your career as a teacher mother but you know you're the exception."

"Sorry, lass. You know I love you," her father said to lighten his comments. "I'm proud as can be what you've accomplished. College educated. Your talent at art. Speaking French. Makin' your own way in a foreign place. And you found this fine Irish gentleman to marry. He must be somethin' special."

Maureen looked over at Sullivan and smiled taking the opportunity to avoid resuming an old argument with her father. An older generation. Mother at least intellectually understood even if it hurt to have her daughter so far away.

"That he is, father. An engineer. A good one apparently. Works for the French government. Only thing he could improve on is his French. Has a terrible American accent."

Eoin O'Farrell poured whiskey all around, including for Maureen and his wife.

"And Terrance and Nora?" Mary O'Farrell asked her husband.

"Stopped off to wash up at their place. They'll be along presently. But right now I need a drink with my new son-in-law and my wandering daughter. Welcome to the family, Trevor."

Terrance O'Farrell and his wife Nora arrived a short time later. Terrance was a well-built man, tall like his father. His wife Nora could be considered plain. After the hugs and greetings it was clear they were both of a quiet nature. Dillon and Maureen stood in sharp contrast.

Eoin O'Farrell said, "Now that everybody is here, you must tell us about what you did in the Great War, Trevor. Maureen's letters said you were decorated for valor."

Sullivan tired of the retelling of his war experiences. But for his and Maureen's family intimately involved in this shooting war, interest in his military exploits served as an indirect bond to those risking their lives.

"Well, Sir, I saw combat by accident. My regular job was building and running railroads. Anyway in the last year of the war I was temporarily assigned to accompany an American infantry battalion. They were to capture or destroy a railroad line held by the Germans. I was there as a railroad expert for whichever eventuality."

Dillon said excitedly, "It was in all the newspapers around the world. Even here. The *Lost Battalion* they called it."

"Lost because we weren't expected to survive after being surrounded by the Germans."

"Trevor rarely talks much about those five days," Maureen said. "Had to pry things out of him. Especially what he did to win medals. Go ahead and tell them, Trevor."

"A lot of soldiers did their duty during that fight," Sullivan said then proceeded to expand with a general account of the battle.

"Trevor is too modest," Maureen said. "What he did was kill a lot of Germans. Killed them because he's a marksman. Dillon is dying to hear the gruesome details, Dear."

Sullivan reluctantly recounted his experience with the *Lost Battalion* in the Argonne Forest. Even though he condensed the narrative as much as possible he captivated his audience for half an hour. Dillon frequently asked questions to pry out more lurid details.

At the end of his story, Eoin O'Farrell said, "My god. Two thirds of your battalion fell as casualties?"

"Yes, Sir. Including me."

"How many Germans did you kill?" Dillon said.

"Not sure. Perhaps as many as twenty."

"Holy shit!" Dillon said.

"Mind your language, Dillon," His mother said.

Eoin O'Farrell poured more whiskey. "Why'd you leave the American Army? Maureen said you were educated at their military academy. Promoted to major when the war ended. Seemed a real future there."

"Well, sir, I realized that I liked engineering better than soldering. I only went to West Point because I was able to get a free education. Secure employment doing engineering work. Then the Great War came along. The Army's engineering corps became the first units to go to France when the United States entered the war in 1917.

"My job was building and operating railroads. Moving supplies to the front line. Wasn't being shot at but I could see what was happening with great numbers of wounded evacuated by the train. Stupid leadership all around. Good men dying unnecessarily in the tens of thousands. There is no glory in war, only horror.

"Caused me to rethink spending the rest of my life in uniform. Before the war, army life was full of regimented boredom. Living all over the country at different postings. Some not so pleasant places. And the engineering work I was doing eventually became repetitious. Technically no longer challenging. Anyway, while recovering from my wound I took stock in what I wanted for a future. Realized the army wasn't it. Didn't have ambitions to become a general.

"But no regrets. West Point gave me a first rate engineering education. The Army gave me enough experience to seek a good opportunity in civilian life. Didn't turn out badly at all.

"But most of all there was Maureen. She might have followed me back to America but army life would have stifled her artistic ambitions."

Maureen came over to him, bent down and kissed him.

"Well now I can see why you won her heart," Mrs. O'Farrell said. "That and your uncommon good looks."

Joined by Terrance O'Farrell and his wife Nora, the rest of the night passed with the joyous bonding of a reunited family on a special occasion. Maureen as emotionally engaged as her parents and brothers. For at least those few hours the violence of the Anglo-Irish War and the local sectarian strife receded to the background.

The following day saw Eoin O'Farrell back to work at the shirt factory. Mary O'Farrell was off for the summer school break. Dillon being unemployed tagged along as Maureen took Sullivan for a walk to show him the three hundred-year old historic walls of the historic city. The intact walls provided a one-mile elevated promenade with views of Derry and the River Foyle.

Passing a tobacco shop, Dillon said, "I need to buy some tobacco for Da. Go along and I'll catch up with you."

Before proceeding, Maureen pointed across to a pub. "That's a favorite of father's. Let's have a spot of lunch there after our walk on the parapet."

A set of worn stone steps ascended to the thirty-foot high parapet.

"What an extraordinary view. This is magnificent," Sullivan said.

"Not exactly Paris, my love, but it has its charms."

Sullivan glanced back inside the walls toward the tobacco shop. Dillon was chatting with a young woman out front. Both were smiling, holding hands.

Sullivan thought that's right young man, there's more to life than war.

———

An altogether pleasant sunny day. No hint of the hostilities swirling just underneath the surface. They lunched at the pub suggested by Maureen. The barkeep, an old family friend, was overjoyed seeing her and her new husband. Heard about her marrying this Irish-American war hero from her father. They were feted as celebrities and served a hearty lunch. All on the house. To which Sullivan bought several rounds of drinks for the other patrons.

Walking back to her parents' house, Maureen said, "Makes me sad all that's going on but I'm glad we came, Trevor."

They spent the evening with Maureen's parents. Dillon excused himself early saying he was meeting some of his chums. Sullivan guessed it perhaps was the pretty young woman from earlier in the day.

As the night turned late, Eoin O'Farrell yawned. He had an early call to be at work the next morning. Repeatedly looking at his pocket watch, Sullivan suspected it concerned Dillon's absence.

Mary O'Farrell had the same concern when she eventually said, "Eoin, it's time we all got to bed. You've got to get up early for work. Can't be worrying about Dillon. He can sleep late. He's a grown man. Not the first time he's come home in the wee hours of the morning."

With that everyone retired. Maureen however became progressively agitated with the passing hours, refusing to undress for bed until Dillon returned. Sullivan struggled to keep his eyes open. Too much food, too many pints of stout.

"He'll be along, Maureen. Saw him talking to a girl outside that tobacco shop earlier. Both seemed more than just friendly. He's young and she's pretty."

"Probably what he's up to. But still, he's IRA. That means the police may know. And they're in league with the Ulster Volunteers. The UVF are the real danger."

At the sound of a motor vehicle, they both went to the window. It was three o'clock in the morning. No other traffic in the Bogside streets. A dark overcast night. No street lights in this poor section. No vehicle headlights yet they could make out what looked to be a delivery lorry.

Sullivan opened the window hearing the sound of the engine idling. Then a sound followed like a sack of potatoes dropping to the street. A raspy whisper, *Out of here! Be quick!*

Maureen was out the bedroom door ahead of Sullivan.

"Wait a second. Don't go outside, Maureen."

Still dressed in his trousers but without shoes, he took the moment to retrieve his service pistol. Not about to duck into the night unarmed in this war zone.

Bounding down the stairs, the noise brought Eoin and Mary O'Farrell out of their room.

"What's going on?" Eoin said.

"Someone's outside, Da," Maureen said.

Sullivan opened the front door while crouching low.

No vehicle. No one in the street. Dark but for a faint illumination from a quarter moon appearing through a break in the cloud cover.

In the middle of the street lay a shape.

"Shit," Sullivan said under his breath. "Stay back, Maureen."

He walked toward the body. His gun still poised but not expecting anyone to be about.

He bent down and looked at the face. Must be Dillon O'Farrell. At least he thought it was. Badly beaten. Swollen beyond easy recognition. A gaping hole in the right eye socket. Obviously Dillon O'Farrell.

He stood as Maureen rushed toward him. Eoin and Mary O'Farrell followed. Sullivan stood aside as all three knelt down and poured out their grief.

As the shrieks of the women's wailing pierced the night, lights started to come on.

Neighbor women soon pulled Maureen and her mother from the body, escorting them to another house. Eoin and several men carried the body of Dillon O'Farrell into the parlor.

Sullivan had seen terrible wounds during the Great War. But the condition of Dillon O'Farrell's body revolted him. Not the wounds of battle, rather the effects of torture before a final bullet to the back of the head.

The gaping right eye socket the exit wound of the bullet. Blood seeping from the wound now congealed in a great black stain soaking the front of Dillon's shirt. A dirty rag tied about his mouth. Hands tied behind his back with a chain. Shot in both knees, his trousers soaked in blood below those wounds. Sullivan heard of the cruel maiming technique called knee-capping. Meant to inflict suffering often before a final bullet to the head.

After forcing himself to examine his dead son, Eoin O'Farrell sat down in his favorite chair. Staring into space, he remained silent. The men helping to carry the body now felt awkward looking at the stricken elder O'Farrell. Not knowing what could be said they quietly left the house except for one man.

The man bent down and whispered something into O'Farrell's ear.

Eoin O'Farrell made no response.

The man nodded to Sullivan then left.

Expecting the return of Maureen and her mother, Sullivan found a blanket and covered the body. At least it seemed not to be leaking any more blood.

Within a half hour the front door thrust open startling Sullivan. Terrance O'Farrell stepped next to the covered body. Kneeling down, he gently lifted the corner of the blanket. His head slumped and he began to sob.

A priest accompanying Terrance O'Farrell said to Sullivan, "I'm Father Sheenan."

The priest immediately went to the elder O'Farrell still sitting in his chair. Saying nothing he laid his hand on Eoin O'Farrell's shoulder.

To Terrance O'Farrell the priest said, "See to your father, Terrance. I must attend to your poor brother."

The priest removed a clerical stole from his pocket. Draping it around his neck he knelt and began reciting a prayer in Latin.

CHAPTER 9

Fergus Croft returned from service in the British Army's 36th Ulster Division at the end of the European war in 1918. He survived three years of trench warfare rising to sergeant. Seeing action at the Battle of the Somme in 1916 and the Battle of the Lys in 1918, he was among the lucky. Wounded by artillery shrapnel during the German Spring Offensive in early 1918, he never returned to the front. Weeks in a hospital but alive. No long-term effects except for a set of ugly scars.

Yet returning to his home in Derry provided little peace. He rejoined the Ulster Volunteers as the issue of Irish Home Rule again came to the forefront with the end of the war in Europe.

The Ulster Volunteer Force formed as a militia when the prospect of a semi-autonomous Ireland almost passed Parliament in 1912. Home rule was popular in all of Ireland except the northeast Ulster six counties. Home Rule was London's way of resolving the Irish problem. To Ulster Protestants that meant they could rely less on British Crown forces to protect them from the restive Catholics.

By 1914 when the bill passed in parliament, UVF membership had reputedly grown to 100,000. A good percentage of all Protestant adult males in Ulster. That year 25,000 rifles and 3,000,000 rounds of ammunition were smuggled into Ulster. A serious rebellion loomed in the north. Yet the British government found itself thwarted in asserting control. When the British military commander for Ireland was ordered to move troops into Ulster, 57 of his 70 officers at headquarters chose to resign rather than enforce Home Rule by confronting the loyalist Ulster Volunteers.

With war declared against Germany in 1914, the British suspended implementation of home rule. Resources must be directed to the Continent and most Irish put aside their differences for the duration of the Great War. Unresolved, the latent sectarian animosities in Ulster reemerged in 1919.

Revisiting the Irish problem, the Fourth Home Rule Bill of 1920 divided Ireland into two separately governed entities. Six counties of the province of Ulster would become Northern Ireland. The remaining twenty-six counties would become Southern Ireland.

The northern counties of Antrim, Armagh, Down, Fermanagh, Tyrone, and Londonderry had a Protestant majority. Overwhelmingly they favored continued union with Great Britain. Therefore partition grudgingly allowed them to accept home rule. They could at least control their own provincial parliament while remaining part of the United Kingdom. In contrast, the nationalist Catholic dominated South overwhelmingly rejected home rule. Only full independence would satisfy Irish Catholic republican aspirations.

Further aggravating hostilities, the sectarian demographic distribution of the northern six counties was uneven. In County Londonderry, Catholics held a narrow majority. In the City of Derry, even more so. That constituency favored Irish independence. For a virulent Unionist like Fergus Croft, circumstances at home appeared more threatening than before he went off to war in France.

Although Croft secured a supervisory position at the Derry's Foyle Port, his entire being centered on UVF activities. No conflict with his work duties since a senior UVF official controlled the port.

In April, 1920, rioting erupted in Derry. As elsewhere across Ireland, the IRA pressed their attack against British rule. In Derry they faced the Royal Irish Constabulary backed by British Army regulars of the Dorset Regiment. In June the Ulster Unionist Council officially revived the paramilitary Ulster Volunteer Force.

Recruitment to the postwar UVF however met with only limited success. Their numbers never approached the numbers of their founding in 1912 before the Great War. That failure further emboldened the IRA. But those that did heed the call to the resurrected UVF were among the most extreme. Many were ex-British Army veterans of the Great War. Not only ultra-Unionists, the UVF represented Protestant anti-Catholic racist militancy. Animosity to such an extent that some UVF units amounted to nothing more than armed killers acting as ethnic vigilantes. Fergus Croft commanded one such notorious group.

———

Two men from Croft's unit loitered about the Carlisle Bridge on this summer night. With a cool breeze coming down the River Foyle it was a good place to take a smoke after a night of drinking. Hanging about on the eastern side of the bridge they saw a couple walking arm in arm across the bridge from the west side. The city quiet at close to midnight. Street lamps on the bridge revealed no one else about.

As the couple came closer they stopped on the bridge. After kissing and embracing they stood looking out over the water. The man held her close with his arm around her waist.

"Look at that will ya?" one man said in a whisper. "Doin' his best to get in her drawers."

"Maybe already has," the other said. "Great knockers. Can see that even from here."

The two concealed themselves behind one of the stone columns anchoring the end of the bridge.

The romantic couple eventually resumed their walk. As they walked past the concealed men, one man whispered, "Well I'll be dipped in shit. That's Abagail Ahearn."

"And who might that be?"

"You stupid shite, don't you know? She's the one that Croft's sweet on."

"Huh. Well it looks like she's not. That bloke's got his hands all over her. Know him?"

"Fuck no."

"But we need to tell Croft."

"Yeah? That his sweetheart is being buggered by someone else? Not me, you arsehole."

"Just the same, Croft will want to know. Right away I should say."

"Well it's your neck. He might still be at Duffy's."

Duffy's was a nearby Waterside Protestant pub they left a short time ago after drinking with Fergus Croft. The two took off at a jog covering the three blocks quickly.

Both were winded from the run as they entered Duffy's. Fergus Croft was still seated at a table with two other men. All were slightly drunk.

"Why the fuck are you pissers out of breath? Somethin' scare you?" Croft said. The other seated men laughed.

"It's that woman, Abagail Ahearn. The one you like, Fergus. Just saw her."

"Saw her? What the fuck's that mean? Where?'

"On the bridge. Walking. From the Bogside. She wasn't alone."

"Who was with her?"

"We didn't recognize him. Maybe because he was one of them."

"One of what?"

"Catholic maybe. They were coming from the Bogside, Fergus."

With that Croft fished out money and slammed it down on the table as he stood. "Show me what the fuck you're talkin' about."

———

86

Abagail Ahearn turned pale. Five men dressed in working clothes came out from an alley. They said nothing but clearly appeared threatening. Even from several feet away the smell of liquor obvious.

Dillon O'Farrell realized he and Abagail had been foolishly careless. Derry with its troubles was not the place for romantic strolls. Especially with the sectarian heresy they were practicing. Abagail was Protestant. As a Catholic, much less IRA, he was clearly in the wrong neighborhood.

Fergus Croft pushed aside two of his men and stepped close to Ahearn.

"What's this, Abby? Kind of late to be walkin' about isn't it?"

Terror caused a wave of nausea. She knew Fergus Croft. Not bad looking but she knew his violent reputation within the UVF. Knew also his attempts at romancing her. The very thought of him touching her made her skin crawl. While always polite the few times he had approached her, she never gave the slightest encouragement to his advances. Caught now with Dillon O'Farrell under these circumstances could only turn out badly.

Croft continued. "Who's your boyfriend, Abby? Haven't seen him before."

She didn't know what to answer fearing to make the situation worse.

"Name's O'Farrell," Dillon said. "We mean no trouble. I'm just escorting Miss Ahearn home."

"From where?"

"Miss Ahearn was visiting my mother. She's been sick. She's a friend of Miss Ahearn's mother."

Croft just stared menacingly saying nothing for several moments.

"Well now, we both know that's a crock of shit don't we? Tell you what I think. I think you're a bloodsucking Catholic. Live in that shithole the Bogside. The pretty Miss Ahearn doesn't find her own kind to her liking it seems. I think she's been out all night spreading her legs for the likes of you."

"You sonofabitch!" O'Farrell said and foolishly stepped toward Croft.

Croft landed a debilitating fist into O'Farrell's midsection sending him to his knees.

Ahearn attempted to go to O'Farrell but Croft grabbed her arm. Two of his men grabbed both of O'Farrell's arms dragging him to his feet.

"O'Farrell you say? Related to a Fenian scum named Eoin O'Farrell? Perhaps brother to an IRA fucker named Terrance O'Farrell?"

O'Farrell made no reply. Croft landed another vicious blow to O'Farrell's lower abdomen.

O'Farrell sagged vomiting while still held by Croft's two henchmen.

Stepping back to avoid being dirtied, Croft said to his men, "Young Mr. O'Farrell here is undoubtedly IRA himself. The whole family stinks of popery and sedition."

To O'Farrell he said, "But you are an audacious fucker. Or just blinded by Miss Ahearn. She is a looker isn't she? That could make you do the most stupid of things. You'd never make it in my outfit, O'Farrell. Dumbass Catholic IRA walking a Protestant girl back to her neighborhood in the middle of the fuckin' night."

Croft shook his head. "It's a war we're havin' while you two are out rutting like dogs in heat. Now you both have to pay for such stupidity. Take 'em both, lads."

"Make a move you IRA prick and I'll put a bullet in ya," one huge man said from behind O'Farrell. Two others held him by the arms.

Croft took charge of Ahearn grabbing her upper arm roughly.

"Fergus, don't harm him. Please," Ahearn said.

"Shut up, Abby. It's yourself you need to be worrying about. Not only a whore but maybe an IRA spy? Serious matters that need to be dealt with."

After a short walk they came to a shabby automotive garage. Automobiles in various states of dereliction ran along an alley to the side of the building.

One of Croft's men opened the office door with a key.

"No lights," Croft said. "Don't want any peelers to come nosing around. Get everyone into the back. Stay here, John and keep a lookout. This shan't take long."

The garage interior was cramped. Enough room to work on just one vehicle at a time. A service van imprinted with a logo occupied the workspace.

"Tie O'Farrell to that chair, boys," Croft said. "His legs too."

Once O'Farrell was immobilized with some chains, Croft grabbed a greasy rag from a workbench. "So you don't make a fuss." He tied the rag over O'Farrell's mouth as a gag.

Walking up to Abagail Ahearn he stood within inches of her face. He was a tall muscular man. Reaching both hands to each side of her blouse he ripped it open to the waist.

She attempted to fight back but he slapped her several times hard enough to cause her to slump back against the bench. Without hesitating, Croft grabbed her undergarment tearing it away. She slumped forward covering her exposed breasts with her forearms.

"Rooney, got that razor you always carry?" Croft said.

"Yeah," the big man said hesitantly. He knew Croft's vicious nature. Not someone to fuck with. Provoked like this no telling what he might do.

"Then get over here."

"See here, Fergus. I ain't goin' to cut no woman."

"Nothing like that. Just want you to give her a haircut."

Abagail Ahearn's eye widened. She prized her long auburn hair. Worse, the shame of being branded a traitor.

"Make it a short style, Rooney. No need to be too fussy though. Sit on this crate, Abby."

When she hesitated, Croft said, "Do it, Abby or I'll make it much worse."

Sobbing uncontrollably she sat down on a crate pulled in front of O'Farrell. Croft undid her hair letting it fall to her shoulders.

"Now Mr. O'Farrell, since you're in store for much worse, I'll give you a treat. The wish of a condemned man so to speak. Abby, sit up straight. Put your hands in your lap. Let your boyfriend feast his eyes on those glorious tits for the last time."

———

Once Abagail Ahearn's humiliation was complete things turned sadistic.

"Need to send a message O'Farrell. Can't be havin' lowbred Catholics defiling Protestant women. Doesn't look so pretty now does she?"

Croft stepped over to Ahern and lifted her head with his hand under her chin. "You need to watch this, Abby. This is your doing."

Putting on a pair of leather work gloves, Croft began a relentless pounding to Dillon O'Farrell's face. Blood splattered about. After twenty minutes, O'Farrell was unrecognizable.

"Don't you be passing out on me you fucker. I'm not finished yet," Croft said breathing hard from the exertion. Nodding to one of his men, "Not yet through with your boyfriend. Now pay attention, Abby."

The man pulled a revolver. Croft pointed to O'Farrell's knee. The round blew away a good deal of the knee joint. A crippling wound causing unbelievable pain.

O'Farrell twisted in agony, grunting through the gag.

Abigail Ahern shrieked and nearly fainted.

"Half a cripple? That won't do," Croft said and nodded again to the shooter.

A second shot to the other knee caused O'Farrell to pass out. Ahern turned away from the horrible sight now hysterical.

Minutes later both she and O'Farrell were bundled into the empty delivery van. O'Farrell was still bound and gagged. Ahearn wept quietly with her head down covering herself during the short ride through the deserted night. The van jerked to a stop in front of Ahern's parents' home.

"You'll not be letting on who did this, Abby. If I get any trouble over this it'll go badly for you. At least your hair will eventually grow back. A razor to your face would be permanent. So you mind your tongue, bitch."

Without time to say anything to O'Farrell she was pushed out of the van by Croft.

As the van began moving away she got up holding her shredded clothing, "Dillon? What are you going to do to him?"

Croft closed the rear doors of the van without answering.

To her horror, the van driver repeatedly sounded the horn. Lights came on along the street.

CHAPTER 10

Peadar O'Donnell arrived at the O'Farrell house the day following Dillon O'Farrell's murder. He did not come alone. A cadre of armed IRA took up positions outside.

After introductions, Eoin O'Farrell explained Sullivan's background including his military experience as well as his Fenian family credentials.

"Show Peadar the note that Collins gave you."

Sullivan handed the slip of paper to O'Donnell. After reading the note, "Well, the Big Fellow says to render any assistance to you, Mr. Sullivan. That would seem to make you one of us."

According to Collins it was O'Donnell's efforts that forcefully restored order in Derry in June. His IRA battalion successfully confronted the UVF and the British Dorset Regiment ceasing two months of attacks on Catholic residents.

Sullivan chose not to debate O'Donnell's overstating of his sympathies. As bitter as Dillon's murder was, this was still not his fight.

"Do ya know who murdered my brother, Peadar?" Terrance O'Farrell said.

In the room was Mary O'Farrell, Terrance's wife Nora, and Maureen.

O'Donnell looked at them and said, "Perhaps we should step outside."

"It's alright, Peadar," Eoin O'Farrell said. "Mary lost a son but her heart is black with rage same as mine. We'll do the proper things. Mourn our poor boy. Go to mass. Watch him put in the ground. But then it'll be about delivering a terrible retribution on these murdering bastards."

O'Donnell nodded his understanding.

"Very well, Eoin. Here's what we know. Seems Dillon and a girl were seen together at the Bloated Goat, that pub the younger people like on Carlisle Road."

"What girl?" Mary O'Farrell said.

O'Donnell pursed his lips not wanting to present more bad news.

"Her name's Abagail Ahearn, Mary. A Waterside girl. Protestant. Father owns a butcher shop. Unionist of course. That's why Dillon never told you about her. We know they left the pub round midnight."

"How do you know this?" Eoin O'Farrell said.

"Because one of our lads was there last night. Knows Dillon. Didn't approach him since he could see he was romancing this girl. Came to me this morning after hearing about Dillon.

"Fortunately our lad was nosy. Probably a little drunk. By his account he was taken with … with how pretty this girl was. Said he thought he best keep an eye out for Dillon, his being exposed this late at night with everything that's been happening.

"Anyway he followed Dillon and the girl to the Carlisle Bridge where they proceeded to cross over the river. Knowing better, he didn't follow them any further. Not the sort of neighborhood for a Catholic IRA man to be walking with a Protestant girl late at night. Damn foolish thing for Dillon to do."

"So how's it you now know her name?" Eoin O'Farrell said.

"That's the interesting part, Eoin. I contacted a confidential source we have on the Waterside. We know the girl's name because it's the talk of the neighborhood what happened to her last night. Seems her hair was shorn. Dumped in front of her house in the early morning hours. The car or lorry blew its horn to wake the neighborhood. Obvious humiliation for fraternizing with the enemy.

"The description of the young lady matches that of the fellow that saw them together. But there's more, Eoin. According to rumor it seems that Fergus Croft had eyes for this Ahearn woman. I think somebody tipped him off. Looks like something Croft would do. Especially being personal and all."

Fergus Croft was well known to the Derry IRA. He was the local face of the UVF. More reviled than the RIC or the British soldiers.

Eoin O'Farrell said, "Are we going to do somethin' about it, Peadar?"

O'Donnell nodded. "That we will, Eoin. After the funeral."

"Want to get those that murdered my boy that way. Not just a reprisal attack. Are you sure it was Croft?"

"Had to be, Eoin. His boys wouldn't have touched this Ahearn woman without his approval."

———

"This was supposed to be a happy time for us, Trevor. I'm so sorry," Maureen said.

Sullivan hugged her as they undressed for bed. "Can't be helped."

"Dillon was always the wild one. Never cautious. Just like him to be blind to the dangers."

"A pretty woman can do that to a man."

Maureen returned a weak smile. "After the funeral tomorrow I want to leave. It's this sort of thing that caused me to leave Derry in the first place. Now father and Terrance are bent on revenge. It'll never end. It'll be their funerals next. But it's mother I most worry about."

Sullivan felt relief that Maureen did not feel compelled to stay in Ireland. As much as his sympathies lay with the republicans, he was not part of this. This sectarian violence in the North was even more foreign. Although favoring Irish independence, ethnically he was New York Irish not Catholic.

"We'll leave the day after tomorrow then. I'll check the train times tomorrow. Maybe even get a ship out of Belfast to get us back to France."

The requiem mass for Dillon O'Farrell was held at Long Tower Church, the O'Farrell family parish church. Even with the wave of deaths in the last several months, the IRA made an effort to encourage a large crowd. Martyrdom made for good propaganda. It was strongly *suggested* that shop keepers close their establishments for the day. Word passed that the young man was the victim of torture before his murder. The UVF were responsible. All good Catholics needed to show solidarity by turning out. In a show of military prowess, the Derry IRA battalion assembled in strategically located groups openly displaying firearms. A direct provocation to Crown forces.

Following the mass, the crowd of several thousand followed the coffin the short distance for internment in the vast Derry City Cemetery. The RIC and British Army wisely avoided a visible presence.

The obligatory paying of respects at the O'Farrell house followed in the afternoon. By evening most visitors had departed. Only a couple of women remained to help Mary O'Farrell with managing the outpouring of donated food. Behind the house in the small yard the men had congregated. Whiskey flowed freely in a semblance of a wake. This day, Eoin and Terrance O'Farrell did not drink.

As dusk approached, Sullivan observed only armed IRA remaining in the backyard. A few women congregated inside the house. Eventually Peadar O'Donnell returned.

"Okay, lads. Everyone ready?" O'Donnell said.

One man said, "Sure you want to be doin' this on the day you laid Dillon to rest, Eoin?"

"I'm ready. My blood's up. Won't do to prolong this."

O'Donnell interjected, "You're right, Eoin. Croft and his bunch won't be expecting an attack this night."

Collins had praised O'Donnell's leadership but implied he could be rash. Sullivan could see that O'Donnell was itching for a fight.

"By the way, Mr. Sullivan is an ex-American Army officer. Served in the Great War. Friend of Michael Collins."

"Comin' with us, sir?" one of the men asked.

Sullivan shook his head no but said nothing. This reprisal that O'Donnell was planning could easily reignite the rioting of recent months. He would protect Maureen and the O'Farrell women while Eoin and Terrance did what they felt they had to. God what a hellhole he'd been drawn into.

He was aghast when O'Donnell explained the plan of attack. Recalling his academy training, it lacked tactical fundamental military precepts. No operational intelligence on the enemy. Unsure of their numbers or how they might be deployed. The enemy undoubtedly in a defensive posture.

O'Donnell planned to mount his attack directly on the home of Fergus Croft. Yet he had no way to confirm that Croft would be there. If he was, O'Donnell did not know the strength of Croft's forces. And the attack would take place within a Protestant neighborhood. Hostile territory. Their own safe lines back across the River Foyle, accessed over the Carlisle Bridge. A choke point when making their withdrawal after engaging with the UVF.

"Once we get close in on Croft's house six men will lob grenades through the windows. All at the same time. Once they explode then they'll enter the building and shoot anything that moves. It's Croft we're after, lads. If he's among them drag his body out. Then retreat taking his body of course. Listen for three blasts of a whistle. That's the signal we have Croft.

"This is not just a reprisal. Fergus Croft is the objective."

Sullivan refrained from criticizing the poorly planned mission. Not his place nor did he have stature with these fighters. It was their war. Yet his military training told him this could easily end badly even if they killed this guy Croft.

—

O'Donnell and his IRA fighters set off at ten o'clock that night. Sullivan went inside as Eoin and Terrance O'Farrell bid farewell to their wives. Both women were stoic. They shared the commitment of their husbands, terrified while reconciled to the inevitability of what their men must do. Maureen's emotions were not as contained. This endless cycle of violence over-whelmed her. She feared the possible added loss of her father and other brother. If not tonight then another time. After em-bracing them she rushed to clean dishes in the kitchen.

For the next three hours the three O'Farrell women and Sul-livan sat in the parlor keeping a silent vigil. He made no pretext of hiding his .45 service pistol which he held in his lap. He also placed himself next to the front window with a clear view of the street. The moonlight afforded a good view. Not the sort of night conducive to a secretive night raid by O'Donnell's IRA.

Sullivan said, "Best if we turn the lights off here in the parlor. Need to see anyone approaching. The light from the kitchen will be sufficient."

Mary O'Farrell made a pot of tea. Something to do.

A strange sight sitting in the semi-darkness sipping tea. No one said anything. The silence more pronounced by the ticking of a wall clock.

The stress had sapped the women. Their eyelids fluttering fighting sleep. Sullivan remained fully alert. Flashes of those ter-rible nights in the Argonne Forest. The same gnawing dread.

The clock chiming two o'clock in the morning startling the women.

Mary O'Farrell finally said, "Might be a long night. I'll make us some more tea."

"Would you be havin' any coffee about, Mrs. O'Farrell?" Sul-livan said. "A bit more effective than tea at keeping one awake."

"I believe I do have coffee. Good idea, son."

Minutes later the silence shattered.

Sullivan saw them first through the window. Terrance O'Farrell seemed to be holding up his father as they crossed the street. Abruptly he pulled open the front door.

"My father's wounded! Something bad. Hit in the stomach," Terrance said.

Sullivan jammed his pistol into his waistband and grabbed the elder O'Farrell's other arm.

From the doorway Mary O'Farrell looked aghast at her wounded husband, his shirt a mass of red. But repressing her distress she calmly said, "Can you get him upstairs onto the bed?"

It proved a struggle. Weakened from the wound and breathing heavily in severe pain, his son and Sullivan took most of his weight.

"Stay awake, Da. I'll be fetchin' a doctor right away. Just hang on."

Sullivan could tell it was a bad wound. Probably fatal unless he got medical attention soon.

As they managed Eoin O'Farrell up the stairs, Terrance breathlessly said to Sullivan, "Everything went wrong. Never even got close to Croft's house. Expecting us. An ambush. Everyone scattered when they poured fire at us."

"Oh my god!" Maureen gasped after seeing the condition of her father in the light.

Mary O'Farrell took charge. "Nora, get me some towels. Got to stop the bleeding. Maureen, get us a washbasin of hot water. Now! Be quick about it the both of you."

"I'm going for a doctor, Ma," Terrance O'Farrell said. "Trevor, you'll …"

"Get to it, Terry. I'll watch over things here. Now go!"

Maureen and Sullivan both hurried down the stairs.

"Is he going to die, Trevor?"

"Don't know, Love. Seen it go both ways in the war. Depends on what the bullet hit. Just help your mother do what she can until the doctor gets here. I need to keep watch. This might not be over. Lock that backdoor to the kitchen."

Could things get much worse? Derry had descended into civil war. Catholics against Protestants. All the politics eventually aligned along ethnic divisions. If he'd known how bad the situation was they would never have come to Ireland. He didn't feel very Irish at the moment. Just a foreigner in an alien land. Ironic to again be stuck in unexpected dangerous circumstances.

That danger escalated almost immediately. With Maureen in the kitchen heating water, he heard the sound of an automobile braking suddenly, Visible on the opposite side of the street, four men jumped out. Two of them took up positions next to the car as cover pointing rifles at the O'Farrell house. The other two rushed toward the house crouching low, hand guns visible.

A UVF counterattack? In an IRA sympathetic neighborhood? Peadar O'Donnell didn't know shit about tactics. Certainly underestimated his enemy, this Croft fellow.

Instinctively Sullivan backed away from the window. After kneeling behind a chair he trained his .45 on the front door.

"Maureen, stay in the kitchen. Get down flat on the floor."

"What? What's wrong?"

Before he could explain the front window shattered. A Mills fragmentation grenade bounced on the floor.

Sullivan took a step and threw himself through the archway into the kitchen ducking behind the interior wall.

The deafening noise and the concussive blast disoriented him for a couple of seconds. Before he could see to Maureen a second explosion followed.

Smoke wafted in from the front room. He could see Maureen on her knees on the kitchen floor her eyes wide with terror.

"Stay down. They may try an attack from the back."

The front parlor was destroyed. The lower runners of the staircase blown away leaving the upper remnants hanging precariously.

Silence followed for a full minute.

Next came a petrol-filled bottle thrown through the window opening smashing close to the stairway. A second flaming bottle followed. With no way for Sullivan to attempt extinguishing the flames, the fire quickly took hold.

The sound of the front door being kicked in announced the attackers' next move. Intent on finishing off everyone expecting any threat eliminated by the grenades.

As the doorjamb splintered swinging the door inward, Sullivan held his fire. He meant to eliminate these attackers not scare them off.

One man entered cautiously brandishing a revolver. Sullivan concealed himself just inside the kitchen doorway. He put his finger to his lips signaling Maureen to remain silent.

"Come on, Bertie, place'll be going up in a couple of minutes. Take a quick look about so we can tell Croft we did what he said."

A second attacker said, "Fuck all. Never seen what a grenade does. Tear a man…"

In a crouch on one knee, Sullivan moved his other foot into the kitchen doorway. Taking the necessary time he took aim on the furthest man for a steadied head shot.

The large caliber pistol bucked dropping the man in mid-sentence. Two quick rounds followed catching the other man in the chest.

As Sullivan stood up he said to Maureen, "We're going out the back, Follow right behind me. Any shooting, get on the ground."

"But mother and father are upstairs!" she said stepping to the doorway. But the heat from the now fully engulfed fire in the front room drove her back.

Sullivan grabbed her arm. Unlatching the back door they exited quickly. Looking around he saw no attackers.

"Got to find a ladder. Only way out is the upstairs window. Stairs are gone."

Maureen looked back toward the house. The flames of the growing inferno evident through the kitchen window.

From the open second floor window, Terrance's wife Nora screamed, "Help us!"

Smoke already billowed out the window around her.

Sullivan took off at a run yelling 'fire' from the rear of the line of row houses.

Windows opened. "Know of a ladder handy? The O'Farrells are trapped upstairs. House is burning," he said to a man several houses down leaning out his window.

"Jesus! I've no ladder but a telephone. I'll call the fire brigade."

"Be quick about it. Place is goin' up fast."

Having seen no ladder in the nearby backyards, Sullivan turned back toward the O'Farrell house. Soon the far off clanging of the fire brigade could be heard. He doubted they would arrive in time.

Returning to the house he looked up. The situation had worsened. Smoke poured vigorously from the opened upstairs window as Nora O'Farrell jumped out.

Unhurt from the fall, Nora got to her feet coughing uncontrollably. "Ma won't leave your da, Maureen. Had to leave…smoke…couldn't breathe."

"Ma! Ma! Please!" Maureen screamed. "You must jump out!"

Seconds passed before Mary O'Farrell appeared through the heavy smoke then fell from the window in a clumsy fall as one foot caught on the sill. A horrible sight with her dress in flames. She landed on the ground at an awkward angle.

Sullivan got to her first. Removing his coat he extinguished the flames. He saw the burns. Her hair had largely burned away. One side of her face and neck were badly blistered. Removing his coat he could see burns to the backs of her legs and shoulders.

Maureen fell to her knees wanting to touch her mother but afraid of hurting her.

"Get wet towels from the neighbors, Maureen. Need to keep the burns moist. Quickly!"

She rose to her feet, took a look at the now fully involved upper level and went to fetch the towels. Obviously her father could not survive.

Terrance O'Farrell returned with a doctor. Falling to his knees and weeping next to his stricken mother he too realized his father perished in the fire.

———

Even with her burns Mary O'Farrell clung to life. Doctors however still held only a poor chance that she would not succumb to infection.

Preparing for yet another mass for a murdered family member, Maureen was stricken with frustrated rage along with grief. Father Sheenan found that out.

"I remember your first communion, Maureen O'Farrell," Father Sheenan said. "Do you remember that first time when you took Jesus Christ into your heart?"

Maureen did not respond. She sat between Nora and a friend of her mother's in a corner of the west transept of the Long Tower Church where the casket of her father rested.

"These are trying times, my child. Only giving yourself over to Christ's mercy can bring peace to your soul."

"Peace to my soul? Shall I turn yet another cheek? This is my second family funeral within a week. My mother may also soon die. All murdered."

"Your family has certainly suffered grievously. But as true Irish patriots. Gave their full measure in this holy fight to free Ireland?"

"That's pious bullshit, Father. This is no holy war. This is people who call themselves Catholics or Protestants fighting over who is to lord over the other. Fergus Croft is a murdering pig not because he's Protestant but because he's a murdering pig. And for that matter the likes of Peadar O'Donnell aren't much better. Both of these bastards caused my loss. That's why I left this accursed place. Should never have returned."

The priest blanched at her tirade using such language inside the church. Making the sign of the cross he mumbled something in Latin and moved on to speak to other mourners.

"You shouldn't be so hard on Father Sheenan, dear," her mother's friend said. "He's a friend to the IRA."

"The Church isn't a friend to the IRA or even Ireland. It looks after itself," Maureen said.

The same ritual as with Dillon O'Farrell's funeral. This time ending with people paying respects for Eoin O'Farrell at the home of his son Terrance. Sullivan and Maureen arrived in the evening after spending the day at the hospital bedside of Mary O'Farrell.

Unfortunately, Peadar O'Donnell was among those there.

"Maureen, so sorry about your father and mother," O'Donnell said to her.

"Sorry? That's all you have to say? It was your stupid fault. Father looked up to you as a leader. Which you're not very good at it seems. Others were killed. Never even got close to Fergus Croft Terry said. Now my mother may also die."

O'Donnell's jaw stiffened. He wasn't used to being dressed down, especially by a woman.

"Know how you must feel, Mrs. Sullivan. Our lads did the best under the circumstances. Your father was bent on killing Croft. So were others after what he did to your brother."

Turning to Sullivan, he said, "You need to explain to your wife that plans sometimes go awry in war."

"Don't be draggin' my husband into this. What you call a war is just murderin' groups of men. Like the ancient Gaelic clans. The IRA and the UVF are cut from the same cloth."

O'Donnell glared at Maureen then turned and left.

Soon after Terrance O'Farrell came over to her and Sullivan.

"What did ya say to Peadar? Said you had harsh words for the IRA. You need…"

"I need to what, Terry? Mind my tongue? Fuck your IRA. It got Dillon and Da killed. Are you next? Ma may not make it. All for what? Are you fighting for Ireland or just killing Prods?"

Sullivan said nothing. Maureen's wrath was understandable. His view was more nuanced being less a personal loss. Not sure where to assign blame to this sectarian violence in the north, but he held strong anti-British views. The product of his militant Fenian heritage. Naturally he sided with the ideal of a sovereign

Irish republic. The parallel no different from America's war of independence against the British 150 years ago seemed obvious.

He and Maureen spent the night at the home of Mary O'Farrell's friend. Before retiring to bed, Maureen said, "You know I can't leave mother. At least not yet."

"Yes, I realize that. Been thinking on what to do. Could be some time before your mother recovers."

"Recovers? If she recovers you mean."

"Of course, but let's hope she does. She's a strong woman."

"Even if she lives, she'll never truly recover, Trevor. Those burns. It'll be horrible."

Sullivan knew what she meant. The doctor told him what it would be like. She would never walk without a cane with the burns to the lower leg muscles and tendons. Both hands would have limited mobility. Half her face forever grossly disfigured. All bad enough, yet she'd also be forever reliving the gruesome deaths of her husband and son.

If her mother survived, it would be a very long time before Maureen felt emotionally free enough to return to Paris.

"I think the best thing to do is send letters to our employers explaining our circumstances. We'll each request a leave of absence. May not be granted but we've nothing to lose."

"Oh, Trevor, I'm so sorry to have brought us here. Dragged you into this nightmare. My god, if you hadn't shot those men we'd be dead too."

She hugged him and tears flowed.

"Listen, I married you for better or worse. Had this happened while in Paris, we'd still have come to Derry."

"Do we have enough money?"

He sighed. That would eventually present a problem.

"Depends. We'll have to live somewhere while staying here. I think we both agree that won't be permanent. Both of us love Paris too much. But we may be here for many months. That means sending rent money to Paris to keep the apartment. A place here to live. Other living expenses. Of course medical care for your mother. We've got adequate funds but not enough to do all that for very long."

"So what do we do?" she asked.

"I'll send off the letters to Paris in a day or two. I'll ask for a six months leave. If it turns out less before we can return then no problem. If it looks to be longer I'll try to extend the leave.

"Let's give it two weeks. By that time we'll know better about your mother. Then I'll look for work here."

CHAPTER 11

Several weeks after the fire, doctors guardedly pronounced Mary O'Farrell out of danger of dying. Infection avoided but she would still remain hospitalized indefinitely. Even after release she faced a long convalescence and a life of severe disabilities.

With a sense of despair Sullivan sent off the letters to their respective French employers. After the bright prospects of a new life with Maureen in Paris this turn of events upended everything. Not only stuck in this war-torn foreign place, but now forced to seek employment.

Unfortunately he quickly learned Derry offered few employment opportunities for his skills. Textile mills and clothing factories dominated industry in Derry. Poor prospects for someone with a civil engineering background. After weeks of fruitless searching he was forced to turn to broader opportunities in Belfast. Even railroad operations where he had experience were headquartered in Belfast. The three-hour train distance from Derry meant at least weekly separation from Maureen.

Unlike Derry, Belfast was a vibrant and diverse industrial city. But it too suffered the same sectarian unrest. It had only been a week since a terrible riot killed 22 with hundreds injured in the west Belfast Catholic slums. Unlike Dublin, the war in Ulster was ever-present in everyday life.

Yet Belfast offered all manner of opportunities for an engineer. Assuming you were pro-unionist and of course Protestant. With distaste he would play that subterfuge. He could easily pass that test citing his father's Protestant lineage from Belfast. Engineering experience at age thirty-four meant he wasn't a youngster. A former professional military officer with a prestigious war record should confirm his leadership qualifications.

The trump card was applying for a position where his grandfather had worked, the great shipbuilding works of Belfast's Harland & Wolff. Builders of the great ocean liners for the White Star Line including the 50,000-ton Olympic-class ships Olympic, Britannic, and Titanic. Gerard Sullivan, his father's father, was one of the original employees when the company formed in 1861, retiring as a senior millwright supervisor after forty years of service.

Trevor Sullivan's credentials provided a powerful resume. What was needed was a cover story. Best to stick with as much of the truth as possible. Most of all he needed to alter the account of the circumstances in Derry. Build a believable fiction that made Belfast always the intended destination to settle with his new wife.

The constructed legend turned out to have plausible underpinnings. Following the war he met an Irish woman studying art in Paris. After resigning his commission in the army he took a job in Paris while his new wife completed her studies. Becoming homesick she wished to return to her native Ireland. Unfortunately, her mother suffered a serious accident during the recent rioting.

The recent wave of sectarian violence made Derry into a frightful place to make a new life. Especially with his Protestant background. Although from Derry, his wife found it too provincial having spent several years living in Paris. With prospects of securing a proper professional position better in Belfast that became their choice. Unfortunately, his wife's family circumstances temporarily force a long train commute to visit her on weekends. Once her mother's condition allows, she will join him in Belfast.

The fabrication would stand up if he could avoid having to elaborate more fully on circumstances in Derry. Understandable why no one in Belfast would meet Mrs. Sullivan. The weekly train trips taken out of Belfast explained. Credible at least for a few months.

As for their real plans, both he and Maureen intended to return to Paris as soon as the situation with her mother allowed. If not Paris then the prospects of New York might be an alternative. Remaining in Ireland was not an option. The Anglo-Irish War began to look more like a real war in the autumn of 1920. A war Sullivan feared would tear Ireland apart for years.

Their personal involvement in what was going on in Ireland was quite enough. Being forced to kill those two UVF was not sufficient to draw him into the conflict. His Irishness did not extend that far. Nothing more than self-defense while caught in a tit-for-tat reprisal between the IRA and UVF.

Tellingly of the government's bias in the sectarian violence, there had been no police inquiry into the deaths and the firebombing of the O'Farrell house. Newspapers reported only the barest of facts. Only the death of Eoin O'Farrell, no mention of the two unaccounted bodies in the burned house. No connection made to the torture and murder of Dillon O'Farrell. Rule of law did not exist in the north. Civil authority in the form of the British Crown firmly biased by painting all Catholics as sympathetic to the IRA rebellion.

—

Sullivan prepared his resume. He would take any engineering job but felt the best tactic was to aim for a managerial role consistent with his background. This was to appear a career move consistent with his cover story to make Belfast his home.

Harland & Wolff should offer the best opportunity. The largest Belfast employer with broad needs for experienced engineering professionals. An ironic choice being the very bastion of Protestant domination in Belfast. He had no illusions about the cultural environment. The recent rioting had its origins at the shipyard. Thousands of Catholic workers were violently driven out by Protestant workers. Many of the fleeing workers died along with victims of the looting and burning of Catholic neighborhoods south of the Falls Road. Eventually the British Army reestablished order. Harland & Wolff management ignored the ethnic purge.

But tensions remained heightened. The IRA killing of an RIC detective in nearby Lisburn a month later set off another round of sectarian rioting killing 33.

With conflicted emotions Sullivan drafted a cover letter to accompany his resume stated his career objective.

As a civil engineering graduate of the United States Military Academy, I have thirteen years of managerial engineering experience. Concluding my military service after serving in France in the Great War with the rank of major, I chose to pursue a civilian engineering career. With extensive railroad experience in the U.S Army, I was employed for two years by the French Ministry of Finance as Deputy Engineering Director for Railway Construction.

I am a first generation Irish-American with roots in Belfast. Having recently wed an Irishwoman completing her academic studies in Paris, we both wish to return to our homeland to make our home in Belfast.

Harland & Wolff has a particular personal attraction since my paternal grandfather spent forty years of service with the firm beginning with its founding in 1861. It would be fitting to return to my ancestral home and begin what I would hope to be my own long career with the venerable Harland & Wolff Company.

Arriving in Belfast he checked into a small hotel. Using the desk clerk's typewriter he typed the resume and cover letter. With a newly pressed suit he visited Harland & Wolff the following day handing the receptionist an envelope addressed to the personnel manager.

He spent the remainder of the day researching other potential employers at the Belfast Library in the city center.

The following day he paid visits to several prospective employers. The railroad, municipal electric company, and the port authority seemed to offer the best prospects. But nothing appeared promising, only junior entry positions. Most senior job openings often did not appear in advertisement. Networking and personal recommendations typically filled such positions. As a foreigner, he could only cite a remote connection to Harland & Wolff to add leverage. At least the industrial climate in Belfast seemed robust. Demand for skilled workers was a continual challenge. Hopefully that included experienced engineers.

Of course he would take any position if the pay was adequate. But a more senior position better aligned with his cover story. It might also provide some diversion for what he expected could be months with the long commute between Belfast and Derry. Leaving Ireland seemed an uncertain distant hope.

Before a tearful departure from Maureen at the train station, she said, "Perhaps you could look up your father's family while in Belfast? Might be less lonely."

"No I don't think so. They ostracized dad when he married into a Catholic family from Limerick. Then Uncle Tom and Uncle Ned became notorious in 1916. Even as a child I recalled my father's anger toward his loyalist family."

Sullivan never met his father's siblings. Grandparents deceased. Didn't know if there were cousins. If they were to meet how could he possibly discuss the events in Derry? No reason to resurrect a decades-old family schism.

Prospects brightened on his third day in Belfast. A letter arrived at Sullivan's hotel in the morning. The delivery messenger said he was instructed to await Mr. Sullivan's reply. On Harland & Wolff letterhead, it read:

> In response to your letter and resume presented, Mr. Malcom Llewellyn, Managing Director respectfully requests the favor of meeting with you this afternoon at two o'clock at his office. Should that time prove convenient, please advise the courier accordingly.
>
> I remain yours sincerely,
> Alfred Pimm

Personal Secretary to the Managing Director

Well how about that? To present the best impression, Sullivan purchased a new white shirt and tie. Hotel staff pressed his suit. After a shoe shine followed by a light lunch he presented himself at the Harland & Wolff offices on Queens Row. In the heart of the massive shipyard, the large red brick building was anything but grand in appearance. A working building housing hundreds including the great hall with its rows of drafting tables. Harland & Wolff was the largest employer in Belfast with a workforce of over 20,000.

The immense lattice work of the Arrol gantry cranes dominated the Belfast skyline. They were erected years earlier to service the two new slipways where the great White Star Line sister ships Olympic, Titanic, and Britannic were constructed years earlier. At well over two hundred feet in height, an even more remarkable sight this close up. For an engineer, this was the place to work in Belfast.

Directed to the third floor, he found Mr. Pimm. Situated at the corner of the building, he sat at a desk commanding a large waiting area paneled in dark wood. A double door marked the managing director's office.

"Mr. Sullivan?" Pimm said extending his hand and offering a smile.

"At your service, Sir."

"Delighted this proved convenient. Mr. Llewellyn is looking forward to meeting you."

Sullivan followed Pimm to the director's door where he knocked then opened the door to announce Sullivan.

Malcom Llewellyn came from around his desk to greet Sullivan.

"Thank you for coming, Mr. Sullivan. A pleasure to meet you. Please take a seat."

Llewellyn motioned toward an informal sitting area with comfortable chairs.

"I'll get straight to the point, Mr. Sullivan. Your background is impressive. You seemed to have consistently advanced in your professional career."

"Thank you, Sir. I have been fortunate to often be in the right place to take advantage of opportunities."

"I appreciate your modesty but I suspect your success has not been entirely due to luck. I have friends in the British Army. I took the liberty to check on your military record. I believe you substantially understated your professional accomplishments.

"I'm not only talking about your prowess in combat that led to decorations for valor, but that they were awarded for participation with the famous Lost Battalion. The entire world read accounts of your desperate circumstances.

"The official wording of your citation reads like sensational fiction. And to think you had stumbled into this horrific situation by accident."

"Valor sometimes is simply a result of desperately fighting for one's life. Evidenced if you will by the *Lost Battalion* being awarded more individual citations than any other American unit."

"Again, your modesty expresses character. But if I may ask, why did you leave what appeared to be a promising military career?"

"As with much in life, unanticipated factors often converge to alter one's course. For me it was the Great War. It held no glory just horror. Unimaginative military leadership sacrificing hundreds of thousands of lives following unrealistic strategies. Cast a pall over continuing a career in the military."

"Yes, I know what you mean of events altering one's course in life. My own circumstances took such a path. In 1912, I was manager of marine construction with the Glasgow firm of William Beardmore & Company. Two things happened that year. Harland & Wolff acquired Beardmore, and the Titanic was lost. A victim of that disaster was my predecessor, the managing director Thomas Andrews, making the great ship's maiden voyage. But excuse my interruption."

Sullivan continued, "However my military career provided exceptional experience. First rate engineering training. The chance to exercise my abilities. Opportunity to manage projects and people. I felt the future would probably be more of the same. Building military installations, bridges, damns. I was an engineer first, a soldier second. The private sector seemed to offer more interesting future opportunities."

"Yes, I understand. That you secured such an important position with the French government validates your capabilities," Llewellyn said.

"Well, Sir, it helped having an extensive background in railroad operations. France is in need of much rebuilding. I suspect that many good French engineers lost their lives in the war. France's need is great."

"You speak, French?"

"Yes, Sir. Learned from my wife. She was also a reason to alter my career path. A soldier's life of continually moving about every few years would not have suited her. She has her own career aspirations in the arts. We met when she was completing her studies in Paris."

"That is a remarkable coincidence. My daughter speaks French. Also studied in Paris. But back to you, Mr. Sullivan. It seems that events similar to those that brought me to Harland & Wolff may also prove fortuitous to both you and the company.

"Not three weeks ago I lost one of my key subordinates, Tobias Hannigan. Old Toby was my facilities superintendent. Sudden heart attack. Took him in the night. My age. Makes one think seriously about their own mortality. Anyway, no obvious replacement presented itself.

"Your technical background seems well suited. Civil engineering degree, extensive managerial experience, project management, proven leadership.

"I thought highly of Hannigan. But to be candid, Mr. Sullivan, while he was a competent enough manager he had certain shortcomings. Followed instructions but did not bring new ideas into his work. Projects under his responsibility often missed deadlines. Difficult for him to commit to a schedule."

"At the risk of being immodest, I would cite my proven skills in those responsibilities, Sir. For the last few years I have been supervising the planning and construction of new railways. During the war, a task constantly faced with demanding challenges and deadlines. After the war, similar chaos in the ever-shifting priorities of rebuilding devastated French infrastructure."

"I can well imagine. Certainly not chaotic here but nonetheless a continuous effort to meet schedule and budget in the construction of vessels on our order book. Efficient operation of the facility is central to the construction schedule."

Llewellyn looked over his shoulder as the door opened. An older gentleman with short gray hair and a well-groomed closely cropped beard entered.

"Malcom. Forgive my intrusion but I have another commitment I must attend to shortly. I wanted the opportunity to meet Mr. Sullivan. Pimm said you two had been getting along for an hour so I decided to barge in before I needed to leave."

"Not at all, Sir. Glad you did. Mr. Sullivan, may I introduce the Chairman of Harland & Wolff, Sir William Pirrie. His peerage title, Baron Pirrie."

Sullivan stood and shook hands with Pirrie.

"We were speaking of coincidences, Sir. The first of which being the untimely loss of Toby Hannigan. The second was Mr. Sullivan appearing out of nowhere with his interesting background. The other coincidence, Mr. Sullivan, involves Sir William directly."

Pirrie said, "That's correct. You see, Mr. Sullivan, your letter mentioned the employment of your grandfather, Gerard Sullivan. I have been here a very long time going back to 1862. My first year at Harland & Wolff was as a gentleman intern having just matriculated from university. Some would treat young fellows like me as dilettantes. Not real workers. Just enduring an unpleasant necessity of getting our hands dirty before putting on a shirt and tie to take our place behind a desk.

"Thanks to your grandfather, he disabused me of such snobbery. Explained how the fundamental workings of the process interconnected from laying the keel to sending the completed hull rushing down the spillway. How things really worked. Showed me how a grasp of the hands-on would prove invaluable in my career *upstairs*. He was right. Your grandfather was an extraordinary mentor. And to think his grandson is now looking to join us."

"Thank you, Sir," Sullivan said. "I shall cherish your comments. Unfortunately I never had the pleasure of meeting my grandfather. My father immigrated to America where I was born."

"But you are Irish. A Belfast man I should say with your family background. Malcom has related your professional background to me. I share his enthusiasm.

"I must apologize for overstepping myself with my comments, Malcom. I don't mean to prejudice what is your call. But no reason to beat around the bush. I sense you have gotten on well this past hour? But I will affirm, Mr. Sullivan, that your employment is entirely Malcom's decision. He runs operations here. I try not to interfere with his prerogatives."

"Not at all, Sir William," Llewellyn said. "I have never had any issues on that account. As for your comments regarding Mr. Sullivan, I shall also not be circumspect. He impresses me greatly. I would like to become better acquainted with Mr. Sullivan, but I concur with your comments, Sir. I think we may have found our man."

"Excellent. Mr. Sullivan, I shall take my leave. I hope I will be seeing you here soon. Good day, Malcom."

After Pirrie left, Llewellyn said, "May I suggest you join me for dinner at my club this evening? It will provide an opportunity for us to get to know each other better. At this juncture you may perhaps wish to ask me many questions about Harland & Wolff. Certainly more about the job. Compensation of course, which I believe should not be a problem. You must also be certain about wanting to join us."

"I would enjoy that very much, Sir. And thank you for the opportunity. I shall look forward to this evening."

"Very good. You can then tell me more about your personal life. And where might your wife be? Still in Paris?"

"No, Sir. She's currently in Derry. Unfortunately, her mother was in a serious accident. A fire during the riots. Suffered terrible burns. She remains hospitalized still in critical condition. It hastened our coming to Ireland months earlier than planned."

"Good heavens. I'm sorry to hear that. Derry you say?"

"Yes, Sir. An unfortunate circumstance. The fire took the life of my wife's father. Her mother couldn't save him but suffered severe injury in the attempt. My wife attends to her every day at the hospital.

"Your wife is from Derry?

"Yes. Although for the last five years she has lived in Paris. With all the violence in Derry, the riots this year, I confess I'm concerned. However my wife insisted I proceed in securing a position in Belfast."

"Derry is a difficult place. If I may be so bold, is your wife Catholic or Protestant?"

"Neither actually. Like me, she's from a mixed background. Her father like mine was Protestant, her mother Catholic. Ironically it is not known which side was responsible for the fire. Her parents were not politically active. Collateral damage I'm told. Other homes were burned that same night a couple of months ago."

"That is truly terrible. Especially at a time when you chose to make your new home in Ireland. How long before your wife can join you here in Belfast?"

"Not certain. Doctors say her mother still faces months in the hospital. After that it depends on the level of care she might require. At any rate I plan taking the train on the weekends to be with her however briefly until... Until her circumstances become more defined."

"I understand your meaning. Most commendable. Both of you. A temporary situation that will only enhance your marital bond once your wife is able to join you in Belfast."

Sullivan experienced a sense of unease. Misleading Llewellyn by implying a long-term commitment felt ethically compromising. The man was warm and friendly. Undoubtedly qualified to run this great enterprise. Appeared to be someone good to work for. Seemed to take a genuine liking to him. The deceit bothered Sullivan.

But apart from disappointing Llewellyn when he soon left, the shipyard with its strong unionist anti-Catholic workforce might prove an uncomfortable environment given his political feelings. He would be an outsider forced to continually present a false flag.

CHAPTER 12

The Ulster Club occupied an ornate three-story limestone building on Victoria Street just north of the Albert Memorial clock tower. The male only membership included the Belfast powerful of business and government. An elegant restaurant occupied the first floor along with administrative offices. The bar and vast reading room with a well-stocked library occupied the second. On the third floor various sized meeting rooms were available to members. The interior throughout was paneled in walnut with crystal light fixtures. A prestigious men's club.

The business of not only Belfast but what was to soon be a separate Northern Ireland was informally conducted here. The shaping of public policy directed by the economic power structure. The quintessential place to conduct backroom deals. Business, politics, and now the response to counter this insurrectionist war were all directed from the Ulster Club. So too the tactical plotting to manipulate London to favor Ulster unionist ambitions.

On this brisk evening with a chill blowing out of the north, six of the most influential men in Ulster sat in a private room on the third floor. Seated in cushioned leather chairs, most held crystal glasses of brandy or whiskey. A fire blazed within an oversized fireplace, now late in the evening following dinner downstairs.

"Gentlemen, I appreciate that everyone could make time this evening. An important development has occurred. A singular opportunity that must be exploited," a tall distinguished middle-aged man said. Phillip Atwood stood to address the five other men of similar age.

Atwood ran the extended enterprises of Atwood Textiles. From production of linen to finished clothing manufacture in Belfast and Derry, the enterprise started by his grandfather also had substantial textile investments in Australia and Egypt. The second largest employer in Ulster after Harland & Wolff. Sir Phillip was also the number-two man in the leadership of the Ulster Unionist Party.

The UUP was the dominate political power in the six northeast counties of Ulster. While Sinn Féin swept parliamentary seats for all the other counties in greater Ireland, the UUP with its majority Protestant electorate controlled the north. UUP members continued to serve in the British House of Commons, where Sinn Féin MPs boycotted the body and instead set up an independent Irish parliament. As the sole Irish parliamentary voice in London, the UUP was therefore able to further their aims from inside the British parliament without republican Irish opposition.

"And this opportunity results largely from the efforts of Sir James Craig," Atwood said. "I will let Sir James explain."

"Most kind of you, Phillip," Craig said.

James Craig headed the Ulster Unionist Party. Stocky with a large bullet-shaped head with a receding hair line and gray mustache, he looked the image of an aging pugilist. His political militancy fit that physical appearance analogy.

"Gentlemen, two weeks ago as you read in the newspapers, the Prime Minister authorized the formation of what is to be known as the Ulster Special Constabulary."

Craig was a junior minister in the House of Commons. He advocated that the apparatus of government and security be invested in Ulster before home rule became law separating Northern Ireland from the other twenty-six Irish counties. Even under home rule he argued Northern Ireland must remain firmly wedded to Britain.

Selling British Prime Minister Lloyd George on the creation of an Ulster Special Constabulary was not difficult. For a number of reasons he found it appealing. First of all, Special Constabulary Acts dating to 1832 and 1914 already authorized their use in times of war or insurgency. No new legislation need be passed, or debated. An executive action that could be authorized from the British administration in Dublin Castle.

It was also cost-effective. This new police body would immediately come from the ranks of existing Protestant paramilitaries. Irish citizens, not costly imported manpower such as the Black & Tans and Auxiliaries now operating principally in southern Ireland. Most of these special constables unpaid except during part-time duty. And the Ulster Volunteers and various other paramilitaries were already well armed.

"Thank you, Phillip," Craig said. "This singular move will allow for a coordinated counterinsurgency response to the IRA and its supporters. Furthermore, it brings those resources under our own police control. I mean no slight against your regiments, General."

Craig looked at Brigadier General Kenneth Hopkins. "We appreciate the difficult task of His Majesty's forces. Certainly not like anything the 15th Brigade experienced in the Great War. A distinguished war record I might add."

General Hopkins acknowledged Craig's comments with a nod. His British Army 15th Infantry Brigade had been formed in Ireland at the onset of the Great War. Now assigned to police Ulster, the Anglo-Irish war couldn't be more different from the trenches of the Western Front. The IRA conducted guerrilla attacks predominately against the RIC but occasionally against British Army regulars. Hopkins hated this policing duty. Not a fit role for his battle-tested regiments. Keeping order in Ulster often amounted to keeping Catholic and Protestants from killing one another. Yet his troops consisted of men of both ethnic backgrounds.

The Protestant paramilitaries, especially the well-armed UVF, although unionists, presented a different set of problems. He held them in contempt as nothing more than vigilantes. Now they were to be invested with policing powers?

Craig continued, "I have already spoken with all the important unionist groups. Wilfrid's Ulster Volunteers are fully onboard."

Wilfrid Spender, a founding member of the UVF and its current president said, "Wholeheartedly. I expect most of our members to join. It will allow them to operate more freely to maintain order now as an official adjunct to the RIC."

Craig said, "In addition to the UVF, I've been in contact with Basil Brooke and his Fermanagh Vigilance people. Also John Redmond and his ex-servicemen in Ballymacarrett. And of course the Ulster Unionist Labour Association with its workers from Harland & Wolff.

"And thank you for your efforts in that regard, Malcom. I know you have your own business issues with the Labour Association. At least they're firmly unionist and anti-socialist," Craig added acknowledging Malcom Llewellyn.

"Not so sure about their views on socialism based on their recurring wage demands," Llewellyn said. The others chuckled. "But yes, I suspect most will join. At least for the part-time Special Constable category. I have agreed to make allowances for absences at the shipyard when they're called to perform policing duties."

"Most generous, Malcom. We all need to note that and get other employers to similarly agree."

Turning to the last man in the group Craig said, "This must be welcome news to you I daresay, Colonel Wickham. This insurrection has certainly taxed the resources of the RIC. Now you will finally have the means to crush this rebellion."

"I believe so, Sir James," Wickham said. "At least in what will soon become Northern Ireland. Once the special constabulary forces are deployed we can take the offensive. As the situation now stands, securing RIC barracks from IRA attack demands much of our manpower."

Lieutenant Colonel Charles Wickham of the British Army had been brought to Belfast as the RIC Divisional Commissioner for Ulster a year earlier. Serving with distinction in the Second Boer War in South Africa he moved into intelligence toward the end of hostilities in 1902 as a young officer. Intelligence related work would remain his calling throughout his career. Before being assigned to Ireland, he served with the British Expeditionary Forces supporting the anti-Bolshevik White movement in the Russian Civil War.

Wickham came well indoctrinated in British colonial rule. The brutality inflicted by British forces on the South African enemy, including the concept of penal concentration camps for the indefinite non-judicial internment of suspected enemy sympathizers, would soon be repeated in Ireland.

Unlike General Hopkins, Wickham harbored no qualms about bolstering his police forces with large numbers of poorly disciplined Protestant paramilitaries. His seasoned RIC officers could maintain order while using these inexperienced ranks in support. Even most Catholic RIC officers considered the IRA a murderous gang of rebels. The sheer impact of immediately adding thousands of well-armed resources provided the ability to aggressively go on the offensive. Although the Special Constabulary would be under an independent command structure, the regular RIC expected to still direct operations.

Wickham added, "I dare say in a couple of months after integrating these new recruits you shall see results. We have good intelligence on the IRA. Now with the means we will decimate their ranks."

"You make it sound a simple question of manpower, Colonel," General Hopkins said. "The IRA is part of the populace. Like any guerrilla force they depend on popular support. Concealment, food, intelligence. This new band of recruits will all be Protestant. Drawn from the ranks of those the IRA is currently fighting. This will make every Catholic an IRA sympathizer."

"That is not far from the current situation, General. Even if there are Catholics that dislike the IRA they are powerless. The IRA kills collaborators. Every Catholic is terrorized into silence."

"This is not simply a war of guns, Colonel. I agree with General Macready and General Wilson. Both think this move to be counterproductive. Others do as well. The Under Secretary for Ireland points out, and I quote, *you cannot in the middle of a faction fight recognize one of the contending parties and expect it to deal with disorder in the spirit of impartiality and fairness essential in those who have to carry out the orders of the government.*"

General Sir Nevil Macready, Hopkins superior, commanded the British Army in Ireland. Field Marshall Sir Henry Wilson was Chief of the Imperial General Staff. Both vigorously opposed establishing the Special Constabulary in Ireland. Prime Minister Lloyd George however liked Craig's idea from the beginning and overrode not only the generals but many senior British administrators.

Atwood said, "But this is more than a faction fight, General. Secretary Anderson uses soft diplomatic language to convey a different impression. This fight in Ulster may have ethnic overtones but at the heart of the matter the real divide is between nationalists and unionists. No different than in all of Ireland. Traditions of union with Britain are simply stronger here in the north."

"Gentlemen, I sincerely hope you are correct in the expected results of this move," Hopkins said. "While I remain skeptical, there is little I can do but follow orders. I can only emphasize that deployment of these new forces be conducted judiciously. And lawfully."

Hopkins held little chance that would be the outcome. Up to now his troops had been in support of the beleaguered RIC. Trying to suppress IRA active service guerrillas but mostly maintaining civil order. As much a sectarian issue as nationalism. His soldiers might now find themselves supporting an out-of-control legalized police state. Bitter garrison duty for a seasoned British officer rising to the rank of brigadier through his combat leadership in the Great War.

Lloyd George's government seemed bent on making matters worse in Ireland. First these RIC Special Reserves, the Black and Tans. Then the Auxiliary Division. Now putting militant Irish Protestant paramilitaries into uniforms as this Ulster Special Constabulary.

CHAPTER 13

Commissioner Wickham sat behind his desk at RIC's Ulster headquarters in a nondescript building on Waring Street in Belfast. Behind him a Union Jack and the RIC flag flanked a portrait of King George V.

His adjutant knocked then opened the door, "Inspector Doyle is here, Sir."

"Show him in."

The tall RIC officer entered coming to attention and saluting. "Sir, you sent for me?"

The RIC maintained military protocols. Even their dark green uniforms with black buttons and insignia resembled those of British Army rifle regiments.

"Yes. Please sit down, Inspector."

Inspector John Doyle had the same military bearing as Wickham. Similar age. Mustache. But distinctly different in physical stature. Wickham was slender where Doyle was muscular. The three stone difference in weight impressive at his height of over six feet.

Wickham said, "Needless to say you're aware of the planned establishment of this Ulster Special Constabulary?"

"Of course, Sir. Everyone is talking about what it will mean. A manpower windfall I'd say."

125

"Yes and no. It'll be under separate command from the RIC. Seems London doesn't trust us enough. Too many Catholics in our ranks. Too many divided sympathies. These Specials will all be former UVF or other Protestant Unionist groups."

"I assure you there're no Catholics in the Intelligence Division, Sir"

"I'm aware of that, Inspector. So the challenge will be to integrate these Specials into coordinated operations under our direction. I don't intend for them to take over from us. The 'A' category specials will be full-time. They'll serve in their own home neighborhoods. We can rely on them to relieve us of some of the patrol work. But it's the 'B' category that will provide us numbers on the scale of a small army. Part-timers. Motivated to act aggressively against republican sympathizers.

"They'll be organized into platoon sized well-armed mobile units. Equipped with transport. Crossley tenders with mounted machine guns. They'll provide us mobile capability like the Auxiliaries in the south. Search and destroy operations. It's these guys I want to make use of. We'll use your intelligence unit to identify targets of opportunity then deploy these new Specials to help execute operations."

"Who'll command these guys, Sir?"

"A former colonel by the name of Crawford."

"Well that's good news."

"I believe you and Crawford worked together in the past?"

"Yes, Sir. A tough guy. Not afraid to crack heads."

Doyle had fed intelligence to Crawford when he wished to distance himself from dirty work. A former British Army officer, Crawford was a senior officer in the UVF.

"I would agree. That's what I wanted to discuss, Inspector. With this massive recruitment, Crawford will have his hands full. A difficult challenge I should imagine. I'm looking to leverage those resources. To accomplish that we need more intelligence on the IRA. That's our bargaining power with Crawford."

Doyle said, "Of course, Sir. I've a good group of lads. Won't let you down, Sir."

"I have no doubts on that account, Inspector. I'll need you to greatly expand the flow of intelligence. A difficult task requiring your unique skills. A promotion to district inspector as well."

Doyle registered a smile. "Thank you, Sir."

"Let me be more specific. With these added special constables we will go on the offensive. That requires new tactics to yield more actionable intelligence. Do you know why I selected you for this job, Inspector Doyle?"

"Well, I ...I believe I get things done."

"Yes you do. Certainly that's a good part of it. But it's because of your aggressive tactics, Inspector. To increase the intelligence value I need someone not afraid to bend the rules. In short, get results. Like you did in South Africa."

Wickham witnessed firsthand John Doyle's violent skills during the Boer War almost twenty years earlier.

"Take off the gloves, but I don't want to know the details. Just get results."

Doyle nodded his understanding. "I get your meaning, Sir."

"There's more. I want you to create a special action squad. Constables to act on intelligence without bureaucratic sanction. The same as a secret unit Dublin Castle created to go after Michael Collins and his IRA leadership. Detectives working undercover but licensed to take violent action. Do the same thing here in Belfast. Eliminate the IRA. Stamp out their base of support. You have a free hand. Dead or alive, doesn't matter. Get down to Dublin and look up a Lieutenant Colonel Wilson. He commands this unit. Duplicate that in Belfast."

———

Only days later and before Doyle's planned trip to Dublin, circumstances changed. A singular event upped the intensity of the secret side of the Anglo-Irish War. It also eliminated the need for Doyle to go to Dublin.

Comprised of 18 or 20 ex-British Army and RIC officers, the group referred to by Wickham began operations in Dublin in early 1920. Receiving intelligence training by Scotland Yard Special Branch in London, their mission was to decimate Sinn Féin and IRA leadership. Specifically Michael Collins. Cut the head off the snake. Officially designated the Dublin District Special Branch, the group became known to the IRA as the Cairo Gang for their frequenting of the Cafe Cairo at 59 Grafton Street in Dublin.

The Cairo Gang detectives lived unobtrusively in boarding-houses and hotels across Dublin. Their mission was to prepare a hit list of known republicans then carry out the assassinations.

However on the morning of Sunday, November 21, 1920, events turned against the D Branch detectives. In a series of sim-ultaneous attacks engineered by Michael Collins, the IRA shot dead twelve operatives of D Branch in a well-coordinated mis-sion at different locations across Dublin.

Collins' intelligence network and his IRA hit team known as the Squad got there first. An intelligence coup of the first-order. The daring success of the IRA stunned the British administration in Ireland. It effectively crippled Dublin Castle's intelligence gathering capability for the duration of the war.

The IRA's success came at a price. Collins' good friend Dick McKee and another senior IRA were detained by Crown forces the previous night. In reprisal for the assassinations both were tortured and later shot dead with the typical justification, *while trying to escape*.

Worse yet, a mixed force of RIC, Black and Tans, and Auxil-iaries descended on Croke Park that afternoon. As a harassing retaliation, the Crown forces intended to surround the football stadium where 5,000 spectators watched a Gaelic football match between Dublin and Tipperary. From the onset the troops went on a rampage firing indiscriminately. Thirteen spectators and one footballer died.

Bloody Sunday claimed 31 lives and further stoked the rebel-lion. The British Government later suppressed the findings of two military courts of inquiry condemning the reprisal.

For Doyle the annihilation of the D Branch in Dublin acted as a warning. Do not underestimate this enemy. He wouldn't make the same mistake. Bloody Sunday meant that he could also justify the most extreme measures. Wickham would get his results.

———

John Doyle needed no training in applying brutal tactics. It came naturally. Always large for his age, his inclination toward violence found frequent outlet. Not only a bully, his intellect allowed him to avoid accountability.

He inherited an imbed hatred for Catholics, often targets of his school years' fights. He became a terror with his natural physical abilities. Even his own father shied from pushing his son too far.

After completing secondary school no career avenue enticed him. The idea of working at the shipyard like his father held no interest. The siren call of adventure and foreign places made joining the army a natural choice. Joining the British Army at the age of eighteen, within a year he found himself on a troop transport to South Africa in 1899, attached to the Norfolk Regiment. A new conflict had broken out in the economically important colonial region.

In what was to become known as the Second Boer War or simply the South African War, the British wanted to annex the independent Transvaal Republic and the Orange Free State. Their prior attempt failed in the First Boer War less than twenty years earlier with the Dutch settlers defeating the British in a minor four-month conflict. Since that time an uneasy truce and conflicted rights of ethnic British settlers festered within those republics.

This new three-year conflict had obvious parallels to the Anglo-Irish War. As fighting intensified, British frustration mounted. Eventually close to half a million British regulars and colonial troops attempted to crush the native Boer forces estimated at only 88,000. A guerrilla war ensued replete with atrocities of every kind. The British Army resorted to torture of prisoners to extract information. To break support, Boer civilians were interned in concentration camps. Food and sanitary deprivations within the camps resulted in nearly 50,000 internee deaths.

In this environment, someone of Doyle's psychological makeup became useful. He was intelligent and violent yet that violence was not purely sadism. More a sociopath, Doyle simply saw violence as a means of producing a result. That's what he had done all his life for personal reasons. He simply held no sympathy for those he harmed. A trait useful to British Intelligence.

Doyle's skills at making resistive prisoners talk quickly gained notice. While Doyle worked on a prisoner tied to a chair, an immediate supervisor once commented to another officer, "Now watch this guy. He's the best. Knows exactly how to inflict pain without losing the prisoner. Knows the psychology behind torture. Never seen anyone stand up to his work. Everyone always talks. And he has a sixth sense to determine if it's the truth."

Those skills resulted in promotion to sergeant by the end of the war in 1902. Toward the end of the war he came to the attention of a young intelligence officer named Captain Wickham. The brief association would later prove fortuitous for Doyle.

Returning to England, peacetime army life turned tedious. Barracks life with repetitious drilling and training recruits proved a jarring change from combat in South Africa. He couldn't see twenty more years of this to retire on a paltry pension as a senior sergeant. Resigning before his next reenlistment, he returned to Belfast. With his background the only civilian occupation where his skills might apply was policing.

Doyle and his small group of selected constables had been using rough tactics outside the law for some time. Wickham's new initiative was nothing more than officially intensifying the application of brutal methods. Terrorize the IRA support base.

The first task was to gather a select group of RIC officers from the intelligence division. Give them new marching orders. Unleash the dogs of war.

But something more was needed. While Wickham gave him full discretion, there were still fetters. Laws would be routinely violated. People murdered. Wickham made it clear that he didn't want to know details. Plausible deniability. But if the shit hit the fan it would be Doyle doing hard time in prison. If the British government found it politically expedient, he would be thrown to the wolves. He may have fought for King and country but he sure as hell didn't trust politicians.

The fix was to bind his unit together in a manner that would insulate against any outside threat. Loyalty first to the group on pain of death for betrayal. Doyle could invoke that kind of fear. Then give it a name to foster esprit de corps. A name when whispered that would invoke fear. All British regiments had a nickname. His old Norfolk Regiment was known as the *Holy Boys*. A dumbass nickname. After some thought he settled on the more threatening sounding *Boer Hunters*.

His staff of fifteen constables fell into distinct groupings. All were loyal to him as he had culled out those that did not embrace his style of policing over the years. All shared his anti-Catholicism. While many Catholics served in the RIC, none were part of Doyle's intelligence unit. Two were clever intelligence analysts that worked best from behind a desk. Next were the core ten street-smart clever men that knew how to extract information from sources. Hard men skilled in turning citizens into informers through threats and intimidation. The remaining three constables were muscle. These men gravitated to violence whether by gun or other means. Often working separately as a group, they served as Doyle's hit squad to conduct off-the-books murders. It was to this last group where Doyle sought to recruit additional members. Create a feared strike force to take the fight to the enemy.

The most immediate pool of candidates would come from the ranks of this new Special Constabulary. Coming largely from the Protestant paramilitary groups, Doyle knew he could find individuals already experienced in the skills he was seeking.

———

A tall man entered Inspector Doyle's office. Dressed in a cheap workingman's suit, he wore the armband of the newly created Ulster Special Constabulary. Uniforms had not yet become available. He was as tall as Doyle and obviously strong with a wiry stature contrasted to Doyle's muscular physique.

"Mr. Kendrick. Take a seat. I see you've already been issued a sidearm. Know how to use it?" Doyle said.

A heavy Webley revolver was holstered at the man's hip.

"Yes, Sir."

"Your superiors speak highly of your performance with the Volunteers. They say you don't shy from violent action. Even seek it out. What do you say to that?" Doyle said leaning back in his chair.

Kendrick wasn't sure how to respond.

"Do what needs doin', Sir. This is war. The IRA is killing unionists. Only way to fight them is be more violent. I'm all for killing the fucking bastards."

"You're a millwright at the shipyard?"

"Yes, Sir. A senior millwright."

"What exactly do you do?"

"I repair and install machinery. All sorts of machinery in the shipyard. I run a crew. I make sure my mates do their job."

It was just small talk. Doyle could care less what Kendrick did for a living.

"The Ulster Unionist Labour Association has a big following among the shipyard ranks. They have an unofficial special constabulary of their own yet you chose to join the Ulster Volunteers. Why's that?"

"Bunch of louts those Labour blokes. All pub-courage. Big talk when they're in their cups but useless as old ladies in a real fight. My UVF mates are the real thing."

Doyle smiled and nodded. "Apparently others think so too. Know why you're here, Kendrick?"

"No, Sir. Assume it's important though because your name's known about, Sir."

"In what way?"

Kendrick didn't know how far he should go. "Well, Sir, there's talk that your constables are a fearsome lot. Shadowy stuff. Feared by the IRA and Catholic sympathizers. Boar hunters they're called. Like you're after wild pigs. Mind you, Sir, I hope it's true what's rumored."

"And how do you feel about being a special constable? Just part time with no pay?"

"Glad to be part of the official police establishment. Didn't get paid with the UVF either. Got a job. Harland & Wolff will give us leave when we're called up for duty. Not sure I'd want to be a full-time peeler anyway. No offense meant, Sir. Just want to put down these Fenian bastards."

"I run the intelligence unit. Know what we do?"

"Well, gathering information I should think."

"I mean how we go about gathering that information? From people that don't want to give it up."

Kendrick didn't know how to answer.

Doyle answered his own question. "All sorts of methods must be employed. The objective is to create as many informers as possible. The most useful are among the Catholics. Since they're not willingly going to give the RIC information they must be forced. That is accomplished through fear. All sorts of ways to invoke fear. That's what my constables do best.

"But gathering intelligence is only part of our duties. In certain situations we are required to act on that information. Striking the IRA. Specifically going after their leadership. Cutting the many heads off the mythological hydra so to speak."

"Yes, Sir," Kendrick said. He had no idea what the fuck a hydra was but he understood Doyle's meaning.

"We've a small mobile strike force. Mind you we're not about arresting these vermin. We remove them. Do you understand my meaning, Kendrick?"

With Doyle's candor Kendrick knew why he was asked to come here. "Yes, Sir. Makes sense. Once you get a fix on these bastards you must move quickly. No time to go through a chain of command."

Doyle grinned, "Right you are. You've grasped the nub of the issue. Want to be part of that?"

Kendrick smiled broadly. "Certainly, Sir."

"Before you agree you must understand what you're getting into. This is a dirty war. IRA murderers melt into the population. We can't crush them by observing legal niceties. No one will ever give evidence against them. The government cannot tolerate that. But many in the government wouldn't agree with our methods. Those that do don't want to know any details. If anything embarrassing becomes public the politicians would look for a scapegoat.

"So we must protect ourselves from any repercussions. Are you willing to commit to the unit no matter what?"

Kendrick looked puzzled. "What exactly do you mean, Sir?"

"Once you're in, you must be absolutely loyal to the unit. Always obey my orders even if distasteful. And never give information that will harm any of us in the unit. Not to other police, not to a judge, not to your wife, not to anyone."

"Yes, Sir. I understand."

"Do you, Mr. Kendrick? So there's no misunderstanding, I'll put it in clear language. Once you become part of the unit the code of silence is absolute. Any breach of loyalty to your fellow officers will result in your immediate death. No escape possible. Remember, we are the police."

Kendrick was suitably stunned by Doyle's blunt pronouncement. Even if he declined Doyle's offer he might now be at risk after Doyle told him so much. But what the fuck? He'd killed before. Would never turn against his mates. He was meant for this rough business.

"Yes, Sir. That's very clear. I'm still your man."

CHAPTER 14

"Good morning, Sir," Sullivan's secretary said with her typical smile for the boss.

"Morning, Alison," he said.

"Tea is on your desk, Sir. Yesterday's maintenance reports too."

Alison Kendrick took an instant liking to her new boss. The handsome polite American was not only the talk of the office but a welcome change from his cantankerous older predecessor.

For Sullivan, he valued Kendrick's quiet efficiency. A pleasant if somewhat sad woman. This morning the vague appearance of a bruise on her upper cheek troubled him.

Being Monday, Kendrick asked, "Did you see your wife this weekend, Sir?"

"Yes I did, Alison. A pleasant time although always too short."

Kendrick shook her head and bit her lip. "So sad. Hope she can join you here in Belfast soon." Then realizing the implication of what she just said, "Oh lord, I didn't mean to wish anything should happen to her mother."

"Of course not, Alison. I know what you mean. I appreciate your kind thoughts."

This was his third trip back to Derry in his first weeks at Harland & Wolff. Everyone was most solicitous, including his boss

Malcom Llewellyn. Sullivan immersed himself into his new job to distract from his depressing thoughts. Though staying in Ireland was temporary, it could be months before the situation with his mother-in-law became clear. Then the uncertainty of what to do for her care.

After dealing with the morning's paperwork, Sullivan approached her desk. "I'll be in the shipyard the rest of the morning should anyone ask."

"Very good, Sir. Don't forget you're to lunch with Mr. Llewellyn at twelve-thirty."

Llewellyn had taken a particular liking to him. Talked of introducing him to his club. As soon as Maureen could join Sullivan in Belfast he was eager to introduce her to his daughter, Caroline.

Llewellyn remarked to Sullivan on his first day at the shipyard, "When your wife is able to come to Belfast please let me know. I'd like her to meet my daughter. Sounds as if they might have much in common. Caroline also speaks French. Fancies herself a writer. Your wife might prove a tempering influence to her rebellious inclinations.

"Caroline is an independent thinker. Advocates for women's rights. Enjoys provocative intellectual argument. Delights in contrarian views. Can't say she sides with Irish republicans but clearly Caroline's not a unionist. You can imagine the friction and awkward moments within our social circle."

The pronouncement secretly amused Sullivan with its irony. Another reminder that his tenure was only temporary as he settled into the job. Although not sharing Llewellyn's political views, the man seemed decent enough. Sullivan liked him. Disliked betraying his trust. But he needed to survive this ordeal arguing to himself it was only a business arrangement.

But just trying to get along overshadowed everything. The separation from Maureen created a constant ache. Knowing the emotional toll of daily caring for her mother while being alone in war-torn Derry added constant worry for her safety. The demands of any new job always stressful. And of course concealing his views in politically charged Belfast.

While his relationship with Malcom Llewellyn couldn't be better, contending with his boss' overt unionist politics presented a constant challenge. Llewellyn's liking of him made it all the more difficult to stake out a political middle ground. He wasn't about to feign agreement to the pro-union, anti-Catholic dogma prevailing among Belfast's ruling class. Too demanding to fake with conviction. He already set the groundwork but knew that pressure would mount. As part of the Harland & Wolff management team, he became part of the Belfast establishment. Llewellyn's acquaintances were all committed unionists.

Lunch with Llewellyn today would be his first real test. It was to be at Llewellyn's club with other powerful men. Men Llewellyn wanted him to meet.

———

Sullivan rode with Llewellyn in his chauffeur-driven car the short distance over the river to the Ulster Club on Victoria Street. They were lunching in a private dining room adjacent to the restaurant.

"Gentlemen. I'd like to introduce Mr. Trevor Sullivan," Llewellyn said entering the room. "As some of you know, he's recently joined my management team at Harland & Wolff. In charge of the shipyard facility. Good Irish stock. Father's from Belfast. Irish-American I should say to be precise. An engineer by profession.

"Graduate of the United States Military Academy. Served with distinction in the European War. Survived that famous unit the *Lost Battalion* that made all the newspapers near the end of the war. Rank of major."

Sullivan circled the table shaking hands with the four other men.

Phillip Atwood the textile magnate said, "Malcom speaks highly of you. Already making your mark I understand. He explained the difficult circumstances involving your wife."

"Thank you, Sir Phillip. Yes it is difficult. My wife's mother is still undergoing care in the hospital. Doctors say it might be some time before she can be released. Even then her condition is uncertain. I make the journey to Derry by train on weekends."

"Derry's a violent place. A hotbed of IRA activity," James Craig said. "Obviously you know that firsthand. My sympathies, Mr. Sullivan. Right choice to make your home in Belfast."

"Not sure what you mean, Sir James. Belfast has certainly had its share of violence," Sullivan said.

"True, but nowhere near the powder keg of Derry. Derry is the largest Catholic city in Ulster. More economically connected with County Donegal to the west rather than here in East Ulster. The IRA can retreat into rural areas. Catholics occupying what is known as the Bogside on the west side of the river in Derry provide shelter for the IRA. The RIC can't even police those neighborhoods for fear of being shot."

Sullivan said, "Well I haven't spent all that much time there. Stay mostly by my wife's side when I visit. She rooms at a boardinghouse close to the hospital"

"I've had many a conversation with Mr. Sullivan about his views on matters here in Ulster," Llewellyn said. "Enlightening to hear his opinions from a different perspective. Tell these gentlemen what you expressed to me just the other day when I pressed you on the matter of this war."

Sullivan had rehearsed his narrative. Put as much truth in as possible while declaring an acceptable position. Yet portray a view that did not pander to the combined extremes of Protestant racism and virulent unionism with Britain.

"Quite simple really. Bear in mind that I was born in America. Irish roots, Irish identity, but not emotionally invested as the Irish living in Ireland. I'm also not political. A soldier's training. From observation as an objective view, the sectarian violence in Ulster is counterproductive. Bad for business. Ulster needs to look to its economic future. Politics I believe follows economics. For that matter, wars are ultimately economic in cause."

Craig said, "But business is still thriving at both Harland & Wolff as well as Atwood Textiles. Besides, this insurrection has been thrust on us. By Catholic agitation, Catholic militancy. By Dublin provocateurs with this Sinn Féin political party backed by gunmen of the Irish Brotherhood.

"The Catholic South is largely uneducated, rural and backward. Peasants not capable of transitioning into the industrial age. Easily hijacked by political opportunists."

Sullivan responded, "And that could be framed as having an economic origin masked as nationalism. I submit, Sir that if this conflict continues in its present form, commerce will eventually suffer. The world is now economically international. Trade and investment are paramount to growth.

"This war is bad politically for Britain as well as Ulster's industrialized base. Especially in America. Millions of Irish now live in America. Most are Catholic. Stories of the suffering passed down by parents and grandparents blame Britain for much of the deprivations of the last century that caused the mass emigrations."

"Including your parents?" Atwood said.

"Not exactly. My father emigrated for two reasons. Simply more opportunities existed in American industry. But also for social reasons. He met a young woman. Since my mother came from a Catholic background, that would never work out in Belfast. In America that did not represent a social distinction. So you see I have a personal reason to look unfavorably toward the religious tone of this fight."

"Interesting. And how were you raised?" RIC Commissioner Charles Wickham said.

"You mean Catholic or Protestant? Neither. My parents were not religious. Not an issue in America. Proud to be Irish though. Irish politics was a constant household topic."

Brigadier General Kenneth Hopkins said, "And how was the Crown viewed by your family?"

Sullivan smiled to buffer the nature of his forthcoming blunt statement. "Heavy-handed, clumsy, arrogant, imperialistic.

Words to that effect. The executions after the 1916 Rising furthered those sentiments in America just as they did in Ireland."

Hopkins dropped his smile.

Sullivan continued, "You see from the Irish perspective it's more a matter of national identity. That and fair treatment. Irish-Americans have a keen interest in the affairs of the old country. Much of the funding for the IRA even comes from America I understand.

"Britain wants to rule Ireland whereas their real focus should be economic. Both British and Irish economic interests can be satisfied even with an independent Ireland, and certainly under home rule."

Words of near heresy to this group.

Atwood said, "A Dublin government led by revolutionaries will never allow economic life to continue as before in the north."

"But the fact remains that continued economic interaction with Britain will be essential to Ireland and will therefore ultimately dictate politics," Sullivan said. "Ireland needs Britain more than the reverse. Besides, with this new bill just passed by Parliament, partition will make the six counties of Northern Ireland independent of Dublin."

Craig said, "That overlooks the reality of such a small state as Northern Ireland competing independently. Far better had we remained a fully integral part of the United Kingdom."

Waiters poured glasses of wine to accompany the first course of soup.

"And from your outside perspective, Mr. Sullivan, how would you suggest we proceed against this insurrection?" Commissioner Wickham said with clearly a condescending tone.

"This armed rebellion must be put down of course," Sullivan answered. "Difficult I should imagine without making matters worse. Need to find conciliatory means to blunt popular support for these republican guerrillas. The present repressive measures directed toward the entire Catholic population only plays into the hands of the IRA."

Wickham said, "That presumes that only a small percentage of Catholics support the rebels. That simply is not the case. There is widespread tangible support. A criminal conspiracy involving thousands. If that wasn't the case, the IRA would collapse."

"Whether that is accurate or not the long-term ramifications remain the same," Sullivan said. "Ultimately you can't govern effectively with most of the population living under a police state where the rule of law is applied unevenly. Negroes in the United States live under such conditions. One day America will regret that legacy of discrimination.

"But to your question, Commissioner, I have no opinion as to how to strike such a delicate balance. I'm not a policeman. Difficult task, if not perhaps impossible. However, most working people everywhere are just trying to get by. They're mostly nonpolitical unless driven by some fundamental issue affecting them directly."

"As I see we're about to be served our first course, let's enjoy our lunch," Llewellyn said. "You can all see that Mr. Sullivan is most articulate on Irish matters. While I don't agree with all his positions, he makes thought provoking arguments. But of course he's first and foremost a business manager. I hired him for those talents not his political views."

After a second beef course followed by a custard dessert, Llewellyn, Atwood, Craig, and Sullivan adjourned to the upstairs lounge for brandies, coffee, and cigars. General Hopkins and Commissioner Wickham excused themselves claiming the need to return to their duties.

A cool goodbye and handshake to Sullivan by Hopkins. Probably still smarting from Sullivan's remarks about the British. Probably not wise but Sullivan couldn't resist the opportunity to express what he really felt.

Sullivan stuck with coffee, no liquor. He had matters to attend to after returning to the shipyard.

Craig said, "Not sure the General appreciated your comments about the British. He's not Irish of course. How do you feel personally about the British?"

"From a business perspective I agree with you, Sir James. Best if Ulster remained a part of the United Kingdom. However that ship sailed with partition and the declaration of a semi-autonomous Northern Ireland going into effect next year. Southern Ireland will never reconcile to that. But if managed right, Ulster's economic future need not change. Perhaps even finding new opportunities depending on what happens in Southern Ireland.

"The unknown will be the British government. They're a clumsy lot. Suffer from extreme hubris as they face loss of empire. Witnessed that first hand during the European war. An unimaginative general staff aggravated by inept political leaders. They believe they'll be successful in Ireland the same as in South Africa. Ireland is different but typically the British seize on past tactics even when the circumstances are different."

Craig chuckled. "Since I'm a member of parliament I share some of your opinions of the British political leadership. Perhaps just as well that you didn't pursue that earlier though. Commissioner Wickham is also a former British officer. Saw service in the Second Boer War. Like Hopkins, he's not Irish. Good man though."

Llewellyn said, "You can see why I'm glad to have found Mr. Sullivan. An engineer that thinks like a businessman."

"I concur, Malcom," Atwood said. "Mr. Sullivan is also American so perhaps less tainted by our historical baggage. In view of her personal tragedy, where does your wife stand with respect to what is going on?"

This is where it became dicey. Not as easy to cover Maureen's background if anyone dug more deeply. The key was to offer as little information as possible.

"She grew up in Derry. Found it too provincial, too conservative. She gravitated to the arts so she ventured understandably to Paris to attend university. A degree in art history. An accomplished painter in her own right."

"Mr. Sullivan's wife apparently has many similar inclinations as my Caroline," Llewellyn said.

"Hopefully not your daughter's political views, Malcom," Atwood said jokingly.

Sullivan avoided the political question. "But at heart Maureen is Irish. We planned on making our home here in Belfast even before what happened with her parents. Derry was never a consideration. To pursue a career in the arts in Ireland meant only Dublin or Belfast. She knew Belfast which also placed her closer to family in Derry.

"But of course I've not answered the fundamental question of her religious background. She like me is not religious. Perhaps that is owing to a family background similar to mine. You see she too is from mixed religious parents. Father Protestant, mother Catholic. Neither pressed their children toward either faith. Carefully avoided politics.

"However, the long-standing sectarian antagonisms of Derry proved another compelling reason for her to leave Derry. Being neutral on the question allowed her to view the damage inflicted on the entire community. A bleak future for a young woman with ambitions in the arts.

"Now this. As I explained to Mr. Llewellyn, the origin of the fire that killed her father and badly injured her mother is not clear. It occurred during a night of rioting. May have been the work of either the IRA or the UVF. Or simply just mob violence. What is certain it was the product of a civil war based on a social divide that uses religion as an excuse."

Sullivan thought he struck the right tone. The lie about Maureen's parents only reinforced what he had already alluded to about his own background. Wouldn't stand up if someone looked deeper into her family background. But no reason anyone should. If they did, so what?

On their ride back to the office Llewellyn said, "I must say you acquitted yourself remarkably well today. I do believe both Craig and Atwood were impressed."

"Not sure I made any friends with the General and Commissioner Wickham. Should have been less openly critical of the British."

"Say no more about it. All of us have at times found ourselves with differences over London's policies. The one point of agreement is this creation of an Ulster Special Constabulary."

Sullivan did not know what Llewellyn was referring to.

"And what might that be, Sir?"

"An immediate expansion of the Constabulary. Great numbers of reserve officers. Most will act as part-time police. Available as required. These IRA outlaws are a police problem. Better the RIC deals with them than relying on the army. The British Army is better suited to conventional war not confronting IRA guerrilla tactics."

"And where will all these new police come from?"

"Mostly the Ulster Volunteers. Already trained. Already engaged. Already armed. Now they'll be newly equipped. A force exclusively to maintain order here in Ulster."

Sullivan suppressed his reaction. The UVF officially sanctioned as police? London was clearly taking sides in the sectarian violence in the north. Unconscionable to vest murderers like Fergus Croft with policing authority.

CHAPTER 15

It was midmorning on a Saturday. Two weeks since Sullivan had seen Maureen. Although a chilly overcast day, anticipation buoyed his spirits. Arriving in Derry he took a bus from the train station to Saint Patrick Hospital in the Bogside.

He knew the way to Mary O'Farrell's room. She occupied the rare single-patient room on the upper floor. Because of her condition, staff determined the sight of her disfiguring injuries too disturbing for other patients in adjoining beds.

A wise consideration Sullivan agreed. Each time he saw his mother-in-law required an effort not to recoil having seen what the bandages concealed. Although still loosely bandaged, her exposed features outside the dressings suggested the terrible disfigurement underneath. The damage to the left side of her face then down to the neck muscles and tendons had already started to distort the undamaged areas. Tasked with periodically changing the dressings, Maureen had managed to subdue the natural instinct of revulsion.

Maureen was reading to her mother when Sullivan appeared in the doorway. She rushed to kiss him.

"Trevor's here, Mother. She's doing so much better since the last time you saw her, Trevor."

Trevor put on a smile and lightly patted Mary's right arm above the bandage still covering her wrist and hand.

"The danger of infection has passed. Now just a matter of time to heal."

Sullivan suspected Maureen said that for her mother's sake. As if her injuries could ever fully heal. Once the burns had scarred over the poor woman would face a difficult life. Unimaginably difficult for whatever remained of her days. Candidly the doctor said she may never fully walk again. Her left arm and hand were totally destroyed. The right hand would eventually gain limited use after several operations. But her face. Nothing could be done for the emotion distress caused by such gross disfigurement.

The routine when Sullivan returned to Derry was for Terrance O'Farrell and his wife Nora to relieve Maureen at Mary's bedside as much as possible. The respite from days in the hospital room was critical for Maureen's well-being.

He could see the deepening effects on his wife. Her face seemed drawn. Dark circles around her eyes. Looked as if she had lost weight. At a pub Sullivan forced her to eat some stew.

Their usual routine during his visits was to enjoy a light lunch at a particular pub on Saturday. An afternoon of lovemaking followed in the evening with drinks and a late dinner. However, Sullivan doubted Maureen was in the mood for making love this afternoon.

"How's the job coming along?"

"Fine. A good job. Llewellyn's a good man to work for. You should see the shipyard, Maureen. Covers a vast area. I get around in a motor car. It's quite the sight. A real challenge. Too bad though."

"What do ya mean?'

"Because it's only temporary. You don't think for a minute I'd want to live in Belfast do you?"

She looked at him with sadness in her eyes. "No. Of course not. It's just ..."

Her thought trailed off to silence.

146

Sullivan needed to bolster her spirits. "Listen, Maureen. We're returning to Paris. That's a given isn't it? Once your mother's condition is stabilized."

"Stabilized? Trevor, she'll be a cripple. Horribly disfigured. Where will she go?"

"Terrance and Nora will take her in. They've said so. We'll arrange for a nurse to see to her special needs. Bathing, that sort of thing. Every day if necessary. We'll cover the expense."

"Not sure I'll be able to leave her, Trevor. I'd feel like I would be abandoning her."

Sullivan too was under more stress than he perhaps realized. His response came out stronger than intended edged with a tone of frustration.

"Listen, Maureen, you can't devote your life to the care of your mother. She'll need professional care. We have a life too. You left Derry to pursue your kind of life. Derry's so much worse now. First the riots now the war. Your father and brothers made their own choice to take up arms."

"Mother didn't."

Whether Mary O'Farrell embraced the cause for independence or just felt compelled to stand by her husband made no difference. She remained a casualty of her convictions.

"Of course. I didn't mean for that to come out so harshly. Your mother's a good woman. She'd always stick by your father. Just like I'll always be at your side."

He placed his hand over hers on the table.

Smiling weakly, she said, "I'm so sorry, Trevor. Our future seemed so bright just a short time ago. Now everything is changed."

"Stay strong, my love. These circumstances are not forever."

"It's been two months since the fire, Trevor. How much longer do you think?"

"Maybe a couple of more months. By then we'll know what sort of arrangements must be made for your mother's care. Think you can manage a while longer?"

She touched his face. "If you can. This must be just as diffi-cult for you. How is Belfast?"

"Belfast's no better than Derry. But apart from being separat-ed from you, the most difficult thing is every minute living a lie."

"You mean about what really happened with the fire?"

"No, I've covered that pretty well with an alternative expla-nation. No the real difficulty is being among these unionists. Not just unionists but the powerful men behind that side of this struggle in Ulster. Worse yet, as a senior manager at Harland & Wolff, I've been accepted into their circle. I've told you how Llewellyn has taken a particular liking to me. Now he's intro-ducing me to his cronies."

"Well at least it's not a hostile environment. How do you ex-plain your political views?"

"That's where things become difficult. Must always be on my guard. Got grilled pretty good a week ago just after I saw you last. Lunch at the Ulster Club. Where the rich and powerful do business.

"Claimed to be non-political. From mixed backgrounds of Catholic and Protestant parents. Same for you. Invented the cir-cumstances of the fire. Blamed it on the earlier riots. Mother burned while trying to save your father. Not certain which side's fault. Just mob violence.

"Since I'm American, I'm not as emotionally invested. Told them the war was bad for business. That struck a chord especial-ly with Llewellyn and another business leader. Also pandered to them by saying Ulster was better-off staying firmly attached to the United Kingdom.

"I feel like I'm leading a double life. Which I am I guess. Glad it's probably for only a few months. My very fiber stands against these racist bastards. I hope the Irish achieve their inde-pendence from Britain. But that's never going to happen in Ul-ster. No matter what happens in the south, Ulster will never know peace."

"Terrance and Nora keep trying to get me to stay with them. I must be so lonely. Says it's an unnecessary expense to stay at the boardinghouse."

"Absolutely not, Maureen. Promise me that. Far too dangerous. Terrance is sure to be as active as ever in IRA activities. He must be a target of the UVF."

"I won't. Already told Terrance your fears. He didn't take it very well."

Terrance and Nora were at the hospital when Sullivan and Maureen returned early that evening to check on Mary.

Nora brought up the subject of Maureen staying with them to Sullivan.

"I understand, Nora, but I won't have Maureen in danger while I'm away in Belfast."

"Danger?" Terrance said. There had been a growing tension between the two during Sullivan's last visits. Sullivan didn't understand why. Did Terrance blame him for not saving his parents, especially his mother? He chose to ignore it not wishing to aggravate an already tense situation.

"Okay for my wife to be in danger but not my sister?"

Sullivan's eyes flashed. He wanted to lash back with *'you ungrateful sonofabitch'* but said, "Not here, Terry. Let's go out in the hallway."

Both men stepped out followed by Maureen and Nora both with concerned expressions.

Once out of earshot of Mary O'Farrell, Sullivan turned on Terrance pushing him against the wall with a hand on his chest. He could smell alcohol on Terrance's breath.

"Listen well, Terry. Don't ever pull that shit again."

Terry was taller and heavier than Sullivan but something intuitively cowed him by Sullivan's aggressive response.

"You and your dumb fuck IRA pals are responsible for this. A stupid raid to avenge your brother. Foolish enough for Dillon to put himself obviously in harm's way. Not that he deserved an end like that."

"Dillon gave his life for the cause."

"No he didn't. He foolishly threw it away. Then you and your father with your stupid commander O'Donnell got shot to pieces. Making matters worse you return home bringing all this down on your poor mother."

Terrance O'Farrell brought his right arm up launching a punch directed at Sullivan's jaw.

Sullivan ducked the blow then grabbed O'Farrell's arm twisting it behind his back. Bringing it up sharply, O'Farrell yelled out in pain and dropped to his knees. Sullivan pushed further forcing O'Farrell's forehead to touch the floor as he groaned from the pain in his shoulder.

"Do that again, Terry and I'll break your fuckin' arm. You can't fight a war by doing stupid emotional things. Get a grip. I'm not the enemy."

The following day, Nora showed up at the hospital after mass to relieve Maureen. She apologized for her husband's behavior yesterday. The poor woman was undergoing her own ordeal. Maureen had confided to him that Nora was in constant fear for Terry's life. Didn't know of his affiliation with the IRA before they married. After Dillon and her father-in-law died at the hands of the UVF, that fear became all consuming. Married only one year, the hopes for raising a family only added to her anxiety.

Sullivan had a few more hours before taking the 3:30 train back to Belfast. The day was cold with a brisk wind blowing out of the north. It only added to the subdued gloom of his impending departure.

Over tea at the boardinghouse, Sullivan said to Maureen, "After yesterday the thought of having your mother convalescing at Terry's and Nora's seems a bad idea. This war will only get worse. No telling what might happen to Terry."

"What's the alternative?"

"Not sure. Must be someplace for people to receive long-term nursing care?"

"A convalescent home? I can't do that, Trevor. That would surely kill her."

Sullivan pursed his lips. "What choice do we have?"

"What about if mother returned to Paris with us?"

Sullivan winced at the thought. Caring for a disabled person? A twinge of guilt brought him up short. Would he not do the same for his mother?

"I don't know. Maybe. Tell you what. Why not start working on all the possibilities? Talk with the doctor. What will her condition be when she's released? When might that be? She won't be able to navigate stairs. What level of care will be needed?"

"Okay. It'll be good to occupy myself with a task."

"Maureen, if we were to take your mother to Paris, would that be good for her? I mean a foreign country? She doesn't speak French. Won't know anyone."

Tears started to flow down Maureen's cheeks. "I fear she'll be just as isolated here in Derry. Even with the bandages, visitors struggle to look at her. Fewer visitors as the weeks pass. Image the full sight of her disfigurement. You've heard what the doctors have forewarned to expect."

Sullivan had no words of comfort. Time to leave. As usual, he took the bus to the train station across the river. Hostile neighborhood for Catholics. Bad enough Maureen had to stay in the Bogside but at least she was among her own.

A difficult parting. More emotional than the last time. Neither of them could continue this indefinitely.

—

Depressed as usual after returning to Belfast, the Monday morning boring routine of reviewing last week's maintenance reports offered little diversion. Things however changed midmorning. While inspecting work being done to repair the hoist gearing on one of the large cranes, he witnessed what appeared to be a fight.

Sullivan rushed to the scene on the run. One of his foremen was trying with little success to separate two pairs of men grappling and throwing wild punches. But just beyond, a ring of men ignored this scuffle. Their shouts suggested yet another fight.

Sullivan shoved one battling pair knocking them both down with a well-placed foot tripping them up. Heads turned. Recognizing the boss, the other pair broke off their confrontation.

Sullivan then elbowed through the encircling ring of men watching two other combatants. Unlike the other brawlers these two circled each other squared off in a boxing stance. One man was a head taller and heavier in build than the other man. The shorter man was also much older.

While the ring of men quieted after seeing Sullivan, the two fighters made no move to disengage. Before Sullivan could step in, the larger man took a wild swing at his opponent. The older man deftly ducked the blow while delivering one of his own into his attacker's midsection. This was followed by a succession of rapid jabs to the bigger man's face.

Like the others, Sullivan stood captivated by the exchange. It wasn't an equal fight. The older guy clearly was besting his younger, bigger opponent.

The foreman came up next to Sullivan. "What's going on Mr. Bishop?"

"It's Kendrick again. Picked on the wrong guy this time."

"Kendrick you say? He's the big guy? Any relation to my secretary?"

"Yes, Sir. Her husband. A troublemaker. Hates Catholics. Taunts them. Not sure what provoked this but Kendrick should have known better."

"How's that?"

"Duncan Gallagher's an ex-boxer. Lots of years ago. But looks like he still knows what's what in a fight."

Sullivan let the fight continue long enough for Kendrick to get a thorough thrashing before stepping in to break it up.

"Mr. Bishop, get everyone back to work. Except for Kendrick and Gallagher."

The crowd of men moved off returning to work. Kendrick remained dazed sitting on his butt. Blood dripped from his nose onto his shirt. One eye was closing. A badly split lip. He was slowly catching his breath.

Duncan Gallagher stood off at a distance. Although he too was breathing heavily, he suffered no obvious damage.

Sullivan looked down at Kendrick. "What started this?"

Kendrick looked up recognizing the new boss.

"Somebody in Gallagher's crew dropped a hammer from above. Nearly hit one of my lads. Stupid *Taig*."

"So how'd the fight start?"

Kendrick glared at Sullivan. An asshole in a suit. A fucking foreigner. Wife says he's a wonderful boss. Stupid bitch.

"You know, heated words. One thing led to another."

"Figured you could kick the shit out of an old guy? Guessed wrong it appears. Clock out and get your ass home. But I'll expect you back on the job tomorrow morning."

Kendrick made no response.

Sullivan approached Gallagher. Up close he looked even older. Weathered face with lots of lines. Nose slightly out of line. Grey showing in his hair. Wiry strong though as evidenced by his well-developed sinewy arms and large hands. No apparent damage other than scrapped knuckles.

"Kendrick said this started over a near accident. That right?"

"Yes, Sir. One of my men dropped a hammer. Careless. Gave the bloke hell. Tried to tell Kendrick I was sorry once I got down from the crane. Wasn't good enough. Wanted the guy who dropped the hammer to come down and face him."

"And?"

"Couldn't have that now could I, Sir? My guy's a little fella. No match for someone as big as Kendrick. Knew he'd hurt my lad. Kendrick's got a real mean streak."

"So you took him on instead?"

"Tried to calm Kendrick down but he wasn't having any of it. Started in on me. Pushing me about. You can ask the other men. Well I knew he wasn't about to give up. Gave me no choice."

Sullivan smiled. "Yes I watched the last of it. You're not so big yourself but Kendrick didn't have much of chance did he? Haven't lost your touch it would seem."

153

Gallagher looked at Sullivan not sure how the new boss knew of his pugilistic background. Or why he seemed to be taking this so well.

"You're Catholic, is that right?" Sullivan said. "Your crew too?"

"Yes, Sir. Mr. Bishop's tries to keep the Catholics separate from the Prods."

"One's religion is none of my affair. Makes no difference. When it interferes with the work then it becomes my affair. Let the word get around, Duncan."

"Yes, Sir." *Duncan*? The new boss knew his first name?

"Better get your crew back to work. Tell 'em I expect no accidents. I'll go hard on any carelessness."

CHAPTER 16

R esentment toward British rule had a markedly different tone in Ulster than the rest of Ireland. The Anglo colonization in the southern counties over the preceding several hundreds of years created class distinctions to be sure. Yet those invaders of the English plantation structure eventually became Anglo-Irish, although the landowning gentry class. To a large extent they saw themselves as Irish. Many of the earlier rebellions of the 19th century were even led by Anglo-Irish. In the South it was an issue of Irish nationalism.

Ulster had a different experience. Here the colonization was predominately by Scots. From the earliest times, these new Presbyterian-Scots were intent on replacing the indigenous Gaelic Catholic population of Ulster. While the native Catholics were never entirely replaced, they became a minority in six of the counties. Ruled by the Protestant usurpers, there was never an assimilation of these separate cultures as in the south. Racism lay at the heart of Ulster agitation.

While the six northeastern counties of Ulster were Protestant, and therefore firmly unionist, the city of Derry held a Catholic majority. With this newly created partition of Ireland to take effect in 1921, Derry would become a border city. Just to the west was County Donegal, heavily Catholic and soon to become part of Southern Ireland.

Well into the second year of the rebellion, the Anglo-Irish War was going badly for the British. The infusion of the Black & Tans and the Auxiliaries did not tip the balance in their favor. This rebellion, firmly supported by a majority of the Irish in the southern counties, meant a protracted conflict. A conflict too unpopular, too costly to politically sustain support within the British Parliament. Prime Minister Lloyd George understood this. Ever the pragmatist, he therefore maneuvered to retain British hegemony in Northern Ireland. With a majority unionist population, partition would allow for a continued hold on Ireland's industrial base. His scheme was to enable Ulster to absorb the brunt of responsibility and cost to defend against this nationalist insurgency.

If that meant turning Northern Ireland into a police state to keep it within the United Kingdom, so be it. In this, the Ulster Irish power brokers were in total agreement.

The creation of the Ulster Special Constabulary would provide the means for unionist forces to defend RIC barracks in the Catholic rural areas. For urban Derry and Belfast it provided well-armed resources to pursue offensive operations in the hostile Catholic districts. The newly organized Special Constabulary leadership was largely comprised of former British Army officers but the ranks were exclusively Irish Protestant-unionist volunteers.

The full-time 'A' Specials swelled the regular RIC ranks bolstering manpower for patrol and barracks security. The larger number of 'B' Specials were part-time officers serving one day a week or as required for emergencies.

Since the Special Constabulary was created overnight by legitimizing the vigilante Ulster Volunteer Force, there was no real vetting. UVF command structure essentially remained intact.

Fergus Croft therefore took command as head constable for a platoon of special constables in Derry City. His unit consisted of four sergeants and sixty constables. No uniforms yet available, just insignia armbands. When going on duty they would requisition weapons from an armory. A full array of newly supplied military revolvers and rifles. The weapons to be returned to the armory after going off duty. Croft's former UVF however had their own weapons. Nothing changed other than they now acted under the cover of police authority.

In the west of Ulster the district commander responsible for the counties of Derry, Tyrone, and Fermanagh was Lt. Colonel George Irvine, a former British officer having served with the new head of the Special Constabulary Wilfred Spender. Irvine was a fervent unionist. Motivated to crush the rebellion, he saw his force as a means of denying the IRA sanctuary and support.

Colonel Irvine addressed Croft and his sergeants in the mess of the Derry's RIC barracks on the Protestant controlled Waterside. With him was the RIC district inspector for Derry.

"Your group has a fearsome reputation I'm told, Mr. Croft. I expect your activities will now fall in line with the law," Irvine said.

The RIC District Inspector Regan Lynch had briefed Irvine. Lynch detested Fergus Croft as a common criminal. A natural leader but a nasty piece of work. Far more than just a troublemaker, he relished violence. An instigator of the riots of May and June directed against Catholics. Personally suspected of murder. No evidence of course for Lynch to act on.

"When on duty, Mr. Croft, your special constables will support Inspector Lynch's regular RIC."

"We're to follow Inspector Lynch's orders then?"

"That's correct, Mr. Croft," Lynch answered.

"Then you'll be in command personally when we do this supporting, Inspector?" Croft said sarcastically with a smirk.

"Listen, Croft. When your people are on duty you'll follow orders from whoever of my constables is in charge of that particular operation. You're acting as police no longer as vigilantes," Lynch said.

Irvine hadn't realized the extent of bad blood between Lynch and Croft. He said, "Mr. Croft. We all share the same common goal. Defeat this rebellion. Eliminate the IRA threat in Ulster. We are not at war with the Catholic citizenry."

"Begging your pardon, Sir, but it's that Catholic citizenry that lies at the heart of the problem. Every one of them supports the IRA. Terror must be inflicted on the whole lot of these papists. Fear is the only remedy. Remove their base of support, you defeat the IRA."

Irvine generally agreed with that approach. That's why he took on this job. The Ulster Volunteers were neither soldiers nor police but they were already in place. Already in the fight. If Northern Ireland was to remain firmly within the United Kingdom, it needed these fighters.

Inspector Lynch saw things more broadly. He had no wish to see his isolated rural RIC barracks come under IRA attack as in the southern counties. Constables ostracized from Catholic communities, virtual prisoners confined to their barracks.

Overall, Catholics represented less than half the population. They did not represent a sector requiring subjugation. They were already subjugated into a peasant class through centuries of discrimination. Unfortunate perhaps but not to be changed by this war of independence. A more practical rather than ideological matter for Ulster. Here the conflict was civil war. The IRA was only part of the problem. In the end, Ulster's Catholics would be part of this new Northern Ireland. Some means of governance and fair policing needed to be achieved. If not, Ulster would forever suffer sectarian violence.

Lynch said, "Now that you're acting as police I expect that when not on duty you shall also observe restraint. Not resort to your old ways, Mr. Croft. Do you understand?"

Croft barely held his anger. "I'll take my orders from Colonel Irvine, Inspector."

"Listen here, Croft ..." Lynch began to respond but was cut off by Irvine, "Mr. Croft. When on duty you're tasked with following RIC orders. As to your off-duty conduct I expect you to also view your actions in the larger context. By that I mean you're not to act independently. If you have actionable intelligence then your constables can be called to duty to act on that information."

Croft gave only a nonchalant nod and shrug of the shoulders.

Retiring to a warehouse that acted as their armory under their UVF days, Croft held forth. The other four men were not only his sergeant-constables, but his most trusted associates for the last couple of years. Tough violent men. A bottle of whiskey passed between them.

"Listen up, lads. Forget all that bullshit you just heard. Irvine is just some fuckin' British officer that doesn't know what's what. Likes to run things like he's still in the army. Maybe born Irish but he still thinks his shit don't stink.

"As for Lynch, he's a Catholic-lovin' pussy. Doesn't know shit either. Thinks he can *police* the Bogside. Best thing is for the Bogside to be burned to the ground. Remove that pesthole and all its vermin. That's what I think those smart-ass bastards in Belfast intended by making us constables. Make what we do sound legal. Imagine, boys, we're now fucking peelers."

Everyone laughed.

"Nothing changes. We still go about our affairs as we see it. When we go on duty we'll act the part. Maybe even get a chance to shoot some *Taigs* all legal like."

"You're sayin' we're still going after IRA on our own?" the big guy named Rooney said.

"Of course. Nothin' changed about that. But now we do it as part of our official duties. Those dumb fucks in Belfast think we'll just back up the RIC when needed. We're independent as far as I see it. Better we're not issued uniforms. Go about as normal like undercover coppers. Things are about to get more interesting, lads."

———

Maureen hadn't seen her brother or sister-in-law since the incident on Sunday. Nora then stopped by the hospital midweek after work. Appearing still upset over her husband's behavior the prior Sunday with Trevor, Maureen sought to downplay the incident.

"Nora, put it behind you. Trevor's mature enough to under-stand Terry just lost control. Both of you are under awful stress with all that's happened. I'm sure Terry regrets his actions."

"Oh my, he does, Maureen. I lit into him somethin' fierce when we left the hospital last Sunday. He took it without mak-ing excuses. You're right about the stress. But it's more than mother, father, and Dillon. Terry would never admit it but I think he's afraid. Always lookin' over his shoulder when we're about. Drinking more."

Nora then began weeping as if something broke inside her. They were sitting alone in a small lounge area at the hospital.

After Nora recovered her composure, Maureen stood up and said, "Left me see if I can find us a spot of tea."

"There's something I need to discuss first, Maureen. Need your advice. I'm at my end. This is all too much."

Maureen sat back down and held Nora's hand. What new ca-tastrophe?

"I'm going to have a baby."

Gripping Nora's hand tighter, "Oh my, that's wonderful!"

"Is it? What if something happens to Terry?"

Maureen had no good answer to that. With the rest of the O'Farrell family destroyed, Nora would have to fall back on her own family if something happen to Terry. Maureen also knew that represented no comfort. She came from a dirt-poor sheep farming family in County Donegal. The youngest of six children. A widowed mother. Scattered relations in the hardscrabble west of Ireland, all desperately poor.

"Does Terry still ... not sure how to ask it. Is he gone at times going about IRA business?"

Nora nodded yes. "He's out many a night. Weekends some-times. Never says what. I don't ask anymore because it starts a row. But it's IRA business for sure. He never comes back smell-ing of drink."

"Does he know you're pregnant, Nora?"

Nora shook her head no. "Just found out a couple of weeks ago. Been afraid to tell him. Been wanting a child since we married. Now all this. He talks about getting revenge on Croft. Then he talks of taking your mother in when she's released from the hospital. How do we manage that with a baby?"

Maureen closed her eyes. Another depressing Irish story of a young woman trapped by circumstances. What counsel could she possibly give?

"Maybe the baby's the answer. Terry must be made to realize that he can no longer fight with the IRA. Not with all that's happened. He must understand that his first responsibility is to you and the child.

"Let's do this. Tell Terry I want to see him. Want him to understand there're no bad feelings about last week. Tell him I need his company. He's all that remains of my family. This coming Sunday afternoon. Trevor can't come this weekend so it'll just be us. Terry's favorite pub. That place on Strand Road. The place with that big giant of a guy tending bar."

"Clancy's?" Nora said.

"Yes. Terry took me there before I left for Paris years ago. My treat. After mass."

"And I'll tell him about the baby?"

"Yes. We'll make it a celebration of the grand news. Then I'll try to convince him that he must no longer risk his life. It's his family he must be looking after. That fanatic Peadar O'Donnell and Terry's mates can't deny the O'Farrells haven't made enough sacrifice."

The prospect of a new beginning raised Nora O'Farrell's spirits. She hugged Maureen. "Thank you. You're like my own sister. I love you, Maureen."

———

Maureen waited outside the Long Tower Church prior to the eleven o'clock mass. An odd feeling of nostalgia for her youth tinged with less benign feelings. She resented the Church. Not for any personal incident but rather the institutionalized relegation of women to second class status. The Roman Catholic Church did not condone any form of birth control, preferring instead to promote unrestricted births to bolster the population devoted to the faith. All in the face of crushing poverty through-out Ireland. The Church not only didn't align itself with the women's rights movement but denigrated it almost as heretical. Husbands, fathers, and priests stood at the top of a male hierar-chy dominating all things economic and spiritual.

Although not keen to attend mass, she was here for her brother and Nora. A place of faith might maneuver Terry into a more pliable mood. Terry was not overtly religious but like many Catholic Irish, the Church remained a symbolic refuge of identity.

Seeing Maureen, Terrance immediately embraced her. He was about to say something when Maureen placed two fingers gently to his lips.

"No need to say anything, Terry. Let's go inside. Been awhile since I've been to mass. This'll be a good start to a wonderful day together."

Terrance O'Farrell nodded as he escorted his wife and sister each on an arm into the church.

That good beginning remained evident after the service as Terry smiled while chatting with Father Sheenan outside the church.

Like all Irish pubs, Clancy's was a place for social gathering for both men and women. Often the favored place for taking a meal. Simple menus with generous servings. The Sunday mid-day clientele included many couples. The special outing for the week. For most, Sunday was usually the only day off from jobs whether that was factory, farm, or household.

Today, Clancy's was already filing up. Even with everything pressing in Maureen felt her mood slightly brightened. Although cold, an unusually sunny December day so close to Christmas put everyone in a festive mood.

The ambience inside was well-worn dark wood from the ta-bles and booths to the bar. At night it would have shadows giv-ing it an intimate atmosphere. Even the midday sunlight now streaming through the windows seemed absorbed, muting the place in a soft natural illumination.

Behind the bar was the extraordinary large man Maureen remembered. Terry told Maureen that Clancy, the son of the original Clancy, went something over twenty-one stone. Arms larger than her thighs. Bald shaved head. What could have been a frightening countenance instead turned engaging with his smile and infectious laugh. Clancy was the attraction. For the family crowd, his presence insured a safe place, free of anybody ever getting out of hand by starting a ruckus.

Terry found a vacant table and seated Maureen and Nora. It was his watering hole so he made his way to shake hands with Clancy and other regulars he knew. Stopping before a young man seated at the bar he said, "Kevin McNeal? Is that you?"

"Well I'll be. Terry O'Farrell. Fancy seeing you," the man said turning to shake hands.

"It's been years, Kevin. Heard you went off to the war in Europe. Never knew what happened to you. What brings you back to Derry?"

———

O'Farrell and McNeal had played on the same Gaelic football team. McNeal left Derry abruptly in 1915 after the death of his sister. Never even said good-bye to O'Farrell. Orphaned at a young age, she had been his only family. McNeal once told O'Farrell they were from a rural village in County Tyrone. Sent to a Catholic orphanage in Derry with the passing of both parents in an unusual typhoid fever outbreak.

Terrance O'Farrell knew all too well of the sister's suicide. Knew the cause. Another teammate and his best friend Grady frequently made lewd remarks about pretty Caitlin McNeal. At times the remarks turned nasty. At issue was her seeing another footballer. A Waterside Protestant from a rival team.

One night Caitlin McNeal was found naked in a park. Her hair crudely shaved off. Heavy crankcase oil poured over her. Grady boasted to O'Farrell that he and two others had taught the whore a lesson about sleeping with a Prod. "Definitely a fine piece of ass. Showed her a real good time before we cut her hair off. Not so pretty now."

163

"You stupid sod. You raped McNeal's sister?" O'Farrell said. He wanted to kick the shit out of his friend. "The coppers will be down on you for that."

Grady shook his head. "She can't identify us. We wore masks. Unless she can describe my big cock." He smiled sarcastically.

Caitlin McNeal killed herself the next day. Slit both wrists and bled to death in the bathtub according to the newspaper. Terrance O'Farrell quit the team and told Grady he never wanted to see his ugly face again.

The incident would haunt him for not doing something. Grady joined the British Army the following year. Rumor had it he died at the Somme. O'Farrell buried the troubling memory.

O'Farrell never again saw Kevin McNeal until today.

—

McNeal said, "Just visiting for the day. First time back in years. Been working in Belfast since mustering out in '18. Got a job with the Constabulary. I'm a copper now. Been transferred to a barracks in Donegal. Thought it about time I paid my respects at my sister's grave. Remember Caitlin don't you, Terry?"

"Yes of course. A terrible tragedy all those years ago." The memory sent a shudder through O'Farrell. Now his old acquaintance was an RIC constable? Even as a Catholic that made him an enemy of the IRA.

"Heard about your own misfortune, Terry. Your da, your brother, and your poor mother. Also heard you're whole family took up with the IRA, Terry. Bad business this revolution. Dangerous to be on the wrong side of the law."

"Tough job being a peeler I should imagine," O'Farrell said with an edge to his voice. "Even Catholic RIC constables aren't welcome in the Bogside, Kevin."

"That's what I've been told. So I didn't wear my uniform. I'll just be finishing my pint then make my way to the cemetery. Be gone from Derry before I rile anybody. Been a long time. Good seeing you, Terry."

As McNeal's made to leave, O'Farrell shook his hand again then said, "Take care, Kevin."

McNeal said nothing as he starred into O'Farrell's eyes before leaving the pub.

Seeing Kevin McNeal was unsettling. O'Farrell's good mood vanished. He returned to Nora and Maureen. While he'd been making the rounds greeting people he knew, the two women preoccupied in their own conversation did not notice his conversation with McNeal. Since they didn't ask about the guy at the bar he avoided any mention of McNeal. Now his former teammate was a constable? Even knew he was IRA. Good that McNeal was not staying on in Derry.

———

Across the River Foyle, Fergus Croft was also enjoying a pint of Guinness at his favorite pub. His four newly appointed sergeants of the Special Constabulary were there as well. They'd been there long enough to be into their third pints.

The barkeep called over to Croft's table. "Telephone call for you, Fergus."

The barman placed the black candlestick pedestal telephone on the bar.

The call was brief. Returning to the table, Croft said, "You blokes sober enough to go on an outing?"

"Where too, Fergus? A Sunday social?" Rooney Moffett said laughing.

"Nothing so boring. Some old unfinished business across the river needs attention."

With the new excuse of being Special Constables, the men always carried their Webley revolvers.

———

Terrance O'Farrell beamed when his wife told him about the baby. A source of concern since they'd been trying for some time.

"That calls for a real drink. Maureen?"

"Sure," Maureen said.

He laid his hand over his wife's. "And for the new mother?"

"Just some tea, Terry. Read somewhere that expectant mothers shouldn't drink alcohol."

Terry went to the bar. "Clancy, I'll be havin' two whiskeys, your finest. And a cup of tea. Celebrating today. Goin' to be a father."

Clancy and two men at the bar congratulated him. Clancy said, "Drinks are on me, Terry."

Returning to the table with the drinks, Maureen launched into her planned speech.

"I'm so happy for both of you. After all that's happened, it gives hope for your future." Then in a whisper, "But you realize you must end your IRA activities."

Terry set down his drink. "I can't do that. After what happened to Da and Dillon?"

"They died for the cause, Terry. You will too if you keep at this. Support the IRA but no longer do whatever it is you do that could get you killed. Put down the gun, Terry."

Terry shook his head no with his lips pursed.

Nora reached out and touched his hand. "I'm begging you, Terry. For me and the little one. I can't be worrying every time you go out. We've no one if we lost you."

"Nora's right, Terry. Must be others that can't be active in the fight because of higher obligation. The O'Farrells have done more than their share for this cause."

The argument ebbed and flowed until Maureen said, "Nora broke down when she told me she was going to have a baby. The happiest of times yet it was fear that overrode all else. I'm your sister so I can say this to you. Do what's right for your family, Terry."

Terry started to respond but Nora said, "No more arguing right now. I'm hungry and I want to enjoy the rest of this day."

The joyous mood however spoiled. Nothing resolved. Eating something at least postponed continuing the argument. Maureen fumed silently at her brother's devotion to this war of independence above all else. She'd like to strangle that fanatic Peadar

O'Donnell. If Terry continued to follow him she might lose her entire family.

———

It was mid-afternoon when they left Clancy's. It remained sunny so they decided to walk back to Terry and Nora's house. Maureen had every intention of pressing her brother further. But she needed to find additional leverage. If the welfare of his wife and unborn child were not enough, what else might persuade him?

Across from Clancy's a parked delivery lorry had its bonnet raised. A man was looking at the engine fixing some problem. When the O'Farrells exited Clancy's the man closed the bonnet then got behind the wheel.

"O'Farrell is coming out of the pub. Two women with him," the lorry driver said turning his head into the rear of the darkened lorry.

Fergus Croft said, "All right lads. We finish off the last of the O'Farrells. Send a message to that IRA prick O'Donnell. None of his IRA mugs are safe even in the Bogside."

The guy named Rooney and another man knelt on the lorry floor poised to open the rear doors when it stopped.

"Goin' to snatch him like we did his little brother, Fergus?" Rooney asked. This was the same lorry used the night they murdered Dillon O'Farrell.

"Fuck no. We're just goin' to shoot the bastard. Make it quick then be gone before anyone knows what happened. Now put your masks on."

The men pulled up bandanas to hide the lower half of their faces.

"What about the women?" Rooney said.

"Try not to hit 'em you stupid shite," Croft said.

Two blocks from Clancy's the lorry pulled to the curb behind the O'Farrells walking on the sidewalk. Croft, Rooney, and a third man exited the rear. Terry O'Farrell turned. Instantly he knew what was happening. After pushing both women away he pulled back his jacket reaching for his own revolver secured at the back of his waist. It took too much time.

Several shots rang out. Two bullets caught him in the chest dropping him to his knees. His revolver fell from his hand without getting off a shot. The three assailants approached to finish him.

Maureen instinctively reached down for Terry's gun at her feet. A fatal misjudgment.

She raised the weapon pointing it at the closest man and squeezed the trigger. The pull pressure jerked the aim off target. But the shot was enough to prompt Fergus Croft to react by shooting her twice.

As another assailant pointed his weapon to shoot Terry in the head, Nora threw herself over her husband causing the round to instead hit her in the head.

"Shit!" Croft said looking at the two women.

But even though this had gone badly, Croft was calm enough to finish the assassination. Pulling Nora's limp body away from Terry, he put a round in Terry's forehead at point blank range.

The entire attack spanned no more than fifteen seconds.

Back inside the lorry the driver gnashed the gears, accelerating rapidly.

Croft barked, "Take it slowly you stupid bastard. Get us across the river without drawing attention." Under his breath, "Sonofabitch."

CHAPTER 17

Trevor Sullivan did not hear of his wife's murder until Monday afternoon. The police traced Maureen to the hospital caring for her mother. That led to her boardinghouse where a search of her personal effects revealed a husband employed at Harland & Wolff, Belfast. RIC headquarters in Belfast dispatched a constable sergeant to deliver the news to Sullivan.

Alison Kendrick opened Sullivan's office door without knocking. "Mr. Sullivan. There's a constable here to see you."

"A constable? Show him in."

The constable entered then closed the door not allowing Sullivan's secretary to enter. The officer removed his cap and put it under his arm.

"Mr. Trevor Sullivan?"

"Yes."

"Constable Sergeant Norcross, Sir. You've a wife residing in Derry? A Maureen Sullivan?"

Sullivan turned pale. "Yes. What's happened?"

"Very sorry, Sir. I have the regrettable duty to inform you that your wife has been killed."

Sullivan's placed his hands on his desk for support. Finding it hard to breathe he gasped, "Killed? How?"

"Yes, Sir. Shot I'm afraid." The constable pulled a notebook from his pocket. "On the street leaving a public house yesterday

169

by unknown assailants. Her brother Terrance O'Farrell and his wife Nora were also murdered in the same attack."

Sullivan eased himself back down into his chair behind his desk.

"Did you know the O'Farrells?"

Sullivan nodded. "Only briefly. My wife and I have been married only a short time. Living in Paris. She was in Derry to help with her injured mother. Burned in a fire not long ago."

"Yes, Sir. A Mr. Eoin O'Farrell also died in that fire," the constable said referring to his notes. "My colleagues in Derry also said that another of your wife's brothers was recently murdered. Know anything about that, Mr. Sullivan."

"No. All those things happened before we came to Ireland. Never met the O'Farrells before that."

"Rumor has it that Terrance O'Farrell was IRA. Perhaps your wife talked about him. Would you be knowin' if that was true, Sir?"

"No. She never mentioned that. They weren't close. She'd been gone from Derry for years. Communicated mostly by letters to her mother."

"Who did this, Sergeant?"

The constable shook his head. "Don't know, Sir. No witnesses have come forward. Hard to say with all the troubles in Derry. Catholics and Protestants been at each other's throats somethin' fierce. Then again, if O'Farrell was IRA then it could be unionists. Or maybe even the IRA."

"Why would the IRA kill a Catholic?"

"Well, Sir with this war for independence raging all over Ireland people are forced to choose sides. Maybe O'Farrell did something that went against the IRA. They've been known to shoot Catholics accused of being informers."

After the constable left, his secretary came in. "Is everything alright, Mr. Sullivan?"

Sitting behind his desk he looked up at her and shook his head. Tears followed down his cheeks.

His extreme distress caused her to gasp putting her hand to her mouth.

"It's my wife, Alison. She's dead."

———

Sullivan left the office immediately. Leaving his weeping secretary, he instructed her to tell Mr. Llewellyn he'd be in touch as soon as he could. With only a brief stop at his boardinghouse Sullivan told his landlady he'd be away at least a week. Gathering some clothing he caught the last train to Derry.

Once into the journey the anguish of realizing Maureen was gone settled deeper. Life itself seemed extinguished. Even during those desperate nights in the Argonne Forest a spark of hope remained. He invested everything in Maureen.

The human mind has all manner of contending with grief. As the train neared Derry in the early evening Sullivan struggled to confront his profound pain. Only a black rage with thoughts of revenge provided an emotional handhold. No different from Eoin O'Farrell after the murder of his youngest son.

Maureen died of no illness or accident. She was murdered. Didn't matter whether a causality of this Anglo-Irish War or ethnic hatred. No matter the reason, no matter which side, the murderers must be brought to justice. Unlikely that would happen given the circumstances. Therefore he must be the instrument of justice. If he didn't make the attempt how could he live with himself?

The first practical thoughts for seeking revenge pushed grief into the background as he disembarked at the Derry rail station.

Overcome by the trauma, he had given little thought of what to do next. Where was Maureen's body? Who to see about burial arrangements? No relatives he knew of in Derry to take charge. Had Maureen's hospitalized mother been told? Her entire family now gone. Was there extended family?

Arriving at eight o'clock at night there was little to be done until the following day. Best to find a hotel. Take up the task in the morning with a clearer perspective.

The night proved an ordeal. Sleep never came. Rage consumed all thoughts. His mind began plotting how to identify the murderers. Somehow he would devise a way to kill them. At the cost of his life if necessary.

While those emotions dominated, he found the will to address the practical details requiring his attention. Christian funereal rituals. Always saw them as another torment to those grieving. Seemed more to satisfy some societal need than to provide any comfort to the family.

He would do the minimum necessary to endure this added ordeal. No personal solace existed for him in these ceremonies. Maureen was simply gone. Everything ended there.

With the discipline of his military training he forced himself to eat breakfast before the hard day ahead. The next stop was the pastor of the Long Tower Church. Father Sheenan would now say requiem mass for three more O'Farrells. What words of faith could possibly provide comfort to the mourners?

Sheenan proved to be not only a spiritual leader, but a worldly shepherd for his congregation during these terrible times. He recognized that priestly ministrations would be misplaced with this Irish-American. Immediately he sensed Sullivan's stoic demeanor held more than grief.

To Sullivan's pragmatic questions, Sheenan dispensed with his usual efforts to comfort the grieving. The bodies of his wife, brother-in-law, and his wife were at a mortuary. The parish had taken the initiative uncertain when Sullivan might arrive. A terrible burden to suffer without support. But Sullivan looked as if he neither needed nor wanted spiritual advice.

"We have scheduled mass for Thursday. Assuming of course that is your wish. Interment will be in the family plot next to Eoin and Dillon O'Farrell."

"Fine."

"Are there other relatives that might be arriving, Mr. Sullivan?"

"None that I know of. Know nothing of Nora's family. Don't know of any of Maureen's relatives. Certainly none of mine."

Sheenan nodded. "Is there anything else that I can do to help?"

"Yes, Father. Does Mary O'Farrell know?"

"I believe not. After hearing the news I sought out her doctor. He thought it best not to tell her yet. Said it might complicate her recovery. He'd like some time to plan how to best manage her reaction."

"Thank you. There of course is no one that can now attend to her long-term care needs. Is there a ..." his words trailed off searching for the correct term.

"A care institution you mean? I've already found a couple of suitable alternatives. I will gladly offer my services to help you with making arrangements."

"Most kind of you, Father. Now to the most difficult of tasks. I'd like to see my wife. Can you direct me to this mortuary?"

"Certainly. In fact I'll drive you there myself. Least I can do since you've been set adrift alone in a foreign place, my son."

Seeing Maureen lying on a gurney at the mortuary numbed his capacity to function for several minutes. His trance broken only by the sensation of his farewell kiss to her cold lips. The shock sent a visible shudder through him.

Father Sheenan was waiting to drive him wherever he needed to go. Outside the mortuary he asked, "Where can I take you, Mr. Sullivan?"

"The police barracks. Need to see what the RIC have to say. The officer that broke the news to me in Belfast was vague. Made it sound like it might be anybody that did this. Means they don't know or don't care to probe deeper."

"So I'll ask you, Father. Who did this? I'm aware the O'Farrells were IRA. Was this the local UVF?"

Sheenan said, "Of course it was the UVF. Both sides in this war are committing the same sins. Goes back and forth. This is murder not warfare. Meant to terrorize. I damn such atrocities whether by the IRA or UVF."

"And which war might that be, Father? Seems the Catholics and Protestants been at each other in Ulster long before this rebellion."

"That is true. But it doesn't matter. God doesn't recognize justice by acts of murder. No matter the cause. Even though Terrance O'Farrell was IRA, his wife and your wife were innocent casualties. But I fear the situation will only get worse for Catholics."

"How's that?"

"The British and the unionist Protestant Ulster leadership in Belfast mean to crush Catholic resistance. A pogrom I fear just like perpetrated on the Jews in Eastern Europe. They've made these Ulster Volunteer thugs into special police."

"And what do you think will happen, Father?"

"The IRA will now step up the violence. No longer even the illusion of a protective police force. Now the RIC is clearly just an instrument of British oppression. Catholics must fight to survive."

No more than Sullivan expected, the RIC offered nothing in the way of encouragement in solving the murder of Maureen.

"Sorry for your loss, Mr. Sullivan. However we have no information on the perpetrators," a constable sergeant said. "No witnesses have come forward."

"Clearly it was the UVF," Sullivan said. "Terrance O'Farrell was IRA." He expected little from the RIC but if he was to be brushed off then why not provoke? "Therefore he was murdered probably under orders from the local UVF commander Fergus Croft. Or is Croft now one of you? One of your special constables?"

"For an American you seem to know a lot about Derry politics."

"Don't have to be here long before you realize that the Derry Constabulary couldn't find a pile of dog shit if they stepped in it. But of course it was just some Catholics gunned down on a Sunday afternoon. So what the fuck?"

174

At the insult the sergeant bolted out of his chair from behind the desk.

Sullivan stepped in close fixing his stare into the officer's eyes with his anger suggesting the real threat of physical assault.

The maneuver caused the officer to fumble while attempting to unfasten the flap to his revolver holster.

"You going to arrest me or shoot me, Sergeant? That how you police in Derry?"

The officer's face went red. Never had anyone dared confront him like this. Yet he hesitated to escalate the confrontation further. This was an American. A war hero he was told. The man had just lost his wife. The crazed foreigner seemed upset enough to do something stupid meaning all sorts of trouble from his district inspector.

"The unfortunate death of your wife is under investigation." The officer paused then added a bureaucratic caveat that summed up the RIC perspective. "However I will tell you that we currently have no leads. No suspects. These are difficult times with countless acts of violence. You'll certainly hear from us should the investigation uncover more promising information, Mr. Sullivan."

For Sullivan, the venture was merely an exercise to confirm what he already suspected. He could expect nothing from the RIC. Even before absorbing the UVF as Special Constables, the RIC was not neutral. In Derry the regular Constabulary was overwhelmingly Protestant. It proved incapable of quelling the sectarian riots earlier in the year.

In Derry legal protection was stacked against Catholics. For Sullivan, justice would take a much narrower path. He was not part of this war. He was not part of the Irish struggle whether independence from Britain or civil rights for Ulster Catholics. He simply intended to identify then kill the murderers of Maureen.

———

On the day of the funeral, two days before Christmas, Sullivan waited outside before the start of the requiem mass for all three of the O'Farrells. It was overcast and cold. Although uncomfortable it provided him the means to avoid the mourners. The endless expressions of condolences grated. His grief a personal matter. He was not one of them, not of this place.

As he entered the church walking down the side of the aisles to take his place in the front pew, he stopped in surprise. Seated there was his Aunt Kathleen.

He bent down and embraced her.

As he did he noticed Peadar O'Donnell seated two pews back. Several young men flanked him. Undoubtedly armed IRA.

"I'm so sorry, Trevor. Does your mother know?"

"Not yet. Haven't had the opportunity. A difficult letter to write."

"Of course. Perhaps I should do that for you?"

"Yes, please. I need some time before I can write her. Don't even know what to say other than Maureen's dead."

"I understand, dear."

"How did you hear?"

"Peadar O'Donnell contacted Michael Collins."

———

Following the funeral, Sullivan sat with Aunt Kathleen in someone's parlor. Her brief stay in Derry accommodated under the protection of Peadar O'Donnell.

"Last I heard you were working in Belfast while Maureen saw to her mother," Kathleen Clarke said. "So what now, Trevor?"

"Not sure Aunt Kathleen. Probably return to Paris. Need to see if Maureen's murderers can be identified. Not hopeful but ... can't just leave."

She touched his arm. "This is war, Trevor. You know who did this. They were after your brother-in-law. O'Donnell told me the whole history. Does it matter who precisely?"

Sullivan reacted by saying, "To me it does. This is not war as I know it, Aunt Kathleen. These are not soldiers. Kill two innocent women to assassinate an enemy? I want to know the names of those that pulled the triggers. The person that ordered the killing."

"And if you were to discover their names then what, Trevor?"

"Hard to say. Depends on circumstances. Would at least need to see if I could … resolve the issue."

"Resolve the issue? You can't take on the UVF. You're just one man. You don't even know Derry. Don't be silly, Trevor. That's just anger looking for release."

"Not sure what I mean, Aunt Katherine. Certainly don't intend going about trying to shoot down these murderers in some American old west gunfight. Just need to do something. Maureen's murder will never be *solved* by the police."

But to himself, why not take matters into his own hands? Shot a lot of Germans all by himself. Already killed two UFV in Derry that firebombed the O'Farrell house. Deadly with a gun.

Kathleen paused for a moment before saying, "Perhaps if you want to avenge Maureen you might do so by helping the cause. Remember your conversation with Mick Collins?"

"Helping the cause won't appease my sense of revenge. I mean to see the particular bastards who did this at the end of a rope. Or with a bullet to the head."

"You're a smart man, Trevor. You know Maureen's murder is part of things much larger. All this stems from the Irish bearing the heel of oppression from Britain for hundreds of years. I know the pain of your loss. After my Tom and my brother were executed, I chose to fight all of Britain rather than go after the one bastard responsible, General Maxwell."

"Tell you what, Aunt Kathleen. Get a message to Peadar O'Donnell. Tell him I want the names of those that took part in these murders. Already fairly sure it was ordered by some guy named Croft. Names and addresses. If O'Donnell's any good he can do that. In exchange I might be able to provide useful information for the IRA from my position in Belfast. I've a job there rubbing shoulders with Ulster unionists."

"I know O'Donnell only through Mick Collins. Not sure I have any pull with him."

"He knows I'm connected to Collins through you, Aunt Kathleen. What's O'Donnell got to lose? Should impress Michael Collins at headquarters if he can infiltrate a spy into the enemy camp in Belfast."

———

Following the graveside interment, Father Sheenan pulled Sullivan aside.

"Peadar O'Donnell asked me to give you this, Mr. Sullivan."

The priest handed Sullivan an envelope.

"A word of caution, my son. Peadar O'Donnell is a fanatic. Perhaps not in the same mold as that barbarian Fergus Croft but still blind to anything but his war. I fear this note is not a letter of condolence. O'Donnell's a crafty devil. I suspect he'll be wantin' to exploit your grief in some way. A siren song. Do not listen.

"I know you're not religious, Mr. Sullivan. When I say that only God can deliver vengeance it perhaps rings hollow. You've lost much. However the memory of your wife will not be served by your own senseless death."

"Thank you, Father. I appreciate your concerns. Be reassured that I used to be a professional soldier. Not inclined to impulsive action. I've seen death and learned to live with it."

Once Sheenan left, Sullivan opened the note. *The promenade on the top of the wall surrounding the historic center. East side facing the river, 3:00pm.*

Sullivan saw O'Donnell standing alone on the wall. Few people about on this damp cold day. Sullivan passed two young men that eyed him as he walked toward O'Donnell. Two more stood just beyond O'Donnell. Obviously IRA.

"So I give you the names of those that killed your wife. What can you possible do with that information?"

Ignoring O'Donnell's question, "Do you have those names?"

"Yes."

"How? Guesses or real intelligence?"

O'Donnell thought for a moment before answering.

"Very well. But only because the Big Fellow asked that I assist you. It was Fergus Croft's UVF bunch. No surprise there. But a reliable source says that Croft himself fired the shots. Bragged about it apparently. As to the others we can't be sure. Probably his key men. Guys made sergeants as special constabulary under his command. Big bugger named Rooney is the worst of the bunch."

"Care to say how you came by this information?"

"A source inside the local RIC. Some informer called the RIC. Told a certain constable that Terrance O'Farrell just showed up at Clancy's Pub. Terry was the last of the O'Farrells. Croft had a particular grudge against the O'Farrells. This RIC constable was then overheard placing a telephone call to Croft."

"How do you know Croft himself did the shooting?"

"Same constable that fed Croft the information about O'Farrell being at Clancy's talks a lot. He's also UVF. Brags about being tight with Croft."

"You'd like to kill Croft just as much me, right? Tried before. Mucked that up. Started all this with the O'Farrells." Sullivan harbored resentment against O'Donnell's complicity in the ill-conceived attempt on Croft.

O'Donnell clenched his jaw. Fuckin' arrogant foreigner criticizing him? Having lost his wife, O'Donnell let it pass.

"Couldn't refuse Eoin. Bound to try something foolish on his own if I didn't help. After all they tortured his youngest before killing him."

"Look, I'm offering you another chance, O'Donnell. What've you got to lose? I kill Croft you get the credit. If I fail, Croft is forever looking over his shoulder."

"One man? A foreigner? That's ridiculous. You'll never get close to Croft."

"Well that'll be the trick won't it?"

O'Donnell remained silent thinking through the ramifications. He knew Sullivan was consumed with getting revenge yet there was something about him. A confidence. A clear resolve. An ex-soldier. Rumored to be some sort of marksman. Stood his ground in a tight spot to shoot down two of Crofts' men that attacked the O'Farrell house. And like Sullivan said, what did he have to lose?

"So you know it was Croft. What else is it you want?" O'Donnell said.

"Intelligence of course. Croft's habits, movements, places he's known to frequent. How does he get about? Wife, girlfriend? His key guys? Who was with him when he did this? Their addresses. Places of employment. Can that be done?"

With no downside O'Donnell decided to help. Sullivan would probably try without his support. Michael Collins wouldn't take kindly if O'Donnell abandoned him? So an easy choice. And even with Sullivan's likely failure it would give Croft something to worry about. And Sullivan was expendable.

"Perhaps. Take a few weeks."

"You have sources that well placed?"

O'Donnell did not. The only informer of value was the one RIC constable. A few other casual sources in the Protestant neighborhoods. Getting this information would be a challenge. But he wasn't about to admit that to Sullivan.

"I'll get you the information, Mr. Sullivan. How do I communicate with you?"

Sullivan came prepared. He handed O'Donnell a business card. "Call my office. Say you're Father Sheenan. As for the information I need, send it by post to my residence. I wrote the address on the back. Show the sender as the priest."

"Sarcastically, O'Donnell said, "Anything else, Mr. Sullivan?"

"Yes. Only you're to know my connection with this. No one else. None of your people. If I'm successful, you take the credit as the mastermind. Somebody up from Dublin did the deed. I never existed."

CHAPTER 18

Sullivan's first day back at Harland & Wolff proved another trying experience. Staff stood and shook his hand as he made his way to his office. Several voiced the normal phrases of sympathy. Uncomfortable, most said nothing.

Arriving at his secretary's desk, Alison Kendrick again broke down with flowing tears. However with staff looking on she did not embrace her boss, holding his hand instead in both of hers for several moments.

"Mr. Llewellyn requested I take you to his office the minute you arrived, Sir."

Ushered into Llewellyn's large office by a visibly shaken Alfred Pimm, Llewellyn jumped to his feet circling the desk to grasp Sullivan's hand, placing his other hand on Sullivan's shoulder. Pimm quietly closed the door.

Once seated, the two men quickly dispensed with the awkward discussion of the circumstances of Maureen's death.

Eventually Llewellyn said, "I certainly admire your composure. Indicative of strong character. I must tell you, Mr. Sullivan, that I'm delighted having you at Harland & Wolff. Even with all you've been through you've already managed to make your mark. But I must ask, now with your wife ... well gone, what are your plans?"

Sullivan had rehearsed the expected question from his superior.

"Maureen and I gave much thought before deciding to come to Belfast. I enjoyed Paris but it didn't feel like home. Perhaps more my wish than my wife's to settle in Ireland. For me it was a new horizon. A chance to experience what it meant to be Irish.

"Derry never felt right. Even setting aside the terrible accident that took her father and injured her mother. She left Derry years before, seeking a different environment. I could sense the provincial culture of the place that she wanted to escape. Being from New York there was never any thought to settle in Derry for either of us.

"Dublin seemed a city poised to be the center of rebellion. Belfast seemed a vibrant big industrial city. In many ways like my native New York. My father came from Belfast. Maureen knew Belfast. At heart I'm an urban creature. Never enjoyed the obscure remote postings when I was in the military. So Belfast became the logical choice.

"And now with ... with all that's happened ... well I plan to make this my home. I feel I've found a professional home here at Harland & Wolff. I value the opportunity and confidence you've placed in me, Sir."

"Say no more. It's your skills that speak for themselves. And I shall do everything possible to help you feel comfortable in your adopted city. Of course you can never forget the dreadful events that have happened. But you can begin rebuilding for the rest of your life."

Just a few weeks ago Sullivan felt guilty over deceiving Llewellyn given the man's genuine affection for him. All such charitable emotion died with Maureen. Llewellyn was part of something larger that Sullivan now intended to throw himself against. Llewellyn now just represented an opportunity to be exploited. All of Sullivan's family-indoctrinated hatred for British oppression of Ireland surged to the forefront.

Of more immediate purpose was the need to solidify his circumstances for the singular purpose of killing Fergus Croft.

Amazing how effortlessly the lies flowed. As he spoke he also realized that his fictional construct made for a coherent narrative. The right balance to enable him to hide in plain sight. His Irish-born wife's family misfortune in this war. His Protestant Belfast roots on his father's side. Irish yet an outsider born in America. A practical stance on separate home rule for the North while supporting a continued bond with Britain. No declared sympathies for the independence movement led by Dublin revolutionaries. Personal ambitions governed by a business perspective. His politics therefore pragmatic.

———

Ten days later he received a telephone call at his office from O'Donnell.

"This is Father Sheenan. How are you, my son?"

"Thank you, Father. As well as can be expected under the circumstances."

"Glad to hear that. The reason for my call is a personal item of your wife's was overlooked. Her landlady brought it around to the rectory. A journal it seems. I'll be sending it by post to the address you provided."

"That is very kind, Father. A journal you say?"

"More a diary. I took the liberty of giving it a cursory examination. Hope you don't mind. Details of daily activities, times and places. Information of personal interest you might find comforting."

"Thank you, Father. I appreciate your kindness."

"Good luck, Mr. Sullivan. I hope things go as planned for you."

Three days later an envelope arrived at his boardinghouse. Return address marked as the Long Tower Church, Derry, Father Thomas Sheenan, Pastor.

Sullivan poured a large whiskey and opened the product of O'Donnell's intelligence gathering. Impressed after just skimming through the material. Surprisingly more information than he expected. Names, addresses, a good accounting of Croft's habits. A ledger with times, names, places. Obviously acquired from surveillance. Detailed maps with annotations. Official photographs of Croft and others from police archives as members of the Special Constabulary.

Even with O'Donnell's limited resources his constable source proved most resourceful. The policeman hated Croft. In his view, worse than a common criminal. A murderer. The constable took his role as protector of the public seriously. The IRA rebellion was a political problem not an excuse to turn the police against Catholics. Although a Protestant, he found it profoundly disturbing that the government so decidedly took sides in the long-standing sectarian conflict in Ulster. He had a brother and nephew that shared his views.

The combined efforts of all three produced a first-rate intelligence product that astounded even O'Donnell. If Sullivan was not successful then O'Donnell would use the intelligence to mount his own operation to make another try to kill Croft.

Two hours and a lot of whiskey later, Sullivan was even more impressed. The intelligence enough for him to begin forming possible ideas. Too bad O'Donnell hadn't been able to get Croft with his IRA brigade. Even discounting the hasty raid that led to Eoin O'Farrell's death, it was a question of methods. O'Donnell would think in terms of mounting an attack in strength. Sullivan would be acting alone. While a severe limitation, it also offered certain tactical advantages.

Whether a squad of IRA gunmen or a lone man, both faced the same fundamental challenges. How to infiltrate into hostile territory getting close enough to the target then successfully escaping?

He had all the intelligence necessary but a plan remained unclear. Perhaps he'd find it impossible. Or suicidal. But every problem had a solution.

Always a problem solver, he understood how to break down a problem. Determine the hierarchy of issues and how each was interdependent. What was the critical path? What stood as the foremost obstacle?

The landlady knocked on his door. "Will you being taking dinner with us, Mr. Sullivan?"

Deciding he needed to eat as well as establish some normality, he said, "I believe so, Mrs. Williams. I'll be right down." Needed a break to clear his thoughts before again attacking the problem.

By the afternoon of the following day, the basis of a plan formed. The solution to the infiltration obstacle came to him while taking the tram to work. The British Army was everywhere. He was an ex-soldier. Easy enough to impersonate an officer. Not of the local Dorset Regiment stationed in Derry, but a different regiment. An inspection assignment from brigade headquarters in Belfast? He'd impersonate a real officer. Someone on Brigadier General Hopkins' headquarter staff probably. Midlevel rank.

Find a name by scouring recent back-issues of the newspaper at the library. The uniform? Find a tailor specializing in servicing army officers.

His cover? Just another British Army officer arrived from Belfast. If he ran into any local Dorset Regiment officers, he's from headquarters, wearing a different regimental insignia. Better though to stay clear of the army. Might lead to awkward questions.

Weapons? Although not regular British issue, his Browning .45 could be concealed within the regulation British officer's holster with its covering flap. Spare magazines in his briefcase. Also a smaller caliber weapon, a Belgian .25 Fabrique Nationale semi-automatic pistol. In slang terms, a *whore's* gun. At just over four inches long and less than a pound, small enough to fit into a pocket. Bought it for Maureen in Paris as personal protection.

The final piece of the plan, where and when? Since he'd be alone he must prepare for alternatives. No matter how events developed, unforeseen circumstances would require adapting tactics once underway with the mission.

The July 22nd issue of the *Belfast Telegram* newspaper covered details of the Belfast riots that broke out at the Harland &

Wolff shipyard. British troops eventually quelled the violence. A battalion adjutant by the name of Major Albert Winslet was quoted with an account of the engagement. Irish Guards Regiment by the insignia on his cap. How convenient. Immediately the rest of the plan came into focus. It explained a lone British Army officer moving about the Protestant area of Derry.

From a tailor specializing in uniforms he ordered two. *'Present for my brother's promotion. He's been looking a little shabby I should say. Difficult to dress properly on an officer's pay. He's exactly my size. Anything not quite right I'll send him by for a slight alteration. I trust you can affix the proper rank and insignia markings? A major's pips? Irish Guards Regiment. Next Thursday you say?'*

———

In the week it took for the uniforms he needed to develop the operational details of the plan. Especially obvious contingencies. Each evening was devoted to the project. During the day, the shipyard consumed all his attention. After the brief flurry of sympathies and deference for his loss, the regular demands of his work quickly returned.

One day his secretary said, "Do you have a minute, Sir?"

"Certainly, Alison. Come in."

She entered his office closing the door behind her.

"I wanted to say something but with all that's happened … well I didn't want to intrude. I must say, Sir, you're awfully strong."

"Thank you, Alison. Please sit down. Now what is it you wanted to tell me?"

"Well, Sir, you remember that incident in the shipyard just before hearing that your wife … I mean the fight?"

"Of course."

"I'm sure you know that one of those men was my husband, Edgar Kendrick?"

Sullivan nodded. "Yes."

"Well what I wanted to say, Sir, thank you for not sacking him."

"There were two doing the fighting. Wasn't about to get into why or how it started. Firing them seemed a little severe."

"Thank you anyway, Sir. My Edgar's got a right nasty temper. I'm sure it was him that started the fight. He was in a mighty foul mood when I got home. Told me a cock-and-bull story 'bout what happen."

"From the looks of him, he got the worst of it."

Sullivan paused before saying what was on his mind since that incident.

"I must ask you something, Alison. Don't mean to intrude into your private life but I'm concerned for you. Those bruises I see on you from time to time? Your husband's doing?"

She dropped her head looking down. "It's the whiskey. When he drinks he gets real mean. Lots of things upset Edgar. Takes it out on me. All because I'm not able to give him children."

She raised her head to look at Sullivan. "I'm sorry, Sir. Didn't mean to spill my own woes with all you've suffered."

"No need to feel badly, Alison. I brought it up."

He wanted to say something more comforting, but what? A working class woman trapped in an abusive relationship from which there was no easy escape.

To change the subject she said, "When you first arrived here you told me a little about your wife. Said she left Ireland to study art. But you also made a comment that she strongly supported better rights for women. Said she was a very independent thinker."

Sullivan smiled. "More than just independent. Had her own ideas how she wanted to live. Didn't care what others thought. I'll tell you a secret, Alison. Neither of us wanted to have children."

Visibly surprised, she said, "My word. And why not?"

"Both of us had different ideas what we wanted to accomplish in life. What we wanted to experience. Nothing wrong with raising a family but it means a different sort of life. The weight of responsibility for children would likely overshadow all else.

"The point I'm making, Alison, is there's more to life than children. Whether by choice or in your case circumstances, it isn't everything."

"Not for my husband. "An edge of anger in her voice.

Sullivan wanted to get out of this conversation. There was no advice he could give her. She couldn't go off to Paris as Maureen had done. The people that could help her won't. Her pastor would counsel with platitudes based on narrow church doctrine. Organized religion was male dominated. In conservative Irish society, any women friends were unlikely to provide anything useful other than sympathy. Maureen made him conscious of women throughout the world suffering second class status.

"Felt it was just the natural way of things. A woman married then had children. That was her lot in life. Always fretted something must be wrong with me. But lately I've had my eyes opened to other things.

"Would you be surprised, Mr. Sullivan, if I told you I was secretly active in a women's organization? A women's suffrage organization."

"Of course not, Alison. Why shouldn't you? You've every right. My feelings are in total sympathy with women on the subject. Like most men I never thought much about it until I met Maureen. But if your husband found out, I'd guess there might be unpleasant consequences."

"I wish he'd go to …" She held her anger. "But yes, there would be. Worse if he also found out some of my best friends are Catholic. I just don't see what the issue is. But Edgar hates Catholics as if they're less than human. He's even active in the Ulster Volunteers. Real troublemakers."

"Lot of anti-Catholic feelings here in the North of Ireland. Always has been."

She abruptly ended her cathartic outpouring. Looking intently into Sullivan's eyes she said, "You're not only a wonderful boss but a fine man, Mr. Sullivan. A most unusual man. If there's anything I can be doing for you, especially with your life turned upside down, you only need ask."

She abruptly stood up looking uncomfortable. "I've taken too much of your time, Sir. Thank for your kindness and hearing my troubles."

Sullivan rose from behind his desk. Thank god this ordeal was over. As he came around close to his secretary, she suddenly took his hand in both of hers. Raising it to her face she kissed the back of his fingers.

Embarrassed, she turned without a word and left the office.

———

The plan was the best Sullivan could put together without seeing the geography firsthand. By necessity it dealt only with the broad elements of reconnaissance, time, and place to execute the mission then successfully escape. Details must remain flexible in order to adapt to circumstances on the ground. If reconnaissance proved the plan unsound, or Croft wasn't where expected, or not suitably vulnerable, it might require a second trip to complete the mission.

Assuming the identity of this Major Winslet also provided the plausible cover to account for a single British officer walking about Derry. *I'm an expert on riot control come to Derry to lend my expertise. Conducting a survey to develop tactical plans in the event there's a repeat of the riots of May and June. Did the same work after the July disturbances at the shipyard in Belfast. Brigadier Hopkins wants the entire brigade better prepared.* He'd cultivate typical British military arrogance.

Since receiving O'Donnell's intelligence, he knew where this must take place. The only location reliably to expect to find Croft was at his job on Derry's docks of Lough Foyle. Croft was operations manager for the harbor facilities. Not unlike Sullivan's larger scale job at the Harland & Wolff shipyard.

Croft's residence was out of the question. Undoubtedly well protected. Deep within a Protestant neighborhood. No reason for the presence of a lone British Army officer. The possibility of innocent casualties like Maureen and Nora. Other than the names of Croft's accomplices, most of O'Donnell's surveillance intelligence therefore proved unnecessary. O'Donnell was looking at it from a tactical military perspective, not a lone infiltrator.

The docks provided the perfect place to do this given Sullivan's subterfuge.

At the harbor Sullivan would pretend to share with Croft his experiences of the disturbances at Harland & Wolff having learned of those events in detail by conversations with Duncan Gallagher. The perfect ruse to get up close to Croft. Perhaps even to get him alone.

As for the others, if any were with Croft they'd be targets of opportunity. Thanks to O'Donnell's RIC photographs, Sullivan committed the images of Croft's henchmen to memory.

Particularly Rooney Moffett who also worked on the docks. Listed as a stevedore foreman. Croft's right hand muscle. A big mean sonofabitch according to O'Donnell's intelligence. The massive neck in the photo suggested a big man. Mentioned as one of the probable perpetrators of Maureen's murder by O'Donnell's source. Fair game.

But Fergus Croft was the mission. Couldn't hope to kill all the bad guys. He'd feel satisfied in knowing he'd cut the head off the snake. Satisfying the primal imperative to directly avenge Maureen's murder.

A few details remained. Would he announce himself to the local RIC? If he didn't might that prove risky? Either way he should have fake orders to support his story.

Having seen countless military orders he knew the stilted syntax and the construction. Should be the same for the British Army. He typed it at the office on one of the clerks' typewriters after hours. To make it look more official he scavenged a couple of children's rubber stamps at a stationary store to create an official looking header insignia of a crown and swords. Completely fictitious. The swords suggested cavalry rather than infantry. But if not scrutinized too closely, it should prove good enough to pass inspection from a constable or a British soldier in the ranks. Perhaps not from a keen-eyed British Army officer used to seeing real orders from headquarters.

HEADQUARTERS HER MAJESTY'S 15TH INFANTRY BRIGADE
BELFAST COMMAND
BRIGADIER GENERAL KENNETH R. HOPKINS, KCB DSO COMMANDING

Major Albert J. Winslet, Adjutant 1st Battalion, 15th Infantry Brigade, is hereby ordered to perform a survey of the city of Londonderry for the purpose of developing a tactical operational plan by which Her Majesty's Armed Forces can control and contain any widespread civil disturbance or insurgency threat.

All members of Her Majesty's Armed Forces are to render all possible assistance to Major Winslet in the performance of this assignment.

By order this *8th* day of *January* ,1921

J Fleming

Col. John C. Fleming
Chief of Staff 15th Infantry Brigade

There still remained the task of escaping once the deed was done. Best to make some attempt at altering his appearance. Something simple yet enough to further obscure his identity once he shed the uniform changing into civilian clothing.

A theatrical shop provided a trim military style mustache along with spirit gum and solvent. Similar to the newspaper photo of the real Major Winslet. A pair of clear eyeglasses would further alter his appearance.

He would carry Maureen's small caliber .25 pistol as a back-up weapon. He'd heard of ankle holsters. Made sense for concealing the pocket-size weapon. If things went wrong, it might even be overlooked if disarmed and searched.

A harness maker accepted the commission to fashion a good quality British regulation Sam Browne belt with regulation holster.

'Brother just got promoted. Wanted him to sport something finer than the government-issue rig. Can you do better? Also need something for a back-up weapon.'

Sullivan showed him the small pistol and explained his idea for an ankle holster. The craftsman said, "You'll be wanting something soft like kid leather. With an easy way to snug it to the ankle comfortably. A bit unusual but I'll create you something fine."

As the time neared to depart for Derry, Sullivan found himself surprisingly calm. A fatalistic lack of fear? From training, not a healthy state of mind preparing for combat. Remain focused on the task. Don't let emotion of any kind override the pragmatic execution of what he was about to do. There was no future to contemplate unless he killed Maureen's murderer. If he died in the attempt, so be it, but this wasn't to be a suicide mission.

CHAPTER 19

O'Donnell's intelligence showed Croft at his office on the docks the last three Saturdays. To set up the background cover, Sullivan arrived at the Derry rail station at noon on a Friday. He would meet with the local RIC district inspector Regan Lynch. Couldn't risk roaming about and being questioned by some constable. A real British officer on such a mission would check in with the RIC and the local army command. He had no intention of doing the latter. Unlike the RIC, the army did not patrol the city and he could probably avoid contact.

To insure his independence for moving about, he made advance arrangements for a hired car at the train station. Didn't want the RIC inspector to insist he be chauffeured about by a constable.

Armed with a detailed map of Derry he drove to Derry RIC headquarters. The car was an old Crossley sedan that had seen better days. Sullivan also had only limited experience driving automobiles. Some experience with trucks in the military. Used buses and trains in France. The temperamental gearshift while driving on the left trying to navigate from the map committed to memory preoccupied his attention.

By design, the meeting with the RIC district inspector was not prearranged. Still a risk if the inspector were for some reason to contact army headquarters. Since there was an actual Major Winslet that should still satisfy a cursory telephone enquiry.

For that matter it didn't matter if the district inspector was in the office. Any sergeant constable would do. He was just checking in out of professional courtesy.

Inspector Lynch was available.

"Won't take much of your time, Inspector," Sullivan said.

His first test. Did the mustache look real? Was his slight Irish accent enough to mask his American speech? Having dealt with many British officers during the European War he thought he had some of the mannerisms down. Some practiced British phrases to throw about. Could always explain that his mother was Irish-American. Spent early years in America. The British palm-forward salute. An air of self-assurance.

"Not at all, Major. What can I do for you?" Inspector Lynch said.

"Nothing specifically, Inspector. Just checking in as a courtesy. I'm from Belfast brigade headquarters. Not with the local Dorset regiment. Have orders to draft contingency plans to protect vital infrastructure for both Belfast and Derry."

"Protect? From what?"

"Well the sectarian violence for one. The riots last year caused widespread damage."

"Yes, but mostly to residential and small business."

"Nonetheless, Inspector, it could easily get out of hand should it reoccur. But of course it's also about the increasing IRA threat. Things are getting quite dicey in the south. We might see increased action by these rebels here in Ulster. Many attractive economic targets."

"Will you be needing someone to show you about, Major?"

"Don't believe so, Inspector. Have a good map and a hired car. Intentionally avoided notifying the local army command. My orders are to make an independent study. Confidentially, Inspector, headquarters thinks the Dorset Regiment's emergency response methods are in need of overhaul. Want a set of fresh eyes on the problem. Just completed revised plans for Belfast.

The shipyard rioting there in July provoked concern by General Hopkins. Then a recent sabotage attack made the possibility more urgent.

"Shipping facilities and railways are of particular concern. Not only the economic blood of commerce but vital for military logistics. Perhaps you could suggest whom I might contact to expedite my survey, Inspector."

"Certainly. The railroad station master is Charles Devlin. He can best direct you to appropriate staff familiar with rail lines, bridges, that sort of thing. As for the docks, that'll unfortunately be a chap named Fergus Croft."

"Unfortunately? How so, Inspector?"

"Croft is the local head of the Ulster Volunteers. Now he commands a platoon of over forty of these so-called special constables. Croft's former UVF thugs. An unruly nasty lot. Many are war veterans like Croft a former sergeant in the Ulster Division."

"Should think you'd welcome additional reserve constables, Inspector. Doesn't that reinforce your regular police?"

"To the contrary. No offense, Major but you're in the military. Policing is a whole different matter. Under normal times, my constables patrol among the people. Both Protestant and Catholic. Now of course with this rebellion they're pretty well confined to barracks except for responding to trouble. The IRA are apt to target a constable, or a soldier for that matter. Suggest you don't go about the Bogside in uniform, Major."

"To my point, Inspector. With this war these IRA rebels are turning Ireland into a lawless land."

"In Derry it's more about Catholics and Protestants at each other's throats. Look at the riots. The IRA just provokes the bad blood."

"Therefore doesn't this special constabulary provide you better resources?"

"More a problem I should say. Not trained as police. Under separate command from the regular constabulary. The Catholics see them as Protestant thugs with badges. Which they are. Led by the likes of Croft. A mean bastard with a sadistic streak if there's any truth to some of the rumors. Pretty sure his lot was instrumental in provoking the rioting last year. Croft runs his own criminal enterprise. Can't prove that of course or I'd have him arrested."

"Criminal?" Sullivan's eyebrows arched up.

"Runs the docks. Docks everywhere in the world suffer theft and smuggling. Derry's no different. Croft controls all major theft. Engages in smuggling. Rumored to extort kick-backs to move goods unimpeded. Enforces silence through threat of violence to prevent anyone complaining. Only Protestants are allowed employment on the docks. Most are UVF. The Derry docks are an armed camp run by a crime boss."

Obviously why O'Donnell would never consider an attack there.

"Well I daresay that's a right hellish state of affairs. But I suppose for my purposes this Croft fellow might prove helpful."

"Good lord, how's that?" Lynch said in surprise.

"Sounds like the docks already have a certain level of armed protection."

Also meant he was planning to do this within the stronghold of an armed criminal gang.

—

Concluding that formality, Sullivan drove straightaway to the docks. They covered a stretch of the east side of the River Foyle north of the city. Several entrance gates along the quays. He did not know what exit he would use but it didn't matter. All connected to Port Road. The purpose of this reconnaissance was to imprint his escape route to memory.

The rail station was six miles to the south. Same side of the river. He made the round-trip twice that afternoon. The Port Road a potential bottleneck if barricaded by police when making his escape but geography provided no alternative. Checking into a hotel near the train station, he took an early dinner. In the morning he'd only have appetite for coffee.

Even a couple of whiskeys did not bring sleep. To pass the hours he listened to music on the radio while cleaning both weapons. Full magazines each with one round in the chamber. Two extra magazines for the .45 in his brief case. The extra fire-power only necessary if all went wrong. Lastly he wrote a letter explaining everything to his mother, to be found should he not survive.

Sunlight streamed into his room window at dawn waking him from a fitful hour's sleep. Outwardly calm, anxiety mixed with agitation to dominate his fevered thoughts. To think he was about to kill a man in cold blood should have shaken him to the core. But for Maureen's murderer, rage pushed aside any moral qualms. Don't intellectualize just get on with it.

If Fergus Croft remained alive it would haunt him forever. An impossible life.

After a shave and wash he affixed his fake mustache with the spirit gum. Fastening the ankle holster to his right leg, he prac-ticed raising his pant leg using his left hand while drawing the small .25 with his right. Might prove to be more than just a backup. The sound it made was drastically less than the loud report of the .45. But the .25 had no stopping power. Only effec-tive at very close range. Deadly only as a head shot.

His satchel contained a civilian suit, tie, shoes, and felt hat. The fake glasses of course. At eight o'clock that morning he set-tled his hotel bill. By arrangement the hired car would be left at the train station. The train to Belfast left at noon. Then again this day might not offer an opportunity. A disturbing prospect if forced to postpone until the following weekend.

Nothing remained other than to get on with it. From here on out he needed to adapt to whatever circumstances dictated.

At the first entrance to the Foyle Port he was stopped at the gate. The man wore the armband of the special constabulary and wore a revolver on his hip. Inspector Lynch had been correct. An armed camp. He pushed aside immediate concerns about escap-ing.

"Major Winslet, 15th Brigade headquarters. I was told to ask for a Mr. Croft."

"Your business, Sir?"

"That's none of your affair."

The man decided to push the issue.

"Can't help you then."

Sullivan pulled the parking brake handle and got out of the sedan.

Standing one foot in front of the young man he yelled, "Listen you cheeky shit, I'm here to see your boss. Confidential army business. If you don't direct me to him I'll make sure you're next job is cleaning toilets since you're not any fucking good at doing this job."

The bluster had the desired effect. Angry but cowed, the man said, "Wait here."

Returning after a minute from the guard shack. "Manager's office is down a ways past this next warehouse. You'll see a sign. He's expecting you."

Finding the operations manager's office, Sullivan took a deep breath to calm the respiratory and heart rate. If the opportunity presented itself, he might kill Croft without further reconnaissance.

Entering he found a large room with several desks. Clutter abounded. Piles of paper were stacked on top of a row of filing cabinets. A potbelly stove gave off an uneven heat. Stale cigarette smoke punctuated the air. The only person visible was a young woman typing at a desk.

"Can I help you?" she said looking up at Sullivan braced upright with an air of arrogance.

"Major Winslet. I'm here to see Mr. Croft. District Inspector Lynch sent me."

"Yes, Sir. Mr. Croft's in his office. I'll tell him."

The secretary walked to a rear office with a frosted glass door stenciled *Operations Manager*.

His first obstacle. If he shot Croft how would he escape? She'd raise a frightful alarm. Not about to shoot the woman to get away.

Returning she said to Sullivan, "Please follow me, Sir."

On seeing Croft in person, Sullivan's stomach took a turn.

The tall well-built Croft stood to shake hands.

"Please take a seat, Major. Inspector Lynch sent you?"

"Not exactly. He just said you were the man I should see. Said you ran things here at the port. Am I correct?"

"You could say that. Keep things moving as they should. Busy place."

"Excellent. I'm from army headquarters in Belfast. Been tasked with making contingency plans for the army to protect vital infrastructure. Foyle Port is certainly that. The commanding general feels the current plans are outdated. I just completed new plans for Belfast. Need the same for Londonderry."

"Contingency plan you say? Against what?"

"Civil unrest. And the IRA of course. Things have gotten much worse in the last six months. Turning into a real war."

Croft smiled. "I think we can protect the port from the likes of the local IRA. Many of the men here at the port are special constables. All armed. Lots of them former soldiers. Myself included."

"I respect your preparedness, Mr. Croft. But what if the IRA were to mount a large-scale attack? Say a hundred men like what's happening in the South around Cork? You've a port to run not man a defensive stockade."

Croft considered Sullivan's statement.

"You say you were in the military, Mr. Croft?"

Croft nodded. "Saw action at the Somme. Wounded at Messines in 1917. Mustered out as a colour sergeant."

"Colour sergeant? Then you know something of military thinking. I'm pleased the state of affairs here at the port is so advanced. Makes my task that much easier. Before even taking a look around I'd venture this broad strategy.

"In the event the IRA were to mount a large attack, the first line of defense would be your armed lads. Hold the defensive perimeter. Setting up a clear signaling procedure that would immediately bring army reinforcements. They would deploy at predesignated positions to protect key port facilities."

Croft shook his head negatively. "What would the IRA gain by attacking the port?"

"Create disorder. Damage commerce thereby inflicting economic loss. Make London less willing to sustain the fight against this rabble. It's this great horde of Catholic unwashed rising up in a populist rebellion. It's the Protestants, the Unionists that own the industry. The infrastructure, factories, shipping, rail is what powers Ulster.

"Think of the disaster if a freighter was scuttled mid-channel in the Foyle. Loading cranes dynamited. Warehouses burned. Rail lines and railway bridges destroyed. Imagine Londonderry cut off by sea from Belfast. How would troops be deployed if the rail lines were also disrupted? That's why it could be an IRA target. Mr. Croft."

"Perhaps. So what is it you need from me, Major?"

"Just a little of your time. Need to understand the port operation better. Determine vital structures. How to best deploy the Army. A quick tour would be most helpful."

Possibly an opportunity to get Croft alone in a remote spot. Shoot him using the quieter small .25 point blank in the head. If lucky, the sound not even identified as a gunshot. Simply drive away before Croft is discovered missing.

For the next hour Sullivan accompanied Croft on a tour. He took notes, made sketches. Busy place. Lots of people about preventing any opportunity to do what he came for. Sullivan's anxieties rose. No reason to expect a better opportunity should he return another time and the risk only greater. He must take action soon but not out of desperation.

After exhausting all contrived areas of interest Sullivan said, "Thank you, Mr. Croft. Think I have a good idea of what needs to be considered if it became necessary to deploy the army. Might you have a detailed map of the port facilities?"

"Yes. Back at the office."

If all else failed, he'd shoot Croft there. Just have to risk the secretary fleeing and raising the alarm. The office presented the only opportunity. Hopefully there'd be no one else inside when they returned. Many unknowns. Stay focused. Assess the situation as it developed.

To add to his concern, it was already ten-thirty. If he missed the noon train it meant a risky long wait until the late afternoon train. No telling what kind of chaos would follow the killing of Croft. Inspector Lynch would surely connect him. Even though he'd be out of the army uniform without a mustache, Lynch was still a policeman.

So this was it.

Sullivan and Croft entered the office. Fortunately the secretary was not at her desk. No one else was there.

Croft went to a file cabinet Sullivan recognized for storing large blueprints.

Sullivan raised his pant leg and extracted the small pistol from the ankle holster.

Croft turned to face the pistol pointed only inches from his face.

"What the fuck?"

"Remember the O'Farrell family? The family you killed? Missed getting me when your people burned the house. I killed your two men that night. But you had to get the last O'Farrell. Killed my wife in the process. A fatal mistake, Croft."

Croft's eyes grew wide the instant before the first bullet hit him in the forehead.

Crumpling to the floor like a rag doll, Sullivan fired two more shots into his head insuring he was dead given the small caliber bullet.

Good choice the quieter .25. Hopefully nothing heard outside the office. He replaced the gun back into the ankle holster. He'd drag Croft into his private office. Place the body behind the desk not visible from the door. Might buy him some time if anyone entered the office.

He didn't get far.

As he was pulling the body by the feet, a scream pierced the silence.

The secretary had been in the water closet. Now she stood with her hands to her cheeks making a terrible racket.

Sullivan ran to her grabbing her wrists.

"Stop screaming! I won't hurt you."

She tried to pull away thrashing her head back and forth as he held her wrists tightly.

"Stop making noise. I won't tell you again."

Being small in stature she could do nothing. In a moment she calmed down.

"Mother of god did you kill him?"

"Listen to me. Nothing will happen to you if you remain calm. You'll be leaving with me."

"No!" She started to struggle again.

"No harm will come to you. But I must …"

Sullivan was interrupted by the opening of the front door.

A huge man took in the scene. Rooney Moffett recalling the large man's photograph.

Sullivan let go of the secretary and bent to retrieve the ankle gun. But in the time it took to draw the weapon Moffett closed the distance. As Sullivan attempted to stand Moffett delivered a blow to his chest knocking him backward over a desk.

The big man quickly came around the desk.

The blow took the wind from Sullivan's lungs yet he did not drop the small pistol. Still on the floor, Moffett made an attempt to grab Sullivan's weapon. But Sullivan got off a quick shot. The shot hit Moffett above his right nipple. If it had been the .45 he'd have fallen like a sack of potatoes. But the small .25 round didn't have that kind of knockdown power.

The shot momentarily halted Moffett's attack. Enough for Sullivan to empty the remaining two rounds into Moffett's abdomen.

Moffett staggered for a moment clutching at the wounds. Sullivan scuttled backwards then got to his feet. Bellowing in frustration, Moffett charged. Sullivan sidestepped the raging bull. The added moment allowed him to unholster the .45 Browning.

Moffett turned to face Sullivan now pointing the powerful pistol. Knowing the gunshots from the .45 would undoubtedly be heard, he hesitated hoping Moffett might succumb to wounds.

Staring at the bleeding Moffett, the secretary however resumed her high-pitched wailing. Gunshot reports no longer mattered and Moffett, still standing, posed a threat.

Two shots from the .45 ended the life of Croft's henchman.

With the secretary now on her knees screaming hysterically, he grabbed a spare magazine for the .45 from his briefcase then rushed out the door.

As Sullivan exited the office, a man out of breath from running stopped abruptly ten feet away. Seeing Sullivan's uniform confused him for a brief moment. With Sullivan holding a pistol the man foolishly tried to draw a revolver from his waistband.

Sullivan shot him in the head.

Jumping into his automobile, Sullivan almost flooded the engine trying to start it. Several men were now converging toward the office from different directions. With valuable seconds lost the engine finally caught. Forcing himself to remain calm, he put the car in gear heading toward the gate, careful not to stall as he accelerated while shifting into second gear.

The same fellow at the gate saw the speeding car approaching. The gate arm still down, the car was not slowing.

Sullivan sped up splintering the wood gate pole while the man looked on in disbelief.

He'd pulled it off. Adrenaline surged through him. He pounded on the steering wheel. Sonofabitch! Why did that guy outside go for his gun?

Croft and Moffett were both targets. The third man was collateral damage. Sullivan had no choice. Yet shooting him was troubling. Is this how Maureen died?

But reality returned immediately. His escape was compromised. Word would reach the RIC. Three men murdered at the port by a British army officer. Or someone dressed as one. Drove off in a Crossley sedan. This side of the river was heavily

Protestant. The RIC had no fears freely moving about in this area. Might even encounter the police road block on Port Road as he motored south to the rail station on this side of the river.

His only chance of escape remained getting to the train undetected. Couldn't therefore risk leading them directly there by parking the car at the station. The RIC must assume this to be an IRA hit. So the likely route for the assassin would be to melt into the Catholic Bogside on the other side of the river.

Sullivan preferred some commercial district to ditch the automobile then change clothes. He'd be cutting it close but thought he had time to abandon the car on the other side of the river. It would further suggest the assassin fled into the security of the Bogside.

Not far from the river on Carlisle Road he pulled into a parking lot next to an office building. Several automobiles were parked there. Out of sight from the street he set about quickly changing into his civilian clothes. A struggle while sitting inside the vehicle. Removing the mustache with the solvent was maddeningly slow going.

Looking into the rearview mirror, the glasses presented a significantly different face to the mustached army officer.

Still had to walk back across the Carlisle Bridge to the train station. The same route Dillon O'Farrell took that fateful night. The station bordered the east bank of the River Foyle only a short distance north of the bridge. Without drawing undue attention, he increased his pace to just short of a run. Checking his pocket watch, he might just make it.

He arrived at the train station with minutes to spare. Two RIC constables passed him on the station platform without incident. There seemed no unusual activity. Seated on a bench on the platform, his satchel remained unfastened allowing quick access to the .45 within easy reach. The reloaded .25 of course on his ankle. If forced to use them, only a desperate final gesture with no hope of escape.

As the train rolled past Foyle Port he thought he could see a gathering of people in the distance near what should be the port offices. An hour further north he felt confident there was no way he would be implicated. Successful as it was, now what? Killing the murderer of Maureen only satisfied something primal.

As the tension of the last twenty-four hours subsided, Sullivan fell into an exhausted sleep lulled by the rhythmic sound of the train wheels on the track joints. The conductor shook him awake as the train pulled into Belfast late in the afternoon.

CHAPTER 20

Now what? He'd just killed three men. Not about war. Simply an individual act of revenge. Croft and Moffett deserved to die. As they were immune from legal authority what alternative did he have? A subjective rationalization calling what he did an execution rather than murder? Nothing like his experience in the Great War. For all its horror, those circumstances were clearer. Could he live with himself had he not tried to kill Croft? No.

Did this act now commit him to be part of the larger struggle? Part of what? Irish freedom from Britain, or just taking sides in Ulster's civil rights conflict?

At least the next day was Sunday. He needed the down time before returning to the office. A miserably cold day but still he wandered a Belfast park. What would life now be like without Maureen? Tears flowed down his cheeks. The wind finally drove him into a pub. Better than returning to his small room. Couldn't bear facing the other boarders at Sunday dinner. Their discomfort in dealing with Sullivan's misfortune made for awkward silence.

If he was to stay on in Belfast he must find his own rooms. And although not fully understanding why, for the time being that was his intention. Something fundamental had changed since coming to Ireland. He could no longer deny his Irish heritage. That heritage left no place for the British to hold sway over

Ireland. No longer should Ireland be a colony. Everything bad happening to the Irish since the Tudor conquest in the 16th century bore the foul fingerprints of the British. Now might be Ireland's chance to determine its destiny. After taking violent action for Maureen's death could he deny his sense of Irish identity by walking away?

Perhaps taking up the cause of Irish freedom might instill purpose to go forward. Something more sustainable than vengeance. For Ulster Catholics, freedom meant overcoming ethnic discrimination. Of course that was inexorably mixed with the political divide between Irish nationalism and continued union with Britain.

What role could he play? Provide intelligence for the IRA? He knew nothing about spying. Spies needed networks of informers. Just because he found himself in the middle of the Protestant-unionism power center did not suggest methods to employ. How would he identify potential sources? Willing or unwitting sources? How to mitigate the risks? Means of communication? To whom? Yet had he not already implied his willingness to O'Donnell in exchange for information on Croft?

Another life changing decision. May never work out. But he realized that if he didn't do this, what then? Cut loose from life with nothing to anchor him? For the present, he'd explore this path. Something to take him outside this pressing despair. Perhaps the way to appease his still seething anger.

Newspaper accounts reported the killing of three men at Derry's Foyle Port. All the victims were newly enlisted special constables including a former UVF commander. Few details were given other than the men were shot. The assumed IRA assailants made their escape by automobile. Plural? No mention of a British Army officer.

But his killing of Croft unleashed a reprisal in Derry. Croft's platoon of B Specials went on an unauthorized rampage in the Bogside. Three businesses were burned, several people wounded. No fatalities fortunately. Apparently O'Donnell's IRA Derry brigade braced for the expected retaliation and inflicted casualties among the attackers.

Glad that his action did not result in widespread harm, his thoughts turned to reordering his life. New norms must be established if he intended to enter this fight covertly. Before Maureen's death, the deceit was a temporary construct necessary to seek employment. Now he would be embarking on a much deeper duplicity.

"Alison, I'd like you to do me a personal favor if you would," he said to his secretary. It was only days since his return to Belfast. She was constantly hovering about wanting to help ever since Maureen was killed. He felt equally sorry for her knowing her marital difficulties.

"I've decided to seek larger living accommodations then the boardinghouse. I've selected several flats advertised for lease in the newspaper that appear suitably located. Would you mind taking the rest of the day to look at them and give me your opinion?"

Delighted, she said, "Oh my, I'd be glad to, Mr. Sullivan."

"Excellent. Here is money for bus fare to get you about. Enough to also treat yourself to a fine lunch. I'll see you back here tomorrow morning."

The following morning she was bursting to tell Sullivan the results of her evaluation.

"Clearly my favorite is the one on Brookhill Avenue. Mind you it's three flights of stairs but you'll be on the top floor. No noisy neighbors overhead. Nice view. Furnished to a gentleman's taste I should say. Single bedroom with private water closet. Bathtub. A large sitting room with bookshelves and a fireplace. Small kitchen with a dining table. Pricier than the other three but worth the difference I should say."

"Wonderful. Then Brookhill it is."

"But one of the others may be more to your liking, Sir."

"No, I'll respect your judgement. Thank you so much for the personal kindness, Alison. I'll go take a look at it this afternoon."

He had little interest in his accommodations as long as it suited his purpose. Yet seeking her assistance was more than a gesture to his doting secretary. Her husband was UVF and now a special constable. A violent anti-Catholic. A bad marriage. Without any specific plan, Sullivan harbored the prospect that she might be of use as an intelligence source. Someone close to the enemy. Perhaps willing to pass along useful information. As good a place to start as any.

———

A week later a letter arrived at the office. The sender disguised as Father Sheenan, he knew it was from O'Donnell.

Dear Mr. Sullivan,

Trust you are getting along well considering all that has happened, my son. Impressed by how you managed to resolve what was thought impossible. Great ingenuity on your part. It has come to the attention of others. My superior, His Excellency the Bishop, would like to meet with you if that would be convenient. I believe you know how to contact him.

God bless you,

Father Edmond Sheenan

The *Bishop* obviously meant Michael Collins. Contact of course through his Aunt Kathleen. If he went to Dublin then he was essentially committing himself to the republican rebellion. Killing Croft had been a personal act. Spying for the IRA entirely different. But had he not already decided? Of course he had. Why else plan to stay on in Belfast?

———

The following Sunday he made the three-hour hour train trip south to Dublin. Again greeted by Aunt Kathleen, his cousin John drove them to the same house where he'd met Collins before. John took a long indirect route insuring they were not followed. Once Michael Collins arrived everyone else left the two of them alone.

On entering, Collins shook his hand then embraced him.

"Can't tell you how sorry I am for the loss of your wife. Words are always inadequate. Please sit down. Sorcha was kind enough to brew us pot of tea."

Seated in the parlor, Collins went to a side board to pour the tea.

"O'Donnell told me about … what do I call it, your operation?"

"Had to be done or I couldn't live with myself. Still an ugly business shooting the bastard up close."

"Executions are ugly business. Soldiers die in war while others simply deserve to die. Fergus Croft certainly did. But you did this alone? How'd you get close enough then get away?"

"O'Donnell provided me some intelligence. But once I realized where Croft worked that was all I needed. I knew immediately where to do this. The trick was always getting close to Croft."

"Of course. Yet into what amounted to be an armed camp. And?"

"Had to masquerade as someone official to gain access. Couldn't very well be a constable since Croft was now connected to the RIC as a Special Constable. Obvious to me it had to be a British Army officer."

"Good lord! That's the cheekiest thing I've ever heard. Under what pretext?"

"Sent from Belfast headquarters. Not a local Dorset officer. There to survey for improving the Army's deployment plans to protect vital infrastructure like Foyle Port.

"As a former professional officer I met a lot of British officers during the Great War. Familiar with their swagger. Tailor made me a uniform. Harness maker a Sam Browne rig. Got myself a fake theatrical mustache. Typed fake orders. Checked in with the local RIC District Inspector. He even suggested I go see Croft on the docks."

Collins listened raptly smiling broadly. "Sonofabitch. And for weapons?"

"Had my .45 Browning service revolver. Used my wife's small caliber .25 pistol to shoot Croft. Quieter. In the end it didn't matter. Like most military operations, circumstances often alter the original plan.

"But I managed to escape. After dumping the hired car I changed back into civilian clothing. Got rid of the moustache and wore a pair of clear eyeglasses. Thought together that should alter any description of me."

"Remarkable. Truly remarkable," Collins said shaking his head in disbelief. "I could use a whiskey. Let me she what I can find in the kitchen.

He returned with a bottle and two glasses.

After each of them took a sip, Collins said, "So what's next, Trevor?"

"Things have changed for me since we met before, Mr. Collins."

"Mick. My friends call me Mick."

Sullivan nodded. "You know my republican heritage. Irish independence was a constant topic. My mother and her sister Kathleen were close. My father shared my Uncle Tom Clarke's views if not with the same militancy. The murder of my wife and her family now made that history mine. Being here in Ireland adds to that. Whatever the explanation, I feel my Irishness. Want Ireland to finally be free of Britain. Want to do my part."

"We can certainly use you. Saw that straight off when we first met. Unfortunate your personal loss proved to be the incentive. However, let's talk specifics.

"Don't need to tell you the different fight being waged in Ulster. In the South the majority of the people are for independence. The fight is against the British and their institutions in Ireland. Support is widespread. But in Ulster, half the population is unionist."

Sullivan said, "Unionist translates as Protestant. Ethnic antagonisms go back before all the failed rebellions for independence. How do you resolve that?"

"Don't have that answer, my friend. But first we have to free Ireland from Britain. After all, it's that union that fosters Protestant domination of Ulster. Goes hand in hand."

"But won't partition under home rule hamper your goal of freedom for all of Ireland?"

"I believe the Ulster unionists lost ground. They didn't favor home rule but couldn't stop it. That conniving bastard Lloyd George thought it a clever political move. Deflate the cause in the South by eventually offering some watered down Irish autonomy. Not even dominion status. In Ulster the unionists would continue to control affairs only now with their own local government. Separate from the south, sure to remain tied to Britain."

"So how'd they lose ground?"

"If the South becomes independent they become only six counties. Two small an entity to survive even under Britain's wings. Especially when Britain wearies of spending lives and treasure policing Ulster sectarian unrest. If we win independence only for the South then we'll turn our attention to Ulster. There'll be no rest for the British or their unionist supporters. Eventually Ulster will be isolated."

"Interesting theory. Mick. Wait till Ulster collapses?"

"Wait? Good heavens no. We shall vigorously help that collapse. That's where you may be of invaluable service."

"That's why I'm here, Mick. Willing to do my part but not sure what that is exactly. Or how to go about it for that matter."

"Sweet Jesus we could use your gun. You're a one-man active service unit. But that would waste a unique opportunity. Seems you possess a whole host of talents. My sources say you've landed a position in the heart of Ulster unionism. Accepted into their circle. Obviously you've a talent for deception. So you can help by becoming a spy."

"I assumed something along those lines, Mick. Trouble is I wouldn't know where to start. That's what you do best. But I'm no Mick Collins."

"There's no blueprint for this. Different circumstances in Belfast compared with Dublin. I have a price on my head. You're accepted into their social circle. It's about developing sources. Willing sources as well as duped sources. Developing a network of intelligence into every corner of the enemy's world. It's about lying, cheating, deceiving. Looks as if you're already good at that. Game to give it a go?"

"That's why I came to Dublin."

———

Sullivan anticipated his meeting with Michael Collins with much curiosity. Collins was already a legend. To his followers he was the personification of a near messiah. To his detractors, a demagogue. But all, including his British enemies, considered him brilliant.

After their two hour meeting, Collins had won him over. The man possessed an extraordinary array of skills. His charm, wit, intelligence, and enthusiasm conveyed with boundless energy made him engaging. Yet it was his extraordinary skills at organization, his practical grasp of a range of disciplines, and a herculean capacity for work that produced results. From a darker perspective he was ruthless. Willing to practice any deceit. Willing to kill to advance his objectives. Willing to accept casualties, even sympathetic innocent victims. A master of both tactics and strategy. An innate grasp of the political landscape. He knew Irish sentiments. He knew the mind of the British government.

In this unconventional war Collins led a guerrilla army. A war fought not only in the countryside against a numerically superior enemy, but often a clandestine urban war. A war fought by understanding the mind of his enemy. Inadequately armed, it meant advantaging the battlefield and exploiting British weakness.

Some speculated Collins was running the war single-handedly. Creating an intelligence network far more effective than the British. Circumventing the IRA chief of staff to effectively direct operations. Managing the sale of illegal bonds to fund the rebellion. Collins' imprint was everywhere. If arrested, the rebellion might suffer a near-fatal blow. Talented and fearlessly clever, the British did not even have a photograph of Michael Collins.

Collins said, "The Irish have never been this close to ridding ourselves of British domination. This is our time. I can feel we have the British lion by its bollocks. A matter of how much pain Lloyd George can endure as we squeeze 'em."

"No need to sell me, Mick. I'll do what I can. Can't promise anything of the sort you've accomplished in Dublin but I'll do my best."

"I have no doubt on that account. Now to some practical advice. Intelligence work is about using your instincts. You'll have to find your own way to set up a network of informers. You're clever and resourceful. Identifying potential sources is the most difficult. Every organ of government has potential sources. Those that side with us do so for many different reasons. Sources have all sorts of motivations for helping us. Sometimes it may not even be clear to them. Look at yourself for example.

"I'll share some practical fundamentals I've learned. First, most sources are to be found among the lower ranks of those working in British controlled institutions. Constables not inspectors in the RIC. Secretaries, administrative staff, telephone operators, postal workers, and such.

"Catholics are employed in departments of the government. I suspect it's the same in Ulster but usually in mundane jobs. But don't discount Protestants. This is not about religion. Potential sources exist everywhere. Just have to seek them out.

"Now in your situation you're your best source. Fortunate finding a place among these arrogant sods. The intelligence you might personally provide may not be actionable but could prove strategically invaluable. Sooner or later we'll bring the British to the negotiating table.

"Means of communication must be carefully thought out. Anything in writing can always prove dangerous. And always find ways of obscuring the trail leading to you.

"Not all the RIC are oppressors. However we must treat the institution as the enemy. Make it impossible for them to function. That's largely what the active service units are doing in the countryside. Attack the small outlying barracks. Bottle up the RIC and the Black & Tans in the larger cities. Deny them the geography. Deny them the ability to interact with the people. Treat them as pariahs. For the few constables that favor independence, turn them. Make them into intelligence sources.

"Behind these murdering British mercenaries the Black & Tans and Auxiliaries, and now this Special Constabulary in Ulster, exists a support bureaucracy. By necessity staffing for administrative support functions must employ native Irish for much of the work. Impossible for the British to vet out everyone with republican sympathies. More so as these bloody bastards kill and burn across Ireland. By resorting to mercenaries disguised as police the British government makes every Irish person an enemy."

Without commenting, Sullivan thought that Collins overlooked the situation in Ulster. There the Protestant-unionists could more easily exclude Catholics from sensitive work. A greater challenge he imagined to identify those willing to resist British authority.

"But enough of my lecturing. You'll find your own ways as I did."

"Hope so. I already have some ideas," Sullivan said. "To the matter of communication. Not sure I want to entrust whatever I dig up to just any of the Belfast IRA. For that matter, I want to have only a single contact. Only one person that shall know what I'm doing. I'll be too exposed."

"Yes, of course. I agree. Anticipating your services I've given some thought to that very issue. There's a battalion commander in Belfast. Seems born to the struggle. The British hung his great-grandfather for an earlier rebellion. Would seem to share your views on the plight of Ulster Catholics. Doesn't shy from attacking the enemy."

"Very good. How do I contact him?"

215

"Let me arrange things. There's some diplomacy involved."

"What do 'ya mean?"

"Roger McCorley's the lad I'm talking about. Commands the West Belfast Battalion. Aggressive. But he can be difficult. Often at odds with the Northern Brigade leadership, particularly the Brigade OC, Joe McKelvey. McCorley even formed his own active service unit without consulting McKelvey. McKelvey's always concerned about reprisal attacks on Catholics. A good commander but more measured. McCorley feels he must take the fight to the enemy. Drive a stick in their eye at every opportunity. Reprisals must be expected. Known to take independent action on his personal initiative."

Newspapers frequently reported widespread reprisals by Crown forces on Catholics in Down and Antrim Counties. So this was the work of McCorley? He remembered Maureen's father even alluding to him.

"And who do you agree with, Mick?"

Collins hesitated for a moment before answering. "This is the type of war forced on us. The British outnumber us, outgun us. We must simply be more ruthless. Fight British terror with our own. Make their reprisals too costly."

Given Collins own style his answer was obvious. He praised the most aggressive of the IRA commanders. Making British security forces lives miserable and tenuous. Singling out killings of those Crown forces guilty of wanton reprisals on the general population. A terror war of attrition.

"So it's to be this McCorley chap," Sullivan said. "I'll wait to hear word on how I'm to contact him."

Collins nodded. "For that matter, how am I to contact you?"

"Use O'Donnell. He disguises his communications to me as a priest from Derry. The one who said mass for my wife and her family."

Collins smiled.

Sullivan left Dublin as a convert of the Big Fellow. Collins could make you believe that this time Ireland would win independence. Sullivan however harbored no illusions about what he was undertaking.

CHAPTER 21

"Well, Sergeant, I believe it's about time we made good on our new portfolio," District Inspector John Doyle said to Sergeant George Rafferty. "Game for a Christmas party?"

Rafferty, a seasoned veteran the same age as Doyle, smiled. "What do 'ya have in mind, Inspector?"

Rafferty sported a similar mustache to his boss but there the likeness ended. Doyle was large in stature, handsome with lively dark eyes. Carried himself like a professional soldier. Rafferty was short, the face of a weasel with vacant expressionless pale eyes. What they shared was an equal inclination toward violence. While Doyle's use of violence was pragmatic, Rafferty's fed a sadistic need.

Doyle said, "A little venture into enemy territory. South of here. Newry. Know it?"

"Not really. Just a train stop between here and Dublin. What's there?"

"Fuckin' IRA I should think. An RIC sergeant down there shot a young woman. Seems the sod got drunk, grabs this girl right on the street then shoots her in both legs. Turns out the girl's brother is IRA."

"Oh yeah. In the newspaper a few weeks back. IRA ambushed the sergeant later on. Killed him and another constable. Tied 'em to posts. Shot 'em in the head."

"Well the sergeant was a stupid shite. Deserved a bullet. Threats followed. Kept the local RIC holed up in their barracks. Then the IRA attacked the barracks in strength. Four constables wounded before they surrendered. Burned the barracks to the ground. No Constabulary in Newry at this time. IRA has the run of the area. Commissioner Wickham wants an example made. Says things are not going to be like they are in the southern counties. We'll not be run off by this rabble."

"Who we looking for, Inspector?"

"Seems a senior Northern IRA commander has family in Newry. It was his active service lads that killed those constables. So with no constabulary they're decided it's safe enough for a Christmas celebration. At the local Catholic parish church on Christmas Eve. Followed of course by mass at midnight."

"How'd you get the information?"

"The constables that used to be stationed there gave us some names. Sent Taggart down to check things out. This IRA commander's uncle plainly enjoys his drink. Loose with his mouth. Brags about his nephew being a bigshot. Home for Christmas. A loyalist bartender was only too glad to give up the information for a few quid."

"And who's this IRA commander?"

"Roger McCorley."

"Holy shit," Rafferty said. "Think he'll be there himself?"

"No way to know. But his widowed mother also lives there. Got a list of those to arrest. The houses of the sympathizers get torched. McCorley's uncle gets shot trying to escape. Probably a few others also. Maybe even the local priest. Use your imagination, Sergeant. You'll be in charge."

"If we don't nab McCorley there that'll sure as hell provoke him to retaliate."

"That's the point, Sergeant. Ratchet things up. Give us an excuse to use our newfound manpower with all these Special Constabulary blokes."

Rafferty nodded and smiled. "They'll be havin' sentries posted all about. What's the plan, Sir?"

219

"A large attack force of Specials led by the RIC will attack Newry. The larger force from Belfast will attack from the north. Convoy of tenders. Machine guns. A smaller force from Dundalk will set up a defensive position to the south to cut off retreat.

"They'll probably trench the main roads to prevent a motorized attack."

"Probably. But I have something more subtle in mind. I want you take a team and travel to Newry by train. You'll be there ahead of the larger attack by the Specials. The sharp end of the spear if you will.

"You'll take ten of our lads on the train. Dressed in civilian work clothes. Take up positions surrounding the church. Once the attack commences from the north you'll move on the church.

"Take that new guy Kendrick. Want to see if he's up to this sort of work. You're in charge but let Taggart do the talking on the train. You're to be a railroad maintenance crew. Taggart knows something about railroads from his old man so he can bluff his way with the railroad people.

"Your team will get off the train in Newry well ahead of the attack. Late afternoon. Taggart will explain to the stationmaster you lads were sent down to repair the tracks. He'll have papers to back up the story. Rumor the IRA had ripped up some rails south of Newry proved unfounded. You're just waiting in Newry for the next train back to Belfast."

"Clever," Rafferty said. "An excuse for hanging about. Got a map of the area, Inspector?"

Doyle pulled out a map of Newry.

"Party's being held at a church right here. There's a basement underneath the church with doors to the outside. The church sits on a hillside sloping away to a cemetery to the west. Taggart's also marked the locations of the houses of those we're after. Don't worry 'bout that though. Your objective is to hit the party at the church once the alarm is raised when the Specials attack."

Rafferty looked at the map for several moments. "Need rifles for a proper attack. How's that work?"

"Hidden in canvas satchels. Supposedly tools for working on the tracks."

"You want prisoners or casualties, Inspector?"

"Casualties, Sergeant. Not a fuckin' massacre but enough to make a point."

———

Like Rafferty, RIC Sergeant William Taggart also worked for Inspector Doyle for years. Just as committed to Doyle's extra-judicial methods as Rafferty, Taggart's manner was in extreme contrast. While Rafferty exuded menace, Taggart was deceptively engaging. Yet behind that cunning, he could be every bit as ruthless as Rafferty or Doyle.

To Taggart this was the supreme game. An actor of considerable range in a real life drama. His particular skill was developing informers. The number of sources represented the scoreboard. His methods varied. Protestant Unionists were of less interest. What intelligence could they produce? The few Catholic Unionists held possibilities but were few in numbers. Catholic Republicans represented his targets. The IRA's base of support. That covered a range from active supporters, to sympathizers, to just average people trying to get by with life. People trying to avoid what increasingly looked to be more a sectarian war than one of independence. To this group all manner of motivations might turn them into informers. Taggart's skill was identifying then exploiting weakness.

It was from the average Belfast Catholic population that Taggart developed an effective intelligence network. It started well before the rebellion of the last several years. Different levers applied effectively to fit a given circumstance produced results. Jealousy, greed, revenge, and particularly fear were sufficient inducements for people to pass along information. For many sources, they did not think they were betraying a trust. For those that knew what they were doing, they understood their own particular motivation. Taggart could charm the devil or corrupt a saint.

As the train slowed pulling into Newry, Taggart entered the railcar with his seated colleagues. Dressed in a cheap working-man's suit he had his arm around the conductor's shoulder.

"Glad the information proved to be a false alarm. At least your train will be on schedule."

"And what'll you fellows be doing?" The conductor said.

"Sure as hell not going to ride all the way to Dublin. We'll be getting' off here at Newry. Since we've had an unexpected night off we'll be having a few pints at a local pub. On the railroad's tab of course." Taggart laughed and slapped the conductor on the back. "We'll catch the northbound back to Belfast coming through in a couple of hours."

The constables got off the train carrying the long canvas satchels concealing their weapons.

Loud enough for anyone on the platform to hear, Taggart said, "A moment lads. I'll have a word with the stationmaster. Explain our predicament. We'll be stuck here for a couple hours. At least you don't have to freeze your arses off working the tracks in the cold of the night."

Taggart went off to find the stationmaster's office. Once the train pulled out no one was visible on the boarding platform. But the disguised police carefully maintained their cover. The IRA would surely have lookouts posted in strategic locations.

During Taggart's previous reconnaissance he spotted a lorry with the railroad logo parked at the station. He would ask to use it for a couple of hours if it was still there. If not it meant a long walk for the constables, but they were in luck this night.

The Newry train station was a mile northwest of Newry's center. Their target, St. Mary's Chapel, was a mile further on the south side of the city. The plan called for Rafferty's attacking force to make their way south along the rail tracks well to the west of the town. At a fixed point they'd cut due east to approach the church from the bottom of the hill using the cover of the cemetery. The church basement on the hillside slope allowed for exterior access doors.

With the use of the railroad's lorry the journey was quicker. Safer too by their clear identification as railroad workers. The lorry also allowed for an unpopulated indirect route to their location. Had they been forced to walk the route would take them through a residential area in order to maintain their cover story.

The last several hundred yards were covered on foot using the cemetery grave monuments to obscure their advance. Rafferty positioned his men to cover all exits from the church. They would wait until the sound of gunfire from the north signaled the attack by the Special Constabulary. Any IRA sentries would then reveal themselves and rush to the church basement to raise the alarm.

On schedule at eight o'clock came the sound of distant gunfire. As predicted, an automobile pulled to a stop on the road in front of the church. A man jumped out and ran down the slope and entered the church basement.

First to rush out of the church were IRA brandishing revolvers. Rafferty's constables opened fire with rifles against the easy targets illuminated by exterior lights.

Two IRA fell but the others scrambled up the slope to the road and took cover. From inside both doorways remaining IRA return fire at the attackers. An uneven firepower match for the IRA armed only with revolvers against the police concealed by the dark.

The gun battle raged for twenty minutes. Then from the north of Chapel Street came the distinct sound of machinegun fire. The Crossley tenders arrived with the body of the Special Constabulary forces.

The remaining IRA fighters inside the church basement heard the machine guns. Knowing they would soon be trapped forced a desperate escape into the police fire. Two more fell while three others made it to the road then into the fields beyond. The Constabulary would not chase them on this moonless night.

They were not Sergeant Rafferty's concern. His orders concerned other objectives.

Over thirty people remained inside the church basement. More than half were women. The men all middle aged.

"Who the hell are you?" The priest said since the attackers wore rough civilian clothing.

Rafferty walked up to the priest. "We're the police. Your name, priest?"

"Father O'Connor. Under what authority do you shoot up my church? If you're even the police."

The priest stood his ground despite Rafferty's revolver leveled at him.

Rafferty swung the barrel of his Webley across the cheek of Father O'Connor.

The blow knocked O'Connor to the floor opening a nasty gash.

"Shut the fuck up, priest. This is an IRA gathering. Everyone is under arrest. Stand against the wall all of you. You too, priest."

"Get the names of everyone, Sergeant Taggart."

Minutes later an unfamiliar RIC sergeant in uniform entered the room with two other uniformed constables. "Which one of you is Sergeant Rafferty?" he asked.

"I'm Rafferty. What can I do for you, Sergeant?"

"The inspector sent me down to report back on the situation here."

"And what's the situation elsewhere?" Rafferty said.

"Heavy resistance but no match for our three machine guns. Got a few of the bastards. Rest ran off. Scattered to the west since this street is cut off south of here. So will you be wanting some help with these people?"

"Does it look like we need help, Sergeant? Still got work to do interrogating all these fucking IRA sympathizers."

"So what am I to tell the inspector?"

"Tell him to get on with his fucking job. Search the town for known IRA. Burn their goddamn houses as ordered. I'll follow my instructions to gather intelligence. Now leave us to it, Sergeant."

Among the people detained were Roger McCorley's mother, her bother Gerald Madigan, and his wife Ester. Two others identified by the former Newry constables as being supporters to the IRA were also present.

Rafferty roughly grabbed Mrs. McCorley by the arm then slammed her down on a chair.

"Now where might your darling son be, Mrs. McCorley?"

"He's not here."

With an open hand, Rafferty slapped her hard across the face. Her brother reacted causing a constable to jam a rifle barrel into his midsection.

"I can see he isn't here you Fenian bitch. Where is he?"

Terrified with tears streaming down her face she shook her head from side to side.

To Rafferty it didn't matter what the old woman said. He was here to terrorize.

Once everyone had given up their names, Rafferty called out for McCorley's uncle and the other two reported IRA activists to step forward.

Pointing to three of his unit, Rafferty said, "Dawson, Ainsworth, and Kendrick. We'll be taking these three and the priest along for special questioning.

"As for the rest of you, you'll stay right here and have a chat with Sergeant Taggart. If you're helpful you get to go home. If not, you're in for a very unpleasant long night."

The three named constables shouldered their rifles by the slings and drew revolvers.

Bleeding from the laceration caused by Rafferty's revolver, a defiant Father O'Connor said, "Where are you taking us, Sergeant?"

"Back to Belfast, Father. Like I said, you're under arrest. For giving material assistance to the IRA."

Ten minutes later a sequence of several shots came from the darkened cemetery.

———

The *Belfast Telegraph* reported the incident at Newry two days later.

> BELFAST - The Royal Ulster Constabulary supported by the newly formed Special Constabulary mounted a sweep of Newry on Christmas Eve. The large-scale police operation was successful according to RIC sources although casualties resulted. One Special Constable was killed and three others wounded. IRA defending the location of a clandestine rebel gathering suffered three dead and five wounded before others escaped into the rural countryside.
>
> Newry had been the site of a violent sequence of events earlier in December. An RIC sergeant allegedly drunk shot a young woman, wounding her seriously. Days later a Sergeant Greenwood and Constable Shelby were shot dead, their bodies tied to a lamp post. Evidence suggested they had been severely beaten before being shot in the head. The following night the RIC barracks was attacked by IRA rebels. After the wounding of several constables, the barracks surrendered. The building was then burned to the ground. As a result of the IRA threat, the RIC was forced to abandon the Newry posting.
>
> According to the Constabulary, this show of police force was to restore civil order in Newry. A temporary facility will serve as the local barracks until a new permanent structure is reestablished.
>
> The police action resulted in ten arrests on charges of providing material assistance to the anti-Crown insurgency. The RIC reported that four of those arrested had been shot and killed attempting to escape. No further details were provided since the incident remains under investigation. An unconfirmed report names the parish priest of St. Mary's Chapel, Father O'Connor, as among those killed.

CHAPTER 22

Over the holidays, Sullivan attended several social events. Most encouraged by Malcom Llewellyn. Llewellyn voiced the opinion that Sullivan needed to interact with others especially at this time of year after the loss of his wife. *Time to forge onward. You're young with a long life ahead of you. Excellent prospects. Grief needs to be placed in its proper place. Life must go on.* A stream of well-meaning clichés.

But contrary to Llewellyn's thinking that these social engagements might be therapeutic to ameliorate Sullivan's grief, they only served to magnify his resolve. This was a performance. Every act a conscious deceit while surrounded by those he saw aligned with the enemy. Acceptance into this social environment only provided the means to acquire intelligence useful to the Irish rebels.

Some of those social-professional events took place at the Ulster Club. His boss treated him like a favored nephew. For Sullivan these contacts with Ulster's unionist power elite afforded a challenge to manipulate conversation to acquire information of intelligence value. Not always clear what information might be of strategic value to Collins but he was a quick study.

The real challenge however was developing a network of sources. Sources that could provide immediate actionable intelligence. Tactical rather than the strategic information he might pick up in careless talk among his newfound social circle. Intelligence the badly outnumbered local IRA needed to sustain their guerrilla ground war. A difficult task given no clear guidelines how to even start. Recruitment attempts therefore could carry the greatest risk.

Sullivan was having a late dinner at a pub not far from his flat. It had been two weeks since his meeting with Collins. Few patrons other than some regular drinkers at the bar. A young man approached his table.

"Mr. Sullivan?"

Sullivan looked up without responding, wary under the circumstances.

"Father Sheenan said I might find you here. May I sit down?"

Sullivan nodded. "And you are?"

"My name's Woods. Seamus Woods."

"And how might I be of service to the good Father, Mr. Woods?"

"Well it's actually for a Mr. O'Donnell, an acquaintance of Father Sheenan. Something to do with some legal matters related to the family of your late wife. Requested I look you up. Introduce you to a solicitor here in Belfast who might be of assistance."

"And who might that be?"

"A colleague of mine. Perhaps I could take you to meet him. He's associated with your friend in Dublin."

"Very well. When?"

"I thought this might be a good time. I have a car."

Sullivan wasn't comfortable with this but what did he expect? This was the game he signed on for.

They left the pub and climbed into a sedan.

"Are you armed?" Sullivan said deciding to be assertive.

The man opened his suit jacket revealing a shoulder holster with revolver.

"And you, Mr. Sullivan?"

"Yes."

As Woods swung the automobile onto Falls Road, Sullivan felt satisfied Woods must be IRA. This part of Belfast consisted of Catholic nationalist neighborhoods.

Woods pulled behind an automobile repair business.

Entering the back revealed a typical service garage cluttered with automotive parts on greasy benches.

Woods opened the office door. A young man seated at a cluttered desk cleaning a revolver and smoking a cigarette looked up. Sullivan was struck by the youth of all these IRA fighters. Over ten years his junior. Same age as Woods. Yet why not? Weren't all wars fought by young men? Even Michael Collins leading this fight was years younger than Sullivan.

The man rose extending his hand. "Mr. Sullivan. I'm Roger McCorley. Glad to make your acquaintance. Please sit down."

Woods closed the door standing in the small cramped office.

"Mick Collins sent me a letter. Speaks highly of you. Can see why after hearing about your background. Said you had something to do with killing that UVF bastard Fergus Croft in Derry. Thought Peadar O'Donnell finally just got lucky. Care to tell me how that all came about?"

"Rather not get into the details. Let's keep what happened in Derry strictly confidential." Sullivan said. "If I'm to be poking about I don't need to be worrying about that getting out. And for that matter, No one else is to know of my involvement."

"I understand. Collins made that clear. Just myself and Seamus here. He's my battalion intelligence officer. He'll be your direct contact. Collins even ordered that I not tell the brigade commander. Just as well. Joe McKelvey's an old woman. Afraid to attack loyalists for fear of reprisals."

"Good. Now how do you suggest we communicate?"

"Seamus?" McCorley said.

"Gave it some thought. Think I've come up with a simple solution."

"You should begin using an automobile. Easy to justify with your position and all with Harland & Wolff. I manage this garage. The owner's a friend of the IRA. The car I drove us in tonight he lets out for hire. I'll arrange it. Of course not under your real name. He'll know nothing about you."

"How's having a car help?"

"It's the perfect method to transfer messages. I've rigged a small box with a powerful magnet. Slips into a secure place underneath the boot. When you have something to send me you place a folded blanket on the back seat. Someone will check it daily. I'll retrieve the message while you're at work at the shipyard. Anybody questions what I'm doing, I'm from the garage fixing a problem with the car. Check the box every night for any message for you."

"I don't know. Isn't there a safer method?"

Woods replied, "The alternative is a drop somewhere. Problem with that it might get found by accident. Or you or I are seen at this place looking suspicious. Remember the police have informers everywhere."

"Alright, we'll start with that," Sullivan turned back toward McCorley. "I must tell you, Mr. McCorley, I'm new to all this. I'll pick up stuff I hear from people I interact with no doubt. Things Collins might find useful. But the kind of tactical intelligence you'll be wanting requires developing different sources. Sources closer to everyday goings-on. Not sure how successful I'll be. May take time."

"We're all new to this, Mr. Sullivan," McCorley said.

"One more detail, Mr. Sullivan," Woods said. "You'll need a code name?"

"Code name?" Sullivan said.

"Got to identify yourself somehow but never by your real name. So who shall you be?"

What name? Something obscure, without obvious connection. A character from Shakespeare perhaps? He was fond of the Bard's work.

"How about *Hamlet*," Sullivan said after a few moments of thought. A character bent on vengeance playing a dangerous game of deception. Seemed fitting to his circumstances.

———

"I'll be leaving now, Alison. Hope you have a pleasant weekend," Sullivan said to his secretary. It was Friday the first week of January.

"Thank you, Sir. I'm off to see my sister tomorrow. Taking the train up to Ballymena."

Sullivan sensed a lack of her enthusiasm for what must be an unusual outing.

Trying to detach himself from emotional involvement while pursuing his new life of deceit, he still felt sympathy for his secretary. Efficient, bright, a good person with unrealized obvious potential if not for her husband. The faded trace of another bruise to her cheek from earlier in the week was still visible. Bound by limited alternatives made for a life with only bleak prospects. An unchanging life with an abusive husband.

"And you, Sir, plans for this weekend?"

"Nothing special. Just relax after all the holiday festivities. Know everyone is looking to help me through this difficult time but looking forward to a quiet weekend. Plan to read a new book I just picked up."

Alison Kendrick nodded and bit her lip. "I can't image how difficult it must be, Mr. Sullivan." She looked away almost on the verge of tears before gathering her composure. "Is the new flat to your liking?"

"My yes, Alison. Thanks to you. A perfect choice. Looking forward to sitting before the fireplace with my book enjoying a glass of whiskey."

She smiled. "That does sound nice. I shall see you Monday, Sir. Goodnight."

———

Sullivan spent Saturday working on ideas to develop a network of spy sources. His efforts leading nowhere. While making notes of possible governmental and military targets, he still had no workable ideas for developing sources. Collins suggested looking to functionaries within the bureaucracies. And how was he supposed to do that? A frustrating day.

Deciding on a good dinner he found the diversion an opportunity to take a fresh look at the problem. Reflecting on Collins advice about average people making for the best intelligence sources, he looked about the restaurant. Most of the patrons looked to be people enjoying the occasional Saturday night dinner out. Not working class but a step up on the economic ladder. Office workers, maybe craftsmen. Men in cheap suits. Woman in their Sunday best. Careful how much money they should spend.

The sort of people to mine for sources. People he would have reason to interact with. People that ran the machinery of government and commerce. In turn, they might have subordinates, associates, friends, relatives willing to assist them. Finding a couple of key sources was the best way to grow a network of informants. And following Collin's advice, it afforded the means for obscuring the trail leading back to him.

That progress in thinking however brought him no closer to a plan of action. How to make that fateful first approach? But then he realized there could be no specific plan of action. This was a process. No different from his higher level associations. Get among them in the course of daily life. Develop a social routine. Cultivate interaction. Share confidences to build personal relationships. Learn their political leanings. Understand what seems to motivate their lives. Look for opportunity then seize it.

He felt a sense of accomplishment as he left the restaurant. The restaurant change of setting provided a diversion allowing for a fresh perspective. Needed to relax more. Free his subconscious to work the problem. That new book with a whiskey or two might even improve on developing this new craft of spying.

On a whim he'd picked up Robert Louis Stevenson's *The Strange Case of Dr. Jekyll and Mr. Hyde* while passing by a bookstore. A unique premise, good writing according to the bookseller. Analogous to his own duality?

After the first hundred pages the book proved an excellent choice. Difficult though to keep his eyes focused by eleven o'clock. The whiskey added to his relaxed state. Perhaps the first good night's sleep in weeks.

A quiet knock came at the door. Almost imperceptible. Who at this hour?

He pulled his suspenders back over his shoulders and went to the door. "Yes?"

"Mr. Sullivan, it's me. Alison."

What the hell? This couldn't be good.

Unlatching the bolt, he opened the door.

Alison Kendrick stood there holding a small suitcase.

"I'm so very sorry to trouble you, Mr. Sullivan. I've... I've nowhere to go. No money."

As she broke down crying Sullivan reach out to touch her shoulder in a gesture of sympathy. Feeling his touch she dropped the suitcase and embraced him. He could feel her tears wetting his shirt.

"Alison, come in and sit down."

He quickly pulled her into the room. Picking up her suitcase he looked down the hall. No one was about. Didn't need to start a rumor among his neighbors.

Seating her in a chair he wasn't sure how to comfort her. Tears turned to racking sobs as she held her face in her hands.

He brought over his glass of whiskey.

"Alison, get hold of yourself. Take a sip of this."

She took a swallow. The burning in her throat caused her to cough. Her crying subsided after some moments. Then came a torrent words.

"Edgar's become unbearable. Ever since he became one of those new constables. I had to get away for a couple of days. So I tell Edgar I'll be taking the train to see my sister in Ballymena. See my newest niece. My sister's fourth child. She's having a difficult time.

"Not a pleasant visit as it turned out. Her husband was unhappy. The little one was his third daughter. Hoping for another son. I said something about Edgar that touched my brother-in-law wrong. A big row. My sister's upset, the baby's crying. I'm crying. So I left instead of staying the night.

"Walked home from the train station. Then ..."

She stopped while covering her face with her hands.

"Edgar wasn't expecting me. Thought I'd be spending the night in Ballymena. Thought he maybe wasn't even home, everything being so quiet. Saturday night out drinking as usual. But not tonight.

"Opened the bedroom door. There he was in bed. A girl half his age. Naked the both of them. He looks at me. Pure hatred in his eyes. Says *what the fuck you doin' home?*

"And me looking stupid just standin' there. He'd probably cheated on me many times before, but catching him in our bed I... Anyway, something broke inside me. So I said nothing. Just turned and walked out.

"Started walking. Couldn't think straight. Realized I don't have anywhere to go. No money for a hotel. It's bitter cold so I can't be staying outside the night. All I can think of is your address.

"Might I borrow some money to get a room? I'll pay you back when I get my wages." She stood up abruptly and made to gather her coat without waiting for his reply. "I'm so ashamed. I'll just be going now, Mr. Sullivan."

Sullivan didn't need this unexpected problem, yet he couldn't turn her out with nowhere to go. Even if he gave her money, she would not find a room at this time of night. Already emotionally fragile, in her desperation she might even do herself harm.

"No you're not, Alison. Like you said, you've nowhere to go. Tomorrow I'll help you sort this out. Things will be clearer in the morning."

She turned toward him tears continuing to run down her cheeks. As she looked into his eyes, he offered a reassuring smile in response to her disturbing vulnerability.

Perhaps misinterpreting his kindness for something more, or just throwing caution aside, she embraced him and passionately kissed him.

Dumbstruck, he folded his arms lightly around her unsure how best to respond. She did not release her kiss. Pressing closer to him he could feel her breasts against his chest.

"Do you find me desirable, Mr. Sullivan?"

She did not release her embrace.

"Alison ... I..."

She pressed a finger to his lips. "You can have me if you like."

"I don't think that's a good idea, Alison."

"I'm too old? Edgar says I am. Thirty-six if you want the truth."

"You're not too old. You're an attractive woman. But we work together."

"But not attractive enough to take to bed?"

Guiding her back to the chair gently by her arm, "Not that simple, Alison. Under different circumstances, I could easily give into your charms. But we've both been through trying circumstances. You feel trapped in a marriage to an abusive adulterous husband. This is a wakeup call to make a better life. You do have choices. But right now you're vulnerable. Emotionally off balance."

Sullivan poured her another glass of whiskey.

"Drink this. Now here's what we'll do. Tomorrow we'll find you a place. Maybe my former boardinghouse if there's a room available. You'll find a good friend in the landlady."

"But I've no money."

"Don't worry about that. I'll pay the rent until you're settled. I believe you can afford it on your salary. Then we'll go around to your house. Pick up your belongings. Assuming of course you're ready to leave your husband for good?"

She nodded. "Yes. I'm scared though. I've no one."

"No, that's not true. You told me of friends you made in the Suffrage Society. Now you don't have to hide your involvement."

"And I have you, Mr. Sullivan."

Before that returned her amorous designs, he smiled and nodded. "Now you'll be taking the bedroom. I'll sleep on the sofa. Finish the whiskey. It'll make you sleep. The water closet's over there. Open the bedroom door to get heat from the fireplace if you get cold. It's pretty cold tonight. But the down comforter should keep you nicely."

"I'm sure I'll be fine. You're too kind, Mr. Sullivan."

She picked up her shabby suitcase and walked into the bedroom closing the door.

Thinking he had defused the situation he settled on the sofa. No longer sleepy, but returning to reading was now out of the question. An uncomfortable night ahead followed by a morning sure to be awkward. At least she now appeared settled into bed.

He misjudged. Alison's Kendrick had not abandoned her lust toward him. With everything so altered in her life there was nothing more to lose. Sullivan was her lifeline. From the first time she saw him she harbored romantic fantasies. Sexual fantasies fed by frank talk with her suffrage friends. Underground photographs and sexually explicit publications passed about. Among the other rights lobbied by the suffragettes was sexual equality with men.

Now she saw them as both free.

Alison Kendrick opened the bedroom door standing naked in the doorway for a moment to gauge his reaction. Whatever he was thinking he did not turn away from looking at her.

She walked up to him bending down to take his head in both hands and kissed him. "Please? Make love to me. I'm begging you."

Trapped. He felt overwhelming sympathy toward her. Foolish to even consider succumbing. It could only lead to a complicating entanglement. Could he extricate himself while she pressed against him naked? Some primal part of him however didn't want to. No classic beauty but naked her trim body provoked physical arousal. She pulled him by the arm into the bedroom.

Sensing his reluctance, she touched one hand to his crotch, pushing him back on the bed with the other. After taking the risk of such an uninhibited transformation his rejection now would emotionally devastate her. Torn, he let things take their course.

Removing his suspenders he began unbuttoning his shirt.

Without hesitation she reached down to unbutton his fly. Bending over undoing his trousers provided an erotic sight looking down at her well-shaped breasts. His erection was boldly obvious as she slipped off his trousers.

If he was going to have empathetic sex he'd try to make it a memorable experience for her. A self-serving excuse for having sex with her. He was too aroused and things gone too far. Easier to just abandon himself to the moment and sort things out later.

With her eyes wide in anticipation she hooked her fingers into his underwear pulling them off over his ankles. As his cock sprang fully erect inches from her face she said, "Oh my!"

Instinctively she caressed his erection. "I've never been with another man other than Edgar. I don't know all the things that make a man happy."

"Well for some men that means making the woman happy. That's the difference between lovemaking and having sex. So just relax and do what comes naturally."

He reached out to caress her breast then drew her down onto the bed. Propping her up on the pillow he proceeded to kiss her breasts. When he took her nipples lightly in his teeth she let out sighs. He could taste fresh tears running between her breasts.

"Why are you crying, Alison?"

Breathlessly she whispered, "Never imagined sex... lovemaking, could be like this."

His hand proceeded to explore between her legs. After spreading her legs she emitted small sounds as she pushed against his touch. Feeling her moisture, he gently inserted one finger inside her followed by a second.

The sensation caused her to arch her pelvis in response.

As he stimulated her slowly she began rhythmically riding his fingers vigorously. Eventually the muscles of her abdomen convulsed as she came to orgasm. Before she finished he rolled on top and entered her. His penetration eliciting vaginal contractions and a protracted groan of pleasure.

To prolong the experience for her maximum pleasure he slowed his own penetrations. Sensing his own impending release he felt her contract around him in a second orgasm as he too climaxed.

After catching her breath she said, "Guess it makes no sense now you sleeping on the sofa."

———

To make matters even more intimate, Sullivan woke in the morning to Kendrick getting him hard again with her hand. What did he expect? Should have found an excuse not to carry things further last night. Couldn't however deflate her expectations, or so he told himself.

After making love again she smiled. First ever smile he remembered seeing from this usually sad woman. That at least was positive.

He pulled on his underwear and went to stoke up the fireplace embers and put new coal in the grate. He returned to gather his clothing. An awkward moment with neither knowing what to say.

"Need a shave and a wash." Obviously he needed a wash. "I'll run you a bath when I'm done."

"You're an extraordinary man, Mr. Sullivan. So smart yet so … kind."

"I think after our intimacy you can call me Trevor. Only outside the office of course."

She smiled holding the bedding to cover her breasts.

As Kendrick took a bath, Sullivan brewed a pot of coffee. Once he got his secretary settled in a place of her own he needed to put some distance to this unexpected sexual liaison. He chided himself for his stupid excuse that he succumbed out of kindness. Simply too weak to refuse her. Yet he had no doubt that it did much to restore her damaged self-esteem.

However a darker thought emerged. As a practical matter might there be value in fostering this intimacy? He needed to develop sources. Women were a good source according to Collins. Disgruntled women a prime source. Suffragettes by definition were disgruntled activists. Perhaps Alison could prove effective in recruiting sources. Knowingly or inadvertently? How far did he dare confide in her? Could he keep their affair secret? Was he willing to seduce her into spying? Willing to exploit her vulnerability?

Had he crossed some moral Rubicon? Killing Croft now contemplating exploiting his vulnerable secretary? Did he now embrace these ethical contradictions or was this simply the lot of a spy? None of this would have happened had he left Ireland after killing Croft. Being Irish inflicted its own mental disorder.

Alison Kendrick came out of the bedroom dressed in her typical office attire. White blouse with a high neck, ankle-length skirt, and practical button shoes with a low heel. But with new life in her face. Color in her cheeks. The eyes no longer sad. A measure of self-assurance?

"Coffee?"

"Oh yes. Thank you," she said.

Surprisingly she displayed no self-consciousness.

On the table lay yesterday's newspaper. The *Belfast Telegram* headline read *FOUR DEAD IN SHANKILL DISTRICT*, with a subheading of *Feared as Response to Newry Police Raid*.

Kendrick picked up the newspaper and began reading.

Seeing the intensity of her concentration while ignoring the coffee he set before her, he said, "What is it, Alison?"

She was shaking her head. "These people the IRA killed. Were they Ulster Volunteers or just loyalists? The paper makes you think they were just innocent Protestants."

"One can't be sure," Sullivan said. "The newspaper is biased to the government so it can't be trusted. As for the IRA, they're obviously biased. This is a war of ideas. Political propaganda's a principle weapon for both sides."

"I know something about what happened in Newry," Kendrick said. Gone was the newfound spark in her eyes. "Edgar told me about it. He was there. Told me what he'd done. Bragging he was. Sayin' he was the police now. All legal like to shoot people."

Sullivan set down his coffee cup. He'd read the article yesterday. Another tit-for-tat reprisal. Except in this case it hit closer. Although the reporting was light on facts, it did cite the Christmas Eve Newry raid as the cause for the IRA Belfast reprisal. *'A notorious commander of the Belfast IRA by the name of Roger McCorley was rumored to be there. While McCorley was not arrested, his uncle was killed in the fierce firefight. Among those arrested was McCorley's mother on charges of materially helping the IRA.*

"What did he tell you?"

"Said he shot someone. A bullet to the head he said."

"Who did he shoot?"

She looked at Sullivan, "Said he shot a priest. Then I read about Newry days later. Four men shot trying to escape. One was a priest."

"Who was your husband with?"

"The regular Constabulary. A sergeant named Rafferty was in charge. It was him that ordered the murders Edgar said."

"Did Edgar say which barracks this Rafferty was from?"

"From Belfast. Rafferty works for some inspector. Special work they do according to Edgar. Said he's part of this police unit being he's now a special constable."

"Did he say the name of this inspector?"

She nodded. "Doyle."

He questioned her for every detail she could provide on the Newry incident. She remembered a couple of the other RIC constables' names. More importantly, Edgar Kendrick had bragged about this special police detail that he was now part of. While not specific, it was enough to suggest this RIC District Inspector Doyle was a different sort of policeman. Edgar Kendrick told his wife he had to swear loyalty to his fellow constables on penalty of death. What kind of police unit was this?

The remainder of the day was devoted to getting Kendrick settled in a place of her own. Another night like last night would make it impossible to break free from her. His former boardinghouse room was still available. Her demeanor noticeably changed as she inspected her new living quarters. Last night replaced her horrid existence with a fairytale fantasy. The boardinghouse returned her to harsh reality.

After settling the arrangements came the more delicate part of helping Alison retrieve her personal belongings from her home. Sullivan did not want to confront her husband personally. Far too many complicating ramifications. As it was Sunday afternoon, a risk since Edgar Kendrick would not be at work at the shipyard.

Turning onto the street in his new hired car, Sullivan spotted a constable a block before arriving at the Kendrick's home. Stopping and getting out he told the officer of the plight of his secretary. A violent husband that beat her. The constable was not only unsympathetic but hostile.

"And you want me to get in the middle of this domestic dispute between a man and his wife? And just what exactly is your interest in this matter, Sir?"

"Told you, officer. I'm her employer. Mrs. Kendrick came to me for assistance. Now are you going to do your duty to protect her from harm?"

The officer looked from Sullivan to Kendrick. "I don't know. A bit irregular."

"Tell you what, constable…?"

"Constable McFarland."

"You can help this poor woman or I'm simply going to take this matter up with your inspector, McFarland. Maybe even with Commissioner Wickham himself. Met him a few weeks ago. See if he condones you shirking your responsibility."

Constable McFarland glared at Sullivan but took the threat to heart. "Very well. Let's get this done, woman."

Fortunately Edgar Kendrick was not at home. Piling his secretary's belongings into the backseat of his car, Sullivan thought how little there was. Her entire material world. Surprisingly few clothes. Some pictures in frames and a photo album.

An emotional parting followed back at the boardinghouse. He took her hand and said he would see her at the office the following morning. Avoiding her attempt at a kiss, "Must be careful in public, Alison?"

That evening he wrote down all that Alison Kendrick had remembered her husband telling her about Newry. The following morning he placed it in the magnetic box under his car and placed a folded blanket on the rear seat. His first piece of intelligence to pass along.

CHAPTER 23

Seamus Woods sent back a reply to meet at the garage the following evening.

Roger McCorley said, "This source, your secretary, can she provide continuing intelligence on her husband's activities? We know Inspector Doyle. His murderous bunch of peelers has killed far too many Catholics."

"Sorry for your family's loss, Roger," Sullivan said alluding to the murder of his uncle. "Afraid my secretary left her husband. She only came to me because she couldn't take his abuse and had nowhere else to turn. It was out of anger that she told me of Edgar Kendrick's boasting about what happened at Newry."

McCorley's mother was still in custody awaiting trial. Inspector Doyle was now a personal matter.

"We've been after Doyle for some time," Woods said. "But he's a wily bastard. Doesn't go about much. When he does he always has other constables around him. We know these guys Rafferty and Taggart your secretary mentioned. A nasty lot doin' Doyle's killing."

McCorley interrupted, "We can't allow Newry to go unchallenged knowing Doyle was now behind it. Murdering four people while trying to escape? Even a priest? We need to kill Doyle."

"Shit, Roger, we've not been sitting on our hands," Woods said. Turning to Sullivan, "You see the problem is maintaining surveillance on Doyle. He lives at the Springfield Road barracks. No way to keep eyes on the area without drawing attention. Doyle doesn't keep to a routine as far as we can tell. Don't have any informers near him. To get at him we need to identify a time and place where he'll be out and about. For that we need much better intelligence."

Sullivan nodded. "Well I've just started at this. But I'll make this District Inspector Doyle a priority."

"Of course *you* might be able to get close to Doyle," McCorley said to Sullivan.

Sullivan shook his head side to side. "I'm not part of your active service team, Roger."

"You're handy with a gun," McCorley said. "And of course that matter in Derry."

"Derry was different," Sullivan said. "Killing Doyle will be far more difficult than Croft."

McCorley couldn't wait for intelligence to develop before delivering a reprisal. Doyle might be out of reach but an attempt could be made on others of his team. This Kendrick fellow would be the easiest target but the Newry outrage called for a more dramatic attack on Doyle.

"Then perhaps we'll hit him by going after those two sergeants, Rafferty and Taggart?"

———

A week of furtive glances and knowing smiles passed between Sullivan and Kendrick. She ached to further their weekend liaison into something more. Sullivan wondered how productive a source she might be. Her involvement with the Suffrage Society offered a promising environment from which to cultivate sources of useful information. She represented an opportunity he should certainly seize on if serious about spying. Using her didn't set well however. He was going to exploit this fragile good woman using romantic manipulation? Cruel since it must end at some point. But if he was to produce intelligence he'd have to live with that.

By Sullivan's own experience, morality is a casualty of war. Little of war has a moral underpinning. Patriotism is not inherently moral, just a motivation driven by social association. But he was committed nevertheless. Driven by compelling motivations transcending moral consideration. But using Alison Kendrick in this matter was still disturbing.

His own moral compass was badly distorted. The assault on the O'Farrells in Derry then Maureen's murder aroused a demanding outrage. Killing Croft satisfied an overwhelming primal urge but left an indelible unease. Now using Alison Kendrick? Could he justify such means? To achieve what end? Conflicted circumstances he could debate endlessly.

But whatever the emotional factors compelling him, he'd made his decision. Best to avoid endless philosophical debate and see this through.

Kendrick was understandably nervous around Sullivan the entire week. Yet she was clearly different as if a great weight had been removed. By Friday he prepared to move forward. No room for timidity if he intended this audacious plan to spy on the enemy. In the afternoon he asked her to step into his office.

Out of earshot of other staff under the pretext of organizing papers on his desk, he whispered, "Perhaps you could join me for dinner tonight?"

Visibly flustered with uncertain expectations all week, she struggled with a response.

"Of course. I mean yes. I…"

"Excellent. I will pick you up at 7:00. We'll go somewhere nice."

"Yes. I'll be ready. What should I wear?"

"You're favorite outfit. Oh, and perhaps bring something for later."

She nearly swooned at his implication, propping herself up by holding onto his desk with both hands.

That evening at the only French restaurant in Belfast, Sullivan introduced her to wine.

"Are we having an affair, Trevor?"

"Yes, I suppose you could call it that."

Kendrick smiled. A changed woman since leaving her husband then immediately falling into this fantasy romance. At the office she was clearly different. More outgoing. Smiling. Engaging in conversation with other staff. Confessing she had left her abusive husband brought on a surge of friendliness from other female staff.

"Never could have imagined. Something only in novels. Difficult not to tell my closest friends."

"Some things must be kept secrets however difficult, Alison. I bet your friends also find it hard not to confide their secrets. Like their feelings about the war, all the violence. People take sides in things like this. They express their feelings to their friends. Do some of your friends object to the persecution of Catholics like you do?"

"Oh yes. All of them think what's going on is horrible."

"How about the fact that it's the police and the army doing much of the killing and burning? Even the Ulster Volunteers like your husband are now police. Does that bother them?"

She nodded. "Oh yes. Everyone is either confused or angry. I don't know much about politics but some in the Suffrage Society have strong views against what the government is doing."

"Well I've my own secret to share with you, Alison. Would it surprise you to know that I think Ireland should be independent of Britain?"

"Oh my. I'd never. And you being Mr. Llewellyn's favorite and all."

"Well certainly keep that to yourself. I'm not that political either. Whether Ireland becomes independent or something less means different things to the Irish people. As for me I have my own burning private anger about what's happening to Catholics."

Kendrick's face tightened as she felt Sullivan's intensity.

"I'm from a mixed religious family. My mother was Catholic, my father Protestant. That's no secret. What is a secret is my father severed his family ties. I grew up in an Irish-republican household in Brooklyn, New York. My father as militant about Irish freedom from Britain as my mother's family. But I'm Irish-American, not a true rebel. Just think the Irish should be independent of Britain.

"But the UVF murdered Maureen. Murdered her whole family because they were Catholic. Claimed her father and brothers were IRA. Tortured her younger brother before murdering him. Dumped his body in front of their house. Imagine a mother seeing that.

"A week later they burned the house killing her father and crippling her mother. Later on they gunned down her other brother along with his wife and Maureen. On a public street in Derry on a Sunday afternoon."

"Oh my god," Kendrick said putting her hand to her mouth. "I never heard those details."

"Because I haven't told anybody the whole story. The police refuse to do anything. Common knowledge that the Ulster Volunteers were behind the murders. Now these murderers have joined this special constabulary. Free to now kill as police. I can't live with that."

"But what can you do?"

"I found a way to get my revenge."

"How?"

"Rather not say too much. But all this has changed me. I can't ignore Derry and Newry. Killers masquerading as police. They're like the bloody Bolsheviks in Russia. A brutal police state killing outside the law. Imagine if your husband can murder a priest without legal consequences while under the cover of a police raid. What sort of society is that?"

Kendrick swallowed hard. "I see what you mean. Some of my friends say the same thing."

"Lots of good people do, Alison. I'm not done with my vendetta. Anything I can do to undermine the RIC and these out of control special constables, I will. The British must be held responsible. They govern Ireland. In Ulster they've sided with the Protestants because of their unionist stance. Taken sides in Ulster's ethnic war to serve their own purpose.

"To do nothing against these bastards would dishonor the memory of my wife."

For effect, he paused and took a deep breath. "Since we've shared … an unexpected intimacy, I'll go even further. You can help me."

"Help you? How could I possible help?"

"Your friends at the Society. Do some of them have jobs?"

"Yes. Many have jobs."

"And who might some of them work for?"

She paused for moment realizing the implication of Sullivan's question.

"Are you asking me to pass on their gossip? I won't spy on them. They're my friends."

"Of course. And no I'm not asking you to spy on them." Placing his hand over hers, "I'm asking you to recruit them."

"What do 'ya mean *recruit*?"

"Simply determine if they feel strongly enough to throw sand in the machinery of this police state?"

Kendrick may not be worldly but she was street smart.

"And who gets this information?"

"I won't lie to you, Alison. The Irish government outlawed by the British. Their military, the Irish Republican Army."

"Oh my god. You know these people?"

"After what happened in Derry they approached me. Enraged over the murder of my wife I agreed to help them in Belfast by passing on information."

As Sullivan looked at her she understood he was expecting an answer.

"I don't know, Trevor. This is such a shock. Let me think about it."

"Fair enough. No more depressing talk. How did you like dinner?"

"It was grand. And I loved the wine," she said but was anxious to know about what the remainder of the night might hold. "Your remark at the office about later. Did you mean...?" Afraid to frame her question directly.

"To spend the night? Yes, that's what I meant. But only if you wish to of course."

———

Sullivan's spy network was born. A dual attack on government institutions. While he integrated into the unionist hierarchy picking up broad-based strategic intelligence, Alison Kendrick began recruiting lower-level sources for tactical intelligence.

Once she made the decision to participate, she threw herself enthusiastically into the effort. Sullivan suspected she saw it as a way to solidify their romance. Delighted with the challenge, she proved highly effective. A secret adventure binding them by the thrill of danger and sex.

Not only did it bring them together in a shared purpose, it provided another form of intimacy. With their budding sexual relationship her attachment to him reached obsessed infatuation. A despicable but effective charade to encourage her espionage activities.

That second weekend together he schooled her in the mechanics of spying. The whole business foreign to him as well. Make it up as he went along based on Collins' advice.

"A source must first be placed where she or he has access to useful information. Who among your associates in the Society work at such jobs?"

"Let me see. Two sisters both telephone operators for the RIC."

"That's interesting. Their politics?"

"Not sure. But the older one Regina is pretty outspoken. Then there's Bonnie. She's a typist at Army headquarters. A widow. Husband killed in the Great War. Don't know her too well. A quiet sort.

"I'm friendly with an older woman, Florence O'Shea. I know she's disturbed by all that's going on. Husband tends bar where the police hang out. Tells her gossip he overhears that upsets her. Guess I'll have to fish about."

Far better than Sullivan could have hoped for. Needed to counsel Kendrick to move deliberately and not risk advertising what she was about.

"What do you ladies talk about?"

"Mostly about doing things to get women the vote and other rights." She then laughed. "And of course about men. How they run everything. Get paid more than women. We all complain about that. Then of course gossip. Harassment at work. Harassment at home. Who's sleeping with whom?"

"Don't you be talking 'bout us, Alison?" he said with a smile. "If your friends get too curious about your love life now that you're separated, tell them you're seeing a married man. That'll sound mysterious. Reason enough not to give details."

"Can I talk about how we make love?" she said leaning over to kiss him. "You'd be surprised what women tell each other. But I'll tell them my boss knows about my affair and he's covering for me since it involves someone at work. That'll deflect gossip away from you."

"Very good. You've a talent for this, Alison. Just maneuver the conversation around to the violence. What do they think about all these killings and burnings? You'll soon get a feel for where they stand.

"Beyond that you just have to use your instincts when asking them if they're willing to help. And be clever how you ask. Not too directly. Give yourself an excuse to back away."

"And they'll ask, *helping who*?"

"The answer is the Irish people. All Irish. The enemy is British occupation and their brutal policing. Only without the British is there a chance for peace. If they press you, say you're not sure what happens to the information. You're striking a protest just like for women's rights.

"Use the anger over your husband's physical abuse. His bragging about committing violence with his UVF thugs. His relishing continued violence now protected as a constable. Even those not sympathetic enough to help will at least understand your stance."

"Yes. I understand. It's the truth too."

———

The IRA in the North was up against a different enemy than the south. Collins could rely on an unlimited supply of intelligence sources in the south. People volunteered information. The population was overwhelmingly in support of Irish nationalism. Ulster was different with half the population loyalist. Intelligence harder to come by. The circumstances for double agents more dangerous.

McCorley and Woods recognized the potential value of Sullivan. Not certain however if a foreigner could achieve a network of informers where the IRA struggled to develop intelligence. Regardless, that would take time. McCorley needed to deliver a proper reprisal in response to Newry quickly. This was as much a war of publicity as action. Catholics needed to feel the IRA was a potent military force. They must make the RIC suffer consequences for their actions.

Their hasty attempt to kill RIC Sergeants Rafferty and Taggart however proved a disaster.

Based on one of Woods's sources, both men were to be at a pub on a particular night. Seems they were staging a surprise celebration for a young colleague's birthday. Seamus Woods' source was a pimp. Sergeant Taggart had arranged for a prostitute to be at the pub. She was to come on to the young constable then take him off thinking he got lucky with a pretty girl. They'd all have a good laugh teasing their mate when he returned to the pub.

The plan called for two teams of four IRA each. One led by McCorley, the other by Woods. Two cars would carry the attackers. The pimp would signal by stepping outside, taking off his hat then lighting a cigarette if the targets were inside at the designated time. Woods had a spotter strategically placed who would call a certain telephone number. A five-minute drive to the pub after receiving the signal.

If the targets were still inside when the IRA arrived, the pimp would simply walk away down the street. If he remained, they would abort the attack. One car would circle to the rear of the pub. Two gunmen would enter the front and two others the back with two men remaining in each car to cover their retreat. The attackers were armed with Mauser C96-9mm semi-automatic pistols. The attackers from the rear alley would take their cue from the first shots fired by McCorley entering through the front door.

The assault should last only a couple of minutes.

The call came. It was on. Woods's car pulled to the sidewalk a hundred yards from the pub. The pimp flicked away his cigarette then turned and walked away confirming the targets were still inside. Woods drove off to circle to the back of the pub. The car carrying McCorley pulled up into place. McCorley and another IRA exited the vehicle moments later and walked toward the pub entrance.

A barrage of gunfire erupted as they entered. The gunman next to McCorley fell mortally wounded. Uninjured, McCorley dropped to the floor and returned fire.

Moments later Woods and another gunman entered the rear. Although caught in a cross fire, a prepared contingent of constables inside the pub returned fire from positions of cover. Realizing a disaster, McCorley and Woods aborted the attack retreating to the waiting cars.

Intense rifle fire hit the fleeing IRA cars. The windscreen of the car with McCorley shattered with the round killing the IRA man in the passenger seat. The driver took a bullet in the chest. In the back seat, another round struck McCorley in the arm. The driver managed to control the car long enough to get beyond the gauntlet of Special Constables lining the street firing on them. He collapsed unconscious blocks away leaving the wounded McCorley to make his escape on foot.

The car with Woods fared better with only one man wounded as they sped down the rear alley disrupting the field of fire

for the special constables positioned along the narrow space behind trash containers.

An RIC ambush. Woods's source, the pimp, a double agent?

———

Alison Kendrick proved either to be very skilled or her circle
of women represented a rich pool of anti-government subversive
opportunity.

Over the next several weeks Sullivan added several sources
to his fledgling spy network through Kendrick's contacts among
the Suffrage Society. The usefulness of their early information
however seemed questionable, sounding like gossip of no value
to the IRA. A promising beginning nonetheless.

From Alison Kendrick's explanations, the sources felt they
were fighting as much a civil rights struggle as a war for independence. The widespread sense of outrage over the Crown
forces' heavy-handed methods evident even among Protestant
women. Women especially could not countenance this terror.
Although both sides practiced violence, for many of the women,
legally sanctioned torture and murder condemned the Crown.
Never reported as such in the newspapers, it was common
knowledge. Suffragettes in particular felt a moral obligation to
take affirmative action against institutionalized oppression of
whatever form.

And this was a war of terror. Each side justifying acts of
murder and arson as necessary to counter those of the other side.
In Ulster the Anglo-Irish War often looked more a pogrom
against Catholics. Better armed British Crown forces and
Protestant paramilitaries greatly outnumbered the Catholic IRA
in the northern six counties.

Since his sources would pass information to Alison in writing, Sullivan told her to assign code names. Never reveal anyone's real name.

"Here's a book of plays by William Shakespeare. Pick your
code names from his characters."

Never having read Shakespeare, she did more than that.
Even with the archaic English syntax, the stories and the poetry

of the words captivated her. Therefore she hit on the idea to match a character code name to the source's personality.

———

First came the source *Kate*, as in Katherina from *Taming of the Shrew*, followed by *Bianca* from the same play. In real life two sisters, Regina and Patricia Flynn. *Kate* the older quick tempered, headstrong namesake character of the play, and *Bianca*, obedient, quiet, self-effacing. Both worked the telephone exchange for the Belfast RIC headquarters. Both unmarried. Father worked at Harland & Wolff, the mother at a shirt factory. Infrequent church-going Protestants. Decidedly not strident unionists.

Regina, aka *Kate*, a student at Queen's University, worked nights as a telephone operator. Younger Patricia, aka *Bianca*, thought herself luckier than her mother who kept the books at the shirt factory for less pay. Her day shift job provided the opportunity to meet many men.

Regina had her mind set on a career. Yet no matter where education took her, as a woman she could not even vote. Other male-dictated restrictions infuriated her. The Suffrage Society provided the opportunity to interact intellectually with like-minded women.

Patricia hoped for a good husband and a family of her own. A quiet manner belied a quick mind. She not only admired her older sister but came to adopt many of her militant-leaning ideals.

Regina was an easy sell for Alison Kendrick. After confiding about her estranged husband bragging about murdering those people in Newry, Regina Flynn could not sit on the sidelines. Patricia willingly followed her sister's lead. Using code names made it all seem an adventure. The stuff of novels. They didn't connect their work as directly causing people to die.

Both women began pouring out copious amounts of information. Once Sullivan passed along some self-editing guidelines to Kendrick their intelligence value improved beyond mere gossip. Of particular interest were communications involving District Inspector Doyle's RIC Intelligence Division.

Both became adept at listening in after connecting calls.

"Another set-up? Not doing that again for a lousy twenty quid. After Gilly's Tavern, the IRA would know it was me selling them out," The caller said.

"Listen to me, Frankie. This'll be different. I just want you to arrange for one of your girls to...." RIC Sergeant Taggart said.

Unfortunately Regina could not remain connected on the call for fear of being caught eavesdropping. She reported:

> Sgt Taggart called 61-4558 at 9:10pm, 9 Feb. Taggart spoke to a man answering as Frankie. Wanted him to set up something involving one of his girls. Frankie refused saying £20 was not enough after Gilly's Tavern. The IRA would know he was involved. Removed myself from listening in on call at 9:12. Call lasted until 9:25. Kate

Sullivan later identified the significance of this information. Frankie was Frank Dunne. A pimp well-known to the IRA. His prostitutes useful. A Woods source now revealed to be a double agent. Cost the lives of three good men. Almost cost the leadership of the IRA's 1st Belfast Battalion. McCorley would recover from his wound.

A week later Frank Dunne was found tied to a lamp post close to RIC headquarters. Three bullet wounds to the head. *Death to British Informers* read the placard tied around his neck.

———

"I think I have two more sources among my women friends, Trevor," Alison Kendrick boasted after lovemaking on Saturday night. Another weekend with her lover. Everything about her new life was stimulating. Freed from the horrors of those years living in continual dread of her husband.

Dispelling any doubts about what she was now doing, the week after she walked out on her husband he confronted her outside the Harland & Wolff offices. An angry scene that attracted other workers leaving work. Edgar Kendrick could do little more than threaten as a security guard approached. Shaken but with the presence of mind she remembered Sullivan's instructions to make sure she was never followed to her new residence.

"And what code names have you assigned to these new sources?" Sullivan said.

"One is to be *Lady Macbeth,*" Alison grinned. "So can you guess why?"

"Well let's see. Been awhile since I read Shakespeare back in school. *Lady Macbeth* of course is easy. Strong-willed, cunning, a domineering woman. Am I close?"

"Yes. Wouldn't call Sarah domineering though. Kind of use to being in charge the way I see her. Strong opinions. Confident. She's a teacher. Older than most of the others."

"A teacher? How do you think she can be useful?"

Alison smiled again self-assuredly. "Because her husband's an RIC sergeant."

That got Sullivan's interest.

"Catholic they are too. Married a long time. Grown children. Told me her husband's been on the force for twenty-five years. Proud to be a police officer. Confided he was not proud of what the RIC has become.

"When I told her about Edgar and what happened in Newry she fairly exploded with anger. Said her husband hates Inspector Doyle. Calls his constables criminals. This proves it she said."

"Well that is a coup, Alison. And you've recruited another?"

"I'll call her *Desdemona.*"

"Ah, let's see. *Othello* of course. That's a bit more difficult. She's the daughter of a powerful Venetian. Runs off to marry Othello, a Moorish general in the Venetian army. Afraid I don't remember much about her character traits."

"Shakespeare's *Desdemona* is a beauty. Margaret is rather plain but she's a strong woman with her own ideas. Daughter of a prominent Protestant minister. That's why I connected her to the character. She's had a tough go of it. Widow raising one child. Husband was killed at Gallipoli."

"And where does she work?"

"She's a civilian typist at the British Army Headquarters."

"So what makes you think she'll pass along confidential information?"

"He husband was Catholic. Caused her parents to disown her when they married. Seems to resent the Army. Says the letters she got from her husband before he was killed talked badly about the British High Command. Said they didn't care about the soldiers. Not even enough food or water. Ordered suicide attacks against Turkish machine guns on the high ground as she put it. One such attack cost the life of her husband. She also mentioned some difficulties with receiving the army pension. Blames the Army for a lot of what's happening here. Says the Army enables the Protestants to run amuck.

"Haven't yet asked her outright. But I've hinted. We'll see."

"Just be careful, Alison."

"I will. But I trust these women. Hard to explain but we're kind of like sisters. Even if they refuse to help they wouldn't tell on me."

"Just the same, don't trust everyone. No telling what people might do given the right reason."

Like trusting him for the wrong reason.

———

Damon O'Shea tended bar at an upscale public house in central Belfast. The clientele consisted of business and governmental types. A watering hole where salacious inside gossip was the coinage to impress.

O'Shea was the archetypical barman. Everybody's friend. Ready to listen. Shied away from politics. A workingman just doing his job. Pouring cheer to the happy, solace to the sad. But his heart raged with hatred. He was Catholic working at the lower strata in this bastion of Protestant power. Nothing in common with his clientele. Everything here was ethnicity or social class. He was on the wrong side of both. But a bartender was everyone's friend. A sympathetic confidant after a few drinks.

He'd lost a younger brother in the riots in July of the previous year. House was burned by rampaging Protestants. The fire also killed his brother's wife and two-year old child.

A thoughtful man, O'Shea knew he could not take up the gun. His wife and three children relied on his wages. His wife Florence was an equal in the household. He respected her convictions about women's rights. She confided to her husband that a woman in the Society she was friendly with had recently left her abusive husband. A real bad character now a special constable.

"The bastard told her what he'd done. You remember those killed in Newry?" Florence O'Shea said to her husband *"Told her he's the one that shot that priest."*

"Sonofabitch."

"That's not all. Says she passes on information to the IRA."

"She's Catholic?"

"No. Protestant. Hates what's going on though. She's well-liked by the other women, and many are Catholic."

"Can she be trusted, Florence?"

"So he's *Macduff*?" Sullivan said. "Back to *Macbeth* huh? Why *Macduff*?"

"Well *Macduff* 's family was murdered. Got his revenge on *Macbeth*. Damon O'Shea tends bar. His brother and family were killed in the riots. He's Catholic. I'm close to his wife Florence."

Impressed, Sullivan said, "Remarkable work, Alison."

For Kendrick it was the adulation of her lover, the Irish cause only secondary. Trevor Sullivan had awakened her to a life never imagined. Shakespeare, politics, adventure, and the joy of sex.

CHAPTER 24

On his normal morning inspection of the shipyard, Sullivan invited Duncan Gallagher to accompany him. Standing next to the immense Arrol gantry cranes never ceased to be awe-inspiring. The great latticework of steel spanned slipways numbers 2 and 3, rising over 200 feet in height. The birthplace of HMS Olympic and her sister ship HMS Titanic ten years earlier.

"Look at this great beast, Gallagher. What do you see?"

Gallagher looked up. "The biggest crane in the world?"

"Yes. And a troubling thought just occurred. Could be a vulnerable target in this unconventional war. Imagine what a few well-placed explosive charges might do. Our largest slipways would be out of service for a very long time.

"And that's not all. Every part of this shipyard is vital to our enterprise. My god, look at that rioting here last year. What if that had been IRA provocateurs causing a distraction while saboteurs infiltrated to wreck equipment?"

"Yes, Sir. See what you mean. But how do you protect a place that covers this much ground?"

"That I don't know. But I think we'd better find a way before the IRA beats us to it."

A variant on that possibility formed an idea for Sullivan. A deviously clever idea.

———

Sullivan called a meeting with McCorley and Woods. Again they gathered in the small office of the automotive garage.

"That's some useful information your sources are producing, Trevor. As an intelligence professional, care to tell me how you developed them in such a short time?" Woods said.

"As one professional to another let's say that for security reasons that should remain confidential," Sullivan said, but with a smile implying no offense. But Woods should know better than to ask.

McCorley got down to business. His left arm remained in a sling from the bullet taken in the failed attempt to kill Constable Sergeants Rafferty and Taggart. "You called this meeting. What's on your mind, Trevor?"

"Need you to mount an attack on the shipyard."

McCorley and Woods looked at each other with puzzled expressions.

"For what purpose?" McCorley said.

"For the purpose of setting me up where I have reason to work closely with the Crown's security forces. Imagine the intelligence I'd have access to."

"Alright. You've got my attention," McCorley said.

"First of all, a personal critique. You IRA are going about things all wrong. You just trade killings with the security forces and the Protestant militants. What you should be doing is attacking economically vital targets. That's what Crown forces are doing in the south. Burning Catholic creameries and such. Here in Ulster it is Protestant controlled industry that is vulnerable. You'll get further by inflicting economic loss than trading casualties in a war of attrition."

"Interesting idea but that takes real explosives," McCorley said. "And people that know how to use them. But that aside, how's an attack on the shipyard going to get you close to the Army and RIC?"

"Simply this. I work for two powerful men. I'm trusted. I'm an engineer. I manage the shipyard's facilities. With a real attack as the catalyst, it becomes obvious that Harland & Wolff is vulnerable. For that matter other essential services such as the railroad and the electric power generating station. I convince my boss and his fellow business colleagues that there is real risk to economic interests if the IRA steps up attacks. I propose these pillars of industry lobby the security forces to accept our assistance. Assistance in the form of civilian experts like myself to identify vulnerabilities and jointly develop contingency responses with the police and army."

"Shit. You think it'll work?" Woods said excitedly.

"Can't say for sure. But if you pull off an attack at the shipyard it'll sure as hell will scare the shit out of them."

To that comment, McCorley smiled. "I like it. Problem remains, we've got no real explosives. Just Mills grenades."

"What about asking brigade headquarters?" Sullivan offered.

"Fuckin' unlikely. McKelvey wouldn't help an old lady cross the street without knowing why. He'd demand an explanation. Can't very well tell him the real reason without exposing you. Therefore it's me proposing a whole new strategy of blowing up loyalist targets. That's his prerogative as brigade CO. Add to that we're not on the best of terms."

"Okay. So I'll help devise a plan where all you'll have to use is grenades or maybe petrol. Question is will you do it, Roger?" Sullivan said.

McCorley took a moment to reflect. Woods gave a nonverbal expression, *why not*? "You're on, Trevor. You put together a workable plan, we'll deliver."

"By the way, do you maybe have a man working at the shipyard? That'll be helpful."

Woods nodded yes. "Sure do. A good man, a foreman."

———

Sullivan's plan was simple. The target would be slipway number 3, birthplace of the ill-fated HMS Titanic. The keel recently put down to start construction on a new tanker. With no explosives other than Mills grenades there was little that could cause damage to the huge gantry crane itself. Just as well. Sullivan would have hated to bring down the magnificent steel superstructure.

The electric motor-driven hoists however presented a less drastic vulnerability. Two hoists serviced the slipway. Properly placed grenades inside the electric drive motors would produce enough damage to cause their removal for rebuilding by the manufacturer. Probably delay the tanker construction by as much as two months since the large motors were one of a kind. Enough to spark concern with Harland & Wolff management.

At a meeting a week later with McCorley and Woods, Sullivan presented his plan.

"The objective is to disable the drive motors of the two hoists spanning slipway no. 3. Here's a map of the shipyard.

"The motors and the hoist gearing are housed inside small buildings found here and here." Sullivan pointed to marked places on the map. "This guy you have working at the shipyard should know precisely where they're located.

"The plan is this. Only five men needed. One is your man on the inside. Pick a dark place to enter the grounds from the river. I'm suggesting by boat. One man stays with the boat while the other four cut through the chain-link fence. The slipways are close by."

"What about security guards?" McCorley asked.

"Not many. Mostly concentrated on the buildings to the east of Queen's Road. This is a big place. Just don't make noise. There's no night shift working at the slipways.

"Now the wheelhouses for the hoist drives have padlocks. You'll need large cutters to cut through.

"Once inside, close the door. You'll need a lantern to do the work."

"How long inside?" Woods asked.

"I'd say not more than five minutes. Here's a sketch I made of the electric motors. We want to damage the copper windings exposed through the large ventilation openings in the shaft bearing supports bolted to the winding housing.

"You'll place two grenades inside each motor. Place them between these pole pieces as I've shown in this detail. Wedge them
tightly using pieces of wood hammered in with a rubber mallet."

"No, no. That won't work, Trevor. When you pull the grenade pin you've only four seconds before the grenade explodes."

"I'm aware of that. So here's my trick. Secure the grenade release lever from releasing with a couple of wraps of hemp twine
tied tightly. Previously you've soaked the twine in petrol. After
placing the grenade you pull the release pin then light the twine.
Make sure the handle is free to spring open once the twine burns
through. Light both grenades at the same time. Give yourself at
least a minute to get clear so practice to determine how many
wraps of twine.

"Once back to the boat, make your escape to the docks on the
west side of the river. From there you know better about the best
escape route."

Sullivan looked at both men to measure their reaction.

Woods was still looking down at the map when McCorley
said, "Sounds fairly simple. Not sure how much damage these
grenades will do to those motors though."

"Should be enough to damage not only the field windings
but the armature windings and perhaps some of the pole elements. It'll be sufficient to disable the hoists for weeks, Roger.
The real purpose is not massive sabotage but just enough to
scare these people about their vulnerability. If disabling the
slipway isn't enough to light a fire under them then we will
simply follow up with another act of sabotage. Maybe a real fire
at an Atwood textile mill.

"I'll give them a course of action requiring only they pressure the Crown to accept our security planning cooperation. Not
only will that give me insider access to all manner of confidential
information but it might prove to be a new IRA strategy for Ulster."

McCorley said, "What do 'ya mean?"

"I mean that I'll know the details of all security precautions
at every important economic site. I'll know the response plans

for the Army and RIC. Therefore I'll be able to target your attacks to maximum advantage. This is where the loyalists are vulnerable. It's about money."

———

A week later, Sullivan's night maintenance foreman knocked on his apartment door at midnight. He's to come quickly. Something about explosions at one of the slipways.

After spending the early morning hours investigating the damage, Sullivan made his way to the main office at nine o'clock. The place was abuzz about the explosions.

Alison immediately said, "Mr. Llewellyn's been looking for you. I told him you were most likely in the shipyard looking into what's going on."

"Trevor. Please sit down," Llewellyn said. "My lord, what happened last night?"

"Sabotage it seems, Sir. I called in the RIC after examining the damage. They're sure it was the IRA."

"How bad is the damage?"

"Both hoists on slipway number 3 are out of service. Based on my military experience the saboteurs probably used grenades. Fortunately not something more powerful."

"My god. How long before repairs can be made?"

"Hard to say. Probably have to remove the motors and ship them to the manufacturer in Manchester for repair. Might be weeks I should think."

The damage proved lighter than he imagined. Grenades held only small amounts of explosives. Repair would mostly just consist of rewinding the conductors.

"That means we'll fall behind schedule on that tanker."

"Yes, Sir. But if I may, I believe we might be facing an even larger concern, Sir?"

"What do you mean?"

"Been spending the last few hours making my usual daily rounds. This time however with different eyes. A bit unsettling."

Llewellyn leaned forward in his chair from behind his desk. "Unsettling? In what way?"

"Our vulnerability, Sir. We're in troubled times. People being killed every day. Ulster is just as violent as the south. These IRA rebels are fighting a nasty war because they have limited resources. What if they've now turned from killings to inflicting damage on the Ulster economy?"

"Never thought of that threat. That is unsettling."

"Not sure why they haven't adopted that strategy already," Sullivan continued. "The major economic assets in Ulster are loyalist owned. The Catholics have little to lose in like reprisal. In fact, that's exactly what Crown forces are doing in the south. They're destroying economic targets like creameries and shops to cripple support for the insurgents. What's to stop the IRA from applying the same tactics in Belfast or Derry? This might be the first glimpse of such new tactics."

"I follow your thinking, Trevor. Certainly hope you're wrong though. Regardless, I'm not sure what we can do. Put more security guards on at night I suppose."

Sullivan said, "With all due respect, Sir, I believe this calls for something more comprehensive. After considering how better to protect our many vulnerabilities, I gave the problem some thought. Need your opinion about an idea I developed. A management solution rather than specifics. Something proactive to better protect all of us from such a threat."

"Wait a moment. Sir William is in his office this morning. I'd like him to hear what you have to say."

Llewellyn returned with the elderly Chairman of Harland & Wolff, Sir William Pirrie.

Sullivan was also a favorite of the old man who shook his hand warmly.

After Sullivan briefly recounted the details of the damage, Pirrie said, "Malcom says you have some alarming concerns," Pirrie said. "Is there something worse?"

"I'd call it a broader concern, Sir. Thinking about this war I wondered if the shipyard might be in real danger. Once I looked about from this perspective, I truly became concerned. With the right resources, the IRA could do great damage to Harland & Wolff. Last night's attack could have been much worse. Poorly executed, using ineffectual explosives, yet still enough to put the slipway out of service for a time. With proper explosives and expertise there are numerous targets within the shipyard that could cripple operations for an extended period."

Pirrie looked at Llewellyn with an alarmed expression. "Good heavens, Malcom. A disturbing possibility I should say."

Sullivan proceeded to expand on his concerns citing specific vulnerabilities throughout the shipyard. Annotated with engineering jargon for effect, he wanted to make his case using specifics rather than merely general concerns. Tangible elements Pirrie and Llewellyn could relate to. And to scare the hell out of them.

"I see what you mean, Trevor, "Llewellyn said. "What do you propose we can do to better protect the shipyard?"

"Certainly a major undertaking. Needs lots of study. We cover such a large area there's no practical way to make the works into a fortress. Security for us requires an improved first line of defense backed up by prompt response from the Army and police. In short, a comprehensive security partnering between the civilian sector and Crown forces."

"But don't we already have that here in Belfast?" Pirrie said.

"The resources are there, Sir, but in the event of an attack they respond without predefined deployment plans to match the situation. By then it's too late to prevent widespread damage. Consider the riots here at Harland & Wolff last July. Had that been orchestrated by the IRA they could have done serious damage under the diversion of a riot. The Army's response would not have prevented serious sabotage.

"Detailed study and analysis is needed to identify vulnerabilities. From there we make structural changes for better protection. But most importantly, detailed response planning needs to be developed jointly with the security forces.

"Both the Army and the RIC move slowly. They typically deploy in large force. That just takes too long. Mobile strike forces need to respond quickly to predetermined locations. There are many targets in Belfast that might be crippled if the IRA adopts sabotage as a weapon. Lots of ex-army sappers from the Great War out there with expertise. Preplanned immediate Crown forces response to differing emergency scenarios is the only means of effective defense."

Pirrie said. "You certainly have our attention, Sullivan. So what is it you suggest we do?"

"Go to the Army and RIC and layout our concerns. Suggest that a commission of civilian experts be organized to identify potential infrastructure targets. Assess specific vulnerabilities of those targets. Not just the shipyard but the port itself, railroad operations, power generation, important factories.

"Being ex-military myself, I suspect they will not welcome the intrusion into their sphere of authority. But you gentlemen carry considerable authority. This is not solely a military or police matter, it's a matter of the Northern Ireland economy."

Both Pirrie and Llewellyn agreed enthusiastically with Sullivan's proposal.

"In the meantime, Trevor, please begin work on identifying concerns here at the shipyard. Anything that can be done immediately to improve security is to have top priority," Llewellyn said. "And I'm sure I also speak for Sir William in saying well done. First-rate thinking."

"Uncommonly creative, Sullivan," Pirrie added.

It was not essential for the IRA to adopt sabotage as a strategy in Belfast or Derry as long as the threat appeared possible. Sullivan's purpose was to promote himself into a role where he could interact with security forces on operational issues. If his superiors were successful in organizing the power brokers in Northern Ireland no doubt he would become part of whatever civilian body was formed. The perfect cover from which to gather high-level intelligence.

———

Malcom Llewellyn wasted little time moving on Sullivan's proposal. He first wanted to muster support among other Ulster power brokers on the idea before approaching the British Army and RIC.

Industrialist Phillip Atwood, the number two man in the Ulster Unionist Party, and the President of the Ulster Unionist Party, James Craig, were both enthusiastic after Sullivan explained the idea. It would further provide them more provincial control over security. That would soon prove more critical as Home Rule placed more provincial responsibility on Northern Ireland while officially separating them from Southern Ireland. They also anticipated British Crown security forces might be cool to the idea of working in partnership with civilians.

As the senior political official of the group, Craig recruited two others in advance of approaching the Army and police. Already a target of IRA attacks, the Managing Director of the Northern Counties Railway Committee enthusiastically welcomed improved security measures. The Assistant to the British Lord Lieutenant for Ireland responsible for British administration in the northern counties found the idea consistent with the Prime Minister's efforts to bolster security in Ulster.

Craig accepted the task of assembling a meeting. All agreed that Sullivan should present the plan. Not only did he possess technical expertise as a civil engineer managing the shipyard facilities of Harland & Wolff, but he also had extensive railway management experience. Although a civilian, Sullivan added credibility as a former professional army officer.

The meeting was to be a working lunch at the Ulster Club. When Malcom Llewellyn and Sullivan arrived they found James Craig with another man engaged in conversation in the private dining room.

"Mr. Sullivan, good to see you again," Craig said as he shook hands with Sullivan. "Let me introduce Mr. William Lancaster. Mr. Lancaster is first secretary to the Lord Lieutenant for Ireland. A good friend of Ulster."

The British Lord Lieutenant was the most senior British administrator governing Ireland. Mr. Lancaster split his time between Dublin Castle and Belfast. Important enough to merit two armed bodyguards standing outside in the hallway Craig said.

"My compliments, Mr. Sullivan. Sir James gave me the brief of what you're proposing. Sound thinking. Makes thorough sense to bring together all possible expertise if the IRA should turn to such dastardly tactics. Although I'm told they probably lack the means."

Sullivan said, "Perhaps that's been the case, Mr. Lancaster. But it wouldn't take much to acquire the right explosives. The attack a week ago on Harland & Wolff certainly makes this more than an academic precaution."

"Your point is well-taken. Her Majesty's government wants to do all possible for Northern Ireland to thrive once Home Rule takes effect next year. No matter how things play out in the south."

Sullivan approached Llewellyn and Sir Phillip Atwood. "Gentlemen. Might I suggest that we take seats around the table in somewhat random fashion? Don't want the security people all sitting on one side of the table."

Atwood immediately seized on Sullivan's point. "Of course. That would look like this is a negotiation. We want to win them over before we resort to stronger methods. Mr. Sullivan has the makings of a politician among his other skills, Malcom."

The security commanders were the last to arrive, punctually at eleven-thirty. This included Brig. General Kenneth Hopkins, Commander of the British Army 15th Infantry Brigade, his adjutant Lt. Colonel Samuel Baker, Charles Wickham the Royal Irish Constabulary Chief of Police for Ulster, and Colonel Fred Crawford, newly appointed Commander of the Ulster Special Constabulary.

Sir James Craig thanked everyone for attending then made opening remarks to set the purpose of the meeting.

"Before I turn this over to Mr. Sullivan, I want to stress the concern all of us feel. As much as I believe Home Rule is not in the best interest for Ulster, it will soon come into being. While London will not abandon Northern Ireland, we shall face a somewhat different status within the United Kingdom.

"It is therefore incumbent that Northern Ireland assumes greater provincial control in all aspects of economic and political life. That necessarily includes security.

"The recent attack on Harland & Wolff could be the harbinger of a new IRA strategy to destabilize Northern Ireland economically. The nationalists harbor the illusion that a separate Northern Ireland could be forced to fail thereby becoming part of a greater independent Ireland. That of course will never happen.

"We are here today to propose a plan that we believe will measurably enhance security to vital elements of Ulster's economic structure. It is the brainchild of Mr. Trevor Sullivan, the manager of Harland & Wolff's facilities. Before I turn this over to Mr. Sullivan let me cite his impressive credentials."

After Craig's introduction, Sullivan took over. Unlike Craig, he did not wander into political rhetoric but succinctly laid out his proposal. Recognizing the inherent urgency, he told the attendees he had taken the liberty to create an organizational format from the standpoint of the civilian sector. Identified participating essential civilian expertise. Possible threat targets. Fundamental changes that should immediately prove helpful.

"Let me be clear gentlemen. What I'm suggesting in no way encroaches on the prerogatives of your respective commands. This civilian advisory commission will be tasked only with identifying potential vulnerabilities vital to the economic well-being of Northern Ireland. That process will also recommend improvements that can be done by the private sector to mitigate threats. Yet most of these important assets cannot be protected from sabotage solely by physically means.

"The commission will provide the security forces with detailed plans identifying areas of concern. A system will be jointly devised for alerting the security forces in the event of an attack. That alert can now be analyzed with a clear understanding of the tactical situation. How, in what form, in what strength, to what locations your forces should respond will remain the prerogative of your respective commands, gentlemen. This information will allow you the ability to develop detailed advance threat response procedures. The objective being quick response to mitigate damage by insurgent attack. "

There followed a lively back and forth of questions and answers. Gauging from the tone, Sullivan was pleased with the reception to his idea.

Not surprisingly, the British Army command embraced the idea. With Home Rule their role will soon drastically change. That was the basis for Westminster granting Irish Home Rule. With only worsening IRA successes, the war presented an untenable continuing drain on the British treasury. Winning the Anglo-Irish War through an overwhelming military campaign was economically prohibitive. Nor did the rest of the United Kingdom have the stomach for the continuing Irish problem. That meant Northern Ireland could not solely rely on the British Army.

Wickham of the RIC and Crawford of the Special Constabulary were less enthusiastic. While not outright hostile to Sullivan's proposal they rebutted with bureaucratic organizational arguments. Craig and Atwood forcefully countered leaving the police commanders with the implication that this should not be construed a debate but rather a fait accompli. The decision already made by those that held political power.

A lunch with good French wine created a tone of conviviality. By the end of lunch, making no pretext to poll the commanders of the various security forces, Craig asked Sullivan to explain the next step after announcing that Sullivan would head what would be known as the Security Advisory Commission. "Mr. Sullivan."

"Thank you, Sir James. So as to not become bureaucratic, the Commission will be kept to a minimum. All the members shall be both technically expert and in management positions responsible for their respective operations. No staff. Each member uses his own personnel resources. This of course will include me as well as the operations managers of all the rail lines, the power generating stations, and the port masters and fire brigade chiefs of Belfast and Derry. Mr. Atwood and Mr. Llewellyn will take on the responsibility of identifying important industrial locations and recruiting the appropriate experts.

"From the various security services, I would request a senior officer be assigned to act as liaison with the Committee."

Craig interjected, "Considering the urgency in moving forward, I'd like to suggest perhaps you gentlemen might identify those officers before you leave today?"

Craig was not only pushy but carried political clout. If the police commanders didn't like this they had little choice. Craig had direct access and considerable influence with Lloyd George the Prime Minister. Craig conceivably would head the Northern Ireland government under Home Rule.

Sullivan's inspiration proved a masterful intelligence coup. No need to cultivate social contacts as his sole means of acquiring random pieces of intelligence. He would now enjoy access to army and police headquarters. The fox reconnoitering the henhouse from inside.

Beyond that, the idea of the IRA attacking vulnerable economic targets in Northern Ireland increasingly seemed a logical progression of the war for independence. With his strategic vision, why had Michael Collins not pursued what to Sullivan seemed an obvious opportunity in industrialized Ulster?

Perhaps Collins did not appreciate the inherent different theaters of war of Ulster compared to the rest of Ireland. Or perhaps the wily fox was playing a subtler longer game against the British. Regardless, Sullivan would possess a detailed accounting of economic targets in the North vulnerable to sabotage. He would also know how to circumvent Crown security forces contingency responses.

Communications meant for Collins followed the same route as Sullivan's local intelligence conduit. Seamus Woods was the clearinghouse. Information intended for Collins was addressed for *Aunt Kathleen*. A common enough name. In fact it was conveyed by courier to Kathleen Clarke in Dublin. As everyone had a code name, Sullivan had assigned Collins as *Prospero*. The sorcerer from Shakespeare's *The Tempest*.

Prospero,

Successful entry into the English King's castle. Accepted as a knight ready to protect their properties. With recent event they now fear more such attacks. Perhaps unfounded but who knows? Not at all certain why Ó Coileáin has not seized on such a strategy. Might greatly further the cause by destabilizing the foreigner's northern kingdom. All that is required are the tools and the will. I am the means. Privy to their secrets of defense. I remain in the service of the wizard. Hamlet

CHAPTER 25

"So who did the bombing at the shipyards, Inspector?" Commissioner Wickham said having called District Inspector Doyle to his office.

"Had to be McCorley's bunch, Sir."

"Had to be? That means you don't actually know, am I correct?"

Doyle bristled but gave no visible indication. "All our usual sources seem to know nothing about it. But of course McCorley often goes off independently."

"And of course you still haven't been able to nail him either. Christ, you're supposed to be running an intelligence division. I'm tired of hearing about this McCorley. Now we have a new irritation stemming from this shipyard sabotage incident.

"Spooked the civilians. Especially Llewellyn and Atwood. Afraid the IRA is about to attack their businesses. Got Dublin Castle and Craig on their side. Anyway, they're setting up something called the Security Advisory Commission. A bunch of thick civilians that'll be assessing potentially vulnerable targets the IRA might go after. But I can see it won't end there. Next they'll want a say in our tactical deployment."

"How's the Army feel about this?" Doyle said.

"The Army doesn't give a shit. They'll do what Whitehall orders, and Whitehall will do what Craig says. The Army will be

274

taking a less active rule I suspect under Home Rule. This Security Advisory Commission is just another step to make the IRA our problem.

"I've assigned Inspector O'Brien to be the RIC liaison to this Commission."

"O'Brien? Don't see how O'Brien can be of much use to us, Sir. Too sympathetic to Catholics for my liking."

"His use is to keep these meddling civilians out of our hair, Inspector. O'Brien's a bureaucrat. Just the sort of buffer I want between us and this Sullivan character."

"Sullivan?"

"A new manager at Harland & Wolff. Irish-American. An engineer. Runs the shipyard facilities. Former professional soldier. Qualified enough to be a pain in the ass. He'll head up this group.

"So you're going to take some of the steam out of their overreaction to this sabotage at the shipyard. I need you to arrest the saboteurs. Doesn't matter if they're the right sods or not. But make it look good. Am I making myself understood, Inspector?"

Doyle nodded, "Yes, Sir. Perfectly."

Back at his own office, John Doyle was in a foul mood. The dressing-down by Wickham would flow downward to his subordinates. Sergeants Rafferty and Taggart sat in front of his desk.

"Still no specifics on the fuckers that did the shipyard bombing?" Doyle said.

Taggart answered, "No, Sir.

"As the police intelligence division we're expected to produce actionable information. Wickham's got his knickers in a knot. So I'm not waiting while your people continue to masturbate calling it police work. Here's what you're to do. Find me two IRA employed at the shipyard. If you can't identify any known IRA then just pick two Catholics.

"You're to make raids on their homes. Both are to be shot resisting arrest. Of course you'll find Mill grenades and a map of the shipyard. I want it done at night within the next two days. Understood?"

———

Since the homes of the unfortunate victims were both well inside Catholic neighborhoods south of Falls Road, the RIC arranged for large backup reinforcements from the Special Constabulary. Rafferty would lead one raid, Taggart the other.

One victim had a cousin known to be IRA. The other was just a Catholic.

Two Crossley tenders carrying RIC and Special Constabulary rolled up to the first house.

Taggart pounded on the door. When a young man answered the door, Taggart and Edgar Kendrick pushed into the house followed by several special constables.

"What do' ya want?" The man said standing in his underwear.

"Your name Brian Lafferty?"

"That's my name."

"Work at the shipyard?"

"Yes."

Taggart looked at Kendrick and nodded.

Without hesitation Kendrick shot the man twice in the chest.

A screaming woman rushed down from upstairs. Seeing her husband she knelt down beside him wailing.

Taggart said to Kendrick, "Search upstairs."

Moments later Kendrick came down the stairs with a pillow case containing something.

"Look what I found, Sergeant. Two grenades." Kendrick held up the pillow case.

"Found a gun in this drawer," Taggart said standing next to a sideboard in the parlor. 'Good thing you shot him before he could reach it."

The evidence of course planted. Solely for the benefit of the special constables now crowded into the small parlor to later make official statements.

The second victim was an older man with a wife and four children. Sergeant Rafferty made little pretext about staging a scene for the other constabulary witnesses in his entourage.

Roughly escorted out of his house by a trusted constable, Rafferty simply shot the man in the back of the head on the front steps.

Shot attempting to escape. None of these part-time constables would testify otherwise if this ever came to an official inquiry. Not against someone of Sergeant George Rafferty's reputation.

———

What followed was a continuation of reprisal killings. As both sides settled into this routine the killings became less discriminating, increasingly brutal. Victims didn't have to be connected with any specific outrage just the wrong association in the wrong circumstance.

"Seems that we've already made headway in finding the saboteurs of your shipyard, Mr. Sullivan," RIC Inspector O'Brien said. It was Sullivan's first meeting with the RIC's liaison to his Committee. "Not surprising since our intelligence people report it was a poorly planned attack."

"I would agree with that, Inspector. Unfortunately that doesn't diminish the possible greater threat. Set enough of these saboteurs loose and they could do real damage. It's that sort of attack we in the civilian sector need to better protect against. It's the more well-planned attack that will require support from the security forces.

"However, that was very good police work to have uncovered two of the perpetrators so quickly. How did that come about?"

"Can't of course reveal the details but the credit goes to the Intelligence Division."

Sullivan already knew the two murdered victims had nothing to do with the bombing. Weren't even IRA. McCorley was beside himself with rage. Something must be done about Doyle's police unit. Need to eliminate his whole band of murders like Collins did by killing Dublin Castle's intelligence detectives the prior November.

Sullivan said, "Obviously they're doing effective work. Who heads that Division?"

"District Inspector Doyle."

"Oh yes. I've heard the name. Too bad the suspects couldn't have been taken alive. Might have revealed vital information. Maybe I should introduce myself to Inspector Doyle. He might prove useful in my efforts."

"I'm afraid that is contrary to the protocols directed by Commissioner Wickham. All interaction with your group must come through my office. I'm sure you can understand the work of the Intelligence Division is highly confidential."

"Very well, Inspector. I understand perfectly. Perhaps you might take a few moments to advise me of the locations, numbers, and response time of the RIC in relation to the shipyards and the railyards? Those installations are of the most immediate concern. And perhaps how do you go about coordinating a response with the other security forces in the event of a serious large-scale attack?"

"A large-scale attack? By the IRA? I think that unlikely."

"Perhaps. However things are changing in this war. Settlement of hostilities possibly in the southern counties. Either Home Rule will come about or at least a truce. If that happens, no reason that southern IRA forces might not come north in force. We need to be prepared."

A good argument to make to the Special Constabulary and British Army for his inclusion into emergency response deployment details.

Lt. Colonel Samuel Baker the adjutant for the British Army's 15th Infantry Brigade whom Sullivan met at the kickoff luncheon was assigned as liaison to the Committee. An immediate rapport developed as one soldier to another after sharing respective experiences in the Great War. Seeing little threat to confidentiality, and knowing the commanding general's views, Baker shared surprisingly detailed information.

Unlike RIC Inspector O'Brien and Army Colonel Baker, the Ulster Special Constabulary liaison was less agreeable. Major Morgan Powell, another ex-British Army officer, commanded the Ulster Special Constabulary for the eastern counties of Antrim and Down which included Belfast.

"Mr. Sullivan, I'll do what I can to help you but you must understand I have my hands full. The Special Constabulary was created to provide the hammer to smash the IRA. Our mission is to take the fight to them," Powell said.

"I recognize that, Major. But I too have a mission. Keep the economic viability of Ulster secure. Our respective charges are not mutually exclusive. Consider a scenario where the IRA begins retaliating against economic targets. Your command would be forced to respond by posting guards. Not probably effective, but still a change of mission that might be politically forced on you.

"I'm a former army officer. If I were IRA that's what I'd do. Pin your troops down to garrison duty instead of rapid response like the Auxiliary forces deployed in the south.

"I know how the politics works. I'm just looking to give you better tools to work with, Major."

Powell absorbed Sullivan's logic. "An interesting argument, Mr. Sullivan. Perhaps with some merit. Let's see where your work leads. I'll do what I can without compromising confidential information or diverting resources."

"That's all I can ask, Major. And I should complement you on the fine intelligence work that caught those two involved in the shipyard sabotage. Too bad they couldn't be questioned. Might have revealed who's behind this."

"Well that was the work of the RIC's Intelligence unit. My special constables just supported the raids."

"My compliments then on the inter-service cooperation. I've seen that to be a problem in my experience. I assume that the credit should go to District Inspector Doyle's Intelligence Division?"

Powell said, "You know Inspector Doyle?"

"Only by reputation."

CHAPTER 26

BELFAST, IRELAND – APRIL, 1921

Sullivan woke at the sound of birds from the half open window on a sunny spring Saturday morning. Alison Kendrick continued to sleep soundly. One naked leg stretched outside the bedding. A week of sexual abstinence while working alongside her lover every day made Friday nights special for her. Her newfound sexual identity proved transformative. In the short span of her affair with Sullivan her self-esteem increased in proportion to her lack of inhibitions in bed.

For Sullivan the affair was quite another matter.

Sexual relations with Kendrick were a complex mix of conflicting emotions. Nothing more than sex. A conscious act even though she physically aroused him. Moderately attractive, she was an able sex partner. For his part he was consciously tender in his attentions to appease his guilt for using her in such a cruel deception. His self-disgust heightened with her deepening emotional dependency.

Post coital periods were the most difficult. While she chattered away, he forced himself to act out his conflicted role of lover, boss, and spymaster. Aware that his psychological distress was his own making. Emotionally driven choices not fully understood leaving him contorted into someone unrecognizable. Everything now viewed through a distorted lens.

Unpleasantly he contemplated the premise of *The Strange Case of Dr. Jekyll and Mr. Hyde.* Had he descended into the persona of Hyde? Had Maureen's death unleashed latent dark forces beyond his control?

The weekend routine with Kendrick became a habit. Lovemaking commenced on Friday night usually preceding dinner. She simply couldn't constrain herself. Following each bout of weekend lovemaking became the time to explain her week's espionage activities. Full of more detail than necessary. Her way of sharing in this adventure.

This night she delivered some surprising news.

"I think I might have two possible new sources. Just met them. They're new to our group. Different I should say."

"How's that?"

"Well they're not what you'd call working class," She said teasingly. "You'll know one of them."

"Oh? And who might that be?"

"Caroline Llewellyn. Mr. Llewellyn's daughter."

That was a surprise.

"A real rebel. Been away in Europe the last few months. Wintering in the south of France if you can imagine. Spent time in London. She even met Sylvia Pankhurst there. You know who she is don't you?"

"Prominent in the suffrage movement I believe?"

"More than that. She's a loud voice for all sorts of rights for women."

"So how might Miss Llewellyn provide useful information?"

"Because she rubs shoulders with all the society types. The people that run Belfast."

"But why should she confide information of interest contrary to her social circle?"

"Well you'd have to hear her talk. No fan of the British. Hates what happening to Catholics."

"Does she know you work at Harland & Wolff?"

"Yes. She knows who you are too. Says Mr. Llewellyn speaks often about you. She's a pretty one. So don't be getting any ideas, Trevor."

"And there's another person?"

Kendrick smiled broadly. "And this'll floor you. Her name's Meredith Crawford. Came with Caroline Llewellyn. Anyway, does the name ring any bells?"

"You surely don't mean the Crawford that's the new head of the Special Constabulary?"

"The same. His niece. Works as a personnel clerk at her uncle's headquarters. An unhappy young woman. Expelled from university. Claims it was for political agitation but she wasn't specific. Parents told her she'd have to pay her way in life or get married. Don't think she's the marrying kind."

"Be careful with both these two. They might not have the same motivations as your other sources. Sound like a couple of spoiled rich women. Just listen to their gossip for anything useful. Don't actually recruit them. This is not an adventure. It's serious life and death business, Alison."

But to Alison Kendrick this was a grand adventure. Something out of a romance novel. The spying adding spice to her clandestine affair with the handsome Trevor Sullivan.

"I'll be careful. Anyway I've already selected code names for them. For Caroline, she'll be *Portia* from *The Merchant of Venice*. Rich, intelligent, quick-witted. And for Meredith, she'll be *Jessica*, Shylock's daughter.

"How's that for typecasting?"

"Like I said, you're becoming quite the spy. Speaking of which do you have any information to pass on?"

"Of course."

She bounded out of bed naked throwing Sullivan's flannel robe around her. From her purse she extracted a sheaf of notes.

"Lots this week. Most of it makes no sense to me. Is any of this stuff I gather important?"

"I believe so, Alison. These bits of information are like pieces of a puzzle. Individually they're meaningless. Even to me. But the people I pass them to have more pieces. Together they start to form the picture."

"Well read this one. It caught my attention. About that crooked copper Edgar's working for."

RIC Inspector Doyle has recently taken up residence at the Hotel Grosvenor. Romantically involved with a buxom opera singer, Playbill pictures suggest this most likely is the new Italian singer Angelina Nicoletti. Macduff.

Two RIC inspectors dressed in mufti were enjoying pints of Guinness at the end of the bar. Tending bar was Damon O'Shea, aka Macduff.

"Did you here that bloody Dracula left his mausoleum? The fucker's taken a room at the Hotel Grosvenor."

"Ya don't say? Must be feeling bold to come out into the daylight, him living like a monk in the barracks. What came over him?" The other said obviously knowing Doyle's nickname.

"What else, a woman of course. The fucker's at least human."

"Well I'll be. And who is this Lady Dracula?"

"A singer at the opera I'm told. One of Doyle's intelligence bunch is chummy with one of my sergeants. My guy says he's seen her. Big knockers. Give Doyle a real handful in each of his big mits."

"So the mysterious Inspector Doyle has taken up with a tart.

Both RIC officers had a good laugh.

"Another round, gentlemen?" O'Shea said coming round the end of the bar.

O'Shea had been feigning some task just out of sight of the two officers. This Inspector Doyle was known to be connected with that outrage in Newry.

Sullivan said to Alison, "*Macduff*. The bartender husband of one of your friends?"

"Yes. So this Inspector Doyle's got himself a girlfriend. What good is that information?" Alison said.

"Hard to say. I don't have the other pieces to that puzzle either. But anything related to Inspector Doyle is of interest I'm told."

———

That Monday evening Sullivan was again back at the garage with McCorley and Woods.

McCorley said, "This news of Doyle is encouraging. Maybe now we can rid ourselves of this monster."

"Roger, you haven't been successful with getting any of his men. Doyle himself will be even more difficult," Sullivan said. "Just because he's no longer holed up in a police barracks doesn't necessarily make him vulnerable."

"We still must try. Something has changed. Doyle's becoming bolder. Look at those two he had murdered for your escapade at the shipyard."

"Were they even IRA?" Sullivan said.

"No. Just a couple of unfortunate blokes. Worked at the shipyard so that's why they tagged them."

Seamus Woods said, "It was Doyle's constables that did this. Rafferty and Taggart personally. One of my people showed photos to the grieving widows."

"Trevor, I know that killing Doyle isn't going to stop this murder gang of his," McCorley said. "But this is a war of propaganda. Taking out the random constable or special doesn't even get much newspaper space."

"And you can't win that kind of war anyway, Roger. Too many of the enemy. Too many unionist supporters. They control the newspapers. You can't keep the police bottled up in their barracks in Belfast like what's being done in the rural south.

"Something grander is needed for a propaganda campaign," Sullivan said. "Any word from Collins on sabotaging economic targets?"

"Not really. Sent him the stuff you prepared. The Big Fellow wrote back that it was an interesting idea. Timing might not yet be right though. Said McKelvey wasn't keen on the idea. Fears a backlash from Catholics that might be put out of work. McKelvey warned it would bring out the British Army in force. Well fuck all I say, isn't that what this is all about?"

Sullivan knew the war in the South was entering a critical stage. The British were on their heels. De Valera or even Collins himself might be having secret talks with the British. Perhaps Collins felt it wasn't the time to push harder in the north. At least for now.

"Then I guess that's where things stand. Still, the role I have heading this bullshit Security Advisory Committee allows me all sorts of access to senior security commanders. Get to poke about and ask all sorts of questions. No telling what I'll be able to pick up if I'm creative."

Woods said, "A stroke of genius pulling off that stunt at your shipyard."

"Unfortunately it cost two innocent men their lives. You're right about needing to do something about Doyle, Roger. But his intelligence operation presents an even more pressing problem."

"How's that?" McCorley asked.

Sullivan said, "This Ulster Special Constabulary. Thousands more well-equipped enemy. Mechanized mobility with machine guns. Just as bad as the Black & Tans and Auxiliaries. But they're a newly assembled force. Ill-trained Ulster Volunteers. All are Protestants unlike the regular RIC. Harder to develop informers from inside."

"Right you are there," Woods said.

"But the Specials are newly organized. New command leadership. By necessity they must get their intelligence through the regular RIC. Inspector Doyle's division. Since the IRA isn't enthused about my idea to go after economic targets, let me offer another suggestion. Do what Mick Collins did in Dublin last year, Roger."

"You mean Bloody Sunday? Killing all those detectives from Dublin Castle? Christ almighty, what do 'ya think we've been trying to do?" McCorley said.

"You've been going about it the wrong way, Roger."

"What do 'ya mean?"

"Listen. I'm not criticizing. Just saying you need new tactics. Collins took out the opposition intelligence by decimating their ranks. Enough to scare off the rest. Blinded the British. It took two things. First of all he had a wide-ranging network of spies to develop opportunities to take out his targets. Secondly, he had his own killing squad. A trained group committed solely to the task of selective assassination.

"Now things are different in Belfast compared with Dublin. You don't have the necessary intelligence sources to chart the movements of Doyle's unit. No offense Seamus."

Woods made an acknowledging expression.

"My meager efforts won't change that. But I'll get back to that. And you haven't yet created a specifically trained squad for the task. Guys trained to shoot the enemy at point-blank. Disciplined guys that can follow the plan coolly no matter what's going on. Smart guys able to adapt and improvise."

"A tall order, Trevor." McCorley said with some sarcasm. "You have a suggestion or just making a speech?"

"Easy, Roger, I'm on your side. I'm offering whatever help I can. I know a little about this. Been in some tight spots. Know weapons. I'd guess you have lads just as capable as Michael Collins does. Yourself and Seamus for starters.

"I'm suggesting forget these random reprisals. Leave that to McKelvey and the Brigade. Focus your battalion on taking out high-value enemy targets."

McCorley digested the idea for a moment before saying, "To go this route, what do you suggest we do?"

"Identify every member of Doyle's murder unit. I'll see if I can help there with my sources. Find people to assign to each one of them. Where they live, where they drink, their habits, where might they be vulnerable, everything. Write it all down till we know these bastards like old friends. Start with Doyle now that he's not holed up in the Springfield Road barracks. Rafferty and Taggart especially.

"Identify who might be right for this work. Only need a handful of the right sort. Start training them. Make sure they have the right weapons. Enough ammunition for practice. You'll need an isolated place in the country where these lads can do some shooting."

"Still would like to take out Doyle himself," McCorley said.

"I agree," Sullivan said. "I'll see what intelligence I can add. Since Doyle now has a lady friend maybe he'll get careless."

———

The following day, Sullivan's boss Malcom Llewellyn stopped by his office to ask that he join him for lunch at the Ulster Club. Just Llewellyn and Phillip Atwood. A follow up to see how matters were progressing with the new security commission.

Situated at a back table in the main downstairs dining room, Sullivan said, "A good start I should say, gentlemen. Already started work of course at the shipyard. Met with my counterparts at the port and the power company. Introduced myself to the security liaisons of the various Crown forces."

"How'd that go?" Atwood said.

"Reasonably well. The Army is supportive. The RIC and the Special Constabulary more guarded. Cited organizational constraints about preserving certain information as confidential."

"Stupid louts. Listen, Sullivan, if you need some leverage to prod them, let me know."

"I will, Sir Phillip. Let's see if it comes to that. Would rather they bend to persuasion before I resort to more heavy-handed methods."

As they lifted wineglasses, a female said loudly, "Why there's father."

All three turned toward the voice from the other side of the dining room.

"Ah, my daughter, Caroline," Malcom Llewellyn said a bit surprised.

The men stood as Caroline Llewellyn approached on the arm of a young man about her own age. See kissed her father and Atwood on the cheek. Her escort shook hands with Llewellyn and Atwood.

"My Dear, let me introduce Mr. Trevor Sullivan. And this is Mr. Herbert Townsend."

"A pleasure to meet you Miss Llewellyn," Sullivan said taking her outstretched hand then shaking Townsend's hand.

Malcom Llewellyn insisted his daughter and Townsend join their table.

"So glad to finally meet you, Mr. Sullivan," Caroline said. "Father often speaks of you. My condolences for the terrible loss of your wife last year. So terribly tragic. How is it you've even been able to function?"

"Thank you, Miss Llewellyn. Thanks in no small part to your father, I've endured the unendurable. Thrown myself into my work as it were."

"And I couldn't be more delighted having him at Harland & Wolff," Malcom Llewellyn said.

Turning to Townsend, Llewellyn said, "Good to see you, Herbert. And I'm sure you're glad Caroline is back in Belfast.

"Mr. Townsend is a partner in the law firm of Townsend & Lansdale. His father is the managing partner in London. Herbert runs their Belfast office."

Townsend smiled and placed his hand lightly on Caroline Llewellyn's shoulder.

Sullivan thought he detected a slight expression of annoyance on Caroline's face.

"My daughter has been away in Europe for the last several months. Accompanied by Phillip's daughter, Kimberly."

"Ostensibly acting as chaperons to each other," Atwood said. "I daresay that being an arrangement of convenience."

Caroline Llewellyn took no offense at the remark. "Chaperons? Nothing of the sort, Sir Phillip. Only men think in those Victorian terms. Kimberly's my best friend. Provence and Paris would be no fun all alone."

"You know, my dear, Mr. Sullivan lived in Paris before coming to Ireland," her father said.

"*Vous ne trouvez pas Belfast provincial après avoir vécu à Paris?*" Caroline said in accented French.

"J'aime Paris. Mais Belfast a son propre charme," Sullivan responded.

"We must speak further, Mr. Sullivan. I doubt there's anyone else in Belfast fluent in French. I miss it already," she said offering Sullivan a warm smile. Perhaps subtly flirtatious but he might be mistaken.

Herbert Townsend didn't appear amused by the interchange. Sullivan detected a possessiveness clearly not reciprocated by Caroline Llewellyn.

That impression became further obvious as they left the Ulster Club. Caroline grasped Sullivan's hand in both of hers and said, "I hope we'll be seeing you again soon, Mr. Sullivan. Daddy must invite you to dinner sometime. Mother so enjoys entertaining interesting people. And she too loves Paris."

Returning to the shipyard in Llewellyn's chauffeured car, Malcom Llewellyn confided, "And now you've met my headstrong daughter, Trevor."

"A charming and beautiful woman, Sir."

"No question about that. I'm glad she's back home though. Also glad she didn't become embroiled in some scandal with her roaming about France. Wouldn't have been the first time. And Sir Phillip's daughter is definitely no chaperon. Looks to Caroline like an older sister. A role model that I hesitate to say is unconventional to say the least."

"Mr. Townsend seemed very attached to her. A potential fiancé perhaps?"

"Unlikely. He may harbor such aspirations but I don't believe Caroline does. Too bad really. A good match I would think. First-rate family. Young Townsend's a smart solicitor. But not smart enough to turn Caroline into a wife I fear. I believe she uses him as a convenient social escort. Doesn't seem much of a romance on her part. Can't see Caroline ever marrying him."

So this was Alison's prospective new source *Portia*. Under different circumstances Caroline Llewellyn's flirtation might have touched a responsive note. Instead it only signaled risk as an unnecessary complication.

CHAPTER 27

"I'm not waiting any longer, Trevor. I want a go after Doyle himself. Too good an opportunity to pass up now that he's keeping time outside his headquarters," McCorley said to Sullivan.

This time the meeting was at a safe house selected by Woods. Sullivan requested the change of venue. Told McCorley and Woods he didn't want to keep to a routine where he could be recognized.

"Okay, Roger. But you need a better plan than that fiasco that got you shot."

"That's why I'm asking for your help. You can move about in places that Seamus's sources can't. And you've done something of this sort I'm led to believe."

Sullivan remained silent.

"Been looking for help. People that know how to do this sort of thing. Even asked Michael Collins if he could spare some people to come to Belfast. Know what he suggested?

Sullivan still said nothing.

"Said to see you. Said you were as good as they come. Said you were an expert with a gun. Said to ask you about what happened in France. And what happened in Derry."

Sullivan gave thought to the matter. He was now fully into this war. Maureen was dead. Was the role of gentleman spy sufficient while others risked their lives? Was he becoming complacent with his new place among the Belfast elite? A romantic affair with a passionate woman agent? If he was serious how could he shy from getting his hands dirty again?

"When I was at the United States Military Academy I was pistol champion my last two years. A natural talent I guess. In the Great War I found myself stranded with what the newspapers called the *Lost Battalion*. Got hold of a German sniper rifle. Killed a lot of Germans for which I won medals. So yes, I'm expert with firearms."

"And what exactly happened in Derry?" McCorley said.

Sullivan sighed deciding there was no reason not to recount what happened. He'd already decided to actively help them. District Inspector John Doyle deserved to die every bit as much as Fergus Croft.

"Fergus Croft killed my wife. So I killed him."

"Holy shit!" Seamus Woods said. "You mean you actually pulled the trigger?"

"Yes,"

"And how'd you pull that off?" McCorley said.

"Disguised myself as a British Army officer. Shot the bastard in his office at Foyle Port. Killed two others and escaped in a hired car."

"You did this alone without O'Donnell's help?" McCorley asked with an expression of awe.

"O'Donnell provided the necessary intelligence. But easier for me to make the hit alone given the circumstances."

"My god. I see what Collins meant. Will you help us get Doyle?"

Sullivan nodded yes. "The first thing is to put together your special squad. Same thing as Collins did. Tough men. Smart men. Committed. Proven cool under fire. If they've killed before, all the better. But killing up close is different than with a rifle. Keep it to a small number. Best they're men without families."

"I understand," McCorley said. "Know of three for sure. Myself, Seamus of course, and a fellow by the name of Gallagher. You should know him. Works for you."

"Gallagher? You mean Duncan Gallagher?"

"Yup. Ex-Sergeant Major Gallagher. Veteran of the Boer War," McCorley said.

"He's a little old isn't he, Roger?"

"He can handle himself. One tough bird. The young lads look up to him."

Sullivan agreed with a nod recalling the incident where Gallagher beat the shit out of a bigger Edgar Kendrick.

"Alright. Let me see what I can find out about Doyle's new movements since he's taken up a new residence. Do you have any informers that might help, Seamus?"

Woods answered, "Maybe. I'll get to work on it."

"I know you're fixated on getting Doyle, Roger, but I'd like you to consider a broader strategy. With this new Special Constabulary you are vastly outnumbered. Creating this new hit squad is a start."

McCorley was a committed firebrand but Sullivan commanded attention. Mick Collins thought highly of him. A newcomer to Ireland but he'd already proven himself with what he did in Derry.

"I'm listening, Trevor."

"The enemy is represented now by two key threat elements. First is their intelligence apparatus. That's Doyle's division. His murder squad is an ugly adjunct to that but not the real threat. In the last few months, who's done most of the killings? Even the firepower you faced when you made the attempt on Sergeant Taggart at the pub?"

McCorley said, "The Specials."

"That's right," Sullivan said. "All Protestant. Most ex-Ulster Volunteers. Not riddled with sympathetic Catholics like the RIC. So Doyle has teamed with the Specials. He's the eyes, they're the fist. I met the local commander of the Specials, a British officer named Powell. He confirmed to me the Special Constabulary relied on Doyle's RIC intelligence.

"So I'm suggesting you target both."

"You mean this Major Powell along with Doyle?" McCorley said.

"Not exactly. Not sure killing Powell achieves much more than propaganda value. I'm thinking something more dramatic. Something from a propaganda standpoint that elevates the stature of the local IRA. Raise the terror level on these part-time constables. Make them feel they're targets. Show your support base the Belfast IRA has a nasty bite."

"You've something specific in mind?" McCorley said.

"The Belfast headquarters complex of the Special Constabulary not far from the river. Blow it up," Sullivan said.

Both McCorley and Woods uttered expletives.

"Listen, Trevor, we don't have explosives. Only had grenades to do that raid on the shipyard. And we don't have any idea how to do such a thing."

"But I know how to do such a thing. Just need to get the explosives. If I can construct a workable plan are you interested?"

"Jesus, Mary, and Joseph, that would be something," Seamus Woods said.

"You're a bold thinker, I'll hand you that, Trevor," McCorley said. "And how do you propose we lay our hands on real explosives?"

"Why you steal them of course."

———

In Sullivan's office, Alison stood beside his desk. In whispered tones, he said to her, "Your husband has quit the shipyard. According to rumor he's now a full-fledged RIC constable working directly for Inspector Doyle."

She stiffened at the mention of her husband. Something from an ugly past.

"Not surprising."

"But speaking of Doyle, there's something else, Alison. Seems our friends would like to get all the information we can on his movements. That piece of information from *Macduff* sparked considerable interest. Can you talk to your sources?"

"Sure."

"I'm thinking especially *Kate* and *Bianca* the telephone operators. And of course your *Lady Macbeth*. But what about you ask them to do more than just listen? Maybe they could poke about talking to their friends at the RIC about Inspector Doyle? He's got quite a reputation. Stands to reason there's a lot of gossip floating about."

"Well maybe," she replied with some hesitation. "Must be careful though if I'm asking for something specific."

"Absolutely. Don't be too direct. Use that piece of gossip *Macduff* relayed as a starter. You know, about his taking up with that opera singer."

She brightened. "Yes of course. A bit of gossip about sexual goings-on will get the women talking."

Furtively she looked toward the office open door before laying her hand over his.

"It's so hard to see you every day of the week thinking only of the weekend. How long must this go on?"

"I don't know, Alison. But we don't want our own scandal. Bad for both of us. People wouldn't understand. And you're still legally married. Not to mention the impropriety here at the office. You'd be forced to leave."

"I know. It's just so wonderful when I'm with you. But it would grand for it to become … well normal. Not hiding."

"Perhaps someday, Alison."

The lie stung him. There would never be a someday. No telling when this war might end. Yet that was not the determinate. He wasn't in love with her. Sex was a means of co-opting her to spy for him. That it provided him a physical sexual release only deepened his sense of guilt. When this ended it would emotionally destroy this obsessive woman.

Sullivan would do his part to reconnoiter possible locations for killing Doyle. Start by casing the Grand Opera House which Doyle must frequent given his new lady friend. While in that neighborhood, he would take lunch nearby at the Grosvenor Hotel, Doyle's new residence.

"Alison, would you place a call to the managing director of the Grand Opera House. I'd appreciate a few minutes of his time this afternoon. Sir James Craig suggested I consult with him. Tell him it's a security related matter. Use my new title."

The Grosvenor was only three blocks from the opera house. Many good restaurants nearby. Upscale shops. Sullivan could see why Doyle chose it. And after seeing the playbills displayed at the opera house, he could see what attracted him to the voluptuous Signorina Nicoletti.

"My advisory commission has been tasked with performing a thorough risk assessment of important economic targets. Starting here in Belfast," Sullivan said.

Mr. Hughes, the slight, middle-aged managing director of the venue said, "But the opera house hardly qualifies as an important economic asset, Mr. Sullivan."

"Perhaps not. However, the thought struck me that if the IRA turned to sabotage, might not cultural targets also be at risk? Think of the propaganda value."

"My lord, you're right. It's not their kind that comes here. Those unwashed barbarians would think nothing of destroying an icon of our culture."

Unwashed barbarians? An unapologetic racist. Sullivan just might recommend the opera house should be a target. Petrol placed in the right locations could ignite an uncontrollable conflagration. Would that not make his case for a new IRA strategy?

"Exactly my thinking, Mr. Hughes. Bear in mind, there is just a logical concern. No threat exists. Better though to plan for the worse. Perhaps you might show me about the building? Get an understanding of potential vulnerabilities. Perhaps you might have a blueprint I might borrow? Be helpful to have security experts take a look. We're working closely with the RIC and the Special Constabulary to draft improved security plans."

"Of course. Anything I can do to help."

"I'm most concerned with the building's access points," Sullivan said. "Service entrances, rear doors. And of course behind the scenes areas, stage rigging sets, dressing rooms, that sort of thing."

On a different inspection mission the following day, Alison arranged for a visit to the Great Northern Railway Belfast office.

The local operations manager greeted Sullivan. A young Englishman full of self-confidence with a measure of arrogance. As both civil engineers, Sullivan won him over by relating his years of railroad experience. Recounting his war adventures established a professional respect.

"Obviously the railroad presents a difficult target to defend," Sullivan said. "The IRA's already proven that by tearing up tracks. I can't suggest there's much more you can do. Clearly it's more about the response of the security forces. Their numbers and how quickly.

"But a thought occurred to me. To sabotage other targets requires explosives. Hard to come by I should think for the IRA. Otherwise they'd have used them. Remember that attack that disabled the gantry crane at the shipyard? They used grenades to damage the hoist motors. Had they used more powerful explosives they might have brought down the entire crane.

"So where might they get explosives? Not any mining hereabouts. But the railroads use explosives. At least for putting down new roadbeds, bridge construction, and such."

"Of course. We keep a modest store of dynamite. Not too much new construction going on at the moment. Only that new spur line from Dungannon to Cookstown. Not much blasting required."

"Mind showing me how you keep the stuff locked up?"

"Not at all. Follow me."

Four wooden cases of dynamite sat on shelves in a substantial metal cabinet within a building housing construction equipment. The cabinet itself welded to the building's structural columns. A hasp with a hefty padlock secured the cabinet doors.

"Only the construction manager and I have keys," the man said.

"Very good. Even if saboteurs could get into this building, they'd be a long time getting into this cabinet." Given preparation, not that secure thought Sullivan. "Well I'm sure we'll be seeing each other again. I appreciate your time."

Now Sullivan knew where to find explosives. The harder part was developing a plan to maximize their use.

———

Killing Inspector Doyle remained a singular obsession for Roger McCorley. Sullivan's idea of putting together a squad like Mick Collins in Dublin was a grand idea but would take time. Now that Doyle was not holed up living inside RIC headquarters, there might be new opportunities. He'd charged his intelligence officer Seamus Woods to prioritize such efforts.

"I've got a source on the cleaning staff inside the Grosvenor Hotel, Roger," Woods said to McCorley as they shared pints at a secure IRA protected pub in West Belfast.

"Well that's something. Anything to report on Doyle's habits?" McCorley said.

"Better. One of our people has a cousin who's a waiter at the hotel's restaurant. Our lad thinks his cousin might be willing to alert us when Doyle's in the restaurant."

"Do we know Doyle takes meals there?"

Woods said, "No. But it stands to reason. He's not one to go about."

"Okay, so Doyle is having breakfast, or dinner. Then what?"

"Well our waiter steps out the back through the kitchen for a cigarette. Holds the door open. A lone gunman comes in then goes right to Doyle and shoots him close up point blank."

McCorley looks at Woods.

"No offense, Seamus, but that's a stupid plan and you know it. Even if this guy is successful it's suicide. He'll never get away. I'm not sending someone to their certain death."

"Getting to Doyle can only be done with something like this, Roger. Sullivan pulled it off in Derry. Doyle doesn't venture far.

Only regular routine is to the Opera House to watch his new girlfriend. But Doyle never moves about without several other constables. His own constables. Hardened killers. It would take dozens of men to mount an attack. Poor chances for success I should imagine. Unacceptable casualties. Far too complicated where this is very simple."

"Just the same, nobody is going to give up their own life to put a bullet into Inspector Doyle."

"There is somebody, Roger. That's why I'm suggesting this. It's Byrne."

"Liam Byrne? Your mechanic at the garage?"

"Yes. Been casting about for lads to make up this new squad. Been considering him. Byrne's no virgin. Handles himself well in a fight. Good with a gun. Anyway, he came to me when I told him that Doyle has taken up residence at the Grosvenor. He immediately thought of his cousin a waiter at the restaurant there. Then he says to me, *let me shoot Doyle. Right there in the restaurant.*"

"Thought he was brighter than that," McCorley said. "Don't want this squad made up of fanatics. How does he expect to get away even if he shoots Doyle?"

Woods took a deep breath, "He knows that's probably unlikely."

"Why in god's name would he do such a thing?"

"Those two boys we lost going after Taggart. Seems they were mates of young Byrne. He looked up to them. Tells me he wants to do this. Doyle must be put down like a rabid dog is the way Byrne put it. Wants our help but says he's determined to do this no matter."

"Shit. What the fuck has this come to?" McCorley said. "And you're for this, Seamus?"

"Might be the only way to get Doyle, Roger. We lose men all the time for things less important. This is solely Byrne's idea. Who's to deny what's in his heart?"

———

"Jesus Christ, Trevor. There're all sorts of ways for this to go wrong," Roger McCorley said.

Sullivan arranged for another meeting. The three of them sat alone in the backroom of a hardware store.

"That's always the case going into battle. Don't need to tell you that, Roger. But with this we don't rely on anybody but ourselves. There's only three key parts. Steal the explosives, steal the petrol lorry, and then crash through the gate to the compound after shooting the sentries."

"Simple as all that is it? And what about detonating the lorry?"

"Once we pull the lorry into the compound, that'll be easy and quick." Sullivan said.

"So now we're inside this compound, how do we get away?" Woods said.

"It'll be dicey for the two in the tanker lorry. Critical for them to crash the lorry into the building blocking a door. The objective's to burn the place down. Here let me show you on this sketch I made," Sullivan said.

"You've reconnoitered the location? How'd you do that?" McCorley said.

"In my capacity with this Security Advisory Commission of course. Didn't get a tour like the opera house but I spent some time outside surveying the building and grounds. Through the gate I could see the fenced compound with parked tenders. A fuel storage tank stands a way back so a tanker lorry delivery should be routine.

"The tanker pulls up to the gate. Your lads shoot the guards. They ram through the gate with the tanker and smash it up against the building right here. They light the fuse then run back to the street. You'll have two cars pull up along the street to pick 'em up and provide covering fire. Over in less than sixty seconds."

"Let's back up. Where do we get the dynamite?" McCorley asked.

"From the railroad. Another courtesy tour of the Great Northern maintenance yard. Manager showed me the locker where they keep dynamite. Four cases. Secured with a padlock. We can break it open.

"I'll volunteer to do that. Just need two men to help me. This'll happen only a couple of hours before you steal the petrol tanker. You'll hijack the tanker just after it leaves the storage yard full. Order an early morning delivery from your regular supplier for the garage."

"And you'll know how to rig this bomb, Trevor?" McCorley asked.

"Yes. I saw fuse cord stored with the dynamite. Simple enough. Supervised my own sappers when I was in France in the Great War. Cutting railway beds to lay new track. Trick here is to direct the force of the dynamite upward to rupture the lorry tank and spray flaming petrol all over the building. You any good at welding, Seamus?"

"Of course. Couldn't very well run a garage otherwise."

"Good. I'll need you to fabricate a quarter-inch steel plate to the tanker's undercarriage. I'll give you a rough sketch. Once you lift the tanker, bring it to the garage. You'll weld this steel plate to the lorry undercarriage. It'll sandwich the dynamite up against the underside of the petrol tank. That'll direct the blast upward into the tank. You'll also make the plate large enough to cover the burning fuse making it impossible to reach before it detonates the dynamite. I'll rig everything and show you what to do.

"Try to examine the undercarriage of the same type tanker beforehand. Follow a tanker making a delivery then crawl underneath when it's parked."

Woods nodded his understanding. "You are one clever fucker."

McCorley added, "You are that, Trevor. But the timing will be critical."

"Timing is everything in life," Sullivan said.

———

McCorley and Woods agreed not to share with Sullivan this unexpected opportunity to kill Doyle. They knew Sullivan would argue against Byrne's desperate plan. The only risk was to Liam Byrne.

After Sullivan left, McCorley said to Woods, "Have someone experienced help Byrne. He'll have to keep out of sight in the back alleyway on successive evenings hoping to get the signal from his cousin. Might never happen. Would help if we could at least get a fix when Doyle enters the hotel. Don't want Byrne picked up by some roving constable."

The opportunity occurred sooner than expected.

Although the actual act of killing Doyle might be a simple plan, selecting the opportunity still required intelligence work under difficult circumstances. The Grosvenor was downtown, the heart of Belfast's commerce and government. Doyle's movements were unknown. Woods couldn't have his surveillance team standing about without attracting attention. With the continuing violence in Belfast, RIC foot patrols had noticeably increased.

Byrne was part of each night's surveillance team of three. When Doyle entered the hotel, Byrne would take up a concealed position in the alley behind the hotel to begin his vigil. If Doyle didn't have dinner in the hotel restaurant that night then they would repeat the routine the following night and for as long as necessary.

As Woods suspected, Doyle attended that Friday night's performance at the opera house under the protection of several trusted constables. For security they traveled by automobile rather than walking the few blocks from the Grosvenor Hotel.

This night Liam Byrne stationed himself in front of the opera house ostensibly as a taxi driver joining the queue awaiting the exiting crowd. A well-dressed IRA colleague stood by Byrne's taxi smoking a cigarette as if waiting for someone to prevent anyone from engaging Byrne's taxi. They were to follow Doyle. For Liam Byrne it provided the opportunity to see his target in person.

Doyle appeared after most of the crowd left. Dressed in RIC uniform, he stood out even from a distance not only because of his height, but his companion. The unmistakable presence of Angelina Nicoletti drew attention from a small crowd outside the opera house.

Doyle's car pulled to the curb. A constable jumped out of the front passenger seat and opened the rear door. Doyle and Nicoletti climbed in.

"Get in, Sweeney. Let's see where he's headed," Byrne said to his colleague.

Doyle's car pulled away with Byrne following at a comfortable distance.

A short ride. As hoped, Doyle's car pulled to the front of the Grosvenor Hotel. Taking Nicoletti by her arm Doyle walked to the front entrance with the same tall constable following while looking around vigilantly for any sign of threat.

Byrne looked at Sweeney. "Let's be hoping the Inspector is gentlemen enough to take his lady friend to dinner before he takes her to bed."

Neither laughed at the gallows humor given what Byrnes was about to do.

Byrne said to Sweeney, "You drive. Drop me off in back. I'll tell you where."

Byrne exited the fake taxi taking up a prearranged position just inside the end of the ally a hundred feet from the kitchen backdoor of the hotel. He could easily see if his cousin came out to give the signal while remaining hidden in the shadows.

For yet another time, Byrne checked the six rounds in the cylinder of his Webley revolver. Thirty minutes later his cousin opened the rear door, lit a cigarette then stood there holding the door open.

Byrne had faced danger before, but this was different being alone. Determined to see this through, fear nonetheless gripped him. The revolver trembled in his hands as he walked the short distance.

As Byrne slipped past his cousin, the cousin said, "He's at a table to the left after you come out of the kitchen. Another peeler standing near the front door. Good luck."

Byrne told himself just shoot Doyle straightaway before worrying about the other constable.

Passing by two cooks, Byrne walked briskly through the kitchen. He blinked at the glare of the chandelier lights as he entered the dining room. Spotting Doyle he approached in a couple of strides. Unfortunately at the same moment, Angelina Nicoletti stood up momentarily blocking his view of Doyle seated with his back to the wall.

Byrne lost precious seconds. Out of courtesy to Nicoletti, Doyle immediately stood allowing him to see Byrne's outstretched arm holding the revolver. With Nicoletti still between them, Doyle instinctively pulled his own weapon. A quick, practiced move since he never secured the holster flap over his revolver.

Byrne pushed Nicoletti to the side with his free hand costing precious time. His first shot missed as Doyle dropped to the floor for cover while raising his own weapon.

Instead of first pulling back the revolver's hammer, Byrne panicked and hurriedly squeezed the trigger a second time missing again.

Doyle returned fire simultaneously. His shot struck Byrne in the center of his chest, followed by a second sending Byrne stumbling backwards.

Doyle upended the table to create a barrier, but unnecessary as Byrne was already mortally wounded. Constable Edgar Kendrick insured the assailant's death shooting him in the chest followed by a final shot to the head as he stood over Byrne.

The hysterical screaming of Angelina Nicoletti mixed with the chaotic scrambling of the other patrons escaping the restaurant.

CHAPTER 28

Sullivan read in the newspaper of the failed attempt to kill Inspector Doyle. He was furious. McCorley seemed just another impulsive provincial IRA commander. No appreciation for strategy. Seemingly not that good at tactics either. Didn't have the patience to do it right. No different from O'Donnell in Derry.

Sullivan however realized he was thinking like a professional soldier. This wasn't conventional warfare. The IRA could only fight as guerrillas. Committed citizen soldiers. A war of propaganda. A war requiring support of the citizenry. A war of attrition of will. Force the British to the negotiating table out of sheer frustration. Maybe a viable objective for Collins in the South with only the British Crown as the adversary, but unlikely to work in Northern Ireland. The IRA lacked the capacity to force the Ulster Protestant-unionists into negotiations. Desperate tactics understandable.

Why the hell was he still willing to take up the fight with these fanatics? This went beyond revenge for Maureen. Had he become political by just being Irish? Had he taken the side of Irish Catholics as a civil rights cause? Perhaps for no other reason than Britain turning Northern Ireland into a colonial police state. A place where Catholics suffered state-sponsored discrimination under threat of terror. A complex mix of emotional and intellectual imperatives that demanded his involvement.

304

The City of Belfast proved especially hostile given that Protestants represented three-quarters of the population. A constant economic struggle for Catholics where ethnic unemployment ran 25 percent. Many of those employed working only reduced hours. This swelled the ranks of the IRA's Belfast Brigade where more than half were unemployed. A civil rights struggle for the essentials of life transcended even Irish nationalism.

To fortify the view of an oppressive state, there followed the usual police reprisals for the failed attempt on Inspector Doyle. Indiscriminate arrests. Reported maltreatment by those eventually released. More Catholic houses burned. Several shot dead for *resisting arrest,* or *trying to escape.*

All the more reason to respond with Sullivan's plan to burn the Ulster Special Constabulary Headquarters compound on Ballymurphy Road. A necessity to proclaim the IRA as a capable continuing threat.

Roger McCorley shouldn't however be underestimated. The failed attack on Doyle was characteristic of the IRA Belfast Battalion commander's tactics. As was the try to kill RIC Sergeant Taggart. Woods pointed out to Sullivan these failures must be considered against McCorley's other successes. He was an aggressive commander. Personally right in the thick of action. Bound to be failures fighting against such odds. Casualties part of war. Couldn't allow enemy reprisals to hamper their fight. Woods ticked off the many successes of McCorley's Active Service Unit.

This was a savage underground war pitted against better armed British Crown forces. RIC District Inspector Doyle stood as the icon of the enemy. Therefore his Intelligence Division the principal target of this new assassin squad promoted by Sullivan.

"So we took a chance. An opportunity we couldn't ignore," Woods said to Sullivan before McCorley arrived at their meeting at the garage. "I recommended we do it. My call. Roger didn't like it. Lost a good lad but it was his own idea. We didn't encourage him. We've no shortage of Irish martyrs."

Ragtag, ill-trained, poorly armed, and too few Sullivan thought. But fanatically committed. Willing to give their lives for the cause of Irish independence. The British could not find a successful strategy to quell this rebellion. The IRA needed to ratchet up the pressure.

When McCorley arrived he did not need further prodding to attack the USC compound.

"London will eventually withdraw much of the army once home rule comes into being. But this Ulster Special Constabulary will remain. Time we drew blood. Are we ready?" McCorley said to Woods and Sullivan.

"Yes. Here's the plan, Roger," Woods said.

Sullivan let Woods explain the details. They needed to adopt the plan as their own.

"So we keep Trevor's identity limited, it'll just be me, him, and Gallagher that steals the dynamite. Early morning hours before sunrise, morning after tomorrow.

"I'll order a petrol delivery for that morning. A few of the lads will hijack the tanker lorry. They'll hold the driver someplace until the afternoon.

"Gallagher drives the tanker here to the garage. I'll have the modifications Trevor designed ready to weld to the underside. Got a chance to crawl under one a couple days ago. Take me maybe an hour.

"We move midmorning. Two in the lorry. Myself and Duncan Gallagher. Two carloads of the active service boys for backup to cover our escape."

"Why must you go, Seamus?" McCorley said.

"I'm to light the fuse. Trevor went over everything in detail. Rather not try to explain to someone else."

McCorley thought for a couple of moments before saying, "Very well. We'll do it. You've selected the men you want, Seamus?"

"Yes. All good lads."

"All our lads are good lads. I'll take command of the backup force," McCorley said.

A bright moonlit night. Four o'clock on a Saturday morning. For some inexplicable reason there was no security guard at night for the railway maintenance yard. Sullivan had previously determined that on the two previous nights' reconnaissance. Unbelievably careless given the uncertain security climate.

Woods arrived right on time with Duncan Gallagher in a small lorry. Woods signaled by switching his headlamps on and off. Sullivan replied from a block away then pulled his car to a more secluded spot.

They met at a point along the chain-link fence previously identified by Sullivan.

Woods and Gallagher carried an eight-foot heavy steel rod.

Visibly astonished to see his boss from the shipyard, Gallagher said, "Good evening, Sir. A surprise to say the least."

"Keep it to yourself, Sergeant Major. Woods and McCorley are the only others that know."

Gallagher cut away a section of the fence with a bolt cutter.

At the maintenance building, Sullivan said, "Break the padlock. Don't worry about the noise. Damn fools don't even post a watchman."

Once inside Sullivan directed them to use the bar again on the larger locker padlock. With much greater difficulty the long steel rod allowed the strength of all three to apply enough leverage to break the hasp free from the cabinet.

Sullivan followed the lorry to a secluded spot to prepare the explosives. To avoid revealing himself to the other IRA assembling for the raid, he would not accompany them to the garage. Prepared with a role of tape, he created two bundles of dynamite with six sticks each.

"I've rigged each of these bundles independently for redundancy then twisted the fuse cords all together. But the fuse is even waterproof so it won't easily go out once lit. The fusing attaches to a blasting cap at the end of each dynamite stick. That's what sets the dynamite off. Otherwise it's totally safe to handle.

"The fuse will start to spark when you ignite it with a match. Strike three matches simultaneously to create a strong flame. You've got time so stay calm. This is 30-second fusing. Burns at a rate of one foot in 30 seconds. I'm thinking 90 seconds allows you to get away?"

Woods simply nodded. A brave man with a gun but the dynamite made him anxious.

"Now you position the bundles securely between the steel plate and the lorry bulk petrol tank. That'll direct the explosive force upward. Way more dynamite than should be necessary so this'll be one hell of an explosion. Light the fuse then get away quickly.

"Remember to leave only a short section of fuse exposed within reach. No more than six inches, a fifteen-second burn. That way if any of the Specials gets to the lorry it'll be too late to stop the detonation by disabling the fuse which will continue to burn out of reach."

Sullivan shook hands with Woods. "Good luck, Seamus."

Turning to Gallagher and shaking his hand, "You mind what you're about Duncan. I'm expecting you at the shipyard Monday morning."

———

At nine o'clock in the morning from the passenger seat, Seamus Woods navigated while Gallagher drove toward the Special Constabulary complex on Ballymurphy Road. Woods had driven the route several times in preparation.

A single guard was stationed at the wooden gate when they arrived. As the uniformed special constable approached the tanker lorry, Gallagher raised a Mauser C96 pistol from his lap and shot him in the forehead. Putting the lorry in gear, Gallagher accelerated the few remaining feet smashing into the gate which flew open.

"To the left!" Woods shouted pointing to the section of the building Sullivan designated.

Gallagher crashed into the building, crumpling a door Sullivan observed during his earlier visit, preventing anyone exiting the building by that route.

Woods and Gallagher exited the lorry cab. Gallagher remained covering for Woods as he ignited the fuse. Remembering Sullivan's instructions, Woods waited several seconds for the burning fuse to disappear out of reach into the cavity created by the steel plate before taking off at a run. When he and Gallagher reached McCorley and the backup team less than a minute had elapsed.

As the two cars sped away, McCorley said expectantly, "Well? What's happening? Is it going to explode?"

Pulling out his pocket watch, Woods said breathlessly, "Stop the car!"

All the IRA jumped out of the car two blocks down the road.

"Any second now!" Woods said looking at his watch

A growing number of special constables flowed out of the building preparing for an attack.

Moments later the explosion jolted everyone with not only the noise but feeling the pressure wave of the blast.

"Jesus Christ!" McCorley said as a large fireball rose a hundred feet. Burning petrol splashed over the side of the building and onto to some of the parked armored vehicles.

The grinning IRA remained looking at the spectacle long enough to see the building become thoroughly engulfed in flames. They could see many special constables lying in the roadway knocked down by the terrific blast, undoubtedly injured or dead.

McCorley slapped Woods and Gallagher on the back. "Wonder if maybe Inspector Doyle heard the explosion?"

Sullivan did. As much as he wanted to witness his handiwork, that would be an unnecessary risk. Instead he found a small restaurant a few blocks away. Might as well have breakfast. The violent rattling of the windows confirmed the detonation.

Hopefully mission accomplished. A fine, sunny spring day brought a wistful thought of spending a relaxing day alone. But he promised Alison Kendrick that they would take a ride into the country. Compensation for her disappointment of not seeing him as usual the prior night. His reason vague saying only it was necessary to what they were doing. She of course might connect his involvement once she learned of the bombing. Couldn't be helped.

———

The following week added to Sullivan's acceptance into the unionist power circle of Belfast. His boss asked him if he would come to a dinner party at his home. Some interesting people, not the usual political crowd. The affair organized by his daughter Caroline. She insisted he invite him. As she put it, an interesting and worldly foreigner to complement an eclectic group of intellectual guests.

"She's both intelligent and difficult," Malcom Llewellyn said. "I've long ago given up trying to restrain her flights of intellectual arguments. Rarely do I share her views. But she's clever and charming. I fear that she hopelessly manipulates me. She's a force to be reckoned with and yet I adore her."

"Of course, Sir. I will very much look forward to the event. I'm sure that your daughter is not as daunting as you portray her."

The dinner party was to be the following Saturday. A telling exchange ensued with Alison Kendrick during the week at the office when he told her of his commitment for the forthcoming Saturday night.

"I'm sorry, Alison. Nothing I can do about it. It's the boss. I'll still see you Sunday."

"What kind of party?"

"A dinner party. Probably important people. It's what I do, Alison. I'm part of that world."

"And you're a spy."

"And how do you expect me to maintain the necessary façade?"

Alison lowered her head. "Yes. I know. It's just that ..."

Sullivan reached over and kissed her." "I understand all of this is difficult."

———

The dinner party was at Malcom Llewellyn's estate. A grand mansion located outside Belfast to the northeast near the small village of Holywood. The Victorian house built in the middle of the last century occupied a rural setting with mature gardens. Over a vast lawn, Belfast Lough spread in a spectacular view. Yet the location was only four miles from the Harland & Wolff shipyard.

Malcom Llewellyn confided to Sullivan that he thought perhaps this dinner party was an excuse for his daughter to become better acquainted with him.

"Will Mr. Townsend be there?" Sullivan said.

"Certainly not. Caroline follows her own course. May use her intellect and charm to manipulate others, but she's never cruel so she wouldn't do that. This dinner is ostensibly around the author Edith Warton. Know who she is?"

"Just the name. American I believe?"

"Yes. An ex-patriot like yourself. Lives in Paris. Caroline met her there and invited her to visit. As Caroline put it, you simply must invite Mr. Sullivan, father. A fellow American that knows Paris and speaks French. I suspect however there's perhaps more to her subterfuge. Therefore you've been duly warned."

As imagined from their first encounter, Caroline Llewellyn could prove a complication.

The last to arrive, she was the first to greet him.

"Mr. Sullivan, so good of you to come," she said and warmly took his hand which she held longer than necessary. "Let me introduce you around."

In a large sitting room with vast windows looking over the Lough, a clear nighttime sky sparkled with stars.

The hostess, Henrietta Llewellyn was a mature version of her daughter.

Sir Phillip Atwood of course Sullivan knew. His wife, an elegant if somewhat plain woman.

Caroline introduced her younger friend, Kimberly Atwood, Sir Phillips daughter. A pretty young woman clearly an acolyte of her older dominant friend.

Kimberly introduced her escort, "And this is Major Albert Winslet of His Majesty's Army."

Sullivan was momentarily speechless on hearing his namesake used for the fake orders in Derry. "Good to meet you, Major. I appreciate the professionalism of General Hopkins' staff. Colonel Baker has been most helpful in my role with the Security Advisory Commission."

"Yes, Sir. The Colonel has mentioned your name. Mentioned you also saw action in the Great War."

"That I did, Major. Different army from yours of course."

Caroline introduced a middle-aged woman. "And my special guest, the noted novelist Edith Wharton. This is the interesting gentleman I spoke of, Edith. A fellow ex-patriot and Parisian."

Wharton took Sullivan's hand and said, "Caroline told me the circumstances that brought you to Ireland. My condolences for the loss of your wife."

"Thank you. I confess that I have not read your novels, Madame. I shall remedy that at the first opportunity."

Caroline turned to the slender well-dressed middle-aged man with a bushy mustache, "And this erudite man is Edith's long-time friend, another American Francophile, Mr. Walter Berry. Lawyer, diplomat, former tennis champion, friend to the literary world, and consummate raconteur. He too makes his home in Paris."

The evening proved both stimulating as well as relaxing. However Phillip Atwood could not avoid politics. As a principal in direct negotiations with London on Ulster Home Rule matters, Sir Phillip tended to lecture.

"Lloyd George can't be trusted. Truly Machiavellian. Sharp as a razor and just as dangerous. Wants to cut his losses in the

South and keep the North in the British fold. But the crafty bastard wants us to take on the burden.

"London can't afford this war so it must end. I believe some form of independence will soon be granted for Southern Ireland. You can sense the Prime Minister feels the same. So he's setting up Northern Ireland to take on its own security once Home Rule comes into effect. Hence the creation of the Ulster Special Constabulary. London doesn't have to pay them like those Auxiliary troops operating in the south."

Michael Collins would certainly like this bit of intelligence from someone so close to the British prime minister.

In deference to the famous Wharton, Caroline Llewellyn diplomatically steered the conversation to matters other than the Anglo-Irish War. Not only had Wharton won the 1921 Pulitzer Prize, the first woman to do so, but she was active in relief efforts for refugees and the unemployed in the aftermath of the Great War.

Major Winslet related to Sullivan's combat experience with the *Lost Battalion*. Winslet had gone through his own hell surviving the Battle of the Somme. Like Sullivan, he downplayed his heroics. Even so, their recounting of the horrors captivated the others.

Walter Berry proved an engaging intellectual. Widely experienced, widely travelled. Not sure of his association with Ms. Wharton. Warm to each other but leaving the impression they were not lovers.

Malcom Llewellyn and Atwood were satisfied to let those so enthusiastically attached to France indulge themselves while they sipped their brandies and talked business.

Caroline Llewellyn devoted a good deal of attention to Sullivan.

At dinner, Sullivan sat between her and Edith Wharton. To the delight of both they exchanged comments in French.

"As a writer, Ms. Wharton, how would you describe your affection for Paris?" Sullivan said.

"Even for a writer that is difficult to frame in words. I attribute it to a feeling that seeps its way into one's very being. So many things combine to complement one another. The whole forming something so much greater than the constituent parts."

"Yes I know what you mean," Sullivan said. "Not only the food, the wine, the art, the architecture, but the intellectual environment. Especially for someone such as yourself."

Caroline added, "I found social freedom another defining aspect of Paris. Not only for women, but even for men. The French never embraced the nonsense of Victorian conventions. The very core of which seems alien to the French psyche."

"And how are men more free with the yoke of Victorian oppression removed?" Sullivan said trying not to sound condescending.

"Caroline I believe means that men are free to enjoy women as equals," Wharton said. "Now you are still young, my dear. When you've had all the life experiences of my many years you'll find that most men fear that. Men like Walter here are uncommon."

Wharton affectionately placed her hand on Berry's arm.

"And as a former New Yorker, and Parisian, how do you find Belfast, Mr. Sullivan?" Wharton said.

A tougher question from which to compose a credible lie. He'd leave Belfast in a heartbeat at the first opportunity.

"Well I'm adaptable. As a professional soldier I moved about. Some places better than others. Then of course France, during the war.

"Met my wife in Paris. She embraced Paris and I soon did. Originally planned to remain there. But both of us felt the indefinable tug of being Irish.

"Not sure I can fairly judge my feelings here with all that has happened and this conflict raging. Of course I've been fortunate to find a professional home at Harland & Wolff. That makes all the difference."

A nothing answer to which no one pressed further in deference to his loss.

In French, Caroline said, "And father thinks highly of you, Mr. Sullivan."

After dinner when the men were to take cigars and their brandy, Caroline suggested that Sullivan along with Kimberly and Major Winslet join her for a walk about the grounds. A moonlit warm spring night.

With Major Winslet and Kimberly Atwood engrossed in their private conversation, Caroline said to Sullivan, "I do hope you're enjoying the evening."

"Thoroughly enjoyable. Most interesting people, Ms. Llewellyn."

"Perhaps you might allow us to drop such silly Victorian protocols. In talking to Daddy I feel I already know you so well. Please call me Caroline, Trevor."

"Very well, Caroline."

"And mother? What do you think of her?"

Caroline was every bit the unusual self-assured assertive woman her father made her out to be.

"An engaging woman. Poised, witty. I can see her influence on you."

"You mean my being so forward? Mother of course wouldn't say or do the things I do. Her generation didn't see women as anything but wives and mothers. Mother was educated only because of her social standing. Never with a view to forge off in her own direction. But I agree she's still her own person."

"I can see she and your father are devoted to each other."

"Oh yes. Daddy isn't like most men. Neither are you it seems. Now look at Sir Phillip's wife. Younger than my mother but more a product of her generation. Beyond fashion and social etiquette she seems to have no views. Just as well with a husband like Sir Phillip."

"Sounds as if you're not that found of him?"

"Wouldn't say that. I can intellectually spar with him and he welcomes the challenge. He's smart, a bit arrogant yet likable. I disagree with his politics of course. His wife's a good fit. She's either comfortable or just reconciled to her subservient role.

"I can see Phillip also respects your views, Trevor. You do have a way with people. You follow Walter's complex intellectual arguments adding your own insightful comments. You talk knowledgeably of military stuff and war experiences with Kimberly's major. Daddy and Phillip respect your business judgment. As for the women, you thoroughly impressed Mother and Edith. Kimberly thinks you're dashing. Her words. I'll add myself to that list."

Caroline stopped walking and looked at him. He could see her face clearly in the moonlight.

"Well that's the first time you seem lost for words. Am I again being forward, Trevor?"

He gave a smile and laugh. He should defuse this. But he wasn't sure he wanted to.

"Of course you are, Caroline. But I don't mind."

"Don't mind? Couldn't you perhaps say something more to bolster a woman's ego?"

Taking the bait, he said, "Yes, I should do better. You're an exceptional woman who speaks her mind. Her own person not bending to convention. And a most beautiful woman that can't be ignored."

"And why would you want to ignore me, Trevor."

"I surely don't want to ignore you, Caroline."

As the party concluded Caroline insisted walking Sullivan to his car.

"I'd like to see you again, Trevor."

"Of course," he said noncommittally but knowingly ill-advised by encouraging this.

"You know what I mean. Just the two of us."

"Wouldn't that cause... well problems?"

"You mean with Herbert?"

"Of course. You never clarified that relationship but clearly he thinks there's something to it."

"Yes. I shouldn't be insensitive. Herbert's a fine man. Tried not to lead him to thinking there was any romance. Unavoidable though I guess."

"With someone like you, of course unavoidable. And what about your parents?"

"Both hope I will marry. Suitably of course. However, they no longer press their views on the subject. So?"

"Still might prove awkward."

"You're an interesting man, Trevor Sullivan. How does a woman in this age engage such a friendship without it being construed as romantic? Why not something like what Edith and Walter share? Perhaps because they're Parisian rather than backward Irish?"

"Even in Paris the company of a beautiful woman would not likely be construed as simply plutonic. And not only is this Belfast, but I also work for your father."

"Perhaps you're involved with someone?"

"No. There is no one."

"Your secretary perhaps?"

Sullivan was immediately wary. Why would she say such a thing? Had Alison been indiscreet?

"Why would you suggest that? My secretary is married."

"I know Alison Kendrick. At least we're acquainted. You see we share a common association in the Suffrage Society. She's told a lot of us about that bastard of a husband. How she left him. How you helped her."

"She's a good woman. An excellent secretary. Least I could do was help in her time of need."

"Well she certainly talks glowingly about you. I'd say there's more to her feelings then just gratitude."

"Our relationship is purely professional. Perhaps you are just reading more into her emotional recovery. Difficult circumstances she endured. I often saw the bruising her husband inflicted. She seems a changed woman now."

Caroline shrugged and said, "Well if you're saying you're not involved, can I see you then? No one needs to know."

———

Sullivan regretted his careless encouragement of Caroline Llewellyn. Nothing could ever come of their relationship. His time in Belfast limited. They came from different worlds. What was he thinking?

Yet a social connection with Caroline as a Trojan horse might be productive. In the convivial setting Phillip Atwood was remarkably candid about the complex machinations of negotiations with the British government. Even how British Prime Minister Lloyd George cleverly maneuvered with the various factions within the British Parliament. Candid insights into the conflicting objectives of the Ulster Unionists with the Crown. As number two in the Ulster Unionist party, Atwood even joked about how he and Craig often rehearsed tactics to manipulate London's position to favor their objectives. Vital intelligence for Collins to shape negotiations.

This of course was not about spying. Spending time with Caroline Llewellyn was a tantalizing thought for entirely unrealistic personal reasons. He couldn't possibly carry on two simultaneous romantic affairs while keeping both a secret from the other.

He must end this. Caroline's advances would only become bolder. If he survived this dangerous game then he would surely leave Belfast when this war ended. Ireland could never be home. Nothing but painful memories. Alison destroyed because of his self-serving deceit. Not about to make Caroline Llewellyn another victim.

CHAPTER 29

By the end of June, events brought the Anglo-Irish war to a turning point. The Crown, including King George V himself, finally came to the negotiating table. With the drain on the British treasury worsening, the *Irish problem* proved unsustainable. Continued military-styled policing operations were not yielding results. Prime Minister Lloyd George and Éamon de Valera, the recognized leader of the rebellious Sinn Féin Irish government in Southern Ireland, agreed to a truce. On Saturday, July 9th they signed terms for the truce to take effect on July 11th. Welcome news in Southern Ireland.

However, in Northern Ireland, Belfast reacted in another spasm of violence. Among majority Protestant-unionists of the newly partitioned Northern Ireland six counties, this was a British sellout to Irish Catholic Republicans. Ulster must therefore protect its own interests.

On the night the truce was announced, the RIC launched a raid into the Lower Falls district of West Belfast. The following day, Sunday, July 10th saw ferocious fighting between Catholics and Protestants in West Belfast. Gun battles raged throughout the day at the boundary between the Catholic Falls Road and the Protestant Shankill Road districts. Sixteen civilians lost their lives and 161 houses destroyed, 150 belonging to Catholics.

While the truce was sporadically violated in the South, in the North it was ignored. The differences between Northern and Southern Ireland becoming starkly evident.

In the North, the Crown intended Northern Ireland to remain part of the United Kingdom. The reason for partition. Now the majority Protestant-unionist Ulster population had its own provincial Protestant police force, the Ulster Special Constabulary, effectively enforcing economic segregation on ethnic Catholics by the gun.

The violence subsided by nightfall on Sunday. However on Monday, the day the truce came into effect, three more people were killed. By the end of the week, 28 people died in Belfast. The sectarian violence between the civilian populations overshadowed the military conflict between the IRA and the British.

Sullivan realized this was the new tone of the conflict. Regardless what might happen in the southern twenty-six counties, Northern Ireland would remain within the United Kingdom. Irish independence for Ulster would never happen.

Protestant controlled police brutalized the Catholic minority. The IRA offered the only means of forcing the Ulster power structure to reestablish the rule of law or face a civil war.

Before giving up his Irish fight, Sullivan would assist in efforts to cripple the enemy. The Ulster Special Constabulary became the face of Catholic oppression. Not only for their numbers but for their indiscriminate sectarian violence. Exclusively Protestant, poorly led, legally unaccountable. Yet they still relied on intelligence from the Royal Irish Constabulary. District Inspector John Doyle's Intelligence Division. An RIC unit itself comprised of violent Protestant racists. Within its ranks lurked Doyle's off-the-books murder squad.

Sullivan commented to McCorley about how he saw republican politics playing out.

"I can see why Collins never embraced my idea of going after economic targets here in the North. Too occupied with delicate negotiations with the British. But that also means that Northern Ireland is on its own, Roger. Look at that debacle in

County Cavan with those men brigade headquarters ordered you to send south. Now locked up in Crumlin Road Gaol awaiting the carrying out of their death sentences. Men you could ill afford to lose. Dublin doesn't understand the war in the North."

Sullivan meant to help McCorley assemble his own squad to take out Doyle's. Do what Collins did in Dublin the prior year by killing twelve members of Dublin Castle's intelligence unit and scaring off the rest. Blinding the British.

With his ground level sources through Alison Kendrick's Suffrage Society associations, he had the intelligence resources to target Doyle's constables. All he needed was the means of carrying out the bloodletting.

———

McCorley and Woods were already working to assemble the right people. They would actively participate as part of the team. Since this was his idea, Sullivan realized he must also be willing to directly bloody his hands.

Professionally organized assassination required getting close enough to the target while offering a reasonable assurance of escape. History proved that getting close enough was often easy provided the assassin was willing to sacrifice his own life. Liam Byrne's failed effort to kill Doyle such an example.

Sullivan was an expert on handguns stemming from his days at the military academy. As an engineer he understood the underlying technology. As a practical matter the noise of discharging a firearm changed the dynamics of the situation, immediately making escape more difficult.

He recalled an instructor at the Academy explaining the interplay of muzzle velocity of a round and the mass of the projectile. Not only a function of energy which changed as the square of the velocity for a given size projectile, but the type of damage inflicted. The higher the velocity, the deeper the penetration into tissue. Knock-down power was further shaped by the diameter of the projectile, its mass, and velocity.

In that same lecture, the instructor explained the nature of the sound when a firearm discharged. First came the sound of the escaping gasses from the barrel followed by a *crack* if the projectile exceeded the speed of sound.

The first factor could be substantially reduced by a suppressor, sometimes called a silencer, affixed to the end of the weapon barrel. Worked on the same principle as the automobile muffler. The instructor displayed a commercially available tubular device. Manufactured by a guy named Maxim son of the inventor that developed the modern machine gun used to such deadly effect in the Great War.

The second noise factor was eliminated only by the use of a cartridge generating a subsonic muzzle velocity.

All sorts of possibilities became possible if you could kill quietly. The most assured means of killing a person was from as close as possible. Both the size and velocity of the projectile therefore became less critical. Good penetration in the right location could cause death even from a quieter small caliber projectile.

When Sullivan first proposed the idea for developing a squad of assassins, these technical aspects to select the most suitable weapon became critical. After all, he based his use of the small .25 caliber to kill Fergus Croft on limiting the sound. How to secure the right weapons might prove more difficult. He was looking for a weapon of comparatively lower lethality than the handguns in use by the IRA and British Crown forces. Inherently that meant a civilian weapon like the pocket-sized FN .25, but for this purpose, he needed a larger caliber.

The answer proved to be the United States. Britain imposed severe limitations on gun ownership in 1920. The combined threat of great stores of weapons from the Great War and the Anglo-Irish War forced all civilians to seek permits. Sullivan was not certain of the situation on the Continent. He was however certain of access to weapons in the United States. No restrictions. Criminals even found it easy to acquire the latest in firearms technology. Gun ownership enshrined as a right by the Second Amendment of the U.S. Constitution.

The ideal bullet seemed the .38 Smith & Wesson Special round. A popular cartridge. A muzzle velocity far less than 1000 feet per second using a short barreled weapon, yet with enough delivered energy to be lethal. At close range, more than sufficient for the purpose.

As for the weapon itself, a revolver rather than a semiautomatic. The simple reason being for easy adaptation by machining threads into the end of the barrel to accept the suppressor. Smith & Wesson also produced these revolvers in great numbers driven by demand from police agencies.

By agreeing to assist McCorley in developing a capable hit squad, Sullivan felt obligated to insure they possessed the right weapons for the mission. On his own initiative he arranged the purchase of five revolvers, ammunition, and Maxim sound suppressors from the United States. He left the details of finding the right contacts to facilitate the purchase to his Aunt Kathleen. She had access to Irish-Americans organizations already funding the rebellion. Among the many militant Irish-Americans there should be no difficulty in obtaining these weapons.

Sullivan received word by means of his usual channel once the shipment was in transit. Consigned to Harland & Wolff in Belfast. A single wooden crate marked *Machinery Parts – Handle with Care*. For will-call at the freight forwarding warehouse personally by a Mr. Sullivan. If the shipment were intercepted by customs authorities, he would simply disclaim any knowledge. After all, his name was well known as a manager at the shipyard. Some sort of IRA smuggling scheme with an ironic twist. A manageable risk.

When notified the shipment arrived he did wonder if it might be a trap. Had the crate been opened for customs inspection? Did those packing it in America follow his specific instructions? Two layers of gears securely braced within the box were to be placed on the top and bottom in the crate sandwiching the concealed weapons and ammunition.

Requisitioning his foreman Duncan Gallagher to accompany him, Sullivan drove to Seamus Wood's auto garage. Suspecting a heavy crate, they drove to the docks in the small garage lorry. Both were armed if this should prove to be a trap. They wouldn't survive but that was the point if the alternative was capture.

Nothing happened. The one hundred pound crate appeared undisturbed.

When they returned to the garage both McCorley and Woods were waiting.

After unloading the crate all three of the IRA looked at the contents with some bewilderment.

McCorley picked up one of the revolvers. "Seems a lot of work to smuggle just a few revolvers. And not much of a gun if I do say. What am I missing?"

"Ever seen one of these, Roger?" Sullivan said handing each of the IRA a Maxim suppressor.

"Can't say that I have. What is it?"

"A noise suppressor. Seamus can easily adapt it to the barrel of the revolver in his tool room. Grind off the fixed front sight then machine threads into the barrel to accept the suppressor."

"So it silences the noise?" Woods said.

"Not entirely. But without getting technical, it changes both the sound level and the sound frequency. Makes a duller, lower pitched noise. Like throwing mud against a wall."

"But why such a small gun? And isn't a .38 caliber the same as the 9mm Mauser pistols we use?"

"The 9mm parabellum round has too high a muzzle velocity. The suppressor cannot dampen the crack occurring after the round exits the barrel. And the Webley .455 revolvers are just too big a round to suppress the report enough from the escaping gases at the gun barrel. This .38 round is much better for noise suppression."

McCorley said, "But at the expense of not doing the same kind of damage."

"Roger, the point is to reduce the noise low enough that the shots don't alert others. As for the lethality, that won't be an issue. This is for close-in use. Don't need much knock-down power from only a couple of feet. Especially for a head shot.

"With this you could walk up to someone on the street, shoot him then walk away before anyone realizes what's happened."

Days later, Sullivan received a message to stop by the garage after work that day.

"What do 'ya think?" Seamus said as he showed Sullivan one of the revolvers fitted with the suppressor.

Sullivan handled the weapon. Ungainly in length but surprisingly well-balanced as he extended his arm sighting the weapon.

Woods said, "Want to try it out? I'm curious to hear what kind of noise it makes. I've rigged a target on the far wall."

Twenty feet away hung a burlap bag from the garage rafters. The rope tied near the top of the bag split it into two distinct sections, the smaller top proportioned to the size of a human head.

"Stuffed with rags. Steel plate behind will stop any stray rounds."

Sullivan loaded the revolver with six rounds.

His first shot hit the simulated head.

"Holy Jesus!" Woods exclaimed. "I see what you mean. If you were outside you'd have heard almost nothing. And the noise didn't even sound like a gunshot.

"Now you try, Seamus."

Woods took the weapon and cocked the hammer back. His shot missed the makeshift dummy hitting the steel plate.

"Not that easy to hit without a front sight. You're bloody good with a gun, Trevor."

"Let me show you something, Seamus," Sullivan said taking back the gun.

He tucked it inside his suit jacket and took several strides toward the dummy. Stopping a couple of feet away, he brought the gun to a firing position at the same time cocking back the hammer two feet from the target. The round again hit the dummy's head.

"At this distance no one misses. Two rounds to the head means a sure kill."

Woods nodded his understanding. "I'll have the other guns modified within a day. Wait till Roger and Duncan have a go at this. With these we don't raise holy hell. As you say, done right we can be away before they discover the bastard's dead."

"Do you have a team assembled?" Sullivan asked.

"Right now it's me, Roger, Gallagher, and another fellow by the name of Quinlan. A good lad. Cool under fire. Drove the car that got me out of that mess when we tried to take out Taggart."

"That'll make five if you include me," Sullivan said. "It was my idea. Wouldn't feel right if I didn't lead from the front."

Woods extended his hand to Sullivan. "Now all we need are the targets to cooperate."

"I did this with Doyle's bunch in mind," Sullivan said. "We need to blind the Crown. I'll work my sources but I've no one close to Doyle's division. We need intelligence on their daily movements. Need to identify their habits."

———

"Alison, talk to your sources. Press them further about information on Inspector Doyle's intelligence division. Anything they can pick up, no matter how trivial."

"Why them? Seems as though it's these Specials that're the real problem for the IRA. Like they go hunting Catholics with their armored cars and machine guns. No wonder Belfast has turned to riot."

"But it's Doyle's RIC division that feeds the Specials intelligence. Course we're still interested in anything worthwhile."

"Very well. I'll be seeing some of my friends tomorrow night."

She looked around to see that no one could overhear, "I was so hoping we might do something special this weekend. Be so nice to go out like normal folks."

A secret life of lying was hard for anyone. As much as she enjoyed the lovemaking, forced to remain inside the apartment on their weekends together was no sort of sustainable existence. Hard also on Sullivan to act his role continuously being careful never to let down his guard while closeted with her every weekend. Since that first dinner they rarely ventured out fearing being seen together. Both needed a change of routine.

"Perhaps we might take a short excursion this weekend. Leave Belfast for the day. We can go out and about. Take dinner at a nice restaurant. As you say, like normal folks. What about somewhere by the sea since it's summer?"

Alison beamed at the thought. "Oh my, can we?"

That Saturday they motored to the seaside village of Bangor. Less than an hour's drive northeast from Belfast. A prosperous Protestant town little affected by the recent rioting.

Over lunch sitting outside overlooking Belfast Lough on the warm summer day, Alison's eyes beamed reveling in the day and a sense of normality.

"Look at this. It's from *Desdemona*. She hasn't been willing to get involved before."

"So what changed her mind?" Sullivan said. This was Alison's friend Margaret, a clerk in the personnel department at RIC headquarters.

"This terrible wave of recent violence. The police shootings and house burnings in the Catholic neighborhoods after the signing of the truce. The police protecting the Protestant mobs.

"Anyway, I approached her again when you said to get what I could on Inspector Doyle. She agreed. Knows about Doyle from the office gossip. Thinks he is evil."

Alison gave Sullivan several typed sheets. The names and personal information of Doyle's intelligence division staff. With the addresses of their residences, Seamus Woods could immediately begin mounting surveillance on selected constables to set up plans for their assassination.

Sullivan was visibly stunned. A goldmine. "This is outstanding, Alison."

She smiled mischievously. "Perhaps worthy of treating me to some afternoon delight in our room?"

In Monday's dispatch secreted in the drop box under the car, Sullivan included the information. To Roger McCorley he wrote:

Make proper use of this. A matter now of acquiring detailed reconnaissance. Must look to destroy the enemy's eyes and ears as did our friend in the south. Ready to do my part.
Hamlet

———

"Commissioner, you see what I mean," Sullivan said to Commissioner Charles Wickham of the Royal Irish Constabulary at RIC Headquarters. "This is the second attack where the IRA has used explosives. I fear they'll soon turn to easier economic targets.

"I just visited the railroad's maintenance yard a week before the theft of dynamite obviously used to destroy the Special Constabulary headquarters. Terrible security at the railroad. The explosives just locked in a cabinet. No guards at night. Told the manager he should do something. Where else could the IRA get their hands on explosives? Regrettably prophetic."

All that said to deflect suspicion if the rail yard manager recalled Sullivan's visit.

"I agree it was woefully lax. You in the private sector need to do a better job protecting your assets. Right now the police must concentrate all our efforts on this civil rioting," Wickham said.

"Of course, Commissioner. And I assure you we are actively pursuing doing just that. But I'd like to leave you with some materials the Commission has assembled. It outlines certain actions already taken to bolster security at important sites. Specially the Harland & Wolff shipyards, the Port of Belfast, and the electric power generating station. Improved perimeter fencing, increased nighttime security patrols, less access points.

"We've also outlined strategic points of control for security forces in the event of armed attack. They're identified on these maps with coordinate identifiers. I'd hope we could define a protocol for communication that would facilitate the fastest response by security forces. There remains some uncertainty which forces to alert; the regular RIC, the Special Constabulary, or the Army?"

328

"Very well, Mr. Sullivan. I grasp your point. Always room for improvement. Are you also providing these same materials to the Special Constabulary and the Army?"

"Of course. In fact I'm delivering a set to Major Powell following this meeting. I understand he has taken up offices in this building after the destruction of his headquarters building."

Wickham's expression soured at the mention of the spectacular IRA attack. "You realize of course these documents are highly sensitive. In the hands of the IRA they would provide the ability to execute just what you hope to prevent."

"Couldn't agree more. All my counterparts on the Commission understand these blueprints must remain confidential. Any security measures are vulnerable to leaked intelligence."

"Speaking of which, have you ever met District Inspector Doyle? He heads the RIC's Intelligence Division."

"Afraid I haven't had the pleasure, Commissioner. Know the name of course."

"Let me see if he's available. Perhaps Major Powell can join us and you can further your thoughts with all of us together."

Well that was something. Get to meet *Dracula* face-to-face.

Both Doyle and Powell entered Wickham's office ten minutes later. At well over six feet with a well-built muscular physique, Doyle cast an imposing physical presence. Handsome with a military bearing. Didn't look the part of a murdering villain.

Wickham said, "Mr. Sullivan has presented me with sets of drawings. Various installations of importance. His Security Advisory Commission advises that internal security has been increased at certain important installations. He's suggesting creating a more rigorous protocol to respond to an emergency by communicating precise location information."

"Got our hands full right now just putting down civil unrest," Major Powell said.

"I appreciate that, but the IRA is still conducting military operations. Considering the Special Constabulary bombing, with new tactics I should say," Sullivan said. "This truce may lead to an ending of hostilities between the IRA and Crown forces in the South. Doubt that'll happen in Northern Ireland."

"For an American, you seem well-informed about Irish politics, Mr. Sullivan," Doyle said.

"Irish-American, Inspector. My Irish side knows the republicans will not give up. Not this time. They're too close. My military training suggests that if the war stops in the South than the IRA will shift military resources to the North. Lloyd George needs to resolve the Irish problem. The truce will lead to accomplishing that in the South. He won't be keen on continuing to wage war with Crown forces here in the North."

Doyle said, "That may prove to be the case. Yet what your Commission is concerned with is damage to economic targets. No reason to believe the IRA has adopted that course."

Sullivan raised an eyebrow. "Major Powell may disagree with you, Inspector."

"A military target, Mr. Sullivan," Doyle said. "With the exception of that damage at your shipyard, the IRA has not targeted economic targets."

"That's true. However, considering some sort of independent Irish South, the IRA might take a longer view strategically. They may see the economic collapse of Northern Ireland as a means of eventually forcing it into a greater united Ireland."

Doyle said, "Leaving aside the politics, using explosives still remains out of reach for the IRA. The attack on the USC building used stolen dynamite. Other than that, they only have grenades."

"I understand your point, Inspector. But nothing remains static. What I worry about is a change in IRA strategy. Michael Collins is a crafty bastard. Securing dynamite is not that difficult. In the United States for example where there is widespread republican support. If the Crown no longer has a presence in the South, what's to stop access of all manner of military weaponry pouring into Ireland?"

"An interesting debate, gentlemen," Wickham said. "You do raise some provocative arguments, Mr. Sullivan. However, your idea for better advanced planning to respond to potential attacks on important vital industrial assets has obvious merit. That shouldn't conflict with our other efforts, Gentlemen."

———

With curfew following the rioting in early July, Seamus Woods was having difficulty mounting sustained surveillance on Doyle and his four sergeants as their principal targets. More difficult on Doyle himself. Since the failed attempt on his life, Doyle returned to living at the police barracks. His habits remained elusive. Imposition of a nightly curfew resulted in suspension of performances at the opera house. No longer could they rely on his visits there to watch his lady friend perform.

All the RIC sergeants lived in Protestant neighborhoods. Given their reputations, attacks on their homes would require a large assault force to breach obviously fortified defenses. That meant catching them in public places. Still difficult territory since they carefully confined their off duty movements to established Protestant locales. Both access and escape posed substantial obstacles.

Sullivan would not pursue failed IRA tactics. Using these new silenced weapons demanded new thinking. Getting close to the target to insure quick success then getting away by causing the least chaos. Operations involving few men. A core plan relying on simplicity allowing for adaptation to unanticipated circumstances on the ground.

One of Alison's sources provided a breakthrough opportunity.

Sgt. Taggart has resumed frequenting the Donegal Road Public House. Curfews now confine the clientele mostly to police and military. Taggart seen there last two Friday nights. Always with one or two other constables.
Lady Macbeth

Lady Macbeth' was Alison's source with the RIC sergeant husband. In uniform he could move about after curfew hours. Taggart therefore presented the McCorley squad's first opportunity. Having taken his idea of an execution team this far, Sullivan was eager to get on with it. He could see a time soon when he would quit this fight. Until then he felt compelled to cripple Doyle's murder squad. Where Fergus Croft had been a personal matter, Doyle and his police thugs were an abomination worthy of extermination by the same means. Police licensed to commit extrajudicial murder even against noncombatants. State sponsored terrorism. A legacy of British colonialism.

Reason enough he told himself for what he was about do again. Was this the same as killing someone shooting at you? Or just rationalization by those claiming to be patriots? Regardless, this far committed he'd see it through. By any criteria of justice, Doyle and his thugs deserved execution.

——

Sullivan called together a meeting of McCorley's new squad. Gathered again at the garage were McCorley, Woods, Gallagher, and the new man Quinlan.

"Everyone's had a go taking a couple of shots with those new silenced revolvers," Woods said.

"And we're all impressed, Trevor," McCorley said. "I take it you've some idea for the real trial?"

Sullivan handed McCorley the typed note from the source *Lady Macbeth*. McCorley then handed it to Woods.

"Code name *Lady Macbeth*? Reliable?" McCorley said.

"I believe so."

"So how's knowing Sergeant Taggart is taking a pint at this pub help?" Woods said. "Damn curfew makes maneuvering about impossible at night."

Sullivan said, "Yes, but it also allows Taggart to feel safe enough to go out in public again to his favorite pub. Note the source saying it's populated mostly by those in uniform. So that's how we'll get to him."

Everyone looked at one another.

McCorley said, "Not suggesting we dress up like peelers are you, Trevor?"

"Not exactly, Roger. Just me. And not a constable but an army officer."

"You're joking. How you going to do that? Christ, they'll see your face," Woods said.

"Because I've done this before. Fake mustache will obscure my face. Won't be there that long. Once Taggart shows, I'm out of there in less than a minute."

"Unless you're dead of course," McCorley said. "How you going to get a uniform?"

"Already have it.

"What do you do if there are other army blokes there?"

"Just up from Dublin. General Macready's staff. So they wouldn't expect to know me. If Taggart isn't there I have a pint and leave. In uniform I won't be bothered by any police patrols."

"Okay. Once you shoot Taggart ..."

"And any other constables with him," Sullivan added. "Targets of opportunity if there're with Taggart."

"I mean, if all the patrons are in uniform, that means they'll all be armed. The whole fucking place will be an armed camp. Can't shoot 'em all, Trevor."

"The trick is do my business and leave immediately. The silenced weapon will buy me several seconds. Everyone confused not expecting this was gunfire. Then they'll react hurriedly. Hopefully that's all I'll need."

McCorley shook his head with an expression of disbelief. "Then what? How do 'ya get away?"

"That's where I'll need help," Sullivan said.

CHAPTER 30

Sullivan chose the following Friday night for the move against Sergeant Taggart. Alison was of course disappointed. Without providing details he said he had to meet some people, the implication being it was IRA business.

The curfew in Belfast was from 7:00PM to 7:00AM. At seven o'clock he left his flat wearing a suit jacket and felt hat. In a satchel he carried the uniform tunic of a British Army major, officer's cap, and Sam Browne belt with holster. Driving a short distance, he pulled to the curb. In the dark with no one about because of the curfew, he transformed to a British officer. After gluing the fake mustache in place and adding the clear-lens glasses, a look in the mirror confirmed a significant alteration to his appearance.

His leather briefcase held the .38 revolver with the noise suppressor screwed into place. If things turned out badly, inside the holster was his .45 Browning automatic. On his ankle the small .25 pistol.

Less than a block from the Donegall Road Public House he pulled his car to the curb. He placed the ignition key under the seat. Even with his senses heightened, a fatalistic calm took control. Sergeant Taggart might not even show this night. In that case he would finish a couple of pints and make his way back home protected by his army uniform.

334

If this turned out badly, so be it. He'd do his duty as a soldier and inflict maximum damage. According to plan, Seamus Woods and Duncan Gallagher would be waiting in the car when he exited the pub to cover his retreat. They were to conceal themselves at a safe location not too distant and make their way by foot to the car. The risk came if confronted by a police patrol and forced to shoot their way out. Sullivan could be stranded. A spy behind the lines in enemy uniform.

He entered the pub. A sparse clientele. All in uniform of one type or other as conveyed by the intelligence from *Lady Macbeth's* husband. Everyone eyed him momentarily as he took a seat at a table near the rear. Since he was in uniform the other patrons returned to their conversations paying no further attention.

Looking about he did not see anyone matching the photograph of Sergeant Taggart.

Returning to his table after ordering a Guinness at the bar, two British captains across the room made eye contact with him. One stood up and started towards Sullivan's table.

Already a complication.

"Saw you're by yourself, Sir. Care to join us? I'm Captain Ferguson," the officer said extending his hand.

"Major Smith. Thank you, Captain."

After introducing himself to the other officer, Sullivan pulled up a chair at their table.

He noticed the Somerset Regiment insignia of both officers, glad that his Irish Guards Regimental insignia placed him in a different unit.

"Don't believe I've seen you around, Major. New to the 15th?" One officer asked.

"No. Just here temporarily. Up from Dublin. I'm with General Macready's staff. Supposed to be seeing a Lt. Colonel Baker tomorrow."

"Yes, Sir. Colonel Baker's the brigade adjutant. Dublin you say? What's your take on this truce, Major? Mean we're going to be giving the island to the Sinn Féiners?"

"Afraid I can't comment on such matters, Captain. The General personally told his staff that anything related to the truce was strictly confidential."

"Yes, Sir, of course. Anyway, welcome to Belfast. You'll find things a bit more heated here than in Dublin."

"That's what I hear. Seems a bit quiet now though with this curfew."

"Not likely to last. The pot will boil over again. Civilians here are a pissed-off bunch of blighters. You're the enemy if you're a different religion."

Almost through with his pint, Sullivan recognized Sergeant Taggart coming through the door accompanied by two other constables. After a careful look around, they took seats at the bar.

Sullivan looked away. A few moments to mentally prepare. Showtime.

"Gentlemen, thank you for the company. Must be calling it a night though," he said.

He stood up as did the two captains. After shaking hands, Sullivan donned his cap then undid the clasp of the briefcase.

Hard to predict how this would play out. A dozen patrons in the pub. All armed.

With his back to the two captains, Sullivan took a couple of steps toward the bar while slipping his hand into his briefcase bringing out the revolver with the long silencer. Taggart and his two colleagues sat facing toward the bar. As Sullivan approached, one constable turned around. Seeing the intimidating weapon pointed at him caused his eyes to widen in disbelief.

Sullivan thumbed back the hammer and fired. The round hit the constable in the forehead. Taggart and the other constable turned at the *phutt* of the suppressed discharge.

Sullivan shot Taggart in the face followed by another shot to the other constable as the man placed his hand to his holster.

Only a few seconds elapsed.

The three men tumbled to the floor. Sullivan shot Taggart a second time in the head.

With the muffled sound of the shots, the bewildered patrons made no response to draw their weapons as Sullivan panned the intimidating revolver with suppressor around the room. Two rounds remained.

Exiting the pub, he broke into a run on the sidewalk. From behind, two Special constables followed immediately. Shots rang out from behind Sullivan. He turned and took aim on one of the shooters. The man went down as the round caught him in the chest. The second man ducked back into the pub.

Sullivan saw his car pull away from the curb. Woods and Gallagher. Fifty more yards. At a full run he switched the silenced revolver to his left hand extracting the .45 Browning from the holster with his right.

Reaching the car another shot rang out. A searing pain in his right side. He'd been hit.

The car driven by Seamus Woods turned crosswise in the road and stopped. Sitting in the passenger seat was Duncan Gallagher. Several armed pursuers from the pub let off more shots before Gallagher opened up with a .303 Enfield rifle. The pursuers retreated for cover allowing Sullivan to scramble into the rear seat of the car.

Woods completed a U-turn driving away in the opposite direction. Now a matter of evading motorized police patrols.

"Did ya get him?" Woods said.

"Yes. Taggart is dead."

"Sonofabitch!"

"Seamus, I've a problem. Seems I've been shot."

"Shit! How bad?"

Sullivan lifted his shirt. A heavy flow of blood continued soaking his trousers. A nasty looking wound. The skin badly torn into a deep two-inch gash. Hurt like hell. Probably damaged some muscle. Maybe not too serious if properly treated.

"I'll live. Need to get it fixed though."

"Right," Woods said. "I know somewhere safe. A doctor sympathetic to the IRA."

———

337

It was close to noon on Saturday when Sullivan showed up at Alison Kendrick's boardinghouse. Expecting him earlier, she was beside herself with worry.

Once in the car she looked at Sullivan. "Is everything alright? You look pale."

As he made to lean over to kiss her he grimaced from a sharp pain.

"What's wrong?"

"Nothing serious but I have an injury."

"My god. How bad?"

"Painful. Here on my side. It'll heal."

"How?"

"Can't tell you, Alison. Because you shouldn't know."

Back at his apartment she demanded to see the wound. Lifting the edge of bandage she saw the row of sutures.

"What's this from, Trevor?"

"No more questions, Alison. Don't worry, I'll be fine. How 'bout you fix us something for lunch. I'm starved. Haven't eaten since noon yesterday. Then a bath. Maybe a nap. Then let's drive back out to Bangor for a nice dinner. Spend the night again at that same hotel. Get away from this accursed curfew."

"Sounds lovely. Are you up to it?"

"I think so."

Divert her nursing ministrations and postpone the inevitable questions for the weekend once she read of the killings on Donegall Road Friday night. The wound would implicate his involvement beyond merely supplying intelligence to the IRA. A day at the sea might also help him rethink how to proceed.

By late afternoon he did feel much better. A stiff whiskey took the edge off the pain in his side.

After dinner they retired to their hotel room in Bangor. Registered as Mr. and Mrs. Smith. Tomorrow maybe he'd be up to a short walk by the sea.

With difficulty bending over, she helped him undress. Propped him up on the bed with pillows ostensibly so he could read. The purpose however was to afford him a view of her disrobing. A routine they had tacitly adopted. Served to arouse both of them. She reveled in her newfound sexuality, intuitively making her disrobing all the more suggestive.

Even in his injured state he became aroused. As she stood naked at the side of the bed she placed her hand on his pronounced erection.

"That looks inviting. Don't think you're up to such exertions though."

However she continued to rub him through his underwear.

"Perhaps you could get on top," he said.

As she stripped off his underpants he assumed that was what she was preparing. Instead she knelt on the floor. Her hand massaged his erection.

"Afraid that might open the wound. So I'll pleasure you another way."

Taking him in her mouth surprised him. They had never practiced oral sex before. Where did she learn this? Perhaps a natural response? However acquired, she proceeded energetically, asking if this or that felt good. She delighted in controlling the sexual act, teasingly finding ways to prolong his pleasure while bringing him to the edge.

His messy climax all over her face elicited a squeal of laughter. Affirmation of her newfound self-worth.

Sullivan slept soundly after the lovemaking with the pain lessened by another whiskey. Unfortunately Alison's sexual euphoria lasted only until the next morning. At breakfast, the Sunday edition of the *Belfast Telegram* carried the headline *THREE RIC CONSTABLES GUNNED DOWN IN BELFAST PUB.*

> *BELFAST* - Friday night saw another vicious episode of murders. Three RIC constables were shot execution style after hours at the Donegall Road Public House. At the time of the shooting, all of the patrons were members of various Crown security forces owing to the nightly curfew. Killed were Royal Irish Constabulary officers Sergeant William Taggart, 31, Peter Adair, 25, and Frank Hollister, 26.

Ulster Special Constabulary Constable Lester Griffin, 22, suffered a gunshot wound but is expected to recover. Reports remain sketchy but several witnesses claim the assailant was in the uniform of a British Army officer. All three murdered victims were shot in the head at point blank range. The lone assailant made his escape in an automobile driven by accomplices. A spokesman for the 15th Infantry Brigade Headquarters announced that an investigation is underway. They declared this clearly appeared to be the work of someone disguised as a British officer. General Hopkins said...

She looked up from the newspaper.

He looked at her and nodded to her unvoiced question.

"What happened?"

"For your own safety, Alison, better you don't know any details."

A look of genuine fear transfixed her face.

"This is what we've been about isn't it? That last message was about this Sergeant Taggart. One of those shot. Did my information lead to that?"

"Alison, this is war. Taggart and the others are enemy casualties. I don't need to tell you that Doyle's constables are cold-blooded murderers. Taggart especially. Murderers in police uniforms. You know their kind since your husband is one of them. That's why we're doing this."

"But this. Oh, Trevor, it makes me physically sick. I'm so scared. Never thought it would be so ... so personal I guess."

"I've seen my share of war, Alison. Lots of killing. In France and now here in Ireland. Everybody fights for what they believe. Most are scared. Bravery is overcoming the fear to do what's necessary."

Within days of the killing of the RIC constables, the Special Constabulary once again invaded the Catholic neighborhoods with their indiscriminate motorized terror. These events triggered another round of sectarian rioting at the end of August. In a three-day period, twenty more lives were lost in the west and north of Belfast.

While militarily successful, Sullivan found it difficult to reconcile the killing of Taggart as worth the cost in these collateral civilian casualties. A spiral of retaliatory government reprisals that would not end.

CHAPTER 31

Sullivan was to leave that Tuesday to go to Birmingham, England on business. A day's trip both ways with two days allocated to a final technical review with the manufacturer of new pumps for one of the dry docks. An eight-hour ferry ride out of Belfast to Liverpool then a two-hour train journey to Birmingham. A welcome diversion from his normal professional routine.

Sullivan told Alison he would return Friday evening by ferry. Unless delayed by weather while crossing back from Liverpool, he should be able to pick her up as usual.

"I don't think I can do this spying anymore, Trevor. I'm scared. My sources are too after this. They'll know they had something to do with the shooting of those constables. Not sure any of us thought about the consequences."

"Consequences? What'd they think their information was to be used for? This is not some parlor game, Alison. This is not political protest. People die in war, good and bad. Inspector Doyle's murdering constables are legitimate targets. Look at your husband. Confessed to you about murdering a priest. Imagine, a police murder squad."

She touched his face. "I know. But seeing you wounded. What if I were to lose you?"

"We're just spies, Alison. What happened was just a careless accident. Needed to help out just this one time. Not something I'll be repeating."

She shook her head and pursed her lips. "Please don't lie to me, Trevor. I think it was more than an accident. Been thinking. Was it you that did this? Did you shoot those policemen?'

"Don't let your imagination run wild. Told you it's better you don't know. I'm a businessman, not an IRA gunman. Doing my part because I can't abide what's happening to Catholics in Ulster."

The denial clearly didn't allay her fears.

The ferry to Liverpool departed at 7:30 Tuesday morning. A breath of freedom to be alone and away from Belfast. He'd brought along two books to read. After a leisurely breakfast he would adjourn to the ferry's lounge. Spend a quiet day relaxing.

That was not to be. Into the lounge walked Caroline Llewellyn. The predominately male patrons all turned their heads. She exuded that kind of magnetism.

Walking up to his table, "May I join you, Trevor?"

Startled, he quickly rose and kissed her extended hand while pulling back her chair.

"Of course. A surprise seeing you here of all places. Somehow I doubt that's not a coincidence. Am I wrong?"

Smiling coyly, "Obviously it isn't. Father mentioned last week that you were going to Birmingham on company business. Told him I was thinking of doing some shopping in London. Perhaps I could accompany Mr. Sullivan on the ferry trip to Liverpool. Take the train with him to Birmingham where I'll continue on to London."

"Shopping in London? Really?"

"And why should you think otherwise?"

"Our conversation after the dinner party."

"Well didn't you say I was clever?"

"Said you were intelligent and beautiful as I recall. Don't remember clever but I'll concede that as well. Especially since this opportunity avoids unwarranted gossip."

"That too. And this way we also both have a pleasant experience rather than a lonely boring journey. Don't you think?"

"I suspect it will be that, Caroline."

After breakfast in the dining room they took coffee in the lounge.

"You don't mind that I'm interrupting your solitude? Looks as if you were preparing to spend the time reading."

"Not at all. I've a restless mind. Read a lot."

She reached over and took the two volumes.

"Go lord. I'm impressed. Homer's *Iliad*. Marcus Aurelius' *Meditations*. Weighty stuff. Personally I gravitate more to modern novels. Studied literature at the Sorbonne. You know I'm a writer don't you?"

"Your father mentioned it. Fiction I believe? Are you published?"

"Not yet. Struggling with my first novel. That's why Edith is such an inspiration. She didn't publish her first novel until she was forty. Now she's the toast of the literary world."

"What's the premise of your novel?"

"A fearless Irish woman. Comes from humble beginnings. Overcomes great hurdles. But it's fundamentally about just getting on in life for a woman with ambitions. I mean a life beyond being a wife and mother. A profession or avocation. A thirst for an intellectual component to her existence. A literary rather than plot-based novel."

"Autobiographical?"

"Not really. I come from means. My protagonist is a product of Irish poverty. The hard part is constructing how such a woman prevails against the obstacles of her circumstances. Without means in reality that seems almost impossible. Tests my imagination. And I want this to read as if it could be."

"Well keep at it. With all that's going on, Belfast should provide endless real-life material."

"Interesting characters for sure. Like you for example. We have many hours for you to tell me more of those adventures you mentioned at dinner. Absolutely intriguing. Maybe you can be a mysterious character in my next novel."

Caroline Llewellyn's flirtations alone were a dangerous complication. Now the added burden of hours of endless questions about his past. Dangerous ground to navigate given his carefully crafted narrative.

Sullivan steered the conversation toward her. He couldn't overlook Caroline's similarities with Maureen. Traits that attracted him. Both Irish escaping repressive Victorian social conventions. Women defining their own identity. Both women gravitating to the more liberated environment of Paris. Both harboring artistic aspirations.

Switching to French, he said, "To hear you talk, why stay in Belfast? Especially with all that's going on. Why not live in Paris?"

She delighted to exercise her French. "A good question. One that I've asked myself. No clear answer. Of course I adore Paris. But as much as I rebel against my parents, I enjoy their company.

"In truth I only rebel against father's political views. But we both approach it as intellectual disagreement. Not personal. As equals. And my mother I believe secretly admires my greater freedom. She's a crafty grand dame, able to manipulate my father. After a sherry or two she has shared real mother-daughter frankness with me. She often comes to my flat. Girl-talk, more like friends than mother and daughter."

"Your flat? You don't live with your parents in Holywood?"

"Oh no. That would be stifling. My own place affords a much better environment for writing. They of course worry with all the violence going on but I assure them I live in a safe neighborhood. Makes for a better relationship. Establishes my independence.

"Even father I believe secretly admires my independent streak. Calls me tough minded. Perhaps some measure of parental pride as a substitute for the son he never had. You see I was difficult even in birth. Mother almost died of hemorrhaging. Never able to conceive again."

"So remaining in Belfast provides a suitable environment to pursue your writing?" Sullivan said. "Paris is only a day's journey away."

"Not necessarily. Belfast is not especially suitable. Paris would be far better. But I know so few people there. Writing may be a solitary endeavor but I'm a social creature as well. As freethinking as Paris is, I suspect being a lone female with no close friends is probably lonely."

"But I should ask you the same question," she said. "Why stay on in Ireland after the dreadful experience of your wife's death? Why not return to Paris? Or even your native New York City?"

He shrugged. "Perhaps for the same reason. Never gave it any real analytical thought. I functioned on emotion for some time after Maureen died. Staying on in Belfast had much to do with my position at Harland & Wolff. Easier to go forward without enduring another life upheaval. I like my job. Like working for your father. As the months passed, I felt comfortable in Belfast. Better of course if this violence would end."

The ferry crossing passed quickly. To avoid unintentionally saying something to conflict with his cover story, he regaled her with the details of his military adventures. Recounting the ordeal in the Argonne Forest, she remarked, "I should consider a novel based on your exploits, Trevor."

Once in Liverpool they had enough time to enjoy a quick meal before boarding their train. Two hours to Birmingham where he would get off, leaving her to continue to London.

As the train pulled into Birmingham, he said, "A welcome surprise that you joined me on this trip, Caroline. I enjoyed our day together. Have a pleasant time in London."

"Too bad you must go about your work. I'd love to show you around London?"

"Another time perhaps."

As he stood up and brought down his suitcase from the overhead rack, she also stood. Unexpectedly she kissed him on the cheek.

"I would love that, Trevor."

———

Caroline Llewellyn now represented an immediate dilemma.

In Birmingham, Sullivan immersed himself in the technical details of the new pumps. The English manufacturer explained new design features for improving performance. Thought had also been given to ease of installation and maintenance. A welcome diversion to the predicament facing him once he returns to Belfast.

They insisted Sullivan join them for dinner. An excellent claret served to compensate for the uninspiring English cuisine. He declined his hosts' offer of more drinking after dinner claiming they all had to work the next day.

He returned to his hotel at nine o'clock. At the desk as he asked for his room key, the clerk said, "Your wife arrived an hour ago, Sir. I took her to your room."

"My wife?"

"Yes, Sir. Caroline I believe she said?"

Looking at the quizzical expression on Sullivan's face, concern came over the clerk's face. "I hope that was satisfactory, Sir?"

"Oh yes, of course. Just surprised. Wasn't expecting her until tomorrow was all."

Relieved, the man said, "Well a pleasant surprise I trust, Sir. She also said to send up a bottle of Champagne after you arrived. Would that be acceptable, Sir?"

"Oh, yes."

Given his encouragement to her advances this wasn't a total surprise. Just not this quickly. A remarkably determined woman. Used to getting her way. No denying his sexual attraction to Caroline Llewellyn, but an impossible complication changing everything.

Carrying on with two women. Hiding that fact not only publicly but from each of them? And they knew each other. One or the other, or both, would quickly detect something amiss. He wasn't that good an actor, nor could he juggle another layer of deceit.

The obvious course would be to rebuff Caroline's aggressive advances. That could carry a risk of eroding his professional standing at Harland & Wolff. Emotionally he didn't want to push her away. Up to now he'd enjoyed the game of seduction knowing she too felt the need to keep their romantic rendezvous secret. Circumstances had now moved well beyond a flirtation. Nothing subtle about her waiting upstairs to share his hotel room for the night.

Since she had the key he knocked on the door.

"It's Trevor, Caroline."

"It's open," came her reply.

He opened the door and entered. Caroline was sitting on the bed. Dressed in a black silk chemise, barefoot, her intentions obvious.

"I ordered Champagne. Sound good?"

"The clerk told me, *Mrs. Sullivan*."

"Well you don't want people talking do you?"

A knock on the door sent Caroline into the water closet.

"You ordered Champagne, Sir?" The waiter in a white jacket asked.

"Yes. Put it over there on the bureau."

Sullivan tipped the man then locked the door.

"All clear," he said.

Caroline came out and made for the Champagne.

Pouring a glass she took a sip. Looking at him while standing very close, "You're not sorry to find me here?"

"No."

"Want a drink first?"

"Already had wine with my dinner."

"How about dessert then?"

She peeled his jacket off and pulled him against her while kissing him.

As she undid his belt he removed his tie.

Reaching her hand inside his trousers she massaged his growing erection.

Feeling his full arousal, she stepped back and pulled the chemise over her head.

While he looked at her naked body he quickly pulled off his shoes followed by his trousers.

Removing his shirt revealed the bandage over the bullet wound.

"What's that?"

"Careless accident at the shipyard. Jagged piece of metal. Nothing serious."

Backing to the bed, she pulled him closer. Sitting on the edge of the bed she pulled down his underwear.

As she caressed his fully erect cock, she said, "Certainly doesn't seem to impair your arousal."

"You know this is a mistake don't you?" he said.

"Want me to stop?"

"No."

An hour later they sat propped up in bed sipping Champagne.

"I wanted to make love to you the first time we met. I could see in your eyes you felt the same. Am I wrong?"

He laughed, "No you're not wrong."

"Too bad you must work tomorrow. But at least make an excuse so we can go to dinner."

"And what will you do all day?" He asked.

"Well Birmingham's not exactly London but I'm sure I can find suitable shops of interest. I'll be waiting for you. Don't be late. We'll make love again before we go out for dinner. Tell you what. I'll be waiting for you in the tub. We'll have a good soak together. Clean enough for doing all sorts of things."

———

Hard to focus on work the following day. Fortunately there were few questions and no problems.

To her word, Caroline was in the tub when he returned to the hotel late in the afternoon. Caroline took command of the

349

lovemaking. A Parisian prostitute could not have been more creative or uninhibited.

As much of a complication as Caroline Llewellyn represented, partly because of her Sullivan was coming around to making a decision. Compounding factors, including her, diminished his willingness to continue leading this double life. Helping McCorley develop the means to neutralize Doyle's murder squad proved gratifying but he would no longer actively take part. Killing Taggart felt different than Fergus Croft. Someone else would have to get Doyle and the rest of his RIC murder squad.

Chastising himself for being less than an Irish patriot, he came to the heart of his disillusionment. While the twenty-six counties of Southern Ireland would achieve independence from Britain, the Northern Ireland six counties would not. Likely never given the sectarian antagonisms. Although he sympathized with the oppressed Catholics in the North, he was not willing to commit his life to that struggle.

Was he too quick to discount a possible future with Caroline Llewellyn? Could he just opt out of involvement with the IRA? Would his past activities ever be discovered? He'd committed capital offenses against the British Crown. Wouldn't matter provided he left Ireland.

What about Alison Kendrick? Not that easy to just sever that relationship without destroying her. He bore a responsibility for using her under the pretext of a romantic involvement.

While those thoughts ran through his mind over dinner, Caroline again raised the question about Alison.

"I wouldn't ask you before but after the last two nights I must. Are you sleeping with your secretary, Trevor?"

Shit. His duplicity already dispelling thoughts of a possible future with Caroline.

He set down his fork and took a sip of wine to gain a moment.

"Not sure how to answer that, Caroline?"

"What? How about a simple yes or no?"

"Because it's not that simple. I'll admit to having had an occasional intimacy with her. Happened first by accident. Regrettable."

"Why regrettable?"

"Because she was vulnerable. Just escaped an abusive relationship. Alison's a delicate person. Insecure. All alone. No children, no close family. As you can well imagine, difficult for a single woman. She threw herself at me.

"Anyway, I didn't resist. Whether weakness or sympathy doesn't matter now."

The implication left that it was only an occasional liaison not a regular weekend affair.

"I take that to mean you are not in love with her?"

Sullivan shook his head. "No. But I need to find a way to extricate myself without emotionally devastating her. Worse that she's my secretary. She needs her job."

"You know she's in love with you."

He shook his head in an expression of denial.

"I'm a woman. I know. Among her associations at the Suffrage Society, she makes little attempt to hide her affection for you."

"All the more reason I need to correct the situation. Just don't know how without ruining her self-esteem not to mention the practical circumstances of her job."

Caroline had only picked at her food. Taking a sip of wine, "There's something else about Alison you should know, Trevor."

He wondered if the concern reflected in his expression.

"The questions she's asked some of us at our Society meetings. She's clever but clearly probing about everyone's politics. I fear she might be passing information to ..."

"To whom?"

"Well I'm not sure. Maybe to sympathetic republicans. Maybe even the IRA."

"What makes you think that?"

"She's vocal about her ex-husband. Says he even confessed to killing Catholics. Now he's a special constable. Uses that as a basis to express her hatred for the government."

"Probably just her way of asserting herself. A rebellion to her abusive husband. How would she even have contact with someone in the IRA? She's also Protestant."

Caroline laid her hand over his on the table. "You're not involved in anything political are you, Trevor?"

"Good grief, Caroline. Why would I help the IRA?"

"Because the Protestant Ulster Volunteers killed your wife? That's what father said."

"No, I said they were the most likely. But she was with her brother and his wife at the time. A bystander. Some said her brother was IRA. There was also speculation that it could have been the IRA that did the shooting. Wrong person, suspected traitor, something personal? Who knows? I didn't know her family. No one ever claimed credit leaving everything in doubt."

"Very well, Trevor. The idea of you being an IRA spy does sound ridiculous. But what about Alison? Not sure I'm liberated enough to want to share you."

"I'll deal with that situation as soon as possible. Should have never let it get this far."

Whether a serious relationship with Caroline Llewellyn even became possible, he knew he must end the affair with Alison. End the spying and all else. He'd done enough. Personally executing Taggart was a mistake. Somehow that crossed a line. He was done with this. A mistake from the beginning.

Of course he could not stay on in Belfast. Couldn't just cease being involved. Far too dangerous after all he'd done. Too many people knew. Didn't relish the idea of a British prison, or the hangman's rope. Or the more likely bullet to the head.

The return journey on Friday might have been pleasant with Caroline's company except for the weekend ahead of him. Could he now keep up this charade with Alison until he figured out how to end it? Could he make love to her that night? Was this infidelity? To Alison or Caroline?

He would pick Alison up at her boardinghouse as promised. As for lovemaking, at least for tonight he'd feign fatigue from the trip. Beyond that he wasn't sure how to proceed.

The looming decision to discontinue his intimacy with Allison had a cascading effect. No matter how Alison reacted, he must immediately leave his job and Belfast. Even at the risk of incriminating herself, the proverbial wrath of a scorned woman might provoke her to reckless revenge. At least she could keep her job if he left.

Before disembarking the ferry, Caroline said. "I fear you must think me a spoiled wealthy young woman. However this wasn't just an adventure, Trevor. I'll promise to keep us a secret but I want to continue to see you. I must see you."

"I feel the same, Caroline. Let's just be careful until things can be sorted out." Sorted out? Would she come with him to Paris?

After descending the gangway they walked arm-in-arm before exiting the dock.

"Father's chauffeur should be waiting in front of the terminal building to take me home. Father insisted. So let's say good-bye here. How do I contact you, Trevor?"

"Oh, I'm sure you'll find a way."

"After these last couple of days together you can be sure it'll be soon, Trevor," she said as she embraced him, engaging in a prolonged kiss as he enveloped his arms around her waist.

"And here's my address." She handed him a slip of paper. "Surprise me anytime."

CHAPTER 32

Sullivan drove to his apartment to freshen up and change clothes. Didn't want to risk Alison smelling any trace of Caroline's perfume. Just enough time to get to Alison's boardinghouse and return to his apartment before the curfew. Claiming fatigue from an exhausting week would take little acting. A couple of whiskeys and he could easily fall asleep.

At the boardinghouse, the landlady told him Alison had not returned home since leaving for work that morning. "Not like Miss Kendrick to have not sent you word, Mr. Sullivan."

"Well I've been out of town on business. Probably wasn't expecting me. Please tell her I'll call on her tomorrow around noon."

That was troubling. She of course was expecting him. Something must be wrong. But he cautioned himself not to imagine something dire. Most likely some normal reason for her absence.

Nothing he could do but return to his apartment with curfew approaching. Perhaps he might find her there waiting. Delayed for some reason. Missed each other in passing.

Not the case. She had no key and was not waiting for him. Unless she showed up soon it was unlikely she would try coming here after curfew. Hoped she wouldn't try anything so foolish.

Give it a little more time then maybe fry a plate of eggs and bacon for dinner. Pour that glass of whiskey first. Use the time to plan how he intended to handle matters with Alison.

Tired as he was, three hours later he wasn't that sleepy. Trying to read didn't help. Couldn't help worrying about what happened with Alison.

While still awake after midnight, there came the sound of automobiles stopping outside his building. Unusual at this hour. Under the curfew that could only mean police.

Looking out the window he saw three automobiles pulled to the curb on the opposite side of the street. No markings. Eight men in civilian suits exited the vehicles. Standing together they appeared to be conversing. Several drew revolvers. RIC?

No reason however to believe he was their target. But this was not a neighborhood where police conducted raids. And out of uniform? He couldn't take the risk. Must implement his emergency escape plan. At least he had some warning.

He pulled a satchel from the armoire. His escape kit. It already contained anything important. Along with a clean shirt, underwear, razor, and toothbrush were his .45 Browning service pistol, the small .25 automatic, and ammunition.

Apart from the weapons, he was scrupulous about never leaving anything incriminating in the apartment. Even during the once a week visit by the cleaning lady, he removed the weapons. Except for the hidden .38 revolver with silencer.

His apartment was three flights up. Good exercise without a lift and he preferred the top floor. No creaking floorboards overhead. Better view. If they were coming for him, it would buy some time before the knock on the door. But it also meant he was trapped. The external fire escape ladder at the end of the hallway would be covered below.

With the foresight of planning he had a couple of minutes. Might not be the target but he had a bad feeling. He put on his suit jacket, looped his tie around his neck, put his hat on his head, and entered the water closet carrying the satchel.

From behind the toilet tank reservoir he retrieved the hidden .38 revolver with silencer. Stepping on the toilet and sink as footholds, he opened the window.

The window was a dual affair, hinged on both sides with a latch in the middle opening out. Part of a roof dormer, the window set back a foot from the edge of the pitched roof. Fully opened it allowed Sullivan to step onto the roof. Carefully holding the window frame allowed him to swing his leg to the side of the dormer. Before making the maneuver he reached out and swung his satchel up the roof slope to the side of the dormer. Although practiced twice before, it was still a little unnerving forty feet above the ground.

The only means of obvious escape from the apartment was onto the roof through this window. The other windows of his corner apartment looked out the gabled end wall of the building presenting no access to the roof. To disguise this only access to the roof, he previously drilled holes in the bottom and top of the window jam. Before exiting he put four nails strategically placed on the toiletry shelf into his pocket.

Once outside, putting the nails into the holes required stretching precariously around the front of the dormer while holding on with his other hand.

With the nails inserted, the window sections would appear firmly jammed from opening outward. If someone were to smash out the window, Sullivan would then move to the reverse side of the roof out of view should someone come out onto the roof.

A chilly overcast autumn night. A damp fog moving in. He'd give it thirty minutes before assuming this to be a false alarm.

Minutes passed before he thought he heard knocking below but couldn't be sure. No mistaking the smashing of the door moments later.

What the hell happened? Must have something to do with Alison. Somehow she was found out.

A loud rattling of the dormer window brought attention back to immediate concerns. It stopped after a couple of tries.

Then silence. Fifteen minutes later he watched as men exited the building front entrance. Two men joined them from the back alley. Huddled conversation followed but he was too far away to make out anything.

Soon after all but two men got into the automobiles and drove off. The two left behind lit cigarettes. As the fog rolled in they soon disappeared from Sullivan's sight except for the glow of their cigarettes.

———

Sullivan's thoughts immediately turned to escaping Belfast. His cover blown and only narrowly avoiding arrest. But before entering back into his apartment a thought struck him. These men were obviously police. RIC or Special Constabulary. Dressed in civilian clothing obviously meant deniability for his disappearance if they were seen by witnesses. Easily blamed on the IRA.

Therefore it was not an arrest. An unofficial abduction. Probably tortured to give up his sources. In the end a bullet to the head. Probably Doyle's constables.

Did that mean they were afraid to arrest him? No evidence? Too powerfully connected? If it was about Alison, they would have to assume he'd claim her to be a scorned woman making up lies. Unreciprocated romantic designs. Actual evidence was required for a legal proceeding given his stature and connections.

Thinking it through further, he never divulged to her to whom nor how he transmitted the information she provided. Never any names. Never divulged what happened in Derry. Never admitted to involvement in the Special Constabulary bombing or gunning down the RIC constables. Her testimony the only basis for prosecution? Insufficient for the police to chance the certain backlash, possibly ruining careers.

Much more expedient to make him disappear. The body turning up in a shallow grave in some rural meadow. The death blamed on the IRA given his high profile work to defend Unionist targets against IRA attack. Certainly he wouldn't be the first such murder.

The more he argued the theory in his mind the more plausible it seemed. It also meant that undoubtedly it was Doyle's constables sent to remove him. The Specials were too poorly trained to be tasked with pulling off anything of this sensitivity.

But still just his speculation. Had he missed something? Did he dare risk not making a run for it?

Right now he needed to get off this roof. Think this through after getting to a safe place.

And what about Alison Kendrick? By recruiting her into this dangerous game, he bore a responsibility to warn her. If this did not originate with her then she might not yet be caught up in this disaster. Still could be an unrelated reason to explain her absence last night. He might have been identified by any one of those IRA that knew what he was up to. Unlikely knowing McCorley, Woods, and Gallagher as he did. But Quinlan? Who knows?

Regardless, he must reach Alison to either rescue her or confirm that was too late. His fault for involving her in this. Regret swept over him as he plumbed the depth of his culpability.

Reentering his apartment through the window, he found everything thrown about. Clothes on the floor. Glad he earlier disposed of the incriminating spare British Army uniform. Mattress upturned. The front door frame splintered around the lock.

Ten minutes later he finished packing clothing and other essentials into a single suitcase. The separate small satchel held the .38 revolver and ammunition for all the weapons. He was not returning. Peering into the hallway, he saw no one. As he made his way down the staircase a couple of doors cautiously opened then quickly closed.

Although he had seemingly accounted for all eight of the invaders, he nonetheless exited the rear of the building cautiously. The Browning .45 in his waistband with a spare clip in his pocket if confronted by the remaining two watchers.

In the now dense fog no one was visible as he made his way to his car parked nearby on the street. Easy enough to get to the car but driving off undetected was the trick. Even with the cover of the fog, the sound of his car would alert the men watching his building given the nighttime silence with the curfew.

He stealthily approached his car from the front. Fortunately it faced the opposite direction from where the watchers had taken up their positions still invisible in the fog.

Quietly he opened the rear door and placed the suitcase and satchel on the rear seat. Getting behind the steering wheel he released the parking brake while putting the transmission in neutral. Stepping back out, he found a handhold from which to push the vehicle while steering with his left hand.

He knew the street. Fifty yards further it ran to a long gradual downhill grade. If he coasted down he might make it a couple of blocks before starting the engine.

Strategically placed roadblocks enforcing the curfew made nighttime movement for any distance risky. His plan was to distance himself from his residence then park for the night unnoticed among other parked vehicles. An uncomfortable night spent in the car on this chilly, damp night. But he'd endured worse in the Argonne Forest.

When the curfew lifted in the morning, what next? How would he go about discovering the fate of Alison? The boardinghouse could be a police trap. Take the risk or make a run for it? The rest of a sleepless night to ponder his next move.

———

In the early evening on Friday, Alison Kendrick planned to surprise Sullivan on his return from England. After leaving the office she bought food to prepare a special dinner of lamb chops. Without returning to her boardinghouse she instead caught the tram to the ferry terminal. It was a good hour before the scheduled arrival time of Sullivan's Irish Sea ferry from Liverpool. No matter given her excitement anticipating the weekend ahead. A cup of tea at the terminal's bar afforded something to occupy her wait.

As the ferry announced its arrival by repeated horn blasts, she found a vantage point hidden in the shadows well back from the arrivals area at the bottom of the ferry gangway ramp. She wanted to discreetly surprise him with an embrace away from the disembarking passengers.

As she saw him at the top of the ferry railing her delight shrank to anguish a moment later. Walking down the gangway in front of him was Caroline Llewellyn.

Once they set foot on the dock they moved to the side to let the other passengers pass. Confusion abruptly turned to horror as Sullivan embraced Caroline Llewellyn passionately followed by an extended kiss. Alison Kendrick nearly fainted, physically difficult to breathe as she hyperventilated under the shock. An unimaginable nightmare.

As Sullivan and Llewellyn approached arm in arm, she stepped further back into the shadows. After standing there transfixed for several minutes she located a bench. A bit unsteady, she needed to regain her composure. Transfixed by her distress she sat there for a considerable time.

Eventually she boarded a tram. During the ride it remained difficult to focus on anything except replaying the sight of Sullivan's betrayal. By the time the tram approached her boardinghouse, she regained a measure of control having made a fateful decision.

She would not confront Sullivan tonight as he arrived according to their usual arrangement. Far too easy to allow him to just brush her aside. She'd instead wait down the street out of sight. After he came and left she would enter the boardinghouse. That was the easy part. After that something much more difficult. Such cruel treatment required an equally cruel punishment.

"Mrs. Lansdale, might I use the house telephone?" Alison said to her landlady. 'I've an important call to make. I'll pay for any charges."

"Of course, my dear. Go right ahead. I worried about you not showing up earlier. Mr. Sullivan came by just a while ago. He seemed concerned as well."

"A family matter delayed me. You know how that can be."

"Ah, yes. Now go make your call. I've saved you dinner so you won't go hungry. Come to the kitchen when you're through."

The wall mounted telephone was in the hallway off the dining room. An awkward location from which to maintain privacy but her call was brief.

With some time to kill she ducked her head into the kitchen.

"I'm afraid I'm not very hungry, Mrs. Lansdale. Thank you so much though. I'm expecting a visitor tonight. If you'd be so kind as to call me when he arrives?"

"Why of course. Mr. Sullivan?"

"No. It's that family matter that kept me late getting home. My estranged husband."

"Oh. Good lord. Are you sure you want to see him, my dear?"

Alison had recounted to Mrs. Lansdale the physical abuse she suffered at the hands of her husband. How her boss had rescued her. Provided her the means for a new life. As for Mrs. Lansdale, she remained skeptical about her tenant's relationship with Mr. Sullivan. Seemed far more than a boss just helping one of his employees his stopping by most Fridays and her not returning until Sunday evenings. Maybe poor Mr. Sullivan had found solace in the affections of his secretary after the death of his wife. A bit unseemly, but both seemed good people. Not for her to judge.

It was after nine o'clock when Edgar Kendrick arrived. Mrs. Lansdale opened the front door and looked at the tall well-built man in the uniform of an RIC constable.

"I'm Constable Kendrick. My wife left me a message that she wished to see me."

"Yes. She's in her room. If you'll come into the parlor I will get her."

As Alison entered the parlor a look of dread came over her at seeing her husband after several months. She closed the parlor door thanking Mrs. Lansdale.

"What the fuck's this about, Alison? Information about an IRA spy? Who might that be?"

"Please sit down, Edgar. I'll explain."

A moment of uncertainty. Was she willing to do something so self-destructive? Yet blind rage overrode all else.

"It's my boss. Mr. Sullivan."

"The fuck you say? Sullivan? I don't believe that. IRA? How the hell would you know?"

She bit her lip before answering. Edgar was a violent man. No telling how he might react. "Because I've been sleeping with him."

Kendrick jumped to his feet. "Fuckin' whore!"

"No different from you, Edgar. But I wasn't just mucking about. It was him that seduced me. Helped me get set up here. Besides he's my boss. When I left you what was I supposed to do? Couldn't afford to lose my job too. He wouldn't leave me be."

As the misplaced anger of his absent wife bedding another man subsided slightly, he returned to the reason that brought him here.

"How do 'ya know he's a spy?"

"Cause he's talked about it. Asked me to see if I could help by passing on information from my friends in the Suffrage Society. Information the IRA might find useful."

"The Suffrage Society?"

"Yes, Edgar. The women's rights group. Got to look after ourselves with you male bastards running everything."

"And did you help him?"

"No. Told him I was for union. Didn't abide discrimination against the Catholics but wasn't about to help the IRA. I'm against all this violence, Edgar. Anyway he kept at me. So I passed on some gossip that I didn't think mattered. Enough to satisfy him."

Her husband said, "Sullivan's a big shot. Heard he's even close to Craig and Atwood. Head of this bullshit Security Advisory Committee. You're saying he's an IRA spy? I think you're full of shit, Alison."

"His wife was murdered in Derry by one of your UVF crowd. That's what I think turned him to doing this."

"If you're right then you're in a tight spot, bitch. The IRA kills informers. You'll have to leave Belfast. But true or not, why you doin' this now?"

"I've done nothing wrong. I'm scared. Don't want to wind up in some stinking British prison. I see myself ending badly. Sullivan used me. I made a terrible mistake. He'll throw me to the dogs when I'm no more use. And I think that might be soon."

"Why's that?"

"Because I think he's doing more than spying for the IRA. That puts me in deeper. A week ago when I last saw him he had a terrible injury. A deep wound in his side. Stiches even. Wouldn't say what happened."

Sarcastically Kendrick said, "And how do you think it happened?"

"It was the day after those three constables from your unit were gunned down in that pub."

"You sayin' Sullivan was shot?"

"Can't say. Might have been. Told me it was better I didn't know what happened. Not sure what a gunshot wound looks like but someone stitched him up. Said he had business that night and couldn't see me. I'm sure he had something to do with it. He has a gun you know."

"But you're still fuckin him. Got yourself a grand new life. Same question. Why tell me now?"

"Because he has another woman. Discovered he's having an affair with Malcom Llewellyn's daughter. Wealthy, sophisticated, educated, beautiful Caroline Llewellyn. He'll be wanting to get rid of me then I'll be out on the street with no job. Might even have the IRA kill me."

Kendrick said, "I still think you're a lying stupid bitch. I think you're just pissed off because your boss got tired of fuckin' a stupid, plain-looking cunt like you. The rest of this is just crap to get back at him.

"Tell you what though. I'll pass along what you've said to District Inspector Doyle. Now let me tell you what'll happen whether your lying or not.

"If you're right, who's to say that you haven't been helping your boss by more than just passing along gossip? At the least you'll lose your job. Out in the street. Too old to get by as a real whore fuckin' for money. Worse case, the IRA shoots you or you wind up in a British prison.

"Now if you're wrong," he paused to laugh, "then I'd guess the same thing probably happens. You always were such a stupid bitch, Alison."

Edgar Kendrick stalked out of the room without saying anything further.

———

Early the following morning Mrs. Lansdale answered a knock at the boardinghouse front door. Before her stood a short stocky man in police uniform. Behind him stood Alison Kendrick's husband from the night before.

"I'm Sergeant Rafferty. We're here for Mrs. Kendrick."

"And why should you be pestering her. I know about you," she said wagging her finger at Edgar Kendrick.

"It'll be none of your affair, madam," Sergeant Rafferty said. "Now please fetch Mrs. Kendrick or we'll do it ourselves."

A few minutes later Lansdale escorted Alison Kendrick down the stairs. Her husband grabbed her roughly by the arm. "You'll be coming with us. Lot's more questions."

"Now see here," Lansdale said in protest.

Rafferty stepped in front of her. "Don't be interfering or I'll arrest you too, old woman."

Driving away, Alison made no protest. What did she expect after revealing Sullivan's spying for the IRA to her estranged husband? The entire sleepless night she debated the impulsive move but always returned to Sullivan's betrayal. The sex nothing more than to get her to spy. All thoughts of her newfound happiness destroyed. Sullivan deserved harsh punishment. Didn't matter what happened to her. Prison only one possible unpleasant fate. Life held nothing further.

Detached despair turned to anxiety as the police car pulled in front of her former house. Why were they not taking her to police headquarters? Looking at the sneer on her husband's face, anxiety turned to fear. Certain fates could be worse than others.

Once inside the house, fear turned to terror. Her husband shoved her into the kitchen forcing her into a wooden chair. Next, Rafferty roughly held her shoulders while her husband handcuffed her, passing the handcuff chain between the spokes of the chair back.

"Why am I here?"

"To answer questions," Rafferty said.

"Why here? I demand to be taken to police headquarters."

Rafferty made no reply while grabbing Edgar Kendrick by the sleeve and pulling him back into the front parlor.

In a whisper so Alison could not overhear, Rafferty said, "Sullivan never returned home last night. Maybe your wife had second thoughts and warned him. We're to find out."

"Why did we bring her here rather than headquarters?" Kendrick said.

Rafferty smiled. "The Inspector wants to play this safe. Sullivan's got important connections. So far we've only got your wife's say so about him being a spy. Fuckin' her boss only to find out he's messing about. Might be she's only makin' this shit up."

"So what are we to do?"

"Find out what she knows. Be rough if we have to. Unofficial according to Inspector Doyle. If she just made this up, don't want it to blow up in our faces. Just a nasty argument between a husband and his unfaithful wife. Not the first time you've hit her I'd venture?

"You can step in the other room if you like, her being your wife and all."

Kendrick shook his head no. "Not any more. Just a fuckin' whore. The bitch needs to be slapped around good."

The two returned to the kitchen.

"Now, Alison I'm going to ask you some questions," "Rafferty said. "Answer me truthfully and this will be over quickly. Resist and I assure you it will be the worst experience of your life. Certainly the most painful."

"I told Edgar all I know."

Rafferty delivered a hard blow to her cheek with the back of his hand.

"Don't try that, Alison. You told your husband only what you wanted to tell him. You think I believe you weren't helping your boss, your lover?

"So one more time. I want to know everything you know. Who are Sullivan's sources? How did he communicate with the IRA? Who did he pass the information to? What information did he pass on? Did Sullivan take part in the murder of Sergeant Taggart? What exactly was your role in all this, Alison?"

"I don't know anything more. Please believe me."

Rafferty shook his head. "Don't have time for this shit,"

He reached for a dishcloth next to the sink. Twirling it into a rope, he placed it around her mouth as a gag tying it behind her head.

"Now this is going to hurt, Alison."

Rafferty pulled leather gloves from his hip pocket, letting her watch as he pulled on the tight fitting gloves.

The pounding to her face lasted five minutes before Rafferty stopped. He was a practiced torturer. The blows lacerated both cheeks below the eyes. Blood splattered about. The dishcloth gag showed signs of heavy bleeding from her mouth.

"Now this can go on as long as necessary, Alison. Ready to talk or should I continue?"

She nodded affirmatively.

Edgar Kendrick removed the gag.

Once the gag was removed, she spit a mouthful of blood on the floor. A loosened tooth lodged in the gag.

Outpoured a torrent of information. Every detail of her involvement in a confusing chronology. Yes Sullivan asked her to spy for the IRA. She agreed because she thought she must to keep his interest and her job. She used her friends at the Suffrage Society for possible sources. Tears streamed down her cheeks as she provided names. She held back nothing. Railed against that bitch Caroline Llewellyn claiming to be a friend. Yes, Llewellyn attended the Suffrage Society meetings sometimes. No, Llewellyn never gave her any information.

"Okay. Now tell us about Sullivan. Why did he tell you he spied for the IRA?"

"Because the UVF murdered his wife. Said he couldn't abide discrimination against the Catholics here in the North."

"Who did he communicate with in the IRA?"

She now realized how precarious that made her position by lacking any knowledge of what happened to the information she gave Sullivan. They wouldn't believe she didn't know more.

"He never said."

"Come now. He must have mentioned a name," Rafferty said.

She shook her head no.

"How'd he communicate with the IRA?"

Again she shook her head. "He never told me. Said it was safer for me that I didn't know any details."

Rafferty said, "Appears he was wrong on that account don't you think? I don't believe a fuckin' word you telling me you know nothing more. Just did your spying then passed it along without any idea who he was working with? Yet all this time you're fuckin' him?"

She made no reply just cried with racking sobs.

Rafferty said to Edgar Kendrick, "Put the gag back on."

Alison twisted her head back and forth trying to prevent her husband reapplying the gag knowing it meant a continuation of the beating.

Once the gag was back in place Rafferty said, "I don't have the time to continue as before. You'd pass out then we'd have to revive you. Eventually you'd talk but it'll take too long. Therefore, I'm forced to resort to uglier methods, Alison."

Rafferty withdrew a straight razor from his pocket. His weapon of choice to extract information. Holding the blade inches from her face he said, "Here's what I'm going to do, Alison. I'm going to start cutting you. Your face of course. Every woman fears being disfigured. After a few minutes your husband here won't recognize you. You wish to talk, just blink your eyes rapidly.

"So let's start. I'll make my first incision on the side of your nose. Such a pretty nose too. Last chance. Ready to talk?"

She blinked furiously.

Rafferty motioned to Kendrick to remove the gag.

"My god, please don't cut me! I swear he never told me what he did with the information. I asked but he never said. Oh please believe me. If I knew anything I'd tell you."

Rafferty looked at her several moments making his decision. He ushered Kendrick back with him into the parlor.

"You okay with what went on in there, Kendrick?" Rafferty said.

"Sure. Fuckin' bitch deserved it."

"Well you keep her here. All damn day if necessary. Not sure what's to be done with her. I'm to report back to Doyle."

Once Rafferty left, Kendrick returned to the kitchen.

"You fuckin' bitch. You not only run off with another man you become a spy. How do 'ya think that makes me look?"

He immediately reapplied the gag.

"I'm not going to ask you a fuckin' thing, Alison. Don't really give a shit what you have to say. But I believe Rafferty let you off too lightly. What you've done deserves a proper beating. I don't need a knife. When I'm done with you, no man will ever look at you again."

CHAPTER 33

As dawn broke Sullivan snapped awake. Not from a sound sleep just a succession of short spells of napping. Cold and hungry, the lack of rest only aggravated the stress of uncertainty. He wanted nothing more than drive south. If he could make it to the newly defined Southern Ireland territory, the truce might provide a safe refuge. A long risky drive. But of course he could not desert Alison Kendrick.

Once the curfew lifted at seven o'clock he drove to her boardinghouse. Parking across the street behind other parked cars, he would wait until nine o'clock. By that time the other boarders would have breakfasted. Didn't want to arrive with the dining room full of people. An opportunity to also determine if this might be a police trap.

He'd been waiting an hour when a sedan with RIC markings pulled up in front. Out came Edgar Kendrick and another constable he recognized as the notorious Sergeant Rafferty from his photograph. Obviously here for Alison, Sullivan placed the .45 on his lap. A fleeting thought of killing the two RIC officers and escaping with Alison ran through his mind. But that would make fleeing south impossible with all RIC barracks alerted.

Minutes later the two RIC officers exited the boardinghouse with Alison Kendrick in tow. Her estranged husband held her arm roughly dragging her along then pushing her into the car.

369

So much for Alison's plight. It also meant that somehow the RIC had gotten on to him without her. Now of course the police would coerce her into confessing all she knew. He only hoped the horrific methods of torture frequently reported by male prisoners would not be inflicted on a woman. Not a certainty with the sadistic proclivities of Sergeant Rafferty and his boss Inspector Doyle.

Sullivan followed the RIC car to determine where they were taking Alison. Perhaps with the help of McCorley's Active Service Unit they could mount an escape. IRA prisoners had escaped police custody before.

To his surprise the car pulled to the curb in the middle of a block of brick row houses in Protestant Sandy Row. He knew it to be Alison's former home when he helped her move. All three entered the house.

Parked well down the street, Sullivan waited. As the minutes passed, he wondered why bring her here? Must have to do with him since no one else knew of her involvement. An alternative to arresting her? She obviously didn't leave the boardinghouse willingly.

An hour later, Rafferty exited the house then drove off alone.

This presented an unexpected opportunity with only Edgar Kendrick guarding her. After waiting ten minutes to organize his plan, he exited the car. No one visible on the street. Well-armed with the .45 in his back waistband and holding the .38 revolver with the long silencer inside his suit jacket, it remained only a matter of gaining entry into the house. He would quietly kill Edgar Kendrick and escape with Alison. No choice now but to save her and take their chances by fleeing Belfast.

With the butt of the revolver grip Sullivan pounded on the front door only minutes after Rafferty left.

"It's Rafferty. Open the fuckin' door, Kendrick," Sullivan said. A risk if Kendrick realized it wasn't Rafferty.

For good measure, Sullivan rapped the door a couple more times.

Kendrick opened the door a few inches. "What the fuck...,"
the sentence truncated as Sullivan kicked the partially opened
door slamming it into Kendrick knocking him back.

Kendrick's eyes opened in shock as Sullivan stuck the intimidating silenced revolver into his face. All Kendrick managed
was, "You!"

"Where is she?" Sullivan said.

Kendrick did not answer.

"One more chance, Kendrick. If you don't answer you get a
bullet in the knee."

Kendrick motioned with his head toward the kitchen.

"Give me your gun," Sullivan said. "Lift it from the holster
by your forefinger and thumb. Lay it on the floor."

Kendrick did as ordered.

Sullivan motioned with his gun for Kendrick to move back
into the kitchen as he picked up Kendrick's Webley RIC service
issue revolver.

On entering the kitchen behind Kendrick, a gasp caught in
Sullivan's throat.

Alison Kendrick was seated on a wooden kitchen chair.
Hands behind her back. A gag tied through her mouth. But it
was the sight of her ruined face that shocked.

The dishcloth soaked red. Blood dripped off her face soaking
her blouse. Splattered blood covered the floor. Deep gashes to
her face now grotesquely distorted. One eye swollen shut.

At the sound of her husband entering the kitchen her head
snapped up. Expecting a resumption of the abuse, confused surprise registered in her one good eye as she saw Sullivan.

With Edgar Kendrick's back to him, Sullivan smashed the
butt of the revolver into the back of his head.

Kendrick crumpled to the floor. But the blow failed to render
him entirely unconscious.

Mindful of Kendrick as still a threat, Sullivan placed
Kendrick's revolver on the sideboard next to the sink and went
behind the chair to unfasten Alison. Handcuffed.

Sullivan patted down the semiconscious Edgar Kendrick's pockets locating the key. Returning to Alison, he laid his silenced revolver on the floor as he knelt down to unlock the handcuffs.

"What happened?" He said untying the gag from behind her head.

She didn't reply. Stepping around in front, her face an even a more ghastly sight without the gag. Every feature distorted by the beating. Unrecognizable, she might never look the same.

"Get the hell away from me you bastard!"

"What are you talking about, Alison?"

"I saw you with Caroline Llewellyn. Went off on your so-called business trip to England with her. An excuse to be with your highborn lady friend."

So this chain of disastrous events had been Alison's doing. An act of revenge.

"It's more complicated than that, Alison. No time to explain."

"Explain? Explain what? You take me to your bed so I can spy for you. But all the time you're doing the same with her. Does she spy for you too?"

"Alison, we've no time for this now. We've got to get out of here."

While helping her to stand, Edgar Kendrick groaned loudly attempting get up.

In that instant Alison reached over to the sideboard grabbing her husband's revolver. Pointing it at Sullivan for a moment she then swung it toward her husband.

She intended not to miss. Now on his hands and knees, she placed the gun within a foot of the back of her husband's head. The big .455 round smashed Edgar Kendrick's head to the floor. The large exit wound removed much of his forehead creating a growing pool of blood.

Sullivan made a slight move toward her but she immediately turned the gun on him.

"You ruined my only chance for happiness, Trevor. I loved you. You knew that. I don't think you loved me but I thought that might come. I thought at least you cared for me."

"Of course I care for you, Alison. That's why I came for you. To rescue you. They tried to get me last night. I didn't know this was your doing."

"Doesn't matter now, Trevor. It's all over. I told the police everything we were doing. Spying for the IRA. There's no escape. They'll put you in prison. As for me... well why continue with just more suffering?"

With that Alison Kendrick placed the revolver under her chin and fired.

Her exit wound splattered tissue on the wall and ceiling. A disgusting sight made all the more distressing by realizing he was the cause of all this. Not a time for recrimination. Assessing the scene it appeared a murder-suicide. If he could leave unseen.

Had the two loud discharges been overheard by neighbors? Leave by way of the back alley and hope for the best while concealing the revolver again inside his suit jacket.

Seeing no one he walked quickly to the end of the alley making his way around the last row house at the end of the block coming out to the street. With his hat pulled down covering his eyes he made his way toward his car. Anyone looking out their window should not necessarily connect him with the Kendrick house.

Once well away from the Kendrick neighborhood he pulled to the curb. Decision time. Make a run for it or stay and bluff it out? Run how? Trains and ferries too great a risk if they were looking for him. That meant driving south all the way to Dublin. Possibly police checkpoints along the way. And Dublin might not necessarily be safe. Just because the truce seemed to be holding there he could still be subject to arrest. That meant getting to Collins. Long odds.

Running also meant the risk of a shootout with police. If he survived, tougher yet to make good an escape. If captured? Well that meant certain death.

A likely prospect since the police had no evidence. If they had a case against him then the raid on his apartment would have been with uniformed constables. No question now this was inspector Doyle's doing. Abduct him and make him disappear. Alison's allegations would then gain acceptance as proof since the suspect obviously fled Belfast to avoid arrest.

Now with Alison dead, they had no witness. Admitting to being the source of this, she also couldn't connect him with anyone else. Nor should any tangible evidence exist. He'd been careful never to reveal any details to Alison. No names, no methods. No admission to participating in the events of destroying the Ulster Special Constabulary headquarters. Never acknowledged her suspicions about involvement in the Taggart killing. Even if she revealed her suspicions to the police, no evidence existed. Without her, the only ones that knew of his involvement were his IRA accomplices. Alison's admissions clarified why everything fell apart.

But to stay and bluff it out? By no means a sure thing. Had he covered his tracks well enough? Were his powerful acquaintances enough to insulate him from police accusations? Did being an American provide a layer of protection? This enemy didn't play by any rules.

If he stayed in Belfast he could face a risky legal process. The only reason to temporarily stay being to insure an orderly escape from Ireland safely protected from murderous police retribution. His spying activities done. The Anglo-Irish War for independence seemed about over anyway. At least for Southern Ireland in some form or another. His Fenian heritage did not elicit in him a calling to be part of Northern Ireland's *troubles*.

On balance, Sullivan decided the best course of action was to stay. For the simple reason that a failed attempt to escape Belfast would fatally incriminate him if caught. Push back hard with his bluff. That meant constructing yet another twist on a cover story to explain away Alison's assertions.

More immediately he must find refuge. A hotel meant exposure to possible arrest. If he was now subject to arrest then he meant it to be in a public place with witnesses. He needed to stay out of sight until he could make his way to the office Monday and prepare for events to unfold.

The solution obvious. Digging into his pocket he extracted the piece of paper with Caroline Llewellyn's address.

Would openly acknowledging his romantic interest in Llewellyn help his situation? Malcom Llewellyn already knew his daughter's interest in him. Knew even that she meant to accompany Sullivan on the outbound leg of his trip to England. Obviously didn't object. Llewellyn thought highly of him. Also knew that his daughter's current suitor wouldn't lead to matrimony. Malcom Llewellyn should prove a powerful supporter with compelling professional and personal reasons for defending him. And all this only necessary for a matter of days until Sullivan arranged to safely leave Ireland.

A hell of shock to Caroline when he related events since leaving her only the night before. More adventure than she bargained for and possibly more than she wished to handle. But right now it was his only chance. A shock showing up on her doorstep without warning. He must look a sight. Needed a shave and bath, a change of clothing, and most of all sleep as fatigue began to impair his sharpness. Thirty hours of recuperation would prepare him for the unknown of what Monday might bring.

———

It was late Saturday afternoon when Sullivan arrived at Caroline Llewellyn's apartment building. A more affluent quarter of Belfast than his building. Not far from the Ulster Club. A top floor, large two-bedroom apartment with sitting room and modern kitchen, the building lobby manned by a concierge.

"Please inform Miss Llewellyn that Mr. Trevor Sullivan is here."

The concierge telephoned Caroline Llewellyn.

"She said to go right up, Sir. Number 402."

Standing up, the man looked down at Sullivan's two pieces of luggage. With a faint expression of distain at the impropriety of a gentleman with luggage calling on a single woman, he said, "Do you require assistance with your luggage, Sir?"

"I can manage, thank you."

Caroline Llewellyn was waiting at her door. Seeing his luggage, "Now who's being forward?"

He set down his bags and kissed her.

Stepping back she said, "Come in. Are you alright, Trevor? You look … a little disheveled."

"Been through hell since I left you yesterday. Got any whiskey?"

A look of concern came over her. "Certainly. And I think I'll join you."

Returning with a decanter and two glasses she poured each a drink. "Now, what's happened? You look a sight, Trevor."

"Let me start out by warning you it's a disturbing story. I haven't been entirely honest with you, Caroline. Couldn't. When I'm done, if you insist, I'll leave. Never bother you again. Right now you're my only hope. More than that, I have … What I mean is, I care for you and don't want to hurt you."

"Christ, Trevor, you're scaring the hell out me. Get to it. I'm not that delicate."

"Very well. First of all, Alison Kendrick is dead."

Caroline brought her hand to her mouth. "Oh no! My god, what happened?"

Telling her the details produced a look of horror. For all her worldly, progressive attitudes, even with the violence besetting Belfast, such a fate of someone she knew proved difficult to absorb.

After relating the events since their parting the prior evening, Caroline felt the weight of this new reality.

She said, "I knew that some of the RIC were a bad lot. But this. Torturing a woman. Her own husband even. Trying to kidnap you and do god knows what to you. And it's my fault all this happened."

"No it isn't, Caroline. If anything it's mine. Should never have let things go so far with Alison. Should never have involved her in all this."

"But I don't understand. You mean you're involved in the rebellion somehow? How'd you get yourself into this? Why?"

"Because they murdered my wife and her whole family. And because I'm Irish. I was raised with strong feelings for Irish independence. An Irish-American Fenian you might say. Ireland's been a British colony for too long. Now it's a police state. Never felt how deeply that was ingrained in me until coming to Ireland.

"Ever heard of Tom Clarke?"

"Wasn't he involved somehow with the Easter Rising?"

"Yes. My uncle. Married to my mother's sister. First signatory to the proclamation of independence in 1916. Executed by the British. His wife, my Aunt Kathleen, is just as much a militant republican. Her brother, another uncle of mine, was also executed on the day after her husband. She introduced me to Michael Collins when Maureen and I stopped off in Dublin before going to Derry. So you see I have a family history of connection with Irish freedom.

"Then of course Maureen was killed by Ulster Volunteers. Could not turn my back and do nothing. So I began spying for the IRA."

He did not reveal his many acts of violence since coming to Ireland. Uncertain how she might assimilate such details so alien to her experience. Enough that he is a spy.

"So what are you going to do?"

"Tell me first how you feel about this. About me, Caroline."

She came over to him and bent down to kiss him. 'None of this changes how I feel about you, Trevor.'

"Well I've decided to stay. Bluff my way out of this. Deny everything. Obviously I'm done with all that now. The RIC have no evidence of my spying. Without Alison they have no witness. I can float plausible explanations for any of their allegations."

"And what's your story about Alison?"

377

"A deeply troubled woman. No wonder with the physical abuse she suffered at the hands of her husband. Misconstrued my support for romantic affection. Became unhinged when she realized that my affections were directed elsewhere."

"That's shitty since you did sleep with her. You know you've got a real dark side, Trevor. But under the circumstance I guess I understand."

Would he ever share with Caroline just how dark a side?

"Do you care enough about me to have our relationship become public?"

Giving it a moment, she said, "Sure. Why not?"

"What about your parents?"

To this she laughed. "Under different circumstances I'd say they'd be delighted. Not sure how they'll react to allegations of you supporting the republican cause."

"Can I stay here until Monday?"

"Of course. Won't exactly be the first time we've slept together."

"Thank you, Caroline. Monday I'll take a room at a hotel."

"Close by I trust?"

She flashed a mischievous smile. He smiled in return but looked exhausted.

"Have you eaten anything?"

He shook his head no.

"I'm no cook but there's some cold meat and bread. I'll run you a bath while you eat."

"Then I need some sleep. Hard to keep my eyes open."

"Do you mean to go into the office on Monday?"

"Of course. That's the bluff. Nothing to hide. Everything normal. If they come for me I want it in public with unimpeachable witnesses. Can't trust these murdering bastards."

CHAPTER 34

District Inspector John Doyle spent the last hour explaining to his superior RIC Commissioner Charles Wickham events surrounding Alison Kendrick. Not however in completely candid detail.

"A busy twenty-four hours, Inspector," Wickham said. "However not entirely productive it seems. Sullivan's whereabouts remains unknown. Your only witness has committed suicide after killing her husband. Your arrests based on this Kendrick woman's information have yet to yield any confessions. You have no confirmation that Sullivan is spying for the IRA. Which I might add still seems a preposterous assertion."

"Or a perfect cover, Sir. Sullivan appears to be part of the unionist establishment but what do we really know about him?"

"You were rash however in trying to bring him in for questioning. Had he returned to his residence and been hauled away by your chaps, we'd have hell to pay. Sullivan's not without important friends. You are not to move on him without my express authorization."

Doyle never mentioned Sullivan's apartment was forcibly entered by constables out of uniform.

"Yes, Sir, I understand. My men were under strict instructions only to question Sullivan had he returned home last night, not detain him. For the same reason we chose to question

379

Kendrick at her former home. Had this been found to be only a lovers' quarrel then complications would have been more easily avoided. Based on his secretary's allegations we had ample cause to explain our investigation."

Wickham raised his eyebrow. "Well that certainly turned out badly. What happened?"

"Sergeant Rafferty questioned the woman for over an hour. He returned to headquarters to report to me as ordered. Left her husband to keep her in the house until he returned. Obviously Edgar Kendrick was derelict in his duties. His wife somehow got hold of his gun and shot him. Distraught, she then took her own life."

"You really think this woman was part of a spy ring operated by Sullivan?" Wickham said.

"Yes, Sir. Sergeant Rafferty has interrogated many suspects. Very good at his work."

Wickham knew of Rafferty's methods.

Doyle continued, "Alison Kendrick provided too many details. Revealed things beyond her ability to fabricate under that kind of physical duress according to Rafferty. Too scared and broken to have invented such an elaborate story."

"Nonetheless, hard to accept the IRA having a source so highly placed."

"But I assume you wish that I continue my investigations into this matter?"

"Of course, but discreetly. Have Sullivan followed by your best people." Wickham said. "Monday I will shake the tree. Perhaps cause him to do something foolish. I'll pay a visit to Malcom Llewellyn at Harland & Wolff. Inform him of the events surrounding the death of one of his office staff. If Sullivan is there I'll confront him with his secretary's allegations. Whatever the outcome, that should prove interesting."

———

Arriving at his office on Monday, Sullivan maintained normality by asking other staff about Alison Kendrick's absence. No one knew why the reliable Alison Kendrick was not at her desk.

As Sullivan was going through the accumulated paperwork from his absence the previous week, Malcom Llewellyn entered his office.

"Trevor, would you please come to my office. Commissioner Wickham of the RIC has some disturbing news he wishes to discuss."

Malcom Llewellyn's face reflected acute distress. Sullivan assumed Wickham told him of the murder-suicide of Alison Kendrick and her husband. He prepared to convey his own expression of shock.

Knowing Alison confessed everything to the RIC obviously required investigation. Since it was Wickham personally delivering the news meant the police recognized the delicacy given Sullivan's standing. It also meant they had insufficient evidence to make an arrest. Further confirmation the attempt to abduct him was an expedient to remove him by other than legal means.

After Wickham related that Alison had shot herself, Sullivan shook his head with an expression of disbelief and grief.

"Where did this happen, Commissioner?" Sullivan said.

"At her home."

"At her boardinghouse?"

"No her former home. Appears some sort of domestic dispute. I neglected to say she also killed her estranged husband. A murder-suicide apparently."

"Good lord," Llewellyn said. "Did you know she was having such difficulties, Trevor?"

Sullivan could see Wickham's interest in his response.

"Yes, Sir. Her husband physically abused her regularly. Often saw bruises on her face. Told me one day after arriving at work that she had left her husband. Hard to understand why she would be alone with him. He used to work here in the shipyard. Left to join the Constabulary. He was a constable, am I correct, Commissioner?"

"Yes he was. Which brings me to another matter. The reason for my personal visit. A delicate matter but one I am duty bound to pursue.

"You see Alison Kendrick confided a most bizarre story to her estranged husband. A troubling story. She alleged her involvement in a sexual affair with you Mr. Sullivan."

Llewellyn said, "See here, Commissioner, I won't listen to such slander."

Sullivan again shook his head. "It's alright, Sir. I think I can explain. Alison was a most efficient secretary, but clearly a troubled woman. Apparently with no family she chose to confide many of her difficulties to me. In hind sight I recognize that she misinterpreted my empathy for something more. I never had any sort of romantic affair with her. But not surprising that she held such a fantasy seeing an imagined opportunity following my wife's death. "

"But you arranged to set her up in a boardinghouse. Helped her monetarily she said."

"She had no place to go. An act of kindness. She was an excellent employee. It was my former boardinghouse therefore I knew a room was available. But enough of this nonsense. You didn't come here to investigate gossip, Commissioner."

"No. You're correct. But your involvement with Alison Kendrick may be integrally connected to a more serious matter. You see she told police investigators that you were spying for the IRA."

Llewellyn jumped up from his chair, "That's the most fantastic thing I've ever heard, Commissioner. And you believe such nonsense?"

"Not necessarily but I'm compelled to investigate. Too many things Kendrick said cannot be explained simply as the delusions of a scorned woman. After seducing and coercing her to spy, she was jolted to her senses after feeling betrayed when she discovered Mr. Sullivan's affections for another woman. She reacted by confiding to her estranged husband."

"Enough!" Sullivan said angrily standing up. "I'm not about to have my reputation sullied about based on outrageous accusations. Accusations by an emotionally unstable woman. Now conveniently deceased after taking her own life probably regretting her actions. If you had any evidence you would arrest me. So just what is your motivation for coming here, Commissioner?"

Wickham remained calm. "I understand how you must feel, Mr. Sullivan but I'm just doing my duty. But let me be frank. Your secretary provided names of those she alleged provided her information. Very detailed specifics of information provided. Clearly useful to the IRA. She also provided details to support her allegations against you. Difficult to believe this ordinary woman could invent such an elaborate story. Coincidences involving you that need explanation."

"Such as?" Sullivan said remaining standing as an expression of defiance.

"The theft of explosives from the railroad maintenance yard shortly after you made an inspection visit in your capacity with the Security Advisory Commission."

Sullivan laughed. "Christ, the IRA wouldn't need me for that. Obviously the only source for explosives was the railroad. And I told the operations manager that it was poorly secured. No security guard even at the facility. Damn fool obviously took no corrective action."

"And your absence the night the Special Constabulary headquarters was destroyed with those stolen explosives?"

Clever bastard trying to trap him.

"Absence? From where? Don't even remember what night that was."

"What about a wound to your side the morning following the murder of three RIC constables at a public house on Donegall Road?"

"A careless accident here in the shipyard. Jagged piece of metal. Ruined a good waistcoat. I told my secretary of the incident before leaving work that day.

"Now let me ask a question, Commissioner. What reason did my secretary give as to why an American visiting Ireland decides to take up sides as a rebel spy in a foreign city?"

"Because of your wife she said. Catholic family I believe. Brothers IRA. Your wife killed by local UVF."

"Everyone knows how my wife died. A collateral casualty. Assumed to be UVF but some speculated to me personally at the funeral that it might have been the IRA itself. One person even passed on a rumor using the term 'suspected traitor'. Never knew my wife's brother so I don't know his background."

"What about the murder of her younger brother? And the fire that killed her father and injured her mother?"

"That's why my wife and I came to Derry to see to the needs of her mother."

"One piece of Mrs. Kendrick's story seems telling. She revealed her sources even to the extent of the code names used when passing information to you. Most inventive. Characters from Shakespearian plays. Convincing to the extent she explained ascribed characteristics that fit her real sources."

"And she said I provided these code names?"

Wickham wasn't quite prepared for the question. "I'm not sure. However certainly beyond her educational level to be that intellectually creative."

"Perhaps my secretary was just creating a fictional adventure fantasy. I lent her a book of Shakespeare's plays. Obviously more irrational then I ever imagined."

"I don't think so, Mr. Sullivan. We have detained several of her associates in this Suffrage Society. I suspect someone will eventually breakdown and confess."

"Or you'll probably find nothing more than her acting out this delusion of romance and adventure. For the sake of argument, let's say it comes to light that my secretary was involved in passing information to the IRA. That still does not connect me to her activities. Might she have simply become unhinged by believing me involved with another woman? Bent on revenge even to the extent of destroying herself? Certainly plausible since she was unbalanced enough to take her own life."

Wickham stood up. "I believe I'm through here, gentlemen. Our investigation will of course continue. Thought you were owed the courtesy of this informal discussion, Mr. Sullivan. I regret the unpleasantness of this affair."

"You regret the unpleasantness?" Sullivan said indignantly intending to punctuate his outrage. "In America we'd call that bullshit, Commissioner.

"I believe this whole charade is meant to discredit my work that the Crown's security forces consider meddling in their prerogatives. You in particular, Commissioner. Therefore you can have your way. Effective immediately I'm resigning any involvement with the Security Advisory Commission. Don't want to be accused of spying for the enemy from a preferential position."

Sullivan turned leaving Llewellyn and Wickham standing with different expressions to his outburst. As he reached the door, he turned back and said, "Your police grossly mishandled this unfortunate affair with my secretary. Not sure why you came here to make these ridiculous allegations with no evidence to substantiate her delusional accusations. I can only conclude it's to cover up the gross incompetence of your officers. Now I understand that derives directly from your own command inadequacies, Commissioner."

For effect, he slammed the door as he exited causing Pimm the secretary to jump in his chair.

Minutes later, Malcom Llewellyn came into Sullivan's office and closed the door.

"I'm speechless. Wickham hasn't heard the end of this. I'm so sorry, Trevor. Seems you've suffered nothing but grief since coming to Ireland."

"There's a war going on. Justice is just another casualty. To be expected I suppose."

"Nonetheless, I want you to know you have my full support."

"Thank you, Sir."

Ultimately it didn't matter. His tenure here now shortened to days. Today's theatrics were nothing more than a means to insure escape on his terms. Wickham's visit confirmed a dash to escape Belfast by automobile after the weekend's events might have easily ended in disaster. The police had no evidence. The bluff worked at least temporarily. When he made his escape by rail or sea he might need Llewellyn to intercede if the police attempted to interfere.

He regretted disappointing Malcom Llewellyn. A good man. At least now he would understand Sullivan's departure from Harland & Wolff. Leaving Caroline would be more troubling.

He may have survived this confrontation but the RIC would not give up. He must leave Belfast soon. District Inspector Doyle was at the heart of this. Under torture, Alison undoubtedly revealed his interest in Doyle. That would link him directly to the attempt to kill Doyle and the Taggart shooting. A personal obsession for Doyle that Sullivan understood all too well.

Officially Wickham might have to temporarily back off. But Doyle already tried to kill him and would never relent.

Had he obscured all possible evidence? No way to be sure until it proved too late. Of course others in McCorley's IRA battalion knew details of his involvement. Someone might reveal his secret under police torture. Spying was the least of his capital offenses against the Crown. Multiple murders of police meant the gallows.

"There's another matter, Trevor. It concerns Caroline."

"How's that, Sir?"

"I hesitate to pry but it's obvious my daughter is attracted to you. I'm aware she manipulated the opportunity to accompany you on your trip to England last week."

"Do you disapprove, Sir?"

"To the contrary. What I mean is she must be told. Hopefully these false allegations of an affair with your secretary will not alienate her affections."

Llewellyn insisted they lunch together with his daughter. Said he wanted her to understand that he believed none of these allegations. Sullivan's position at the firm remained secure.

While spending Sunday with Caroline, Sullivan strategized with her to demonstrate suitable shock when being told of Alison Kendrick's suicide. The added conspiratorial element was for her to admit her casual acquaintance with Alison Kendrick. Caroline would elaborate further. With appropriate distress she would confide that she may have unintentionally contributed to Kendrick's suicide by mentioning her affections toward Sullivan.

———

Wickham recounted his confrontation with Sullivan to his subordinate District Inspector Doyle immediately following his visit to Harland & Wolff. Doyle thought it a premature stupid move. Wickham argued it was the best they could manage without evidence. Cause Sullivan to cease his subversive activities and deny the IRA their unique source of information. A ridiculous tactic by a bureaucrat. Doyle felt Wickham probably remained unconvinced that Sullivan could possibly be an IRA spy. Looking to cover his ass if somehow it proved true.

Wickham's final instructions, "Continue to investigate, Inspector. Find evidence. But take no action against Sullivan without first consulting with me. I suspect there will already be some blowback. I'll handle that but do not embarrass me with any mistakes."

Doyle harbored no doubts as to Sullivan's guilt. Although not firsthand knowledge, Rafferty had been with him for years. Knew Rafferty could read the kind of *tells* that a suspect displayed under intense interrogation. He also witnessed Rafferty's methods. Never knew of anyone standing up to the man's brutality. Particularly a confused woman like Alison Kendrick.

Therefore if he believed Sullivan to be involved based on Alison Kendrick's information then it meant Sullivan was part of the IRA's effort to target him and his constables for assassination. Involved with the failed attempt on his life and Taggart's murder?

A week later Doyle's intelligence unit had uncovered nothing directly linking Sullivan to anti-Crown activity. The interrogations of the detainees incriminated only Kendrick. Better progress made on assembling a picture of his wife's family in Derry. Clearly the father and both sons were IRA. Their deaths and the burning of the O'Farrell house undoubtedly the work of the Derry UVF. Unofficially the police knew the two unidentified bodies in the burned O'Farrell house were UVF. Shot according to other UVF involved. Speculation that Sullivan might have been present during the attack could not be established.

The most intriguing information however was the death of the notorious Derry UVF commander Fergus Croft. Intriguing because of similarities to the killing of Taggart. *In both cases a lone gunman in the uniform of a British officer.* Derry now Belfast? A new IRA tactic? A possible different picture of Sullivan. A spy or IRA assassin?

Possible, but even Doyle found it hard to accept. A well-regarded businessman? Yet he was a decorated war veteran. According to the citation, for killing a lot of the enemy. A weapons expert by Scotland Yard's report on his background at the United States Military Academy. Sullivan possessed the capability. The killing of his wife understandable motivation.

Regardless, Doyle concluded uncovering legally incriminating evidence against Sullivan was unlikely. Short of arresting some IRA operative that chose to talk to save his own skin, Sullivan's crimes would go unpunished. Doyle could not afford to wait for such an uncertain eventuality. Sullivan might simply leave Belfast after Wickham foolishly alerted him.

However Doyle could no longer just make Sullivan disappear. The failed try at Sullivan's apartment followed by the incident at the Kendrick house made that impossible.

An idea immerged while assessing where Sullivan might be vulnerable? Perhaps something involving his newfound romantic interest in Caroline Llewellyn. According to information extracted from various sources of the Suffrage Society, Alison Kendrick's allegations concerning Caroline Llewellyn could be correct.

———

Huddled with Sergeant Rafferty in his office, Doyle said, "You still convinced that Sullivan's a spy, Rafferty?"

"Yes, Sir. The Kendrick woman wasn't lying."

"What if she was passing on information to the IRA but not to Sullivan? What if that was just to get even with him for taking up with another woman?"

"No, Sir. It was Sullivan she was giving the information to. She wasn't that smart to cover for someone else. When she eventually started to talk you couldn't shut her up. You'd have to have heard her to understand what I'm saying, Sir."

"What about her suspicions that Sullivan might have been involved with the Special Constabulary bombing? And shooting Taggart?"

"Grilled her hard on that. Said Sullivan never admitted to anything. Told her he wasn't going to tell her anything about what he did for her own safety. But the circumstances fit. He could have been involved."

"Enough to convince you he was involved?"

"Yes. Listening to her I think he was, Sir."

"What about Sullivan's injury the night Taggart was killed? A bullet wound?"

"She couldn't say. Bad looking wound to his side she described. Stitched up so he got medical treatment."

"Why not an accident at the shipyard like Sullivan told Wickham?"

"Couldn't have been. She says he left the office just fine that Friday. Gave her some vague excuse for not seeing her that evening. Had to have happened later when Taggart and the others were shot."

"Think someone with Sullivan's stature could lead a double life as an IRA gunman?"

"Yes, Sir. Pieces all fit."

"Well I think so too, Sergeant. Fact remains I never believed McCorley's bunch capable of the Taggart killing. Something about the weapon used. Too sophisticated. Could of course be someone up from the South? Maybe one of Collin's people. But I don't think so. I agree with you. Sullivan killed a lot of Germans during the war. Knows guns."

"Just wanted to make sure you're convinced Sullivan's dirty because I intend to do something about removing him. Wickham's tied our hands. Sullivan's too well connected. But what I'm planning will circumvent all that."

"What do 'ya have in mind, Sir?"

Doyle smiled. "Involves some unpleasantness with another woman. You up for that."

"Yes, Sir. Whatever it takes to get Sullivan. Don't relish the target he put on my back."

"Must keep this deep and tight. It'll just be you and I doin' this, Sergeant. You okay with me being operational with you?"

Rafferty looked at the big man. He'd seen Doyle in action in the field. One mean sonofabitch that could handle himself in a fight. He grinned at his boss. "Like old times, Sir."

CHAPTER 35

Following the confrontation with RIC Commissioner Wickham the lunch with Malcom Llewellyn and Caroline came off as Sullivan hoped. Caroline displayed suitable distress over the death of Alison Kendrick. She followed by expressing guilt as being the cause of this sequence of events. Recovering her composure, she confessed to her father that she did indeed have a deep affection for Trevor. She was planning in fact to tell Herbert Townsend this forthcoming weekend.

A consummate actress, she took on an angry tone at the absurdity of Commissioner Wickham's accusations. Accusing Trevor as a spy for the IRA was beyond stupidity. Not only were the RIC a bunch of Protestant thugs, but plainly led by gross incompetents.

Of course Sullivan did not share with Caroline his plan to leave Belfast within a matter of days. That would require revealing more than his spying activities to explain the danger Doyle represented. And Wickham only needed something damning enough to silence Sullivan's highly placed protectors to arrest him. Unlikely he would make it to trial. *Committed suicide in his cell* most probably. The only reason to play out this charade was to allow for an orderly safe escape. And however unrealistic, to perhaps continue a relationship with Caroline Llewellyn.

At Malcom Llewellyn's insistence Sullivan did not return to the office after their lunch.

Llewellyn said to Sullivan and his daughter, "This has been a most trying day for both of you. Spend the afternoon with Caroline, Trevor. Drive out to the house later. Need to break all of this to Henrietta. Best we do that all together. We'll have a quiet dinner. With this damn curfew, plan to spend the night of course both of you."

Sullivan and Caroline did spend the afternoon together. Making love. As if Caroline sensed impending doom, she was insatiable.

"It's getting late. Let's take a bath together. Don't want to rely on perfume covering the smell of sex all over us. Mother has the nose of a bloodhound."

While Caroline was applying makeup at her dressing table, Sullivan picked up the afternoon edition of the *Belfast Telegram*.

"Did you see this in the newspaper?"

"What?"

"About what's going on. I'll read it to you."

> BELFAST - In the wake of recent attacks by the IRA, the RIC has responded with stunning success, reporting an important IRA spy ring has been shut down. While the investigation is ongoing, a highly placed source close to the investigation but not officially authorized to comment, provided certain details.
>
> According to the police source a secretary at the Harland & Wolff Shipyard had been a conduit for passing information on Crown security forces to the IRA. A Mrs. Alison Kendrick confessed to not only passing information to the IRA but also recruiting sources using her associations within the Suffrage Society. Some of these sources were in the employ of various Crown security forces with access to confidential information. Several of those named have been arrested and others detained for questioning by the RIC, however no names or details were provided.

Details are also unclear as to the circumstances surrounding the apparent suicide of the principal witness Mrs. Kendrick. The source stated only that Mrs. Kendrick was being held under house arrest at her home in the custody of her husband who is a member of the Constabulary. Apparently distraught over confessions of an adulterous affair gone badly, she somehow got hold of her husband's service revolver. A domestic altercation appears to have followed although there were no witnesses. Constable Edgar Kendrick was shot and killed by his wife. Perhaps out of recrimination for her deed, she then took her own life with a bullet to her head.

When asked if this spy ring was instrumental in the recent murders of three constables in a Donegall Road public house and the bombing of the Ulster Special Constabulary headquarters, the police source said that had not yet been determined. He added that the investigation was only in its early stages.

"This just confirms my concerns, Caroline. Wickham and Doyle will not end their efforts to make a case against me."

"And how can they do that, Trevor. You never told Alison about your end of this spying. Now she's dead. They don't have any witnesses or evidence. That nonsense with Commissioner Wickham was to scare you off from any further spying."

Sullivan didn't want to argue Caroline's naïve interpretation. This would not end.

"Can't be sure something won't surface. Did Alison say something to one of her sources implicating me? What if one of the few IRA that know my involvement is arrested? What if they're tortured? The RIC is certainly not above that."

She turned around on her dressing stool to face him.

"So what are you saying, Trevor?"

"I must leave Belfast, Caroline. Not only for my safety but yours."

"Me? How am I at risk?"

"You knew Alison. You're known to be involved with the Suffrage Society. Most of all you're now associated with me. Life could become unpleasant for you here by unending controversy. But that won't happen if I'm not around to be the lightning rod."

She looked at him. Tears started to run down her cheeks. He went to her and nestled her head against him.

"This can't be. I just found you now you're leaving me?"

She grabbed a tissue and began dabbing her eyes. "Now you've gone and ruined my makeup. Where will you go?"

"Why, Paris of course."

"Paris?"

"That's where my heart is. I was never meant for here, Caroline."

A hard look came over her expression. "But you haven't yet asked me to come along even though you know I'm fond of Paris."

"Well I'm asking you now, Caroline. What do you say?"

"Think it will work out between us? Not sure I really know you, Trevor. Something's missing in all this. Something I fear you don't want to share."

He started to reply when she held up her hand, "Don't say any more. So when are you thinking of leaving?"

Hesitating for moment, "End of the week."

"Goddamn it! When were you going to tell me?"

"Everything just came undone the last couple of days, Caroline. I wasn't planning to leave until this happened."

"But why so soon?"

"Because the risk is just too great."

She stood and embraced him. Eventually she pulled back and said, "I don't know, Trevor. I want to. Such a drastic move. Guess for all my bold talk I still have my own doubts. Run off with a mysterious man I only barely know to live in a foreign place."

"Shouldn't be that foreign to you. It's Paris. Everything you like. You even speak French. And you won't be alone."

"And when will you tell father?"

"Tonight. Might as well get it out of the way. Course I'll have to embellish the reasons. I'll say that Alison's jealous accusations have poisoned my standing with the police. If Wickham was bold enough to come forward and accuse me directly, no telling what the RIC might do. This war and the byzantine political ramifications make for a climate of uncertainty. I'm at risk and therefore so is your daughter.

"And what will you say about your plans? Your parents will naturally wonder if you'll follow me to Paris."

"Let's not go that far at least tonight. I need time to prepare mother. Time to prepare myself for that matter. Last time I left it was just a long trip. This sounds permanent."

Sullivan nodded his understanding. "Remember, Paris isn't all that far from Belfast. Your mother could always visit."

Dinner that night was difficult. Women of Henrietta Llewellyn's social class insulated themselves from ugly realities. Even with the violence of the war and the sectarian rioting the fallout from Alison Kendrick's jealous attack, followed by the murder-suicide, profoundly disturbed her sense of security. When Sullivan revealed that he must leave Belfast for his as well as Caroline's safety, Henrietta seemed comforted to see the matter buried.

Not so for Malcolm Llewellyn. He was devastated. Genuinely fond of Sullivan, he would not only be losing his most outstanding manager but maybe a prospective son-in-law. He made all sorts of overtures to take the matter to Wickham's superiors in Dublin, even to Lloyd George. However, in the end he could see the wisdom of Sullivan's move. If nothing else, his daughter would not be dragged into what might become an ugly scandal. In a few months circumstances may change allowing Sullivan to return to Belfast.

The following morning Sullivan left the Llewellyn residence in Holywood for his office. Caroline intended to spend the day with her parents. Many weighty matters to discuss. But she insisted on seeing him at her apartment that night after he left the shipyard. Father's chauffeur would drive her back into Belfast. She would be home by six o'clock.

———

"Ready?" Inspector Doyle asked Rafferty. They sat in a marked RIC car parked at the curb a short distance from Caroline Llewellyn's apartment building.

"Yes, Sir."

"Had some of the lads tailing Sullivan right after Wickham fucked everything up by confronting Sullivan. Sullivan spent yesterday afternoon with Llewellyn here at her apartment. Later they drove to her father's estate in Holywood. Spent the night there. Sullivan drove to the shipyard this morning. Doesn't appear that she's returned yet. I've been watching the last few hours.

"There's a concierge on duty. After he confirms she's not in, tell him you'll return another time. You leave and signal me. I'll pull down the street about a hundred yards. You enter through the rear door to the building. Still handy with your lock pick tools, Sergeant?"

"Keep in practice, Inspector."

"Careful you're not seen by any of the other tenants when you pick her lock. Number 402. Stay there in the dark until thirty minutes after curfew. If she doesn't show up, leave quietly the same way. We'll try again tomorrow night."

"And if she does, I know what to do."

"It's got to be quiet, Sergeant. If something goes wrong…"

"Nothing will go wrong, Sir."

"After you're done, leave the same way from the rear of the building. Join me in the car. We'll wait for Sullivan. He'll eventually show up here with our boys following him. After he enters we immediately follow announcing to the concierge we're on police business. We arrest Sullivan inside the apartment for murder."

"Yes, Sir. I understand.

———

Caroline Llewellyn arrived at her apartment promptly at six o'clock as promised. Time enough to have a bath before Trevor arrived. Lugging a bag of groceries she would try her hand at cooking dinner. Something simple. A good bottle of wine. Make love before or after? She rebuked herself for acting the silly romantic in the midst of such upheaval.

"Good evening, George," she said to the middle-aged concierge.

"Ah, Miss Llewellyn, let me give you a hand with your parcel."

"Thank you, George."

George was noticeably out of breath with the exertion of ascending the stairs. After unlocking her door, she extracted some coins and tipped him.

"That's how I get my exercise, George. Thank you so much."

She took the groceries to the kitchen then went into the bedroom. After undressing she put on a bathrobe. As she was about to enter the water closet with her hand on the doorknob, she hesitated.

Some music would be nice. After taking time to select a Victrola music disk, she cranked the drive spring then placed the needle on the rotating disk. Mozart's' Violin Concerto No 3. Perfect music for her bath while anticipating the remainder of the evening.

Swinging aside the door to the water closet she strode to the bathtub to run a bath. As she bent down to turn the facet handle her head jerked violently back. Something wrapped tightly around her throat was choking off her breath while pulling her backwards.

Concealed behind the door, Rafferty sprang upon her soundlessly after removing his boots. A man's necktie served as a garrote. It would not cut deeply into the throat and larynx therefore taking at least a minute to render the victim unconscious. Longer for asphyxiation to cause death. Inefficient but suitable for staging the intended crime.

Rafferty pulled the necktie across at the back of her neck, his hold secured by wrapping the tie around each hand.

He was strong but not a large man. Frantic efforts to free the constriction around her neck accomplished nothing. Realizing she had only moments before passing out, her adrenalin-fueled strength pulled Rafferty about the room smashing his hip into the tall clawfoot bathtub. This was followed by twisting her body sideways enough to slam her knee into his groin.

Pain weakened his grip slightly, enough for her to bend downward unbalancing both, sending her to the floor with Rafferty on top of her. But the effort exhausted all remaining breath. Black spots rolled across her eyes. Pinned to the floor she knew there was no escape as consciousness faded.

As Llewellyn pinned beneath him ceased struggling, Rafferty knew just another minute more and it would be over. In the same instant his own head exploded in pain.

———

Sullivan left Harland & Wolff promptly at five o'clock. He was not sure what to expect after the previous day's confrontation by RIC Commissioner Wickham. The end of the workday saw the usual mass outpouring of workers from the yard as well as office staff. Arriving at his car, he surveyed the sea of people wary of any police presence.

To avoid losing sight of their quarry, two men stood out. Dressed not as yard workers which would be more difficult to spot, but more like office employees. Sullivan did not recognize them. They also stood together smoking cigarettes next to a car, obviously in no hurry to leave. All the other employees were intent on making their way home or the nearest pub.

Sullivan eased his car out of the parking lot. The two men followed closely in their car. Taking a circuitous route toward the center of Belfast forced the following car to close the distance to avoid losing him. After several turns it was clear they were following him.

Not wanting to lead them to Caroline Llewellyn's apartment, he parked the car and entered the central library on Royal Avenue. Once inside he immediately left by a side entrance onto Kent Street. Walking two blocks south to Royal Avenue he boarded a tram.

After transferring to another tram he got off two blocks from Caroline's apartment building. If the RIC were following him then it was conceivable they would also have her residence under surveillance.

Sure enough he spotted a marked RIC sedan a half block from her building entrance. No question now about the urgency to leave Belfast within a matter of days. He needed to get to Caroline unseen. Perhaps an unlocked rear entrance if not being watched by a constable? It was after six o'clock so she should be home. He'd try to enjoy his last few days with her. Get his mind around making a new life in Paris. Possibly convince her to join him there. Leave the horrors of the past year behind.

The building's rear service door stood slightly ajar. About time he got a break. Quickly ascending to the fourth floor he knocked quietly on Caroline's door. No response. He could hear music. Probably couldn't hear him. Turning the door knob he was surprised to find it also unlocked. Expecting him of course. Entering, he immediately heard a disturbing commotion from the water closet and what sounded like a man grunting.

Moving quickly to the open water closet doorway, he saw a uniformed man lying on top of Caroline clad in a robe. The sonofabitch was strangling her with something about her neck!

Taking two quick steps Sullivan unleashed a savage kick. The toe of his shoe caught Rafferty in the forehead.

Sullivan pushed a semi-conscious Rafferty off Caroline. He then pulled her away rolling her onto her back. Frantically he removed the necktie still wrapped around her neck.

Putting both hands one on top of the other between her breasts, he pushed rhythmically to revive her breathing. After several repetitions came a sharp gasp as she inhaled desperately to fill her lungs while her eyes sprang open with a look of terror.

Peripheral movement distracted Sullivan. A dazed Rafferty was now on his feet. From his pocket he pulled a straight razor flicking it open then lunging forward trying to catch any part of Sullivan.

Sullivan scrambled backward on the floor rolling on his side. Lashing out with his foot he caught Rafferty's left ankle tripping the stout man to the floor.

Rolling further away in the spacious water closet, Sullivan extracted the .25 pistol from his ankle holster. Rafferty unsteadily got up on one knee still holding the razor.

It took Rafferty another couple of seconds to stand. Enough time for Sullivan to take aim and fire a single round hitting him in the throat.

The small caliber round proved enough to stop Rafferty's advance. Dropping the razor, Rafferty clasped both hands to his throat. Blood gushed in a torrent through his fingers as his eyes displayed bewilderment.

Sullivan got to his feet and with his left hand pushed the still standing Rafferty backward against the bathtub. Another push sent Rafferty falling backward into the tub slamming the back of his head on the opposite side of the cast iron tub.

No sound came from Rafferty's voiceless moving lips as he gasped for air. Removing one hand from his throat he made a feeble try to rise from the bathtub. Lacking enough strength, he fell back. Blood continued to spurt out at a great rate with each pulse of his heart. Rafferty's face noticeably turning pale as he quickly bled out.

Sullivan bundled a weaken Caroline into his arms and half-carried her to the bedroom. Placing her on the bed he said, "Stay here. I'll be back."

Not about to trust Rafferty making another recovery, Sullivan returned to the water closet. Rafferty's open eyes were now rolled back. Removing Rafferty's hand from his throat it became clear that the heart had stopped pumping blood. No pulse confirmed he was dead.

Sullivan returned to the bedroom. Caroline sat on the bed weeping in great sobs with her hands covering her face.

"Caroline. Let me look at your neck."

Her neck revealed a vivid reddening abrasion from the necktie. Undoubtedly badly bruised.

"Can you talk?"

She swallowed. "Yes, but it hurts," coming out in a raspy tone.

"You're going to be fine. No serious damage."

"What happened? That man. What …"

"He tried to kill you, Caroline. One of Inspector Doyle's thugs. But he's dead now."

"Dead? What happened?"

"I shot him."

"Oh god!"

"Listen carefully, Caroline. He was undoubtedly not alone. My guess is after murdering you they planned to arrest me. Claim you discovered my spying and I killed you to prevent you going to the police."

She looked at him with an expression that suggested she didn't completely comprehend what he was saying.

"This is not yet over, Caroline. I need to leave you for a short while. Need to take care of whoever is waiting for the killer to leave. Don't have much time."

"No! You can't leave me here with that … that dead person."

"I must. Stay right here. In the bedroom. I'll return very soon."

He then returned to the water closet. With a coin he unscrewed a wooden access panel on the wall concealing the plumbing shutoff valves. Wrapped in a towel were the .38 revolver and silencer along with ammunition, hidden there two days earlier. Unlike his other weapons, carefully hidden since it represented evidence he could not explain.

On the way out he collected the .45 Browning from the bottom of his briefcase. Might be more than just those in the RIC car outside. Could be walking into an RIC ambush.

Helped that it was now dark. With a cloudless night he could at least conceal his movements. The curfew also provided silence eliminating traffic on Wellington Place.

Exiting the rear of the building he moved behind the adjacent building. Coming through the alleyway onto Wellington should place him close to where he observed the parked RIC car earlier. In luck, he could see the car just ten yards further facing away from him. If he approached carefully avoiding visibility in the rear mirror, he could surprise the occupants.

No question what he intended. The occupants must be Rafferty accomplices. After killing so many RIC a couple of more made no difference. Under this circumstance, no choice. Hopefully there were no others.

Coming up alongside the car on the driver's side, the driver's arm rested on the door through the open window. Sensing Sullivan's presence, the driver turned his head.

Both Sullivan and Doyle registered surprise as each recognized the other. An instant later, Inspector John Doyle's eyes registered something else as he looked at the long barrel of the silenced revolver pointing from only a few feet away.

The muffled shot caught Doyle in the left eye. Sullivan stepped closer confirming Doyle was alone in the car then fired a second shot into Doyle's head.

Looking about, Sullivan worried that perhaps those previously tailing him might have returned to report to Doyle and could be lurking close by. Retreating back into the shadows of the alleyway, he waited several moments but sensed nothing. Just Doyle and Rafferty? Strange.

Sullivan knew he wasn't out of this yet. Wouldn't do to have Doyle's body found outside of Caroline's apartment building. And of course the larger problem of Rafferty's body.

Sullivan pulled the dead Doyle to the passenger seat then got behind the wheel. Risking exposure if encountered by an RIC motorized patrol, he drove south a couple of blocks into a commercial area. He parked the police car on a street with other parked cars. After forcing Doyle's body to the floor to at least avoid immediate observation he left in a fast-paced walk to work his way back to the apartment on foot.

Rafferty's body presented a real threat to Caroline. A time-urgent problem he must solve immediately. But one thing at a time. Foremost was dealing with her state of mind after the assault. Complicated now by realizing he could not wait days before leaving Belfast. No way to anticipate the scope of official reaction to Doyle's murder. Would Wickham see Doyle's death as confirmation of Alison's allegations with another even higher profile IRA assassination? Might Wickham manufacture evidence to support an arrest of Sullivan in response?

—

Returning forty minutes later to the apartment through the rear entrance, he found Caroline's earlier near-hysteria replaced with controlled outrage.

"Where have you been? And what the hell have you gotten me into?"

"Calm down, Caroline. Let me explain."

"Explain? You're not just a spy for the IRA are you? You're one of their killers. Look at that," she said pointing to the revolver with its long silencer screwed unto the barrel still at his side. What kind of gun is that?"

"It's to suppress the sound."

"So you can kill quietly?"

"Exactly. But now's not the time for explanations."

"Who are you? What are you?"

"A soldier. Fighting a war."

"What happened outside? Killed more police?" Her voice rising in a mix of fear and confusion.

"The people I killed deserved to die. Not because they were the enemy, but because they were murderers, not police. Inspector Doyle led a police gang of murderers. That piece of shit in the water closet was one of his constable sergeants. His name's Rafferty. Tortured Alison Kendrick. I saw what he did. Just tried to murder you."

"That means his boss Inspector Doyle must have ordered this. He'll be coming here wondering what happened," she said frantically. "What'll we do?"

Sullivan hesitated before responding. "Well it won't be Inspector Doyle. He was waiting in a car down the street for Rafferty to kill you. But he's dead too. That's what I was doing after I left you."

Caroline was so shocked she could not respond.

"Don't worry. I drove the car with his body blocks away from here. That's what took me so long. The RIC will think it's the IRA. No reason to connect you."

He hoped that to be the case. Regardless, he had very little time to escape Belfast.

Caroline could only shake her head in bewilderment. "But what about... There's a dead body in the toilet. How do we explain that?"

"We can't. He's a dead constable. Nothing else will matter to the Crown's prosecutor. Even you won't be immune, Caroline. So hold yourself together. I've an idea to protect us."

While making his way back to the apartment an idea formed for removing Rafferty's body.

"Let me take a look at your neck. Does it hurt?"

He lightly touched the appearing discoloration of the bruising.

Grunting in pain she said, "Of course it hurts. Let me see."

She stood and brought back a hand mirror from her dressing table.

"Oh my god! It looks awful."

"Doesn't appear a serious injury though. Tomorrow you can hide it with makeup or a scarf. Right now I need to get you out of here. Get dressed. Pack an overnight case. We'll go to a hotel for the night."

"But the curfew. We'll be stopped by the police."

"We'll walk. Risky, but it's a dark moonless night. I know of a hotel not far where I was going to get a room. We'll stay in the shadows and pick our way carefully."

"Can't we just drive in your car?"

"Too risky with the curfew. And my car's not here so it won't connect me to you if found. I was followed leaving the office. Police dressed in civilian clothes. Probably Doyle's constables. Lost them by parking the car downtown. I walked here earlier and came in through the back. No one saw me."

He did not explain that with such police scrutiny his arrest might be imminent. Too many suspicious occurrences coming together once Doyle's body is discovered.

As Caroline dressed quickly. Both packed in silence.

Once ready to leave he said, "Take your jewelry, Caroline. You'll not be coming back."

"But what about …"

"I'll take care of removing the body tomorrow. No evidence left that anything ever happened. Just the same, I don't imagine you'll ever want to be spending another night here."

"Stay with your parents until things become settled. Day after tomorrow send your father's chauffeur and your mother's maid to pack your clothes. Sell the furniture and forget what happened here. Tell them this whole unpleasant episode with Alison has badly shaken you and you don't want to be alone especially with my leaving Belfast."

Leaving through the rear building entrance, they made the seven-block walk to the hotel, careful to avoid any illumination that might reveal their presence. Fortunately there was a room available. Sullivan explained his car broke down stranding them beyond the curfew. The bored desk clerk offered only a raised eyebrow in silent response.

Forestalling any further discussion, Sullivan pleaded exhaustion. They would talk tomorrow with clearer heads. After forcing Caroline into bed, she soon fell asleep as the effects of adrenalin subsided giving way to irresistible fatigue.

As for Sullivan, he took the opportunity for a wash and shave to refresh himself. A change into clean clothes would prepare for a long night. He needed to stay awake. Once Doyle's body is discovered Wickham might turn Belfast upside down.

If a knock came on the door in the middle of the night he would be ready.

Carefully packing only essentials in the small satchel, he thought about everything lost since coming to Ireland. Maureen and the prospect of an unimagined future after surviving the Great War. Maybe part of his humanity lost with his bloody deeds since coming to Ireland. Guilt over Alison. Now a possible future with Caroline Llewellyn gone before it barely began.

The final task was to write her a farewell letter. Once he left at dawn he would not return. Another painful shock to her but necessary. He was now a dangerous pariah that could destroy her.

Dearest Caroline,

You provided a light for a future that I thought forever lost. Now that too is lost. In our short time together I was not able to tell you the truth. Things so terribly ugly as you now know. I regret that because of me you have been dragged into unimaginable circumstances. Events beyond anything you could have ever prepared for.

Hold the memory of our short time together. You are a truly remarkable woman. Hold to your convictions, your aspirations. Do not compromise. Find a life on your terms. Pursue your writing. I would delight to someday read your published novel.

The passing of time will provide a clearer perspective on these terrible events. Too much to hope for but perhaps you might wish to write me in the future. Paris of course.

Although Irish, Ireland did not draw me as home. Nor did my native Brooklyn, New York in America for that matter. Paris became my adopted home. When Maureen was killed I never thought I could return to Paris without her. Yet I could never let go the idea. Now it remains as my refuge to survive, perhaps even make a new life. So I kept our Paris apartment by wiring the rent each month. 8 Rue Laplace. Apartment 509.

May you always remember me, Caroline. With deepest affection, Trevor

P.S. Rest assured I will see to that other unpleasant matter before I leave Belfast. Unfortunately that must know be immediately. For your sake, never speak about what happened to anyone. The separately addressed letter to your father offers my regrets for my sudden departure. Use it to explain your despondency and the reason for your sudden return home.

No telling what chaos the morning might bring after the discovery of Doyle's murder. Each hour he remained in Belfast increased the risk of arrest but he must remove Rafferty's body from Caroline's apartment. Whatever the cost he could not allow her becoming involved.

CHAPTER 36

As the first rays of morning sunlight appeared through the window, Sullivan prepared to leave the hotel room. Caroline Llewellyn was still asleep. Her fretful tossing through the night as he sat awake in a chair finally settled into a deeper sleep by the pre-dawn hours. Better this way. Nothing more to be said. Emotionally wrenching goodbyes could only complicate matters.

During the night he cleaned and oiled all his weapons. Quietly he left the room fixing in memory what might be his last glimpse of Caroline Llewellyn.

Settling his bill he told the desk clerk not to disturb his still sleeping wife. He would return for her later.

At the official time for lifting the curfew he was standing at the nearby tram stop. Close enough to view the hotel entrance if any police should arrive. Nothing happened as he boarded the first tram of the morning.

Arriving early at the shipyard, he deposited his satchel in his office. Office staff would not arrive for another hour. Making his way into the yard, he located Duncan Gallagher.

"Some unexpected things have happened, Duncan. All hell could break out today. Need your help with a delicate matter."

"Certainly, Sir. What's happened?"

They were standing alone near slipway no. 3. The hull of the freighter under construction taking shape.

"Inspector Doyle is dead."

Gallagher's mouth dropped then formed a broad grin. "Sonofabitch. How?"

"I shot him last night."

"Sweet Jesus! Then they'll be coming for you."

"Probably. Maybe not right away since they may not know it was me. I'm hoping I've a little time. But they'll sure as hell lash out at the IRA in retaliation."

"How you planning on getting away, Sir? Need my help?"

"Yes, but that's not the delicate matter. It's a long story, Duncan. Started during the weekend. You may have read about the police discovering a spy ring."

"Yes, Sir. McCorley and Woods been wondering if they might have nabbed you since your secretary's name was mentioned. Glad that didn't happen."

"Well the police are more than suspicious that I'm involved. Rafferty tortured my secretary so she told all she knew. I was there when she shot her husband then herself. No time to explain how all that happened. But I was careful never to reveal anything to her so all they have are her allegations.

"With her dead the police don't have enough evidence to make an arrest. Realizing this, Doyle tried having me abducted Friday night at my apartment. Unofficial since his men were not in uniform. Failing that they tried last night to murder Mr. Llewellyn's daughter. Doyle's doing. Murder her and blame it on me I suspect. Not sure how high up the order may have come from. So at best I'm only one step ahead of these bastards."

"How can I help?"

"I'd guess that Doyle's body has been discovered by now. I shot him in his car. Parked it downtown."

"He was alone?"

"Well not exactly. Sergeant Rafferty was with him. He's the delicate matter I spoke of. You see he was the one that tried to murder Miss Llewellyn. Caught the bastard in the act. Shot him too. Problem is his body is still in her apartment."

Gallagher registered further surprise, "You mean ..."

Sullivan cut him off. "That's right. Need your help removing Rafferty's body from Miss Llewellyn's apartment. I need you to fetch a lorry. We'll stick the little bastard in a steamer trunk. Trust you can find some place to dispose of it? That could be dangerous. No way to tell what the police might be up to. Definitely kicked the hornets' nest with this. "

"I'll tell McCorley. Get the lads to help."

"No time, Duncan. Tell Roger later. Right now I just need you. Can't involve Miss Llewellyn in the murder of a constable so this needs to be done this morning."

Thirty minutes later Sullivan waited outside the main entrance to Harland & Wolff. As instructed, Gallagher arrived with a small delivery lorry. After passing by then circling the apartment building twice, they saw no evidence of police.

To the concierge at the desk, Sullivan said, "Miss Llewellyn asked that I stop by to transport a steamer trunk. Believe she's planning a trip abroad. Said she would not be in so she gave me the key. Apartment 402? Correct?"

He displayed the key for the old man.

"Yes, Sir. Will you be requiring any help, Sir?"

"No, I believe the two of us can manage."

The mess inside the water closet was minimal. Shoved into the bathtub allowed for Rafferty's blood loss to be contained. Still required filling the tub halfway with water then scrubbing with a cleaning brush to remove the coagulated blood residue.

Blankets placed at the bottom of the trunk should soak up any remaining bodily fluids excreting from the corpse. Contorting the body to fit within the trunk proved more difficult. Rigor mortis made the task of forcing the limbs into place particularly unpleasant.

A grisly job to which Gallagher remarked, "Good to see this ugly piece of shit finally in a box."

Once loaded into the lorry, Gallagher said, "I'll take care of Rafferty, Mr. Sullivan. Best you be taking your leave of Belfast straightaway. I must say it's been a privilege serving with you,

Sir. Never seen the likes of an officer such as you. You're one dangerous man. Glad you're not with the enemy."

"Thank you, Sergeant Major."

"What about you, Sir? Need a ride somewhere?"

"No thanks, Duncan. Catching a tram. I'll be leaving Belfast by train or ship. Give my regards to Roger and Seamus. Hope you fellows are successful. Things may come to something soon in the South."

"Seems that way. Truce hasn't changed anything here in the North though. Ulster may never change."

Sullivan nodded his understanding. "One more thing. Since you're carting about a dead body you won't mind taking this off my hands."

Sullivan bent down and undid his satchel extracting the Smith & Wesson silenced revolver. Handing it to Gallagher, "Wouldn't do to be caught with evidence on me."

He pulled the clear-lens eyeglasses from his pocket. Putting them on, he said, "What do you think?"

With a skeptical expression, "Might help a little, Sir. Still armed though I would hope?"

With a smile Sullivan replied extending his hand, "Well armed. And you take care of yourself, Duncan."

———

Leaving Belfast turned out to be uneventful. He ruled out a train south to Dublin. Too much time for the alarm to be raised. And Dublin might not be safe. The choice therefore passage again on the ferry to Liverpool. Unlikely the police would look for him in England. No indication the police were screening passengers at the ticket office after careful observation before he approached.

From Liverpool the train went to Southampton where he boarded the cross-channel ferry to Le Havre. Another three hours train journey brought him into Gare Saint-Lazare on Rue d'Amsterdam. A sunny autumn afternoon greeted him as he stepped outside the train station.

Next to a street vendor hawking roasted chestnuts a busker played a typical French tune on an accordion. Sullivan's first reaction was that of being home. His beloved Paris.

—

It was now several months since leaving Belfast. Winter of the new year 1922. Shortly after returning to Paris, the Ministry reinstated him to his former position managing rail operations. Events of the last eighteen months remained ever present on his mind. A deeply troubling range of emotions he could not dispel. Continual reexamination led to the same dead ends. No longer the same person. It remained impossible to fully come to terms with all that he did in Ireland. Returning to the Paris apartment did feel like home. But the ghost of Maureen and those happy days here haunted his memories, overshadowing any thoughts that life could again hold meaning.

The blood on his hands might eventually lapse into disturbing memories as a necessary part of another kind of war. Not so the guilt over Alison Kendrick. Morally indefensible. The loss of Caroline Llewellyn a just penance.

He never wrote to Caroline since returning to Paris. Lines he would never write continually composed in his mind. No right to press her. Guilty of bringing such ugliness into her life. Almost killing her. Unconscionably selfish not to recognize the ill-fated nature of their relationship.

The manner in which he abruptly left following the assault at her apartment must have seemed self-serving. His inadequate goodbye letter poorly expressing affection. The shock and disillusionment after discovering he was something so utterly unimaginable would only magnify those disturbing memories over time. A violent alien intruding into her ordered world. There was no argument he could make in his defense. No right to expect there could be a future together.

Still, he vainly hoped for a letter from her. Just to hear she was doing well would have brought comfort. But increasingly unlikely with the passing of each month.

Belfast continued to be a violent place. Following her brush with violent death, surely a difficult environment for emotional recovery. How was Caroline coping? Probably living with her parents. Perhaps she had found someone. Whatever her circumstances he was confident in her ability to find a path for moving on with her life.

Sullivan kept abreast of events in Ireland from French and British newspapers. The outlawed Dáil Éireann republican parliament of the South voted to accept the terms of the Anglo-Irish Treaty. The Irish Free State therefore came into being ending three years of war with Britain. While British forces withdrew from the former Southern Ireland and handed over all administrative functions to the new Irish government, Irish anti-treaty factions expressed outrage. They repudiated the treaty claiming it betrayed the Irish people by denying full independence from the British Crown.

The six counties of Northern Ireland opted out of becoming part of the Irish Free State thereby remaining an integral part of the United Kingdom. In violation of the treaty, Michael Collins poured in arms from the South. However the republican schism over the treaty and the British imposing imprisonment without trial, combined to destroy IRA resistance in the North.

However the violence of the sectarian-based *troubles* continued in Northern Ireland.

Having not attained full independence from Britain, the new Irish Free State descended into civil war between opposing factions within the Irish Republican Army and Sinn Féin members of parliament. As an outspoken critic of the treaty Kathleen Clarke split with Michael Collins as the principle Irish negotiator and now effectively prime minister of the new Irish government. Ireland seemed no better off at the end of the Anglo-Irish War.

———

On a cold February evening there came a knock on Sullivan's door. The unlikely but potential for threat remained. He left a wake of enemies in Ireland that might have a long reach. Unlikely they'd come at him in Paris, he nonetheless always kept the

413

small .25 pistol handy. Not on his ankle but in a drawer on the reading lamp table. Concealing it in his rear pocket while holding it in his hand, he stood to the side of his front door.

"Yes?"

"It's Caroline. Open the door, Trevor. I'm bloody cold standing out here in the hallway."

CPSIA information can be obtained
at www.ICGtesting.com
Printed in the USA
BVHW030329150820
586214BV00006B/22